THE WAY THINGS OUGHT TO BE

Books by Gregory Hinton

CATHEDRAL CITY

DESPERATE HEARTS

THE WAY THINGS OUGHT TO BE

Published by Kensington Publishing Corporation

THE WAY THINGS OUGHT TO BE

Gregory Hinton

KENSINGTON BOOKS
http://www.kensingtonbooks.com

KENSINGTON BOOKS are published by

Kensington Publishing Corp.
850 Third Avenue
New York, NY 10022

Copyright © 2003 by Gregory Hinton

All Kensington titles, imprints, and distributed lines are available at special quantity discounts for bulk purchases for sales promotion, premiums, fund-raising, educational or institutional use.

Special book excerpts or customized printings can also be created to fit specific needs. For details, write or phone the office of the Kensington Special Sales Manager: Kensington Publishing Corp., 850 Third Avenue, New York, NY 10022. Attn. Special Sales Department. Phone: 1-800-221-2647.

Kensington and the K logo Reg. U.S. Pat. & TM Off.

Library of Congress Card Catalogue Number: 2003103716
ISBN 0-7582-0174-5

First Printing: September 2003
10 9 8 7 6 5 4 3 2 1

Printed in the United States of America

For Nancy Kelley

For Eric Sawyer

THE WAY THINGS OUGHT TO BE

Boulder, Colorado, 1974

AUTUMN

Chapter One

They'd lost the trail. The last thing King and Lex remembered, they were in this same area, but west of the lake, in a meadow surrounded by two enormous ridges. It was early autumn. Great swaths of yellow aspen trembled, zigzagging up the mountains through somber blue-green pine forests. Golden leaves rained down on them in the late afternoon breeze. The ground cover was red with berries and amber brush.

They were mad at each other, and Lex was stomping ahead, King following, cursing him under his breath. Lex, with amber hair; tall, angular, his backpack jangling with an ornithology student's provisions: binoculars, a book on Rocky Mountain birds, a compass, his camera, and bird seed, nature's blend, purchased at Alfalfa's, Boulder's whole earth general store.

King, Kingston James, the gold one. Gold the color of the fall trees, quaking in the mountain sunlight. Honey skin. Blond hair, just touching his shoulders. Shorter than his friend, compact and muscular—gold. With warm, intuitive eyes, like an old Rambler's headlights, dimming below a careworn hood of a forehead. Young for worry lines, King wasn't carrying anything in his pack but water and solemnity. He'd be glorious with a shallow man's soul.

Lex had been correcting him, insisting on taking the lead. Every idea King suggested, he overruled. Lex was the outdoor expert. He knew where they were and King had to be patient.

"I'm cold," King called after Lex.

"I told you to bring your sweater," Lex said harshly.

King's thought was interrupted by a low-flying, single-engine plane. It barely cleared the pine ridge. He could see the passenger's face from where he stood on the ground. He was probably in his mid-thirties, wearing glasses. He looked terrified.

"It's crashing," said Lex ominously.

And it did, past the trees. They could faintly hear the explosion. They started to run. At the edge of the meadow they picked up the path. Trotting along at a fair rate of speed, they came up behind two strapping members of the Rocky Mountain Rescue Group, out sweeping the trails.

Their burnished cheeks cracked from cold wind and high-altitude sunlight. Their two-day beards were sun-bleached the gold of the hillside. Their denim jeans, faded by last winter's snow, clung to the muscular contours of their calves, hips, and thighs, as if painted on, King noted, and to his dismay, Lex clearly thought the same thing. Like sure-footed, rutting bighorn sheep, they reeked of Rocky Mountain animal sexuality.

"A small plane just went down," Lex said breathlessly. "Only a mile or so west of here."

King nodded in agreement. One of the pair pulled out his walkie-talkie and began shouting information into it. Lex knew these canyons as well as anybody. He loved topography maps, and, in fact, had one on him, which he pulled from his backpack.

King was amazed by this. Why hadn't he brought it out earlier, when they thought they were lost? Had he delighted in King's fear?

Shortly they were all huddled on the ground over the map. Congratulating Lex, they concurred where the plane might have ditched and called in the additional information on the walkie-talkie. Then they continued scrambling up the ridge toward the crash site.

The plane had not exploded, just broken apart. Both wings had sheared off as it crashed through the trees. The tail was intact, the front end crushed. One body, the pilot, remained strapped in a seat, his face twisted away from King's view.

The passenger, the one King had seen, had been thrown from the wreckage. In the violence of the impact, his leg right had been yanked from its socket and was now wrapped behind his shoulders. His neck had snapped; his face was smashed into the earth. King could see the bent stem of his glasses protruding up from his collar.

"I've never seen a dead body before." And King hadn't. He'd

never been to a funeral. His mother wouldn't allow it. King began to hyperventilate. He wondered who their relatives were, who'd be contacted tonight. King hypothesized about their sorrow. The horror of the descent. The face in the window.

Lex grunted, folding his arms.

In a matter of minutes other hikers arrived, as did more members of the rescue squad. There must have been ten or twelve hikers on the scene "Lotta planes get eaten by these canyons," someone observed. "This is the second one in two weeks."

"Well, we better get moving. They aren't walking out of here on their own. Any volunteers to help carry 'em out?"

"I'll do it," Lex said quickly, ignoring King. Five others volunteered. Without them, there were more than enough, even taking turns.

King scanned the darkening sky. It looked like snow. "I don't have a coat," he whispered to Lex. "I'll freeze."

"Then you better go down," Lex said simply. "See you later. I can get a ride with these guys." And he entered the chatting, jocular circle of the rescuers as they prepared the bodies for transport.

After a miserable summer in California, they were back in Colorado, living together in secret, because although King agreed to come back to Boulder, he lied to his parents about Lex. The only way King's mother would continue to pay for college was if Lex was out of the picture, so King told her it was over, when in fact, it wasn't.

Although they wanted to live together, which he'd never get away with, King found two rooms across the hall from each other in a beat-up old boardinghouse on University Avenue. They were very depressing.

Lately, every chance to be away, Lex would take. He studied at the library and ate at the Packer Grill. They slept together but rarely had sex. They didn't have any friends left. They were all born-again Christians and Nicholas had decreed that no contact with either of them was allowed. Lex missed the group. King did, too, but going back was not an option. Not after the call to his parents.

King used to wonder why Nicholas called his parents and not Lex's. Why had he singled King out? One day, King reflected as he trotted down the trail, King would have to ask him. It was an action that informed so much of what was to happen. It led to everything.

* * *

Lex didn't come back till after eleven. King heard him. Got up, padding across the hall, where Lex had stripped to his shorts and was just about to climb into his own bed.

"You aren't sleeping with me?"

"That's your first question?" Lex shrugged, crawling into bed. "Not, did you get them down okay? Did you find out who they were? Were their families notified? Do they know why they crashed?"

"I know the answers to those questions," King said. "It was on the six o'clock news. You've been off the mountain since before then. Five hours ago."

"I never said I wasn't."

"You never said you were."

"I'm tired. I want to go to sleep."

"Fine. Sleep."

King slammed out. Went across the hall. Tried to lie down. Got up. Stormed back across the hall. Snapped on the light.

"Tell me."

"Tell you what?"

"The truth."

"I'm tired, King."

"Can I sleep with you?"

"Not that kind of tired."

So that was it. King blinked once or twice. He cut Lex's light. Crossed back to his room. Lex's door was still ajar. "Why do you suppose Nicholas never called your parents," he called out across the hall. "Why'd he pick on mine?"

"Ask him."

"You ask him! I saw you having coffee with him yesterday morning. Are you saved again?"

"We just ran into each other. We had a cup of coffee."

"You've gotten off too fucking easy!"

"I came back with you," Lex protested. "I tried again. I miss our old friends."

"I'm way out here on a limb and you haven't lost one night of sleep. Nobody hurt your parents. How can you even talk to that bastard after what he did? Fucking coward! *Fucking coward!*" And several minutes later, he heard Lex, dressed now, King figured, running down the hall for his life. So Lex wanted to salvage his salvation.

King liked that line, he reflected. He reached for a pencil and jotted it down on a pad he kept by his side of the bed. He had learned the hard way, no matter how inspired, that it was easy to forget a good line by morning. This would be his last practical thought of the night.

"King?"

King knew his mother Kay napped most afternoons, promising herself she was just going to finish some article on a new shish kabob marinade in this month's issue of *Redbook*. She wouldn't sleep. It was a beautiful fall day, and she wanted to rake the leaves. She promised herself she wouldn't fall asleep.

The bag of assorted candy from the plastic bins at Safeway would undermine her plan. She always weighed herself each morning. In the year before King went away to Boulder, Kay had joined Weight Watchers. She lost twenty-three pounds, three more than her goal. She made new clothes. She felt wonderful. Now it was all back on, plus another eight pounds. Family stress, the culprit.

The marinade looked easy to make. Her old cat had arrived. Bones. He circled three times, collapsing on the blanket against her side. She'd just popped her first caramel. She always ate the caramels first. Bones made a feeble attempt to bat at the wrapper. Then she started with the jellies, first sucking the sugar off, until all that remained was a pliable, gooey, gelatinous medallion. Her blood sugar would shoot up. In moments she'd have her peace.

"It's me, Mom."

"Are you okay?"

Her youngest son loomed into the frame of her bedroom doorway. "You look awful."

"I lied to you about Lex."

"I know."

She felt ridiculous, caught like this. In bed on a beautiful fall day, wanting to rake the leaves. Her neighbor Lily had offered to come over with her new leaf blower. Kay and King's father, Jim, lived on a block of women without husbands. They'd died or the wives divorced them. Where Kay had bet against the odds of Lily adapting, now she knew how to operate a leaf blower. She was dying to show off with it. And here was Kay, in bed with a woman's magazine, a bag of cheap candy, and the cat. At three-thirty in the afternoon. What kind of example was she?

"Don't get up," King offered, reading her embarrassment. "I'm sorry I lied. We weren't really living together. He lived across the hall. It's over. He wants out."

"Oh, I see."

"I need to move. I want to come back home."

The cat started licking himself. He gazed up at King, his eyes half closed in ecstasy.

"I can't really lie here and have this conversation." She wished she hadn't eaten the candy. Her head felt fuzzy. She had been seconds away from swooning into a deep, dream-free, afternoon sleep. "I have to put my pants on," she said modestly.

He disappeared. It was good news and bad news, Kay reflected.

She pulled on her drawstring pants. She followed him into the kitchen.

"I'm making coffee," he told her.

"Lex moves this time," she told him. "I don't even need to ask your father what he thinks. He'll agree."

"What?" King said.

"You've done all the moving," she observed, flicking her cigarette lighter and lighting a Marlboro. "It's his turn. Pour me some coffee, King. Then go back to Boulder and tell him."

"I wouldn't want to stay there after he left."

"Fine. But don't tell him that. He'll go. I promise you. Then you can move wherever you like." She smiled at him then. "I'll carry boxes."

King found a room on College Avenue, in a nice brick house shared by Teddy and Wade, who he'd worked with last summer at Boulder Blue-Line. They were architecture students. They would share the front bedroom, and give King the larger bedroom in the back. The house was only two blocks from campus, five from the Hill. King didn't know them well, but they were good-natured, happy, and dedicated students. Teddy was the handsome one. Wade, the nerdy best friend of the girl-magnet. Wade always hoped for spillovers, but Teddy was a master at never overfilling his cup.

When King's parents arrived in their new Ford Econoline cargo van, with his bed, his dresser, and his boxes, the bedroom door to Teddy and Wade's room was pulled shut. As King and his dad were piecing together the metal frame for his box spring, they could hear moaning. King's dad glanced up.

"I don't want your mother to hear."

"Hear what?" Kay appeared with a box.

"King can take it from here."

Behind Teddy's door, a bed was squeaking, the fever of the love-making picking up.

"I see," said Kay.

"Let's unload the rest of it on the lawn," King offered, escorting them back out to the front yard. "I can get the rest of this. I've done it ten times already."

They laughed.

"Fresh start." His mother hugged him, as King helped her up to the passenger seat. In the center console they kept their supplies. A coffee caddy with a beat-up camping thermos. A carton of cigarettes. Cough drops. Maps. A compass. In back, his dad built benches for sleeping cots. The van was only three months old and it was already trashed. King's gleaming new Mercury Capri shimmered like a silverfish in the driveway. They'd given him the down payment and co-signed his loan. They got a special deal for buying two vehicles.

"I'll call you tonight."

From behind the curtained, slightly ajar front bedroom window, Teddy and his girlfriend howled in climax. His mother gazed questioningly toward the house.

"A girl," she remarked quizzically, as the Econoline roared off.

After his parents drove away, Teddy appeared and started lugging cartons back to King's room.

"Hey, man, Jen and I didn't know your folks were out here. What's with the cargo van?"

A pleasant-looking boy-man, Teddy had strawberry blond hair, blue eyes, and perennial freckles. Women loved him. He had a beautiful girlfriend, a sorority girl named Jen who came over every afternoon when they fucked like rabbits before Teddy's roommate Wade needed to use the bedroom. Teddy and Wade had bunk beds with mismatched cowboy sheets. Teddy and Jen loved their sex together. Like screaming cats, it made no difference to them who heard.

"Well," King said. "I've gotta get to class."

King's advanced writing class met each week in Hellums Hall, the arts and sciences building that overlooked the University Memorial Center fountain court and the outdoor Shakespeare theater. There were only ten students.

Dr. Maddie Sloan was King's favorite professor at Boulder. She was young, had her MFA from Columbia and her doctorate from the University of Iowa at Iowa City. She'd already published a volume of short stories, several which had appeared in the *Atlantic Monthly* and the *New Yorker*.

She had known King as a freshman, had, in fact, along with Stanley Whitcomb, the closeted gay English professor, recommended him for his writing scholarship. Petite and beautiful, she came from Boston and spoke with the most wonderful accent. People often commented that King, too, spoke with a slight, indefinable accent, something he never quite understood, but appealed enormously to his grandiosity. He was a King and spoke like one.

Professor Sloan always gave King A's, but never called on him to read his work. He asked her about this once, hesitating only because it relieved rather than offended him. She explained that she didn't want to unnerve her older students.

For a time, in his freshman year, Hellums was partially closed due to construction. Maddie's writing classes relocated to Old Main, across the expansive campus commons. One of the oldest buildings on campus, Old Main was small, only four stories high, with gleaming peg and groove oak floors, majestic wooden staircases, and a cupola on top.

The classroom was located on the second floor. On the landing at the top of the stairs, King liked to watch for her, her dark hair streaming, striding down the walk in her leather boots and a full-length fox coat. King never knew a woman so sophisticated. He began waiting as a ritual, and as the semester proceeded she, too, would glance up, search the windows, smile magnificently, and wave to him.

Often he'd pass by her office, now back in Hellums, on some pretense, glancing in to see if he could catch her eye. He loved her office. It was cozy; loaded with books, a desk facing the hall, covered with unread manuscripts and two old leather chairs flanking the door. Her window overlooked the open-air Mary Rippon Shakespeare theater-in-the-round. A radiator pumped heat on snowy mornings.

"King," she'd call out after he'd passed her door. "Come back here. I'm boiling water for tea. Can you stay and talk?"

King's heart would soar.

"Did I ever tell you"—she'd smile—"that as a girl we used to go sailing off the Kennedy compound in Hyannisport? My mother was a childhood friend of Rose Kennedy's. I had a fantastic crush on Teddy Kennedy. I was his for the taking, King. So, how are you today?"

And King would tell her what he was working on. How he was faring in his other classes. The success or failure of his living arrangements. She knew he moved often. She always ran into King out on his own, doing something most people only did with companions. Like breakfast at Dot's Diner on Sundays. In a dining room crowded with couples talking and laughing, King would be solitary at a small table in the window, which he always got because Linda, the waitress, liked him; eating bacon and eggs, not even pretending to study, just sitting and musing out the window.

"Do you see friends, King?"

"My characters in my stories are my best friends," King countered. It sounded horribly pretentious.

"Still, I worry about you. You aren't lonely, are you? College can be very lonely for someone sensitive like you."

"How do you know I'm so sensitive?"

"I read what you write. You have a gift. I wonder if you've ever read any Christopher Isherwood. I think you might enjoy his writing."

She wrote down his name on a piece of notebook paper. After it she wrote, *The Berlin Stories.* "These stories are so wonderful, King. They just made a fabulous film based on one of them, *I Am a Camera.* Actually, it was a play. Well, first it was this story, then a play which I was lucky enough to catch in London, and now a movie with Liza Minnelli as Sally Bowles. You must read Isherwood, King! I think he'll have an enormous impact."

Later, as King was hanging his Sierra Club posters, a remnant of his life with Lex, a waft of perfume floated into his bedroom. He turned. This was apparently Jen, vigorously brushing her blond hair. She wore one of Teddy's denim shirts. Her legs were sleek and bare. Inexplicably tan for October.

"Hi." She smiled gloriously. "Sorry if we embarrassed your parents."

King shrugged. He was intimidated by her. A rush of anxiety swept over him. Where was Lex tonight? What was King doing here?

"Are you okay?"

"Yeah," he mustered.

"Are you about to *cry*?"

"No."

"Jesus, Jen. You don't ask the guy if he's crying."

Teddy appeared behind her, nuzzling her neck. She tried to shake him off, but he persisted, groping the front of her. She started laughing. Teddy shrugged helplessly. They disappeared into their bedroom.

Moments later, they were fucking again.

That night, King opened the cover of a fresh college-ruled notebook.

People ask, he wrote, *Who made you King?*

But that was him, and he was still learning to live with all the blessings and burdens being a king entailed. King was a family name and he was glad, because whenever he gave his name, there was always a discussion about it, no one forgot it, and he figured, how often does anyone get to make the acquaintance of a king? Let alone play with one, or work with one in close contact—or make love with a true king.

King always signed his given name, Kingston James, on all his checks, his personal and business correspondence, his writings.

An assignment, given to him by Professor Sloan: a daily journal and six short stories. That night, King typed:

I should tell you what's it like to be saved. I was sitting at Mackey Auditorium with Nicholas, attending an Andre Crouch and the Disciples concert. The place was packed with thousands of born-again Christians, a few I knew from around campus.

It was hot, and the air was thick with emotional passion. Prior to that night, Nicholas and I had spent much time together. He was witty, self-deprecating and charismatic. He generated enormous sex appeal. Sex sweated out of him. Women, I knew, loved him.

I understood clearly that I was being proselytized, but I knew from seeing him in class and around my other friends that Nicholas had a genius IQ and came from a military family; his father was a General in the army, had served in Vietnam. We speculated that liberal guilt was informing Nicholas's decision to follow Christ. His father, too, was a deeply religious Russian Orthodox.

The fact that he'd spent so much time with me was flattering.

He liked to make late-night calls, as late as two or three in the morning. The phone would ring and Nicholas would say, "Oh, were you asleep? Do you want to go for a drive? Have breakfast?" I would always say yes. And we'd drive through the night in his Ford Pinto, sometimes as far as Winter Park or Breckenridge.

And we'd talk about intimate things. Our hope for the future. Our Existential Loneliness. Our fears. I had been terribly lonely my first year at Boulder. Nicholas picked up on that, introducing me to his roommate, Lex. Lex kept his distance at first, which I never quite understood till later. He was fighting his attraction for me. I was tempting. Satan's playground.

The crowd at these events is played to build in emotional intensity. An individual, not part of the group, feels it. Gets caught up. You'd have to be extremely self-contained and aware to fend it off. The emotion is simply so great. People are moaning and talking in tongues, laughing and waving their hands in the air. Some weep uncontrollably. The music propels them. Crouch preaching from the stage drives it to further frenzy.

I remember hearing doubts in my head and Crouch speaking to them as I weighed the invitation to come forward, to come to Christ. A representative would pray with me if I stood up and came down the aisle. The Lord Loves You. He's calling for you. Can't you hear him? Can't you hear him? Confess your sins and accept him. Ask him into your heart. The Lord is your King and he wants to take you home.

Suddenly I felt lifted out of my seat, like the Book of Revelation, compelled to go down to the stage. My feet did not touch the floor. The experience of being saved was truly a physical phenomenon, occurring in one brilliant, miraculous millisecond. Like a nuclear event. The rush of the Holy Spirit. The euphoric loss of loneliness. The power of Heaven! The Glory! The Ecstasy!

I would not have the same experience again till I entered my first gay disco.

Chapter Two

He was surrounded by a small group of good-looking guys, holding court. A few King recognized from around campus, some from the Denver bars. He looked up when King came in, but King gave himself no credit for his interest. He stood against the window, his face in shadows, but he was tall, a head taller than they were, than King was, surely. Behind him, outside, the snow was falling gently. The soft light from the church floodlights illuminated the white snow, and it seemed brighter outside than in. Inside the only light came from the flickering table candles, the dimmed lights from the nearby church hall kitchen.

Backlit by the glow of the snow, Sam wore a dark sweater, blue jeans, boots. His dark hair was shaggy-long, just shy of ponytail length, and he had a subtly hawklike nose and dark, important eyes, though why King could see his eyes, he now couldn't say. It was too dark to make out his eyes, but there they were still. He was framed by the gently falling snow.

Sam was tall and he was handsome and looking at King. He felt new to Boulder, that was for sure. King would have surely remembered him. Sam was new and interesting for that reason, interesting for all the basic reasons. Interesting because he was surrounded by several others King had found interesting at other times.

King sized up his odds and looked away.

It was early October, and snowing softly that night, the first snow of fall. King was wearing a parka. The roads were slippery and he'd been told he didn't need snow tires because his new car had radials; his first new car, the silver Mercury Capri. The car was beautiful and handled well in the snow. Still, the roads were slippery.

The car handled well in the ten-minute drive along Broadway Avenue, capably rounding the perimeter of the softly lit flagstone buildings of the University of Colorado campus. King proceeded slowly down the hill, past the eclectic campus housing of old Victorian houses and flat, postwar apartment buildings. At Arapaho he turned right, continuing past Boulder High School till he made another right on Folsom Avenue. Then King proceeded up a short hill, parking on the street instead of in the parking lot.

Friday night and too snowy to make the drive to the bars in Denver. Not till he got the feel of his new car. They had no gay clubs in Boulder. This was the weekly Friday Night Gay Coffee House. They charged a dollar cover.

King crunched his way up the sidewalk toward the entrance to the recreation hall of Boulder's A-frame Wesley Chapel. It was probably around eight-thirty. He could see his breath in the cold air. He could smell snow and the faint comforting scent of smoke from someone's nearby chimney.

If it was slow inside, King might be willing to attempt the drive to Denver. He came in through the side entrance, and several men were hanging around a table where a guy named Theo was selling tickets. He'd seen Theo around. He was one of the original founders of the Boulder Gay Liberation Front. He was lanky, intellectual-looking, and wore thin, round glasses. He always dressed in black.

King peered inside the rec hall. Busy enough. The overhead lights were off. Candles flickered on tables pushed off to the side. Maybe fifteen or twenty guys hung around the edge of the room. He recognized a few of them, decided to stay. He nodded hello to Theo and gave him his dollar. He walked into the cloakroom and hung up his parka.

It felt strange coming to the church for this reason, in light of what it once meant to King. On the walls of the rec hall, children's artwork depicted stories from the Bible. *Jesus loves the little children of the world.* The liberal elders of the church had offered this space to provide a safe place for gay men and women to gather. Make alliances. Like-minded friends.

King had no gay friends. He didn't know the first thing about how to go about making them. For him, being gay in and of itself wasn't enough of a reason to form a friendship. As he looked back, he better understood his thinking. Coming out had been a personal and social disaster; the *Titanic* of any coming-out story he had ever heard, due largely in part to his considerable naiveté. King once believed that with family support, his trust in God, and lastly, the fact that he was living in Boulder in the mid-seventies, no harm would come to him.

Free love, alternative lifestyles, *Saturday Night Live*. The collapse of the Nixon White House and the end of the Vietnam War. The antiwar movement had won. When King came to Boulder, the campus was in a state of flux.

Whereas only a year before, the Colorado National Guard had tear-gassed Kittredge Commons, the upscale, country-clubby dormitory complex where he lived as a freshman; the fraternity and sorority system became so passé that many houses sought renters; there was no pressure at all to belong to anything. Boulder had no specific identity, at least as far as he was concerned, except for once being rated by *Playboy* magazine as the number one party school in the nation.

King's parents allowed him to attend the University of Colorado only because it was one of three affordable in-state universities. This pissed off his brother Neil, who several years before wasn't even allowed to apply because their parents thought Boulder was too radical and dangerous for him. They dispatched him to a teaching college in nearby Greeley instead.

Boulder was a beautiful city, sloping up along the front range of the Colorado Rockies, and in his time, King watched it evolve from a quaint university town to a bastion for smart and entrepreneurial money. In the mid-seventies, Boulder offered many options: political, spiritual and sexual, it had become a melting pot for innovative thought. An antiwar activist, the Reverend Daniel Berrigan, was rumored to be in hiding there. Influenced by Chogyam Trungpa Rinpoche, wealthy Eastern religious sects were buying up old buildings in downtown Boulder.

Poets Allen Ginsberg, Gregory Corso, Diane Di Prima, and Peter Orlovsky formed the Jack Kerouac School of Disembodied Poetics at Boulder's Naropa Institute. Radical Christian groups, such as the Children of God, had established a foothold among Boulder's burgeoning Christian movement.

At some level King never knew what he had and would regret leaving. Had his emotional circumstances not thwarted a more speedy departure, he might have missed out on the very best time of the five years he lived there.

He would have missed out on Sam.

After standing off to the side and watching several lame attempts by a few coffeehousers to dance, King felt like an idiot. No one approached him. Often his shyness got mistaken as arrogance or conceit.

His body began to feel like so many loose pieces of Lego. If King stayed a moment longer he would disassemble right down to the scarred and yellowing rec hall linoleum floor. He decided to leave. The room had filled to thirty or more. He was still alone. As he made his way along the perimeter of the room toward the cloakroom door, a hand touched his shoulder.

"Leaving so soon?"

The voice was gentle, even slightly tremulous with the slightest East Coast twang. King didn't reply. He was so nervous, he turned, staring in utter deer-in-the-headlights stupefaction. Of course it was Sam. He was hanging in the shadows, gazing down at King and smiling.

King was of average height, just shy of 5'10", but because he had long legs, he seemed taller. King didn't have a proscribed body type when it came to a sexual partner, but to be a male and looking *up* into the eyes of another extremely tall man was, to him, sexually charging. Small talk was clearly not his forte.

"Yeah," King mustered.

"That's a shame," Sam offered. "I saw you and I wanted to say hello."

"It's not too late." King brightened.

"No." He smiled. "I suppose not. I'm Sam."

"I'm King," King introduced himself.

Sam gestured King into the shadows, patting the wall as if inviting him in. King leaned in awkwardly, muttered a few unmemorable remarks, but Sam was clearly happy to be talking with him. They exchanged the perfunctory demographics. King was born in Montana and grew up in Denver. He was getting a degree in English. He was here on a writing scholarship.

Sam came from a small town in upstate New York. He was working on his graduate degree in city planning. He'd arrived in Boulder the previous semester. Sam was as surprised as King that they hadn't noticed each other before.

"A few of us are planning to walk over to the UMC," he said. The UMC was the University Memorial Center. The campus student union. "They're holding some kind of a monthly dance. We thought we'd crash it and dance together. I was wondering if you wanted to come along."

He grinned down at King, but his eyes were earnest. Sam was testing him.

King hoped he didn't look appalled.

"Sure," King agreed, and Sam laughed heartily in response and hugged him.

About ten or twelve of them left the church and headed across the snow-covered field behind the School of Engineering, toward campus. King knew most of the guys. Theo, of course. All of the sycophants King saw surrounding Sam earlier. A preppy-looking guy named Tim. His sweet boyfriend Peter. Rod, a tall, striking, smirking, short-cropped blonde who apparently, as much as King could gather through eavesdropping, had just broken up with his boyfriend, a sexy Italian stud he'd always admired named Tony. Rod owned a local gay rag, a Denver newsletter filled mostly with advertising, a few political articles, and photo teases. The usual shirtless skier advertising a gay ski weekend in Aspen.

King knew these guys because he'd tricked with a few of them. Tim, right after he and Lex broke up, in a bedroom at a party house on the outskirts of Boulder. King hadn't known about Peter. Tim had a cock that curved down instead of up, like a Japanese bridge.

Rod had only been an attempted conquest. King sat gin-drunk on his lap, probably at the same party, where Rod confided that he'd had a crush on King for years. They'd made out passionately. King had quoted a little poetry.

" 'In my Tanqueray recollections, I do not lament rejections, only mistaken identities . . .' "

Rod laughed, made excuses, and left.

Had King come on too strong? He called Rod in the middle of the night. Rod told him he wasn't the marrying kind, which by implication meant that somehow King was.

If King had known how to make gay friends, he might have better understood that every smile didn't imply a long-term commitment; that sometimes sex was for fun and not always for love. He might have developed a sense of humor about the whole thing. Finally King might have known how comforting friends could be, that sometimes it was better to leave a bar with your friends than a strange trick. King personalized every encounter, every false hope, every letdown. The stakes he played for were high.

As King walked along the periphery of the amassed group, he felt very nervous about what they planned to do. His motives were not exactly pure, and the uneasy feeling that he hadn't just been picked up by Sam but recruited by him was beginning to creep into his mind.

Sam wasn't even talking to him. He was walking way out ahead and trying to talk sense into Rod. King's acute sense of survival was informing him to fall back, out of ranks, and slink quietly back to his new Capri and then home. He realized he could never trust anyone, least of all his own intuition.

At the very moment King began to slow down, Sam turned and anxiously searched the group with brooding eyes. Rod continued to march moodily ahead, but Sam stood off to the side, reviewing his troops. Would twelve gay men be any match for five hundred drunken heterosexuals?

Sam caught King's eye. Now King could never escape.

"Hi," he said, as King slowly approached.

"Hey," King muttered.

"Sorry I got hung up with Rod. You know him? He says he knows you. Says you're a great poet."

Terrific, King thought.

"Listen, are you still up for this? You look a little worried."

"I'll be okay," King murmured.

King didn't know what else to say. He'd had enough public humiliation to last a lifetime. So had his parents. It was all too intense and complicated to explain to Sam on the snowy streets of Boulder.

They crossed the campus in silence and began to approach the University Memorial Center. "Look, I'd be surprised if we had any trouble, but I can't guarantee we won't. If you're worried, you don't have to stay. I wouldn't think any less of you."

"I said I'd come and I'm coming."

Sam smiled down at King. "You won't be alone. You have us. Me," he corrected himself, humbly. The others were making their way up the steps to the lobby of the UMC. Band music blared out from inside. The snow was falling heavily now.

Sam waited patiently. He held out his hand. King took it.

They walked up the steps to the lobby where their friends had gathered. They all paid the cover. They entered the dance floor hand in hand. King didn't remember much about the band except the fact that they were local.

Sam led the group through the crowd to a small opening in the middle of the packed ballroom. The dance had started an hour ago, and the energy was peaking. Sam came to a halt and King looked around. The attendees looked mostly like Greeks. King thought he recognized a girlfriend of Jen's, Holly, dancing with a sorority sister nearby. Holly had been over to Teddy's once or twice. She seemed to recognize him, because she nodded just as the band started playing "Eli's Comin'."

Sam held out his hand. "Dance?"

Stepping out, King never took his eyes off Sam. The gay men and women began to dance. King, noticing Holly's shock, watched in amusement as she and her partner fled the floor, afraid of being mistaken as part of Sam's group. She glanced over her shoulder at King, as if to make certain he was who she thought he was. Teddy's roommate. Teddy. Jen's boyfriend.

The surrounding straight couples noticed, rippling away momentarily, but acquiesced to their presence without comment. They weren't scandalous. Only interesting, a mental bookmark event with which to amuse their friends. Boulder, after all.

That night King walked Sam back as far as Sam's room, a graduate school dormitory in the same direction as the church. Sam was enthused about the action, glad for the statement they had made. King, too, felt invigorated. The throngs didn't turn on them. They weren't hung up by their toes. The floor didn't open up and swallow them whole. They only danced a few songs and left. Outside, they all hugged each other. King felt like he had brothers and sisters. A new kind of family. The Boulder Gay Liberation Front.

As Sam and King walked back, King was laughing with relief. Now the sky was clear and cold. The storm had passed and the outline of the Flatirons hatcheted across the starlit sky.

When they came to Reed Hall, Sam's dorm, he stopped.

"This is it. This is where I live."

The end of the evening had come. King took in a deep breath. "You wanna come up?" Sam offered. "I'll make us some tea." King nodded, expecting only tea.

Sam's room had a twin bed, a desk, a dresser, and a drafting table by the window. King feigned interest in a drawing Sam was working on. Behind him, Sam peeled off his coat and sweater. He wore a white T-shirt with dog tags underneath.

"Take off your coat," Sam ordered King pleasantly. "You aren't leaving anytime soon."

King smiled and unzipped his parka. Sam disappeared into his bathroom to fill a small electric percolator with water. When he came out, he plugged it in. King sat on the edge of his drafting stool and smiled at him. Heat pumped from a radiator under the window. The room felt cozy and warm.

Sam's body was lean and he moved jauntily, with joy. He fiddled through a box of herbal teas. Celestial Seasonings.

"Boulder's own," King said.

Sam looked up and smiled. "Sleepy Time okay with you?"

"Yeah," King whispered.

Sam dropped a bag each into two mugs. Then he walked across the room and kissed King from behind. Sam handed King his mug. "I'm feeling a little sleepy. You?"

They made love twice that night, once in the morning. Sam was the first uncircumcised man King had been with. He explained that as a baby his foreskin had been so negligible his doctors hadn't bothered with a circumcision. King had trouble getting the hang of it. Sam instructed him how to hold his cock, taught him where the most sensitive area was to arouse him.

They made love on Sam's single bed, facing each other, on their sides, Sam's arm around King protectively, cradling him as they gently rocked. He had long, dark eyelashes. He closed his eyes when he kissed, and King could almost count each lash as it feathered across his cheek. King liked kissing him. For a man, Sam had especially pretty, perfectly formed lips.

Outside it started to snow again.

They whispered through the night, in and out of sleep. They slept bound together by a flurry of arms, bedclothes, and legs; limbs tangled with limbs. Sometimes they'd drift awake kissing passionately, only to fall back on the pillow and float away.

They blurted out intimate details. They could remember how many men they'd slept with. They could remember names, ages, and the circumstances of how they'd met. They talked about childhood, of brothers and sisters. Of aged parents. They talked about favorite books, music they liked, colors.

They talked about future plans. King's desire to move back to California. Sam's longing to move back to New York. In the morning Sam wanted to fuck King. King had only tried it once, with Lex, unsuccessfully, and because it was Sam, wanted to try it again. King grimaced through the whole ordeal.

They made plans to meet at the gym later that day. Maybe they'd go to dinner after that. That night, King found himself back in bed with Sam.

"Listen, I'm sorry about this morning. Did I hurt you?"

"No," King lied.

"I found a drop of blood on my sheet."

"I'll get you a new one."

"No, King. I'm not worried about the sheet. It washed out. If you don't like being fucked, you should say so."

"I thought it might be different with you."

Sam laughed. "Fucking is a pretty outrageous thing to do. It didn't even occur to me till one night it was happening to me. I didn't know two men did such things! There are other things we can try," Sam smiled kindly. He kissed King on the top of his head. "This is all new to me, too."

King headed to the library with a smile on his face. Something clearly was developing between them. King welcomed it, even so soon after Lex.

Several days later Sam told King he'd made plans to go back to New York for a long weekend.

"In the middle of the semester? Midterms are coming up."

"Just something I have to do, King."

"It's my dad's birthday, anyway."

"Good. Then we're both having family weekends. What are you getting him?"

King laughed, thinking of his father.

"What's funny?" Sam smiled.

"I asked him if he wanted a sweater. Know what he said?"

Sam shrugged.

"He said he already had one. That's my dad in a nutshell." King waited expectantly, hoping Sam would explain more about his trip back home.

Sam folded his arms. It was clear that his mission was none of King's business. King drove him to Denver's Stapleton Airport the following Thursday.

That Saturday, Teddy and Wade hosted a tailgate party in the driveway in front of the house. It was mostly Greeks. King was not invited, which he didn't question, so he took a walk. King reflected how deeply lonely he had been when he first moved to Boulder, walking through the streets, filled with strange desires, clinging so futilely to the idea that he wasn't different from everyone else, but knowing deep down that he was.

He felt deeply isolated. Why was he different? The snow had melted, it was a beautiful Saturday autumn afternoon, and King was passing Folsom Stadium on his way alone toward downtown Boulder. The Colorado Buffs were playing the Nebraska Cornhuskers. Someone scored a touchdown. The entire crowd roared in unison, the sound rising up out of the stadium like a mammoth hovercraft, sound so loud King could see it. Would his voice ever belong?

"King!"

Later, as he started to walk back from downtown, King was surprised to run into an old friend at the intersection of Broadway and Spruce. The streets were getting busy. Rushing cars spackled the sidewalk with broken, dusty golden leaves. The game must be over.

He turned. It was an old friend. Celine. She was delighted to see him.

"I prayed I'd see you. I didn't know where you'd moved."

"I'm sharing a house. The phone isn't in my name."

"I'm leaving Boulder, King. We're going to Austria. I'm so glad I ran into you."

He smiled gently, his eyes reflecting genuine sadness.

Reading him, she smiled at him warmly. "You had a thing for me, didn't you?"

"No."

"Yes, you did. I can tell. You're heartbroken. I knew it. I always knew it! Nicholas was so jealous of you."

Celine was Canadian, older than King by ten years. He met her last year, at Bible study. She'd come to Boulder with a small ministry of sacred dancers, sponsored by a local Christian ballet instructor. They communicated holy scripture through dance.

They were an unlikely ensemble. None started as professional dancers. They didn't have svelte dancer's bodies. They'd been hand-picked and trained by their instructor. They made their living cleaning houses and doing odd jobs. They lived hand to mouth, day by day.

King had been particularly taken with Celine. She had beautiful eyes. She laughed like a wind chime. She was always being criticized by the others for her irreverent wit. Maria von Trapp had nothing on Celine. Celine had a gift for proselytizing with self-deprecating humor. She never forgot how strange her beliefs must seem to the nonbeliever. Hence she could relate to the staunchest atheist.

For a while she dated Nicholas. Because of Nicholas, King and Celine had important history between them. King cut ties with her over the Lex debacle. Seeing her now, he realized that he'd hurt her. Celine had been kind to him. She once taught King the choreography to the Lord's Prayer on the fifty-yard line of Folsom Stadium. She was present when King came out.

"King, you look so sad."

King forced himself to smile. Where was this emotion coming from?

"You'll always be in my prayers." She grabbed his hands. "Not that I'm saying you need to be! I hope I'll always be in yours, too!"

"Will you be coming back to Boulder?"

"Probably not. We're starting a dance ministry in Vienna. We leave in the morning."

King struggled to check his reaction. He wanted to be happy for her. He didn't want her to worry about him.

"I want you to have this," Celine searched her bag. She unearthed a beat-up old Bible. It had been given to her by a janitor in Montreal. King always loved it, because the cover was printed backwards. It was a King James Version. Celine always loved the fact that King's last name was James.

"I can't accept it. It's your favorite possession."

"Well, yes, I do love it. It's my most precious possession. That's why I'm giving it to you." Her eyes twinkled. "Hey, it has your name on it, right? Right?"

She pressed it toward him.

"I don't know where I am with all this. With my faith," he told her helplessly. "Don't give it to me thinking I'll come back someday."

"I know you love it and I have nothing else to offer you." She stroked his cheek. "It's traveled all over the world with me." She smiled beautifully. She forced it into his hands. "I've misplaced it a hundred times. It always comes back. I'd be very honored if you'd take care of it for me."

"Okay," King shrugged.

"I'm late. Remember what I told you King. I *love* you so much." He watched her disappear into a flurry of golden leaves.

King went home for the weekend, calling Sam nervously from the telephone in the hall off the basement family room. Nervous because he didn't want to intrude on Sam. Nervous because he didn't want his mother to hear. The call was short.

"It's cold here," Sam said cheerfully. "Hey, my ma is calling us for dinner. I'm back in two days. You'll pick me up?"

"I miss you," King said, but Sam was already gone. King was lamenting to a dial tone.

His father's birthday dinner was just King and his parents. His brother Neil announced other plans. His mom was shaken. She wanted the four of them to be together. Jim drank heavily under the weight of her sadness. Neil didn't even offer an excuse, or explain what better offer had come along. He just called to say he wouldn't be joining the family this year. King knew why, but certainly wasn't going to elaborate if Neil didn't have the guts to tell them. King was just as happy to have the subject be on somebody else, and not on him for a change.

The four-day break weighed heavily on the family. King had promised to pick Sam up at the airport around one-thirty on Sunday afternoon. He left his parents' house at eleven. He figured he'd knock around the concourse till Sam's plane landed. It ended up being an hour late. When he saw Sam disembark from the jet way, King summoned the wherewithal to check his elation. When he saw Sam, he just knew, that was all.

In the car, Sam draped his arm over King's shoulder while King drove. It was an affectionate gesture, designed to comfort. If anything, it made King feel worse. Sam was a nice guy. Why did he have to be such a nice fucking guy? It made him all the more desirable.

"See, King, I went back east for several reasons. It was a tough trip, but I feel clean now. I cleaned up a few things."

"Such as?"

"For one, I told my ma and dad about me."

"They didn't know?"

"I never said they did."

"I just assumed. You're so radical."

Sam laughed. "Maybe because I'm so far from home."

The traffic on the Boulder Turnpike was picking up. It was Sunday afternoon. Students were coming back. Just after Louisville, the proscenium of the snow-dusted Flatirons rose majestically in the distance.

"It's beautiful, Colorado."

"Yeah," King said thickly. He wished Sam would spit out whatever he wanted to say.

"Did I ever tell you why I wanted to come to school in Boulder?"

"No."

"I read an article about homosexuality in *Time* magazine. It talked about how progressive Colorado was. Boulder had one of the first equal rights amendments extending to gays in the country."

"It didn't pass."

"Still, they had the guts to fight for it." Sam paused. "I've only been out for two months, King. Technically, I guess it's only been two days."

"How did they take it?"

"They were wonderful to me." Sam's eyes glistened.

"I'm glad." The Baseline exit was coming up. King started signaling.

"There was another person I needed to tell," Sam told King. "Say, can we just keep driving? I don't want to go back to my dorm just yet."

"Sure," King nodded. He decided he should just relax. He had no idea what Sam was leading up to. Maybe nothing having to do with King at all. In fact, maybe he was telling King he'd cleared the air so the two of them could move forward. Out of the closet.

"I've had a fiancée. We were planning to get married after I finished grad school."

"You're *engaged*?"

Sam's eyes clouded. "Not anymore."

"Ah."

"She didn't take it so well. It was awful. But it's over now. She can move on, and so can I."

They drove in silence now. King's Capri was crawling through Boulder where the turnpike turned into 28th Street. He wondered in irritation why they hadn't built a freeway all the way to the other side of town.

"You can turn back if you want, King. I'm being selfish. I just wanted to spend a little more time with you."

"You have all night, " King offered.

"Well, see, this is hard. This is the hard part."

Here it was.

"We haven't talked about us," Sam started. "I think you might want something more than I can give, under the circumstances."

"What circumstances?"

"I just broke up with my childhood sweetheart. I came out to my folks. King, don't you want to kick up your heels? It's such an exciting time to be gay. And Colorado is in the forefront of gay rights legislation. Don't you want to be part of that?"

"Why can't we be part of that and be together?" Given that he never really thought he had a chance in hell, this was bold of King. He congratulated himself for it.

"Don't get me wrong, I love being with you. You're a wonderful man. But I think we want different things."

"What do you think I want?"

"Well, I think maybe you're probably geared toward the traditional heterosexual model of relationships and marriage. You won't be happy unless you find someone who thinks the way you do."

"You want your sexual freedom."

Sam smiled kindly. "Yeah, King. I want to enjoy my friendships, sleep around, and fight for our rights. We live in Boulder. It's the seventies. The sky's the limit. Nothing can stop us now. I've thought about this very carefully. I don't want to be dishonest about who I am anymore. I've hurt people. I don't want to hurt you."

"Can't I be a friend you sleep with?"

"It isn't your style, King. You'd be compromising yourself."

King couldn't defend himself. Sam was right.

"Why did you crash the dance with us?"

"Why did you ask me to?"

"I needed the body. And I was hoping to get in your pants. Now you tell me."

"I wanted you to be my boyfriend." King blushed and laughed. They came to a halt in the Reed Hall parking lot.

Sam gazed wistfully at King. "You didn't even know me. You wanted to sleep with me. And that's okay, too."

King shook his head. Sam was right about him. He felt awful.

"Just remember this," Sam added. "I'm a boy and a friend, and I loved making love with you."

"Me, too." King shrugged, and passionately Sam kissed him goodbye.

Chapter Three

The following day, Teddy suggested afternoon drinks at Scornovacco's, an Italian restaurant on Walnut Street in the historic section of downtown Boulder. It was upstairs from a Guatemalan boutique called La Boca, which was filled with sandals, and flimsy flower print dresses which tied behind the neck, and gauzy wedding shirts for the men. Every shirt King bought from La Boca was a clumsy mistake; ill-made, scratchy, reeking of dye. They always shrank and faded after the first hand washing. *Flaws in the weave only enhance the beauty of the garment.*

Scornovacco's tiny upstairs bar overlooked the river and the Flatirons. The Flatirons were singularly one of the most distinctive front range of rugged mountains overlooking any city in the world. Like the flat bottoms of old steam irons, they erupted the entire length of Boulder County. In rain, they burnished a deep red, at sunrise, a fiery orange, but King's personal favorite was winter, when after a sudden heavy snow the clouds would rise, and the Flatirons would glaze with thin, iridescent, sparkling white ice.

It had snowed early that day, and King and his roommate Teddy were drinking and talking. Teddy drank Scotch. King drank Bombay rocks. After several niceties, Teddy introduced the topic of conversation, the reason he'd suggested they meet.

Teddy was always happy; so good-natured. They made small talk. Teddy smiled at King, swilling back his drink so vigorously the ice popped forward and hit him under his nose.

"Say listen, no offense, but we *know*."

"Know what?"

Teddy grinned at him. "We know."

King was stunned. He'd been so careful, even respectful, not to lay his lifestyle on their home. The few times King slept with Sam had been at his dorm.

"So how did you find out?" King wasn't going to deny it.

"Jen's sorority sister Holly likes to dance. She saw your group." He chewed on some ice. "Saw you."

"Oh." King nodded. He didn't need to ask which dance. What song. "Eli's Comin'," probably. A lot of people stared at them on "Eli's Comin'."

"Quite a radical act." Teddy lifted his glass to King.

"Well," King offered, "it was just a dance. We weren't throwing pipe bombs in the physical science building."

"No point, really."

"No. No point." King shrugged again.

"See, it became a point to Jen, because her sorority sister knows we're roommates. She asked Jen if she knew."

"If Jen knew what?" King liked Jen. She was pretty self-confident. Her father owned a chain of Ford dealerships in California. Jen always drove a new Mustang convertible with blue California plates.

"If Jen knew about *me*."

"You mean, about your *roommate*." King stared into the bottom of his glass. It was empty. Teddy noticed and signaled for two more. Outside the snow began to fall again. It was close to five. The sun had been down for twenty minutes but King could still vividly see the silhouettes of the snowy Flatirons, emblazoned across the skyline.

"No," Teddy corrected him, "she specifically asked if Jen knew I was gay, because she saw *you* dancing at the UMC." He was now smiling ear to ear.

A cocktail waitress in a batik dress and Berkenstocks shuffled over with the tray of drinks. King moved to pay, but Teddy insisted. As he placed six dollar bills on her tray, King noticed her study Teddy hungrily.

"What did Jen say?"

"She laughed. Holly's an idiot. They all think so. They're kicking her out of the house."

"Because of this?"

"Nah, her grades suck."

"Follows," King commented.

"So anyway, Jen thinks it's great. She's from California. She has an openly gay second cousin. She thought it was very brave."

"Hmm." King really liked Jen, he reflected. Jen and King could be friends.

"Was it brave? I mean, were you scared?"

"Yeah," King barely whispered his reply because he was thinking about Sam. He felt bad. Missed him.

"Crowd could have turned on you. Beaten the crap out of you."

"Nah." King shook his head. "Not in Boulder."

"You think Boulder's any different?"

"Well," King ventured, but Teddy cut him off.

"Boulder's no different. Maybe it *was* brave"—he studied King— "or just plain stupid."

Now Teddy wasn't smiling. King thought he was going to give him a lecture that he shouldn't be so trusting, that he shouldn't take such stupid chances. King thought he was going to tell him to be more careful, that they were friends, King was his roommate. He didn't want King getting beaten up.

"We're gonna need the room back."

King looked up.

"We're gonna need the room back. Wade wants his own room. He thinks he can't get a date because of the bunk bed. And he can't sleep when Jen stays over."

"You guys have lived in the house for three years. You've always rented the other bedroom."

"Yeah, I know, but my old man is offering to kick in a few extra bucks. He likes Wade. He's been my best friend since grade school. He's worried he'll never find a girlfriend." Teddy paused. Took a deep breath. "Look, we just want the room back, that's all."

"What's Jen gonna say?"

"She'll call me a chickenshit. She may break up with me. Jen likes character. But she can't resist my body. She likes my body better than she likes me." Teddy's eyes twinkled and he smiled.

"Are you kicking me out because I'm gay?"

Teddy didn't say anything, but he pulled out his wallet and produced a few bills. "Keep it." He winked at the waitress. He wouldn't look at King. He just reached for his parka and pulled it on.

King was pretty sure Teddy felt bad, but he also sensed Teddy's great relief. King automatically began to justify him the same way he'd justified all the other gay-bashers King had known in his young years. *Teddy was uncomfortable, he was under peer pressure from the others, I was at fault for being too open.*

When Teddy left, he gently squeezed King's shoulder. Teddy may have felt bad, but he was still kicking King out for dancing with Sam in public.

When King came home, oddly enough, he got a call from Tim, Peter's boyfriend. They hadn't spoken two words since they tricked after a Hidden Valley dance.

"We're throwing Sam a surprise birthday party this Saturday in Denver. It's short notice. Can you make it?"

King stared stupidly at the telephone. It was already Thursday.

"King?" Tim covered the receiver on his end. "God, this guy is so uptight," King heard him whisper to someone.

"I'll come," King said abruptly.

"You will?" Tim gave him directions. "Remember, it's a surprise."

"I doubt I'll see Sam," King observed.

"Yeah, well. Just remember."

The party was held in an opulent apartment in a Cheeseman Park high-rise. The host was a slick stock broker named Skip, who had taken Sam to dinner and would bring him back to his apartment, presumably for an intimate evening. King recognized most of the guests. Rod and Tony. Tim and Peter. It was mostly couples.

"You'll love the cake." Tim grinned at King. He surprised him by kissing King full on the lips. King tasted gin. "Mmm . . ." Tim wet his lips. "I remember that."

"It has all the names of the men Sam's slept with. It's pretty tacky." Peter shrugged behind him. Peter was already drunk. He was a sad sack. He spent most of his energy guarding Tim.

"That's not true," Tim said. "I'm not on it." He winked at King and turned to greet another arrival. Peter gazed longingly after him.

"He's such a fucking flirt."

"Yeah, but at least he's your flirt," King said, surprising them both. They shared a laugh.

"We didn't think you'd come," Peter admitted. "That's why we didn't invite you sooner."

"Why not?"

"You're such a loner. And you're still hung up on Sam."

King feigned umbrage but they laughed again.

"When's he coming?"

"Skip said around ten. Shouldn't be long now."

At five minutes to ten, Tim cut the lights. They all fell silent. Right on time, they heard a key in the door.

"I can only stay a few minutes," Sam was heard protesting. "This is a little soon. I just ended a thing with someone."

Peter nudged King in the dark.

"Someone local?"

"No. My high school sweetheart back in New York."

"I just wanted you to see the view." Skip snapped on the lights. "Surprise!"

An embarrassed but pleased Sam surveyed the room. Friends and admirers rushed to greet him.

At the center of the dining room table, King spied the cake. There were fourteen names monogrammed in green frosting. When he thought nobody was watching, King anxiously searched for his own name. He felt validated to find it scrawled in green frosting, close to Sam's, near a pink rose.

"Hey, King." Caught, King turned to find himself face-to-face with Sam, smiling sweetly down at him with Skip clutching his arm.

"Happy birthday," King mustered, reaching up to kiss Sam's cheek. The group swelled around Sam, edging King to the outside. After a few minutes, King took off. Tomorrow he had to go apartment hunting.

In King's years in Boulder he probably lived in eleven different places. He'd get kidded about it but he didn't mind. He usually moved because of a roommate change or problem. He always bettered his digs. Plus, he knew Boulder like the color of his eyes. Since King was asked on short notice to vacate his room up at Teddy's, his options would be limited. As luck would have it, Theo caught him loitering outside the campus Gay Lib office. King was scanning the bulletin board, looking for places to live.

This business about getting kicked out of his house was starting to eat at him. He was increasingly ashamed that he hadn't put up more of a fight. He was also too embarrassed to admit to his parents why he was moving. They'd be devastated. And angry. King chose to protect them from the truth.

"You looking for something?" The office door swung open. Theo peered out.

King's face flashed hot. He'd purposely come after hours, when no one would be manning the office. "Hey . . ." King managed to sputter.

"I approve all the messages and literature posted on the bulletin board. I can help you find what you're looking for. You come Friday nights. To the Coffee House."

"Yeah." King nodded.

"We appreciate the support."

"Beats the drive to Denver."

"Hopefully you come for more reasons than the long drive."

"Yes," King lied, "I do."

"So what are you looking for?"

"I need a place to live," King muttered miserably.

"What's up? You breaking up with someone?"

"No." His damn voice quavered.

"Look. Do you need to talk? I can open up the office. Or we can go across to the grill and have a coffee."

King didn't think he could ever admit why he was so upset, but Theo seemed like a good guy. The eyes behind the wire frames were surprisingly blue.

"The grill, I guess."

The University of Colorado student grill gained national attention when students voted to name it after Alferd E. Packer, a famous mountain cannibal. It was situated on the ground floor of the UMC, and all the campus clubs were housed in a maze of tiny offices across the corridor from its doors. This area always invigorated King, because the clubs seemed particularly radical, like UMAS, the United Mexican American Student coalition, and NOW, the National Organization for Women.

And BGLF, the Boulder Gay Liberation Front.

The first time he noticed the office as an impressionable freshman, King started to sweat. As he walked away, he had to hold his books down to hide a swelling erection. At that time, King hadn't allowed himself to consciously fantasize about having sex with men. The hallway leading to this door always had a hold on King. He avoided passing it whenever he could, as if he'd be sucked in by its powerful current.

Each office had a small bulletin board announcing meetings, calls to action, elections, and other matters of importance. Outside in the main corridor, another huge bulletin board lined the entire corridor with all manner of notices: campus events, rides needed to California or New York; used books for sale; used furniture for sale; stereo equipment; tutoring; roommates wanted; even a few personal ads.

Logan, come back to me, I'm desperate. Sue

Poor Sue. King knew about feeling desperate.

Sam, come back to me, I'm desperate.

The corridor was always packed with students rushing in all directions. A thin haze of cigarette smoke and incense permeated the hall.

Now Theo led King through the swarming student population toward the doors to the Packer Grill. He put his hand on King's arm as if to pull him along. That old maneuver. King had been poked and squeezed in enough dark bars to know when someone was trying to figure out if he had any muscles under his jacket. King had one guy hold his face up to the light on the street by his car before he finally agreed to take him home.

But Theo didn't grip King with any force. He was merely being gentle. King caught his own reflection in the glass. He looked quite beside himself. They strode past the tables toward the coffee machines. Theo pulled out two tall cups and filled them. Occasionally Theo would glance over at King, smile slightly, then look away. He handed him his coffee. When they got to the cashier, King paid. Although he wanted to resist, Theo nodded thanks instead.

"So how long have you been out?" They took a table in the back, almost in shadows.

"Out?"

"Openly *gay* . . ." Theo chided King.

King hated that word. Was that the best they could come up with? When did they vote, anyway? Nobody asked him.

"I guess you might say last year." King sipped his coffee. "Depends on what you mean by *out.*"

"It differs from person to person," Theo offered. "For instance, I'm out on campus. To my professors. Where I work. All of my friends from before know. My mother knows. I haven't told my father."

"You sure she hasn't told him?"

"He's away a lot. She doesn't like to upset him." Theo gazed up at King. "So what about you?"

"Oh." King shrugged. "Everybody knows. Everybody."

A silence overtook them. They sipped their coffee thoughtfully. The grill emptied out. It was late afternoon.

"So what was upsetting you?" Theo asked. "Why do you need a place to live? The semester's already started."

"It's embarrassing."

"I can handle it."

"I was asked to move out of a house I was sharing. My roommates needed the extra room."

"What's embarrassing about that?"

King didn't answer.

"They didn't know?"

King shook his head.

"Is this the first time you've been discriminated against?"

"I don't know if I'd call it discrimination."

"What would you call it, then?"

"They needed the room. See, they were living together before I moved in. They shared a room. I had my own. They decided they wanted separate bedrooms."

"But they asked you to move after they found out?"

"Yeah."

"It's a hard thing."

"What?"

"The first time you come face-to-face with discrimination."

"This isn't the first time," King replied.

"No?"

"It isn't something I talk about."

Theo's eyes flickered with interest. Interest and respect. "So I don't know if you'd be interested, but a studio just came available in my building. I live on Canyon. It's pretty reasonable."

"How much?"

"A hundred fifteen . . . I'd be your next-door neighbor."

"So when can I take a look?"

They took off across campus, heading for the footpath that cascaded down the hill behind the recreation center to the bridge over the river. The gray sky churned overhead. The air felt brisk. Tonight it would probably snow.

Boulder Canyon fed into Canyon Avenue and the river followed it temporarily till it snaked south toward campus. Theo's apartment complex was relatively new; a two-story brown brick featuring a tiny swimming pool abutting the parking lot. A slightly weathered sign offered: *Studios and One Bedroom Apartments for Rent.*

King liked the overall look of the place.

"The manager here?" he wondered.

"I'm the manager," Theo replied.

He led King down a walkway to a short flight of stairs. They descended to King's waiting apartment. Theo fumbled with his keys, finally unlocking a sliding glass door. He pulled back a drape and ushered King into an L-shaped studio with a full kitchen and a good-size main room. A small bathroom lay wedged behind the kitchen. Theo pulled open the drapes. The room would always be dark, but King could see the sky over the upper railing. He liked the womblike feeling of the place.

"Neighbors are mostly graduate students. Mostly straight. It's a good location. Close to campus. Close to downtown. You like to go out?"

"On occasion," King told him.

"You ever hang around the Boulderado?"

"Le Bar."

"I've seen you in there. We're gonna try to take it over."

"Take it over?"

"Boulder doesn't have its own gay club. The church is okay, but we need a real bar. The Boulderado is perfect. The heteros can have the Mezzanine and the Catacombs."

Boulder's oldest hotel, the Boulderado Hotel, sported three bars; upstairs was the Mezzanine, a white thicket of fan-backed rattan chairs and low divans overlooking the ornate lobby of the old hotel. On the main floor, behind the hotel front desk was Le Bar, a small room with French café tables and a short mahogany bar. King had never been to France, or east of the Mississippi, for that matter, but he found this room very romantic and sophisticated.

On the ground level, under the staircase to the front doors of the lobby, steps led to a maze of dark rooms called the Catacombs. Sometimes the Catacombs could be pretty cruisy, but you ran the risk of hitting on a drunk and sentimental straight frat boy whose friends might intervene and beat the crap out of you.

"On Thursday, a group of us plan to meet there."

"Same group I went dancing with?"

"He'll be there." Theo studied King for his reaction.

"Who?" King knew fully well he meant Sam. His face grew hot.

"He's a handsome man. I can understand the effect he has on you." After a moment Theo asked if King wanted the apartment. He nodded that he did.

"Where do you live?"

"We share a common wall." He gestured to the apartment just past King's. "I'll never be more than a foot away from you when you sleep."

King's testicles churned.

"Come in and sign your lease. You need help moving?"

"My dad has a van. He'll come up and help."

"That's pretty cool." Theo started to walk toward his apartment. King followed him. He slid open his sliding glass door. "He knows about you. I wish my father knew about me."

King followed him in, happy to be out of the cold.

The following Sunday King's mother and father came to help him move. How many times, King wondered, would they continue to make this trip from their snug little brick house situated innocently in Green Mountain, on a hill overlooking Denver, to move him, wild-eyed and neurotic, to another place again.

King always had mountains over his shoulder to give him direction. His father, a fed with the Bureau of Land Management, once confided that although he made his living from the mountains, at heart he loved the Great Plains.

When told of King's impending departure, Teddy and Wade disappeared on the day he moved. Jen, Teddy's girlfriend, astonished him by roaring up in her red Mustang convertible and announcing she had come to help.

"Hullo." She extended her hand to King's mother. "I'm Jen."

"I'm Kay." She nodded, pursing her lips shyly and drawing her sweater close. As Jen grinned vivaciously at King's father, Kay nervously scanned the red car. It was early winter and the top was down.

"Aren't you cold?" she queried.

"I keep an afghan stuffed in the backseat. I also turn on the heat."

"With the top down?"

"It's pretty unecological, huh?" Jen grinned at her apologetically. "I just love the cold wind in my face." Smiling next to her red car against the backdrop of the gently rising black street, the silver-coated winter lawns and the gunmetal Colorado winter sky, to King it was as though the entire world was black and white and only Jen and her red, red car were in color. King never saw red like that before.

He reflected upon the possibility that Jen and he never uttered much more than a hello or goodbye in the month he'd lived there. Yet here she was, offering to help him move because her boyfriend and his buddy were too ashamed to show their faces to his parents today.

"I've never ridden in a convertible," King's mother commented.

"Then you will today! Now, how can I help?"

King stood stupefied next to his father. He nudged him. His father was a sensitive man. He'd never heard of Jen. He knew King was intimidated by her.

"There isn't all that much. Maybe you could carry a few boxes. My dad and I can get the bed."

They finished loading up in less than an hour. King placed his key on the counter in the kitchen. Jen came up behind him. She hesitated, then reached into her pocket for her key ring. She picked out a key and held it out to King, the other keys dangling.

"Can you get this off? I just had a manicure. I don't want to break my nail."

King managed to excise the key and handed it to her.

She took it and placed it on the counter next to his.

"Let's not look back," Jen said wistfully, taking King's arm. "My cousin wants to meet you when he comes to town."

Moments later, in the side mirror of his father's van, King watched Jen tail them in her red convertible, his mom riding shotgun, knit cap pulled tight, her hair blowing in the open car. They were warm under Jen's afghan. Every time King looked back, they were laughing like the best of friends.

Chapter Four

Theo had many visitors at all hours of the day and night. King's curtains were always open and when men showed up they glanced into his room, some more blatant than others. Early one morning King stepped naked from his shower, realizing that his clean towels were unfolded in the laundry basket on the table in the kitchen.

At the same time, a tall, light-haired man was leaving Theo's. He peered through the window, and noticing King was naked, turned and stared boldly in his direction as though through a one-way mirror. King pretended not to notice, but he knew he was being watched. He slowed his pace, and when he reached the laundry basket, slowly dried himself off in front of the voyeur. When King finally wandered back to the bathroom, his peeping tom had vanished but King was aroused by his power to spellbind him.

At night through the shared wall, King could often hear soft music, mostly jazz, and the hushed cadence of lowered voices. Later, speech might transmute to guttural noise, as passions flared on Theo's side of the wall. King got off on it more than once, sometimes pressing his naked body into the scramble of sheets and blankets and jerking off as he writhed along the plasterboard moaning wall. King hadn't had sex since Sam. It was time to break his new place in. He decided to drive to Denver.

The drive from King's front door to the Broadway, a combination cabaret and dance club in the Capitol Hill area of Denver, took about forty minutes if the roads were clear. Hustlers sold themselves in the ellipse surrounding the nearby Colorado state capitol building. As a grade school student he took many trips to the capitol building. The thrilling climb up the rickety stairs to the catwalk inside the rotunda dome caused King's heart to pound. King's classmates pushed and shoved each other against the flimsy railing and contemplated the cold marble floors, five flights below.

Now King came to Capitol Hill for another reason. The Broadway was situated next to the White Spot Café at 13th and Broadway. King parked across the street, coincidentally in the same lot where his father parked his van during the day. King worried he might meet someone, ride home with them to trick, and barely make it back to the lot in time the next morning before Jim would park and walk the several blocks north to work.

If he ever saw King's new Capri parked in this obscure Denver parking lot, his father never said anything. King didn't think he knew that by night the Broadway was a gay bar. They served lunch during the day and catered to a business crowd. Once, after King and Lex closed the Broadway, Jim asked King to join him there, twelve hours later, for lunch.

As King pulled into the jammed parking lot he looked at his watch: 10:48. It was Thursday and the bar was already busy. King found a space in a slippery patch of black ice near the back of the lot. He heard muffled laughter in a car nearby. Two figures, nearly invisible behind the steamy windows of a blue Camaro, smoked a joint, which King could smell in the night air. He crunched his way across the parking lot.

King never wore a coat when he went out because he didn't know how to handle it once he got inside. Although the Broadway had a coat check girl, usually a drag queen, King preferred to ditch his coat in his car. He resisted the urge to jaywalk. Denver cops liked to harass club patrons with jaywalking tickets. With a high violent crime rate, King guessed they had nothing better to do.

Because it was King's first gay bar and King was sentimental, he didn't think he'd ever find another bar as great. As he entered, his eyes adjusted to the smoky cabaret. A few men lined a bar which ran the length of the room. A low wall separated the bar area from the cabaret, where steps up led to crowded cocktail tables. Tonight a Kim Carnes lookalike was bitching for everybody to stop talking during her set. King had to admit, when she sang she was good.

He kept walking, enjoying the cruisy stares of the men lining the bar. He entered the hallway separating the cabaret from the dance room. It was soundproof. When King opened the second swinging door, the dance floor churned like a cement mixer, smoke and poppers wafted to his nostrils, and Barry White singing, " 'You're my first, my last, my everything . . . ' " exploded up beneath him and rocketed him to heaven.

Pivoting left to a small service bar, King always ordered call gins on the rocks—Bombay when they had it, or Tanqueray, which he found a little harsh. That way, if a stranger bought him a drink, he could ask for his usual without taking advantage. Not that many strangers sent him drinks, but when they did, he was ready. King usually drank his first drink very fast. A U-shaped catwalk overlooked the dance floor, four or five feet at its widest. Men lined the walls—on busy nights like Thursdays, they were two or three deep.

The regular disco queens came every night, wearing gabardine pleated pants, Nik-Nik shirts, and platform dancing shoes. They had big teased-up hair, slightly frosted, with enough pancake to disguise acne-scarred cheeks and necks. They were big on designer colognes.

King thought they were beautiful in their way, and since most of them were hairdressers or shop clerks, they made the most of what they had. They all chipped in to live in security high-rises, with parking garages and mirrored elevators. They drove big Buicks and Oldsmobiles with plush velour upholstery and called each other *She* and *Miss Thing*. They were paired off but incestuous, and King was always intrigued to see how the configurations might change on a weekly basis.

To them, King thought he was probably just a boring college kid in French-manufactured Izod tennis shirts, Sperry Topsiders, and jeans. He noted the crowd. Tim and Tony were dancing. Peter and Rod nowhere in sight. King scanned the room for Sam but he wasn't there. They all drove in every night from Boulder, but them together, King alone.

The song changed and the Boulder Men surged with the crowd up near the service bar. Tim nodded. Tony hugged King, kissing him on the top of his head. King overheard Tim exclaim about a man standing in the shadows near the service bar. He glanced over, saw who he was talking about, and quickly looked away.

The dance floor was packed and King was already on his second shot of Bombay when the bartender told him someone wanted to buy him a drink. He looked up. The object of Tim's affection. Late thirties, early forties. East Coast. Quite handsome. Uncomfortable here. King nodded his thanks as the waiter poured his third shot of gin in less than an hour.

King's patron approached. For a moment they stood next to each other, watching the dancers on the dance floor.

"Thank you for the drink," King shouted. He had the bad luck to select a momentary lull in the music, so heads turned.

"What'd I buy you?" his new friend shouted back, studying the clear contents of King's glass.

"Gin."

He took King's glass, holding it up to his nose.

"Bombay. You have good taste."

"What?"

"Maybe we should move to the front where we can talk." He smiled when King nodded. King pictured his cock. King could guess what a cock would look like from a man's smile. A smile on a man's face told King a great deal. Friendly or mean. Bright or slow. And King could always guess the dimensions of their dicks. Not just length or width, but the folds of their testicles, the size of their balls. Without looking down, King could tell that his new friend was already aroused.

King followed him through the tunnel to the front part of the bar. He had rich man's hair. Longish brown with natural gold highlights.

"I'm Matthew," he turned.

"I'm King."

"Who made you King?" Matthew asked, smiling slightly. He held the door for King, his hand accidentally brushing his ass.

They sat at the dark end of the bar, on two stools isolated by a pass-through for the bar backs to load ice and haul beer. A bartender finally noticed them and wandered over.

Matthew took King's hand and held it on his knee while he ordered. This was a confident gesture—assuming quite a bit. Frankly, King liked the fact that he did it. Matthew wore dark pleated wool slacks with a navy V-neck sweater. The wool was fine and King could feel the muscles of his thigh.

"What'll it be?"

"Bombay rocks and a Chivas, neat."

"My friend thinks he's an expert on the bouquet of gin," King volunteered.

"I *know* I'm an expert." Matthew squeezed his hand. King was already a little drunk. The bartender disappeared and returned shortly with their drinks.

"That'll be four bucks."

"It's my turn." King tossed a five on the bar.

"Thank you, King." For the first time, they really saw each other. Matthew smiled. He threw back the remainder of his first drink, leaned in, and kissed King. Matthew's tongue tasted cool and wet.

King's eyes opened. "How old are you?" he asked.

"Thirty-one." Matthew smiled, but his eyes betrayed him. He was lying. "How old are you?"

"Seventeen," King answered, and Matthew reeled back. "I've got a fake I.D."

The bartender, returning with his change, howled.

"I'm really twenty-two," King laughed.

"Thirty-six." Matthew shrugged. "You got me. You have a pretty mouth," he whispered. "A sweet, pretty mouth."

King thought of Sam. *If you like pretty lips, you should kiss my friend*, he thought of saying, but didn't. He needed to be over Sam, he reminded himself.

"If you lined up four different shots of gin, I bet I could tell you which is which."

"Let's do it." Matthew nodded to the bartender. "Close your eyes."

He watched while the bartender poured, so he knew the shots were lined up in alphabetical order. Bombay, Boodles, Gilbey's, and Tanqueray. King guessed as much.

"What are the stakes?" King asked.

"Stakes?"

"What do I get if I do it? If I'm right."

Matthew shifted uncomfortably. "I don't know. Drunk?"

"I don't want to be just drunk. It isn't necessary, you know."

"What isn't necessary, King?"

"You don't need to get me drunk to get me to go home with you."

"I think I'd have to get you very drunk. I live in Pittsburgh. I go back in the morning."

"Yeah?" Before King could check it, his face registered his dismay.

"But I come to Denver often on business. Often," Matthew said again, his voice trailing away.

"Well, to spend the night then. That's what I want if I win."

"You do?"

King picked up the first glass and smelled it. He did the same thing with the next three. "Bombay. Boodles, Gilbey's, and Tanqueray. I win. Let's go."

"We haven't discussed parameters."

"Parameters?"

"You know," he whispered. "The deal."

He thought King was a hustler. By King's reaction, he knew he'd made a big mistake. He felt horrible and King was glad. King shot to his feet, the picture of melodramatic umbrage.

"If you looked like a hustler, I wouldn't be interested." Matthew grabbed King's hand. "I'm sorry, King. Is King really your name?"

"No, it's King. But that has nothing to do with it. Is Matthew really your name?"

"Yes."

"Why did you think I was a hustler?"

"Because I'm so much older than you. I'm the oldest guy in this bar. Nobody's looked at me once. I only think hustlers are interested."

Tim trolled by, his eyes widening when he saw King with Matthew.

"Think again," King commented, leaning over to kiss him, mostly for Tim's sake.

Matthew was staying at the Denver Hilton. King had never tricked in the Hilton before and thought it was probably very sophisticated. It was Denver's finest hotel other than the ornate old Brown Palace, which King dismissed as out of date and shabby. No one had taught him the finer points of crown moldings.

They walked over, leaving his Capri in the parking lot. King promised himself he'd be back before six-thirty the next morning to claim it. The hotel was six blocks west of the bar. It was cold.

"Where's your coat?"

"I left it in my car. I don't need it."

"You're being ridiculous. Take my jacket."

"Then you'll be cold."

"I'm wearing a cashmere sweater and a wool shirt underneath. I'll be fine."

He took off his leather jacket and draped it over King's shoulders. It smelled expensive and probably was. "Would you put it on?"

King studied him under the streetlight. Matthew smiled to himself as they walked. He seemed genuinely happy at the prospect of being with King, who felt a rush of affection for him, but checked it.

"What's wrong?"

"I'm sorry you don't live here," King, feeling his gin, frankly admitted. "I'm already kinda missing you. I think we're gonna have a great time."

"I'm already having a great time. Let's see how you feel in an hour."

They crossed at 14th. The capitol building loomed up. "If you wanted a hustler, you should have started there."

Cars slowly circled, headlights illuminating figures standing back in the shadows. Occasionally pulling to a stop to discuss a deal.

"I think it's pathetic if you think you have to pay for sex."

"I don't think I have to pay for sex," Matthew offered. "But for others there must be practical reasons . . ."

Poor guy, King thought. Had no idea how handsome he was.

"What do you do?"

"I'm a lawyer."

"What kind of lawyer?"

"A divorce attorney."

"That's sad," King said.

"Sometimes, very sad."

"My parents have a happy marriage."

"They're lucky," Matthew said quietly. "Mine didn't." He smiled over at King. "I wish I could hold your hand."

"You can. Go ahead."

"I don't think so, but I want to. When we get to my room, I want to kiss you for about a year. You're a very good kisser, you know that?"

When they got near the hotel, Matthew said without apology, "I'm in room 1209. Wait for a minute and come up." Before King could complain, he was gone. King was angry, but he still had Matthew's coat, which probably cost over two hundred dollars.

King hesitated, not knowing what to do. He thought about leaving, walking back to his car and keeping the fucking coat. It fit him well enough and he could never afford a leather jacket. King started to walk away but he stopped. He began to justify Matthew's behavior. Matthew was afraid to come out. He wasn't lucky to have the parents King had. He was in Denver on business. He was older.

King waited and went up to his room.

"I'm married," Matthew said when he opened the door.

The room was dark behind him, with the exception of a candle flickering bedside. Through his open drapes King could see the lights of Denver from his windows.

Matthew was out of his clothes, standing in a loosely tied checkered robe. He wasn't wearing slippers. His feet were big, and his legs, from what King could tell, muscular and well defined. King was certain if he reached under the robe he would already be semierect.

Matthew was coating his news by trying to seduce him.

"You should have gotten your jacket back first." King was pissed off.

"You won't take my jacket."

"It's too cold to walk back without it."

"I think you knew I was married when we left the bar. I don't think you want to go back tonight at all. But we can get you a cab if you do."

"Don't I get to keep the coat?"

"My wife gave it to me. I'm sorry."

King took off the coat and handed it to him.

My first married man. King could picture him fucking a woman and it turned him on.

A door opened slightly down the hall. A face peered out. An old lady. She stared at him blankly. Matthew motioned for him to come inside. King disappeared into his room and closed the door.

Matthew moved to kiss him. King pushed him away.

"I want to talk things through a little."

Stepping back, Matthew winced, and sat on the bed. His robe fell open and King could see his cock. He'd been right on the money. Exactly what King thought. Big head. Short, thick shaft. But not too short.

"We can talk all night if you want to. I have to be on the plane at six A.M. I can sleep all the way to Pittsburgh. But it's my suggestion, and only a suggestion, that we might explore our physicality first. Talk can spoil sexual rewards."

"Sex can spoil conversation."

"Conversation can also spoil further conversation. Sex doesn't usually spoil sex."

King smiled. Who was he kidding?

"Take a shower with me."

"Don't worry. I'm clean. I took a shower before I came out." King shook his head in disgust.

"Well, I didn't," Matthew said mildly. "I came straight from a business dinner. Join me if you like."

He disappeared into the bathroom and took off his robe. King watched him climb into the shower. He was well made, but not overly muscular. The shower stall was clear glass. He allowed the warm water to cascade over his head.

They made out passionately for nearly an hour. Matthew had dark green eyes. Almost brown. King began to caress his chest, kissing first his nipples and then tracing the tendrils of short hair leading down to his groin. Matthew's cock pulsated up from his body with each flick of King's tongue on his lower abdomen. King wanted to plunge it inside his mouth.

Matthew leaned up and kissed him. Stopping him.

"Wait," he whispered breathlessly. He reached over to the nightstand and pulled open the top drawer. He found a condom and sat up, tearing the foil with his teeth.

"What's that for?" King never heard of two men using condoms.

"I want to wear it if you're planning on giving me a blow job." He looked at King pleadingly. "Look, I get NSU even if I look at a guy. Then I have to go to my doctor, who's an old friend of the family. Please. Let me put it on. Rubbers can be sexy."

"The taste of rubber isn't sexy."

"No problem. I really want to fuck you. You have the best ass on any man I've ever seen. I saw your ass across the room back at the club. I've got to make love with you."

"I don't really like getting fucked," King whispered, remembering what Sam told him.

Matthew moved close to King and began kissing him again. They lay facing each other, but he was propped up on one elbow. "Please. I think you're so lovely, King. I want to see you whenever I come to Denver. I'll stay another night if we can spend it together. Put this on for me."

Unrolling the condom over the tip and down the shaft of Matthew's cock electrified King. Matthew smiled at his reaction. He'd guessed it would.

King lay back on his pillow. Matthew fiddled with a jar of cream, lubricating the condom. He kissed King again, reaching down between his legs. "I'll be gentle," he promised him. "I just want us to be together."

Matthew pressed himself inside him. He waited till King relaxed, and then began rocking gently. Soon he was thrusting as deeply as he liked. King didn't even bother to jerk off. He curled up into him as tightly as he could. King could see the candle flickering, reflecting in the mirror. He could see the lights of the distant foothills of Green Mountain where he grew up. King was happy to be gay. He marveled at this closeness to another man. His breathing hurried.

"Look at me, King," Matthew whispered passionately.

When King looked into his eyes, Matthew came.

Matthew was true to his word. They talked all night. King asked him if his wife knew. He said she knew some of it.

"I travel a lot. She doesn't ask questions."

"Does she see other men?"

"I hope so," he said after a minute.

"*Why?*"

"Things are confused for us now."

"Are you planning to rectify that?"

"No," he said quietly. "She's a great woman. I want her to have what we just had."

"You don't have to keep pretending that I'm anything special," King said.

"I not pretending anything of the sort!" Matthew stood up in irritation. "And don't test me that way. You wouldn't be here if you weren't special. You'd have twenty dollars in your pocket and you'd already be walking home."

Matthew wandered over to the window. He was naked, his hands pressing on the humming heating unit. The head of his penis dangled just below his balls in silhouette, which King loved.

"It's starting to snow."

"Don't change the subject."

"But it's nice. Come back to bed and we'll watch it fall together."

"You hurt my feelings. You don't know how lucky you are this is nineteen seventy-four. You don't have the same pressures to start a family as my generation did twenty years ago. Christ, Stonewall hadn't even happened when I started to explore my sexuality. It's very confusing and oftentimes deeply lonely."

"Then come back to bed."

"I'm sorry I lied to you. I've lied to you about something else. My real name is Ralph. Not Matthew."

"Come to bed, Ralph."

"Last year a store clerk kid tried to blackmail me. You can't blame me for being careful."

"To be fair, yes I can." But then King stopped. "I'm glad you care about your wife. I hope things work out the right way, whatever that is. I'm happy I came here with you. Are you really staying another night?"

Matthew turned and came back to bed with him. King began to kiss him tenderly. He thought he could taste tears on Matthew's cheek. Matthew brushed them away angrily but didn't say anything. They kept kissing. Matthew disappeared down King's body.

"Coming out hasn't been entirely easy on me either," King whispered.

Matthew's mouth found King's dick. He moaned when he tasted it.

"Matthew. Do you want me to put on a condom?"

"No. King." Matthew shook his head. His hair fell down against King's skin. "And tomorrow night, I won't wear one either."

Chapter Five

The following morning Matthew loaned King his jacket and offered to walk him back to his car. Since they were seeing each other later, King agreed to borrow the coat but he wanted to walk alone.

When King was in the shower he heard the phone ring. Before Matthew answered, he came to the bathroom door to pull it closed. King turned, pretending he didn't see him. He listened carefully while he toweled off. He opened the door and went into the bedroom.

Matthew looked up.

"That was my office. I asked my secretary to cancel my schedule tomorrow. This actually gives me a day to catch up while you're at *class*," he added, and his hand went to his forehead in mock horror that King was so young. "I've ordered breakfast for us. Should be here shortly. What shall we do tonight?"

"You ever been to Boulder?"

"No."

"I'll come pick you up. We can spend the night at my place."

"Maybe we should stick closer to the hotel. I might miss a message."

King's face fell.

"It wasn't all that bad, now was it? Staying here. Vacation for you, too, huh? When I come back I'll stay with you."

"How will you do that?" King said sharply.

"By being honest," Matthew told him. There was a knock at the door. He opened it and a room service clerk entered with a tray. He checked them out. King recognized him from the bar last night. Nothing was said. Matthew signed for it and the guy left.

King left shortly thereafter. They agreed he'd be back around six-thirty.

There was one other vehicle in the snow-covered parking lot. His father's Ford van, parked across the lot from King's Capri. His office was in a bank building a block past the Hilton. King hoped he hadn't passed him on the street. He'd been an idiot. His dad always left home early to avoid traffic, especially on snowy days.

He glanced across the street. Two doors up from the Broadway was an old bar called the Tip Top Club. It opened at six in the morning, which King knew from his early morning returns to his car. Only real alcoholics drank there.

His mind raced. His dad had clearly seen his car. Had to know it was King's. But maybe not. It had stormed after all. King was in luck. His car was white with snow.

King trudged across the parking lot in Matthew's leather jacket. He decided he would continue to call him Matthew, a name that made him King's. When he got to his car he saw that his windshield, which should have been covered with ice and snow, had just been freshly scraped.

Knowing his father, it was not to indict him or prove he was on to him. He had done it out of consideration for King's safety. So when King got back, he wouldn't be inconvenienced. King looked around. Across the street, the door to the Tip Top swung open and a man stepped out, shading his eyes from the snow-bright day. He stared at the ground, hunkered down inside his top coat, heading west toward 14th Street. He looked like the loneliest man in the world.

Of course it was Jim, his father, and this was why he left so early for work. To brace himself for a job he hated with a few drinks at the Tip Top. Today an added bonus: finding his son's car in the morning-after parking lot of Denver's most popular gay bar.

King didn't call out to him.

His dad had respected King's privacy as King would respect his. Like Matthew and Matthew's wife, they would each do what they had to do in order to survive the day.

When King got back to Boulder, Theo met him in the passageway leading down to their apartments. "I need to prepare you for something. She was very depressed and said she had nowhere to go, so I let her in."

"Who?"

"She came knocking at dawn. I saw her help you move in. It was nearly four so I figured you wouldn't be back. That you were sleeping away."

"Who are you *talking* about? Is someone in my apartment?"

Out of the corner of King's eye, a figure drew back the drapes. It was Jen. She opened the sliding glass door.

"She was looking for you. I had someone over. We were asleep. When I said you were gone she just sat on the steps. I thought she'd freeze to death. So I let her in."

King studied Jen.

"It's okay." Don't worry about it." King headed down the stairs to his apartment.

"You have a good evening?"

King turned. "Huh?"

"You meet someone?"

"Yeah." King nodded. "I think so. I'm seeing him again tonight."

"Sounds serious."

"Who knows?" King stepped through the sliding door to his apartment.

Jen hadn't slept and she'd been crying. She kept apologizing for barging in on him and King kept telling her she didn't have to worry.

"What's wrong?"

"I'm pregnant," she said. "I made coffee. You want some?"

"Yeah . . ." King struggled for the right thing to say. She poured him a cup of coffee.

"I'm keeping it, in case you're wondering." She stared at him. "Nice coat. New?"

"I borrowed it. You thought it all through?"

"I don't think I'll ever finish thinking it all through. All I know is I'm pregnant, and I'm going to have a baby this spring."

"Teddy know?"

"He knew the day you moved out."

"That was a month ago."

"I was a month pregnant then."

"Jesus."

"No, it isn't Jesus in here. This wasn't an immaculate conception," and she laughed halfheartedly. "You know that only too well."

"You went at it like cats."

"I was gushing with his sperm. I'm surprised it didn't come out of my pores." She paused. "The father of my baby has no character. Do you think I can overcome his genes?"

"Teddy's okay. Won't he help?"

"He offered to pay for an abortion. I considered it, but then he admitted he already had a kid with someone else. I couldn't abort someone's brother or sister. You know what I mean? It creeped me out."

"So you've known for awhile. I called you a couple of times. To say thanks. You didn't call back."

"I'm sorry. Everything steamrolled out of control. I had to leave the house."

"They kicked you out?"

"They would have."

"And your family?"

"My mother nearly had a stroke. I finally had to tell her. She offered to pay for an abortion so my father wouldn't find out. She even flew out to Colorado. She slapped me when I told her no. My father is a very devout Catholic. In any case, he knows now."

"How did he react?"

"I'm cut off. On my own. He even took my car. Had it repossessed."

"Can't your mom reason with him?"

"She's scared to death of him. She gave me a thousand dollars and told me to call during the day when he was out." Jen smiled. "I've learned how to ride the bus." She studied her hands. "I've lost everybody. My girlfriends in the house won't have anything to do with me. Teddy. My family. I'm alone. I have to apply for an emergency grant to finish school. I need to go on welfare."

"Where are you living?"

"Like an idiot, I stayed in a hotel till my money ran out. I thought they'd come around. They haven't. I just got kicked out. This was the only place I had to come."

"Then stay."

"Your mom called, by the way. Early. I thought it was you so I picked up."

"How early?"

"Seven."

"What'd you say?"

"She didn't even ask. She seemed glad I was here. She asked if she could have another ride in my car. Then I burst out crying."

"She on her way?"

Jen nodded.

As if on cue, King heard his mother's voice. "King? Are you down there?"

"Yeah, we're here."

He pulled open the drapes. His mother stood pensively on the patio, smoking a cigarette. King reflected that only an hour earlier, after scraping King's windshield, he'd witnessed his father exit a dive bar in downtown Denver. Now his mother, always terrified to drive in the snow, stood on his front porch to offer consolation to Jen, a virtual stranger who caught her attention in a diminished moment. His parents were kind people, but all King could think of was how he could calm everybody down before his date with Matthew that night.

"Don't just stand there, King. Make a fresh pot of coffee."

It was good advice and gave King time to think. His mom took off her hat and coat. Three people in King's small space was pretty crowded. He wondered if her visit had a dual motive. His father called his mother every morning from his office to tell her he loved her. King speculated on the possibility that he'd told her about finding King's car parked, or abandoned, in his lot in downtown Denver. What must he have thought?

He studied her. He couldn't tell what she really knew, but to his parents, it would be unconscionable to ever cut loose a child. No matter what mistake—what choice—that child made.

Jen was considerably more subdued than Kay might have imagined. Her hair hung lifeless. Washed but unkempt. She wore a too-big maroon-striped ski sweater that King recognized as Teddy's. She'd been so vivacious the day she came to help him move. Knowing what King now knew, it was all bravado on Jen's part. She was frenetic with terror.

"What are your plans?" his mother asked. Kay was a chain smoker, so she sat near the slightly open sliding glass door with her mug of coffee in one hand, a cigarette in the other, and a small saucer perched on her knee for an ashtray.

"Hopefully, I can get a grant to finish school. I graduate in June."

"Have you been to an obstetrician?"

"Yeah. I'm in perfect shape. So's the baby."

"And the father?" She asked this disapprovingly. She knew about the character of the father of Jen's baby. Although she hadn't asked King directly, he was sure she knew why he abruptly needed to find a new place to live.

"What about him?" King asked.

"He wants to stay together, but only if I get an abortion. It's out of the question now, and I'm glad."

"Weren't you on birth control?"

"King! Does it matter now?" his mother demanded.

"Sorry," King muttered.

"I can't go into it." Jen hunkered into herself.

"Will he acknowledge the baby? He has responsibility here, whether he likes it or not."

"He's already supporting another baby," King told her.

"He's done this before?"

"I didn't know," Jen whispered miserably.

"And your parents . . ."

"I'm disowned." And she began to cry. Kay squashed out her cigarette and moved to comfort her.

"Finishing school and getting good prenatal care are the most important things now. Do you need money?"

His mother had spent all their savings getting King through college. He was stunned at her offer.

"I'll probably get a check tomorrow from the university. Your landlord, the guy who let me in, told me he has another studio available. Across from yours. My housing allowance will cover it."

"That's wonderful. King can help you."

"We should ask King if it's okay." Jen looked up at him.

"Of *course* it's okay," King's mother insisted. "It makes perfect sense."

Kay was not by any means a pushy or overbearing woman. In this instance she pressed only to help Jen get her needs met. If she thought Jen might be a good influence, or a good cop, she was sadly mistaken, but for King's part he'd be glad to have her so close.

"I think my mom's right. I think you should do it. Let's go look."

"He left it unlocked."

They stood up and filed out. They came face-to-face with Theo and his trick for the night. Unbelievably, it was Sam. Theo shrugged. He knew King was stunned and Kay picked up on it. Sam leaned down and hugged King.

"I didn't know this was where you lived."

"I told you I moved."

He smiled beautifully. Reading King, they were all uncomfortable. King introduced Sam to his mother and to Jen. He nodded good-bye to Theo, loped up the steps, and disappeared out the back of the complex into the alley.

As Kay and Jen inspected the appointments of the apartment, the exact same layout as King's only in reverse, Theo stood back with King.

"It was nothing." he whispered. "We're planning a march, it got late, and he slept over. That was all. Then your friend came knocking in the middle of the night. I'm beat tired from being so nervous. He's so beautiful."

"Yeah," King nodded. "Yeah."

"It's guys like him who'll make all the difference for the movement."

Kay was promising Jen that she'd make her new curtains.

"Yeah?" King focused on Theo.

"He's smart and attractive in a nonthreatening way. He'll make it okay for everybody else. I think he'll be famous someday."

"I don't want to talk about him anymore. I'm tired, too."

"You want to tell me about your new boyfriend?"

"Sure. He lied about his name, his age, admits he's married, lives in Pittsburgh, and thought I was a hustler."

Theo whistled.

King's mother turned. "She'll take it. Can I give you a check now? I want her to hang onto her cash." From behind her, Jen's jaw slackened with relief.

It looked like it might snow, and after she took Jen to Montgomery Ward to buy sheets, towels, an inexpensive set of dishes, and pots and pans, Kay agreed to drive back home. She came back thirty minutes later with a load of groceries. King walked her to her car.

"Why did they all turn their backs on her?" she asked. She rummaged through her purse for her cigarettes. "She must feel so betrayed."

When King's mother got upset she talked to herself, and he could see her having a mental argument with Jen's father. And Teddy.

"Mother."

She didn't hear him.

"Mom! You're talking to yourself."

"I'm so damn mad. You call me if she needs anything. Understood?"

"She's blown away."

"She's been through a terrible ordeal." She lit her cigarette. "It won't get any easier."

"I mean she's blown away by what you've done for her, Mom." King leaned through her window and kissed her on her hat. A few snowflakes began to fall.

"I love you, King."

He hugged her.

"I'm worried about your father," she said, starting her engine. "But that's a conversation for another day."

"We should have it sooner than later."

"Bring her to dinner next week."

"I hardly know her, Mother. She may feel a little overwhelmed."

"In the car to Ward's she said she knew you'd be the only one who'd understand. Why did she know that, King?" She hesitated and gazed up at him from the driver's seat.

"You should get going. I'll call Dad in case he wonders where you are."

"He knew I was coming. We talked before I left."

"I owe him a call anyway. Call me when you get home."

"Don't you have class today?"

"My writing seminar at three. Call me after that."

She put the gear in reverse and King stepped back from the car. He waited till she drove away. When he turned to head back to his apartment, Jen was standing with Theo in the passageway.

"You're so damn lucky." Jen told him.

"Unbelievable," Theo echoed.

"When I was younger, they embarrassed me," he shrugged. "My brother and I thought we were poor."

The three of them walked back to Jen's new apartment.

"King has plans tonight, so maybe you and I can have an early dinner," Theo volunteered. He didn't know King well, but he knew he'd want to see Matthew given that he was leaving tomorrow.

Jen shrugged. "Hey, I'm just grateful to have a roof over my head." Now she seemed like the old Jen. They assembled in her room. "I have boxes stored in the basement of my sorority house. I guess I better go pick up my welfare check."

"I'm headed to campus," said Theo. "Let's walk together."

"I have to call my dad. I'll see you tomorrow."

"A sleepover, huh?" Jen smiled sweetly. "Kiss him for me, King."

"And me," called Theo.

King went inside to call his father. "She just left. It was snowing a little. She was really something, Dad."

"That's why I married her."

"Dad?"

"Yes, King."

"Thanks for the windshield." He wanted to mutter some lame excuse but didn't. He thought his dad was relieved. "I don't want you to worry about me."

"That's next to impossible, but your mother and I are doing our best not to make you worry about our worry."

"Okay if I come downtown for lunch next week?"

"I'd like that, King. I'm glad we got you into a more reliable car."

King hung up and decided he should change his clothes. He was still wearing last night's outfit. It was no different than the same uniform he'd wear tonight. As King pulled off his shirt, he gazed across the walkway to Jen's apartment. Now he had two friends in the same complex. Theo and Jen. They couldn't be more opposite. A disgraced sorority girl and a gay activist.

King thought about Sam.

Tonight, Matthew was in for the fuck of his life.

Chapter Six

King wore a thick ski sweater underneath Matthew's leather coat, knowing when he returned it he'd be warm enough without it tonight. King didn't have a nice coat. Only a Gortex parka and a jean jacket. When he arrived at the hotel, Matthew was waiting for him in the lobby. He sat smiling on a sofa near the elevators. When he saw King he stood up, marched up to him, and hugged him like he was his best friend in the world. People stared. King squirmed away.

"What's got into you?"

"I'm getting *sex* tonight!" Matthew whispered. "Can we go up to the room?"

King started getting aroused. Matthew looked wonderful. In the elevator someone asked if they were brothers. Matthew laughed and didn't answer. In the hallway they stumbled toward the room. Before he opened the door, he pulled King close, whispering, "Tonight I want it all. I want to make love before dinner, then I want us to go out. Afterward I want you to take me to a few clubs, where I want to hold hands, kiss you in public. Tell anybody who asks we're lovers. Then later tonight I want to come back to our room, where, if you called for room service and gave them your name, they'd look and find you registered with me. Then I'll want to make love with you again. Then we'll talk about our respective days. Hold hands while I read a brief and you watch Johnny Carson. Then I want to sleep with my arms around you. Deal?"

"Deal." King took off his jacket and handed it to him.

In their room they fell into each other, savagely pulling off their clothes. They didn't stop tasting each other for an hour.

"Wait for a minute," said Matthew. He disappeared into the bathroom and returned with warm wet hand towels. He began to swath King gently, starting with his face, his neck, and working his way down his body to his groin. King grew erect again.

"Enjoy your youth." Matthew smiled up at him.

"You're no better," King told him.

"Get dressed. We have a lifetime to pack into the evening."

"Until you come back," King chided.

"Until I come back," Matthew agreed. He quickly toweled off and got dressed. "I'd like to walk tonight. Your sweater won't be warm enough."

He opened the door to his closet. He produced a hanging bag from I. Magnin, Denver's best department store.

"You got a new coat?"

"No. *You* got a new coat." He handed it over to King. Nervously King unzipped the bag. "If you don't like it, you can wear mine tonight and pick up something else another time."

"I didn't bring anything for you."

"Yes," he corrected him. "You did."

The coat was beautiful. A dark brown bomber jacket. Very plain. King looked over at Matthew in astonishment.

"I think with your hair, dark colors suit you. I like blondes in dark colors. Do you like it, King? Try it on."

"This must have been so expensive." King's fingers were trembling. He slipped it on. Matthew was right about the color. "I've wanted a leather jacket for as long as I can remember."

"I hope you'll think about me when you wear it."

"You want me to think about you all the time. Is that it?"

"At least in the winter. Come spring, I'll have to jog your memory with something else."

King hesitated. Slowly he slipped it off and sat back down on the edge of the bed.

"What is it, King? What's wrong?"

"It's nicer than anything I have."

"Is it too conspicuous? That's why I bought something so simple. I remember what it was like in college. I think you wear it easily. It belongs on you. But you can take it back."

"I'd only exchange it for one thing."

"Whatever it is, it's yours."

"It's not right to tell you what I'm thinking. What I want. We hardly know each other."

"We probably know each other better than you think. I'm a good judge of character. You have sweet qualities, King. That's why I changed my plans."

"Maybe it's just the sex."

"It's more than our sex, which happens to be wonderful. I couldn't stop thinking about you today. As a matter of fact, I called your apartment and a girl answered. I just hung up. I didn't treat you very well last night."

King allowed this to sink in. He was right. King admired him for admitting it. King brushed away a lock of thick hair which had fallen across Matthew's eyes. He had a high forehead, and his hairline receded slightly. King could imagine him in a navy suit, addressing a courtroom, a client weeping at a table behind him as he defended her honor to a judge. Now King knew what Matthew looked like under his suit. He'd tasted his semen. He'd tugged with his teeth the tiny hairs trailing down his abdomen to the pink silky tip of his cock.

And what did King owe Matthew's wife? Should he concern himself with her interests? Maybe he wasn't in the driver's seat, but he was certainly riding shotgun. What kind of person did this make him? And Matthew?

"She didn't call this morning like she usually does," he said, as if he read King's mind. "So I called her after you left. She didn't answer. And she still hasn't called me."

"Can I tell you what I want more than the coat?"

"What, King?"

"I know you have a wife, but do you have a boyfriend? Someone you see on a regular basis?"

"I did. I ended it several months ago."

"Do you travel much?"

"On occasion."

"Do you always go to bars?"

"Yes."

"I go out a lot, too. I like bars. I don't always meet people I like. But if I lived in Denver I'd go out every night."

"I'm usually ignored. I'm too old to be doing what I'm doing."

Then King told him about his day. About Jen. His mom's reaction. He told him about his walk from the hotel down Broadway past the capitol building and the civic center. How much he loved the smell of the jacket, not just the leather, but that he could also smell Matthew. King told him about seeing his dad's van in the parking lot, and how surprised he was by the early hour. Matthew gasped slightly at the part about the scraped windshield.

And then King told him about seeing his dad come out of the Tip Top.

"Do you think it's my fault?" he asked Matthew.

"No, King. And I don't think he does either."

"I have a gay brother, too."

"Really."

"He's three years older. He lives with a college professor near DU."

"Are you close?"

King was happy he didn't make a big joke of it. King couldn't say how many times he'd been asked if he and his brother ever tricked together. It was as disgusting as asking a straight guy if he ever fucked his sister.

Instead, Matthew sat next to him on the bed and listened intently, his hands folded in his lap. King wondered if anyone would ever listen so closely to him again.

"Yeah." He nodded. "But neither of us had any idea about the other one. He told me out of the blue. We both came out at the same time. He was private and I was noisy about it. I'm afraid I compromised his privacy."

"How?"

"I didn't know for sure I was gay. In fact, I was afraid of it. I thought I should go to my parents and ask for help. My mom always told me I could tell her anything."

"You must trust them very much."

"It was a stupid thing to do. I guess I figured if I talked it over, it might all seem like a dream. I can't even believe I did such a thing. And then I told Mom about my brother. My mom gets pretty depressed. I remember driving home in the middle of the day and she was asleep in bed. I was going through hell at school. Hell."

"Was your need to tell them over someone in particular?"

"Yeah. My best friend. At the time."

King stopped talking. Just stopped.

Matthew waited patiently.

"You can tell me, King. I've heard incredible stories in my line of work. Get it off your chest."

"We weren't crazy, or zealots or anything—see, the way I figure it, I was just lonely. And these people—"

"You were caught up in a religious cult?" Matthew's eyebrow shot up.

"No. Not a cult. But my parents thought it was a cult." King hunched over and covered his face in his hands. "It makes me sound so weak, but I was lonely. I didn't have any friends. There was this one guy, Nicholas. I met him in a freshman science class. That's where I met all of my friends. One Intro Physical Science class. So, anyway, Nicholas was a born-again Christian. Charismatic."

"He spoke in tongues?"

"Yeah."

"You ever make it with him?"

King shot him a look.

"Sorry," he smirked.

"You're supposed to act jealous, not amused."

"Go on, King."

"And no, Nicholas was no closet case. He was a really horny straight guy. He loved women. But he had an effect on me. On a small group of us. We didn't pass out pamphlets. We just went to church and held Bible studies."

"Who was in the group?"

"My friends Leslie and Celine. Their roommates Kelly and Jane. My friend Lucy. Nicholas's roommate Lex. And me. We were close. I was very, very happy."

"So you were born again?"

King looked up at the ceiling. "I was, yes."

"What's that like, King?"

"It felt so real," King whispered. "Imagine all your cares as if they were weightless, floating up out of your body as if it were an open vessel, and instead of feeling empty, you felt full—completely peaceful. Every need completely satisfied. Wanting for nothing."

"But it didn't last."

"No." King folded his hands and looked down at them.

"Why?"

"Lex, Nicholas's roommate—we were sitting in a prayer circle. Me, Celine, Nicholas, and Lex. Lex and I were best friends. We did everything together. Made Nicholas a little jealous. The other girls were somewhere else that night. Emotion was pretty high. Nicholas was the leader. He always led. We'd start speaking in tongues—"

"Did you really speak in tongues?"

King smiled at Matthew. He leaned over and kissed him, wanting to lighten things up. He was happy that Matthew kissed him back with no reservation at all. "Any more doubts?"

"This is so fascinating. I always wanted to ask somebody what these experiences were like, but frankly—"

"Everybody seemed too crazy."

"Well. Overzealous."

"In retrospect, I probably was, too. I know my dad thought so. They were worried about me. No wonder they never saw this coming."

"This."

"My homosexuality. During that prayer session, Nicholas confessed to his lust for several women. I felt pretty secure with them and we were all . . . overwrought, so I decided I needed to confess a secret I had never allowed myself to express to myself consciously— let alone to another human being. I told them about my feelings for men.

"And Lex's hand started to shake. Violently. I thought I'd disgusted him. I'd caught Nicholas off guard. He wanted to be a minister. We were his first fledgling flock and I throw him homosexuality. So then Lex confesses, too. We couldn't believe it. You can bet Nicholas dropped our hands. He let go of us, instantly." Celine laughed, King recalled then. Then she caught herself.

Matthew chuckled.

"He got pretty scared. He led us in prayer. He started speaking in tongues. He prayed for God to cast away our demons. We hugged each other. He reminded us that whenever two or more agree, God would listen."

"Let me guess what happened," Matthew said. "You and Lex found yourselves in bed together."

"And Nicholas caught us. He told the rest of the group. Lex wanted to break it off. I did, too, but we kept seeing each other. We couldn't stop. I really loved Lex."

"Or thought you did."

"Same difference. I'd never had sex with anyone before."

"Same difference." Matthew nodded, his eyes gentle.

"When it became obvious that Lex and I weren't going to break it off, Nicholas got pretty crazy. He'd get one or the other alone and try to scare the shit out of us."

"Fire and brimstone."

"And more. He threatened to go to our parents. Lex freaked out. I never thought Nicholas would go through with it."

"He thought he was saving souls."

"Yeah. Lex caved in. Told me it was over. He was so afraid. So that's why I told my parents. I didn't want Nicholas having this over me. I guess I wanted them to know."

"How did they take it?"

"My mom called my dad. He came home right away. Then she called my brother. 'I know,' is all she said. And we have to have a family meeting. Everybody comes home. We sit around the table, my mom freaking out. She was terrified we'd both be killed, or worse, live lonely, horrible lives. My brother throws all the statistics he has at her. I keep yelling that I don't want to be gay. My dad doesn't say anything. He sits with his head in his hands. She starts yelling at him. I never heard my mother yell at my dad. 'Don't you have anything to say? Are you just going to sit there? This is the end of the line for the family name. It'll stop with you! Did you think of that? Who'll carry on the family name after the boys go?' "

"What did he say, King?" Matthew smiled kindly at King. He patted his hand.

King gathered his thoughts, his brow knit in memory.

"He said, 'The family name is the least of my worries.' Then he sat up in his chair, looked each one of us in the eye, raised his finger, and said, 'We're a family. We're in this together and we can all just calm the hell down.' "

"And did you?"

King laughed. "No. The worst was yet to come."

"And Lex?"

"Dropped me. Started going out with a girl. I couldn't stay away from him. Nicholas took matters into his own hands."

"What did he do?"

"He called my mom. He told her he'd drive me out of Boulder with whips and chains if I didn't give up on Lex. I heard my mom screaming and my dad picked up the phone. He threatened to kill Nicholas if he ever called them again."

"King," Matthew whispered. "You're trembling."

King looked at his hands. He was. Matthew put his arm around him.

"I wouldn't ever make trouble for you," King told him. "I know what's it like to have trouble made for me. I'd never hurt someone the way Nicholas hurt my mother and dad. He was their worst nightmare. Everything they feared for my brother and me. I just want you to know, I'd never want to hurt you or your wife. Even if I couldn't see you again."

"I never thought you would."

"Do you think that's why he drinks now? Is it my fault?"

"No, it isn't your fault."

"Then what should I do for him?"

"I think you do your best to reassure him that you're happy. That things are okay with you. Affirm your life."

"Is that what you do?"

"I haven't been as brave as you, King. I've copped out. I'm cheating my wife out of time. I want to correct that, but I've been too afraid. We're somewhat prominent in Pittsburgh. We're social," he said, his voice trailing away.

"You have more to lose than I did."

"That's not true at all. I hope your folks respect you for trusting them enough to go to them for help. Even if they didn't initially take it well, remember that they probably had no experience with gay people. No point of reference."

"They don't have many friends now. They keep to themselves."

"Reassure your dad, King."

They sat on the bed in silence. The heating unit under the window began to purr. They were considerably more somber than an hour ago, when they'd burst into the room, ripping at each other's clothes. King's chin and cheeks were flush with the burn of Matthew's day-old beard. He hadn't shaved since the morning.

"Let's not spend more of our time on sadness, King. In addition to the responsibilities we have to our families, we have a responsibility to each other right here and now."

"What I want more than the coat is for you to come back again. Why don't you take it back? Buy another plane ticket. I know we've been pretending a little. But today, I was thinking, in the middle of it all, I want to see you again. That I hoped you'd come back to Denver. And now, after this, I want it even more. I want to be with you."

Matthew kissed him. "You will, King. And you don't have to give up the coat for that."

When they stepped from the Hilton lobby into the cold Colorado night air, King felt deliriously happy. They walked that night. Matthew wanted to take King to dinner at The Broker, an old Denver restaurant built inside a bank vault. King had prime rib.

Then they hiked a good ten blocks over to Doc Weeds, a new dance club built street level on the corner of a big office building. Cars passing the windows could see men dancing with men and women dancing with women. Matthew never let go of King once. When he ordered a round of drinks, he told the bartender that his lover only drank Bombay. Then he kissed him.

"You guys have it bad." The bartender shook his head. "Don't fuck it up."

And that night when they walked back to the hotel, sentimental because of King, Matthew laid out his plan. He'd go home and talk things over with his wife. He'd come clean, he promised, with her and himself. He'd make plans to come back, certainly within the month. He'd call King every day. There was plenty of work in Denver till they saw where they were headed. King just listened. Matthew seemed so happy. Almost born again. That night, high in their room over Denver, Matthew and King made love again, but this time no showers, no condoms, no lies. King lay beneath him with his eyes closed, rocking under the weight of Matthew's body.

"This isn't fair to say to you now, but I mean it," Matthew whispered breathlessly. He was thrusting very gently. He pressed his face against King's cheek. "I'm falling in love with you."

King had to bite his lip to keep from ejaculating. He'd wait for him, he promised himself. Now, and later. When Matthew got close he murmured, "Look at me, King."

And when King opened his eyes, they came.

Chapter Seven

Last night, to avoid running into his dad in the morning, King parked on a side street behind the Denver Art Museum. As King walked down Broadway toward his car, he wondered if he could resist calling Matthew. He'd given King his card. Told him to call whenever he liked, but asked King not to call him at home. Not for a while. His telephone number was unlisted because of the blackmail incident, but Matthew gave King the new number anyway.

Leaving this morning had been difficult for them both. It was always easier on the one going away, but this time Matthew had it much, much worse. He hadn't spoken to his wife in three days. He knew she was okay because her secretary told him she was in and would call him back, but she hadn't, and as he persisted, the secretary admitted she wasn't supposed to put his calls through.

His expression was grave as he watched King pull on his new jacket. King was glad for it. Tangible proof that they'd met. Matthew sat on the edge of the bed with his hands clasped over his knee. It was still dark outside, only five-thirty. King sneaked a glance at him and Matthew smiled the way he smiled when King came back the second night.

King believed that Matthew really had feelings for him. King was in bliss, heading for the door.

"King," he said. "So we understand a few things . . ."

"Yeah?"

"I meant what I said last night. It's my intention to go back and straighten my life out. If I know my wife, and I know divorce, there are probably documents waiting on my desk as we speak. I'll deal with that. I'll also deal with the fact that you are a very young man. My problems and the choices I'll make are not of your doing. You may think after I'm gone that I've used you. Others will say so. Or you may lose interest. All of which is my way of saying that I'll understand. It comes with the territory of being an older man with a younger . . . person. And also the stress of a long-distance relationship."

"I'll wait."

"This is far from ideal. Any of it."

"I'd do it again."

"So would I, and if it's up to me, we will. Very soon."

"Then we will."

And then Matthew started to cry quietly.

King moved to comfort him. Matthew held up a trembling hand to stop him.

"I've made a terrible mess of things," he whispered. "I'm not as brave as you. I'm not as kind as your mom and dad. Some think I'm downright ruthless. I don't deserve you, King."

"Stop talking like I won't see you again."

"Remember that you're wonderful. Deserving of great love. Settle for nothing less. Nothing less, okay? Think of me when you wear the coat." Then he composed himself, clasping his palms together, his fingers touching his lips. King moved closer to him. He lay his head against King's stomach while King stroked his hair.

After a minute King left. He heard the phone ring as he closed the door.

Walking in the cold air toward his car, King wondered if Matthew was watching him from his hotel window. He wanted to seem brave as he walked away. Blocks away he turned, looked up, and waved. King imagined he saw a flashing light, but it was the rising sun reflecting from the east against the windows of the hotel.

King worried that his father might be strolling, slightly intoxicated, through the canyon of skyscrapers a block over, and see him, gigantically reflected in those same windows. King thought about what Matthew was trying to tell him. He pulled his jacket closed as he rushed down the sidewalk toward his car.

Theo was shoveling the walk when King pulled up. He wasn't wearing a coat, only a thin black T-shirt. His body flexed as he worked, his hair falling down over his spectacles. King was surprised that his body was so naturally muscular. He'd thought Theo was just slender.

"Tomorrow night we take over the small bar at the Boulderado," Theo advised King. "About ten of us. Ginsberg may attend."

"Allen Ginsberg?"

"Maybe. He flies in later tonight. He may be too tired."

"But still." King had read "Howl" in a poetry survey.

"So how was your date?"

King pulled off his jacket. Held it up.

"So he's married."

"Yeah."

"Make any promises?"

"We both did."

"I'll bet. He your first married man?"

"Yeah."

"Watch out. The wives bite. Your chin is chapped but your acne cleared up."

King rubbed his jaw. He was right. Matthew's beard.

Theo smiled. "So you'll come? We're meeting here and walking over together."

That day King went to class. Worked in the afternoon. Got home around six-thirty. Theo and Jen came over with a pizza. He told them about Matthew. It was possible that he checked his phone for a dial tone at least fifty times that night. When they left King decided to write a short story about Matthew. He tried to describe Matthew on paper, so he could have some written photo of him. King wished he'd asked him to send a picture. He calculated that he might call after midnight, when his wife was asleep. King stayed up past one. Matthew didn't call. At four in the morning, King had a panic attack.

He huddled in the corner of his mattress, holding his knees, and rocked. When King suffered panic attacks he moaned, unaware that he was doing it, or how loud it was. All he could do was wait it out.

A few seconds later Theo knocked on his door.

"I'll stay with you till you fall asleep."

"He won't call." A statement of fact.

"No, King." Theo smiled gently. "Probably not. That doesn't mean he isn't thinking about you. But no, in my experience with married men, especially if he's from out of town, he probably won't call you again."

King stared miserably up at the ceiling.

Theo lay next to King. "But this will pass. You'll be okay. I promise you. I *promise* you."

Then Jen appeared, her hair in rollers. She scanned the two of them and left. She came back with her blanket and a pillow. She didn't say anything. Somehow they all arranged themselves on King's narrow bed. When King finally fell asleep, he dreamed of Matthew. He was sweet and tender. He asked King to be patient.

In the morning, King's anxiety was gone.

That night twelve gay men and women crowded into Theo's cramped apartment a little after nine o'clock. It was Thursday night. The energy felt carefully jocular.

"Why the small bar at the Boulderado?" This from Pat, a butch lesbian from a ranch in southeastern Colorado, a real cowhand.

"So they'll notice us," Theo answered. "We'd get swallowed up at Tom's Tavern."

"Beaten up is more like it."

"That, too."

"The Boulderado is so uptight," she pressed. "With its little checkered tablecloths and sweet French café chairs."

"No." Theo shook his head. "I think it's perfect."

"It's half gay already. Nobody's gonna bat an eye." Sam's voice. At the door. He towered over all of them. He surveyed the room. Nodded when he recognized King. Behind Sam, his usual posse. Rod, back together with Tony. Tim with Peter.

"I wanted to make a few comments before we head out." Theo stood on his bed. "This meeting of the Boulder Gay Liberation Front is hereby called to order."

"Hear, hear," Sam sang back.

"Remembering the agenda set forth at our very first meeting, our goal to establish ourselves as out and open has taken on a new meaning. Since the Stonewall riots, gay men and lesbians will no longer tolerate living lonely and isolated lives hidden behind closet doors. It is an agreed upon mandate of the BGLF to establish a visible public profile in the Boulder/Denver area—making ourselves known to non-gay members of the society at large while sending a message to fellow closeted gay men and women that we are out and proud and organized. Basic human rights such as housing, employment, and the right to fraternize as openly gay men and women is the main goal of the BGLF.

"Establishing a beachhead in a small bar at the Boulderado Hotel may seem like a tepid step, but nonetheless vital to our momentum as a movement. With a growing gay and lesbian population in Boulder, it should not be necessary to make a forty-minute drive to Denver whenever any of us wants companionship. Boulder should be able to support its own gay bar. Depending on our continued visibility, I see this as a reality in the not too distant future."

"So what are we supposed to do when we get there?" Rod asked. He was riding Theo. "Pull out our dicks and wag 'em around?"

"You just did that in the car on the way over." Tim smirked.

"There's no need to act any differently than you would in any other situation," Theo explained. "If you feel like dancing, then dance. If you want to kiss your lover, then kiss your lover. If you want to get drunk, then get drunk. This is trial and error and I for one am very proud of all of you for supporting it. You're making history whether you think it's all a big joke or not."

Tony elbowed Rod.

"Hear, hear!" Rod shouted.

"This meeting is adjourned!" Theo hopped from his bed to the floor.

The militant group poured out of his apartment. As King climbed the staircase he could see Jen sitting on her bed, staring at the wall. She didn't even react to the commotion. He hadn't called her when he got back from Denver this morning. Her boxes were piled in rows along her wall. She hadn't unpacked.

King waited for the group to amble into the parking lot. He knocked on her window. She turned. Saw him and motioned him in.

"What's up?" King asked her.

She brought her knees to her chest and hugged them. "I had a bad fight with my mother. Then Teddy stopped by."

"Yeah?"

"He says if I agree to give up the baby we can get married."

"Why give up the baby if you'll end up together anyway?"

"That's my point. He says it's no way to start a life together. He wants us to get to know each other first. Not start a family right away."

"He doesn't even want to raise his own kid?"

"He admitted he isn't sure it's really his." She looked away.

"What the fuck did you say?" King demanded.

She studied her hands. Her response was surprisingly mild. "We were experimental a few times. We went to a few swapping parties up in Sunshine Canyon. Not a lot. But enough to make us both wonder. Don't tell your mom, okay?"

"You think I'm crazy?"

"So you think it's disgusting, huh?"

"No. That's not what I meant. Look, the baby's got to be Teddy's. Law of averages."

"He thinks that without being sure, he doesn't want to raise somebody else's kid."

"But it's your kid no matter what!"

"That's why I'm keeping it. I told him to forget me. I'm glad he admitted what he was really thinking. Then we slept together."

King stood, not knowing what else to say. The group must be nearly at the Pearl Street Mall.

"I heard Theo's speech. Funny to think you can't love who you love without fearing for your safety. You should go. Catch up with them."

"Why don't you come with me?"

"You're making a big political statement and you want to bring a woman?"

King shrugged. "Come out tonight. We don't even need to go to the Boulderado."

"Maybe I will go. I should make an effort. But let's go with the group."

"What if Holly sees us?"

"Holly from the house?" Jen cracked up. "I owe Holly everything. This baby owes Holly its life."

"How do you figure?"

"If Holly hadn't told me about you dancing, and I hadn't told Teddy, I wouldn't have known what a shallow shit he is. We probably would have agreed on the abortion. My life would be back to normal. I wouldn't know the truth about my parents, or Teddy."

"Or yourself. You never would have known you had it in you."

"Had *what* in me?"

"Character." King smiled.

*   *   *

Jen and King caught up with the group at 17th and Walnut. Even on such a cold night the open-air Pearl Street Mall was fairly busy. Street musicians played guitars and saxophones. A group of Hari Krishnas jangled by. The softly lit local pubs were lined with drinkers, the windows clouding with smoke and steam. King glanced west to the mountains—the Flatirons sulked against a moonless winter sky.

"It's beautiful tonight," King whispered. "You're lucky your baby will be born in Boulder."

"On a night like tonight I can believe everything will turn out okay."

As they joined Theo and the rest of the group, King was reminded of his walk with Sam toward the dance at the UMC. Same brisk air. Same shining eyes. Same ruddy cheeks and runny noses.

"Who's the beard?"

They turned. Sam stood grinning behind King, kneeing his thigh.

"This is Jen."

"I'm Sam." He smiled down at her.

"What's a beard?" Jen asked him.

"A decoy." He smiled again. "See, if King and I were boyfriends but we wanted to fit in, we might bring a pretty woman along to give the impression we were straight."

"You don't seem straight at all," Jen replied. "Not with ten beautiful women! If anything, you look like a chorus boy."

Sam laughed. "Touché!"

"Besides," she added. "King is *my* beard. Not the other way around."

King hunkered into his new leather coat.

"This is King's second demonstration." Sam smiled. "He's getting very bold."

"Yeah, I heard about his first. Got him kicked out of his house."

"Your parents kicked you out?" Sam's eyes widened.

"No, not his parents. He doesn't live at home anymore. His roommates."

His eyes melted with concern. "Gee, King."

"My sorority sister saw you guys at the dance. She told me and I told my boyfriend, who used to be King's roommate. For that matter, he used to be a lot of things. In any case, he kicked King out. So, see, if King wants to take it a little easy, I don't blame him. You ever been discriminated against?"

"No." He shook his head. He knew she was ribbing him but King could tell how bad he felt. "I was the one who asked him to the dance. Look, can I talk to King alone for a second?"

"Sure." Jen nodded. "I'm gonna go over to that group of ladies and reevaluate my sexual preference. That's what you're after, right? New recruits." She wandered over to a small group of women with short cropped hair and Berkenstocks. They seemed delighted to receive her.

Sam led King around the corner and put his arm around King's shoulder.

"When did this happen?"

"The day after our last serious chat."

"Why didn't you tell me?"

"What was to tell? It got me out and into a better situation. Theo rented me an apartment and now Jen lives across the way."

"She still see that guy?"

"She's pregnant. She broke up with him."

Sam whistled. "I've been thinking about you. I've owed you a call. Even if we aren't dating, I meant what I said. I care for you, King. I'd like to be friends."

And then Sam leaned down and kissed him.

Jen popped her head around the corner. "Everybody's gone ahead."

"Then we should head out." Sam held out his hand to King. He offered his other hand to Jen and she took it.

"I thought the girl should be in the middle," King commented.

"The girl is in the middle." Sam grinned.

Hand in hand, the three of them mounted the stone steps to the main entrance of the Boulderado Hotel.

As they entered the tiny bar behind the mahogany reservation desk, Theo and the others had already claimed four tables clustered in the corner of the room. A few other tables were occupied by several middle-aged couples, probably college professors. Behind a short service bar with only a few stools, a bartender nodded to the group.

"Let's get four carafes of red wine," Theo advised the group. The bartender heard him and began pouring. A moment later he began to deliver the wineglasses. Then he went back for the wine. The group all stared at him. He had long gray hair tied back with a rubber band. None of them said anything. The intellectual couples paid them no mind.

"What are we supposed to do now?" demanded Pat. "Nobody gives a shit."

"Maybe that's a good thing," Theo countered.

"Somebody has to dance."

"It's French café Musak for Christ's sake." Sam laughed.

"King and I will dance," Jen volunteered.

"Oh, that'll make a big statement," someone jeered.

"Then *Deborah* and I will dance," Jen corrected herself. She stood up and offered her hand to Deborah, a tall, shy, homely woman who never said much. They sashayed to the only open spot in the bar, near the entryway, visible to the lobby outside. The tape switched to Edith Piaf. Jen was a head shorter than Deborah, who rested her head in the crook between Jen's neck and shoulder. Her hands dropped to Jen's ass.

"Hey!" Jen squirmed. "Watch the hands."

"Sorry, precious." Deborah grinned.

They all watched and smiled. A few college students in the lobby glanced in, nudging each other. Rod and his boyfriend Tony stood up. They started slow dancing, and pretty soon they were tonguing each other like crazy.

King studied the bartender, who caught his glance and looked away. He didn't care. Soon the whole group loosened up. They began to drink and dance. Sam cut in on Jen and Deborah. Deborah backed away in irritation. Theo asked King to dance. After a few numbers, Jen cut in. She and Theo danced away. King turned and Sam held out his hands.

The older couples left, smirking and laughing between themselves. The invaders were only an oddity. A good story for tomorrow. More patrons came in. Le Bar was always a good place to gather with friends for conversation. To talk about politics. Books read lately. A foreign film. Boulder had a small art house theater down the mall across from city hall.

An older man, officious in a suit and tie, came to the entryway and surveyed the room. Clearly management. He stood for a moment, gathered his thoughts, and disappeared. King couldn't tell what he was thinking.

King got a little drunk from the red wine. It made him sleepy and sentimental. He glanced around at his new friends. Jen was laughing with several women in the corner. They were asking her about her pregnancy. They all knew she wasn't gay and didn't care. King heard them offer her support. One of them told her about a great women's group she should try. She promised she would.

Rod and Tony began arguing in the corner. Looked like they were breaking up.

Theo and Sam were in deep discussion about the course the Boulder Gay Lib should take from there. The evening was positive, invigorating both of them. It emboldened them all.

The tables unoccupied by their group filled with more lanky intellectual types. New York expatriates. Jewish Buddhists. Long black topcoats. Horn-rimmed glasses. King overheard one of them introduced as Gregory Corso, the poet. The intellectuals looked at them and King and his friends looked back.

"Allen's plane was delayed," Corso explained. "He wanted to be here."

Referring to Ginsberg. King wondered if he'd ever become a published poet.

As they walked home, King fell back away from the crowd and watched Sam up ahead. He delighted at being in his company again. He thought of Matthew and felt guilty. Tonight Matthew was home in a bed with a woman he didn't love and probably wondering what direction his life would take him. How would Matthew have fit in tonight? Older. More sober.

Tonight as they left the Boulderado and walked back toward campus, King finally understood that to accept his differences would ensure commonality. He decided to enjoy his feelings about Sam. Even though King would always feel different, even among different men, he would delight in his short-lived intimacy with him. He would accept Sam's offer of friendship.

Take his kisses as they came.

Chapter Eight

The following week King met his father for lunch in downtown Denver. Jim worked as the state chief of public affairs for the United States Bureau of Land Management. Most government agencies were housed at the Denver Federal Center up in Lakewood, where his parents lived, but when he left the Forest Service for a better paying job at the BLM, Jim had to commute. It would have made more sense for them to move to an older house downtown, on one of Denver's beautiful, tree-lined Park Hill streets, closer to his new job. The driving caused both him and Kay terrible stress. Kay worried about any of them driving in the snow. And King's father worried about her worry. Plus, she was afraid to drive outside of their perimeter of Green Mountain, a tract housing development they bought into when they moved from Wyoming to Colorado.

When they were seated by Leo, the Asian proprietor of King's favorite restaurant, King made a mental note about how well-liked his father was. As they walked to their table he was greeted warmly by Leo himself, his bartender, the cocktail waitress, a busboy, and several waiters.

"A martini, Mr. James?"

King's dad hesitated.

"I'll have one, Dad," King volunteered, "If you will. Bombay rocks, twist."

"He's his father's son." Jim smiled.

Leo nodded cordially and left.

Jim James was a complex-looking man with a crew cut and a

space between his front teeth. His complexion was ruddy from drinking. A busboy poured water. He nodded to King.

"My son." Jim gestured to King.

"Your father is a very wonderful man." The busboy smiled. "A very wonderful man." He bowed and disappeared into the darkness.

"He had an immigration problem. I made a call. That's all." The drinks arrived and Jim reached for his. He held up his glass. "Cheers, King."

"Cheers, Dad."

"It's good of you to make the trip in snowy weather."

"Roads were clear."

"I'm glad you're in a dependable car."

They fell silent and studied the menu.

"How's your friend?"

"Which friend?" King thought he meant Matthew.

"The girl I met."

"Jen."

"Her parents come around?"

"No."

Jim shook his head, his forehead knitting in empathy for her.

"Let your mother know if she needs anything. She wants to help."

"They talk every day. Did you know that?"

"Yes." He finished his drink. He signaled for another one. They both ordered fancy hamburgers, Leo Burgers, which he made with onions and soy sauce.

"Jen got an emergency grant. She'll finish school. She's applied to nursing school already. I hope she makes it."

"Seemed like a bright girl. Hard to think she could be stopped."

"She's more vulnerable than when you met her."

"Of course." Jim nodded. His second drink arrived and he drank it fast. King watched him in silence. Before he came to work for the federal government, his father made his living as a small town newspaper editor. He started working in the newspaper business when he was only sixteen, forced to quit high school to support his mother and sisters. Deserted under extraordinary circumstances by his father when he was only eleven, Jim had vowed to do right by his own family. His personal pain now seemed to be exerting itself in his pattern of drinking.

"We're good friends," King added, referring to Jen. "Things are good."

King remembered Matthew's advice to reassure his father. Affirm his life.

"How so?" Jim asked.

"Jen, for one. We see each other daily. We eat dinner together most nights with another friend in the building. Theo. The manager. I've met other friends through him."

"You lost all your friends last summer. We were worried you'd be lonely."

"I'm not, not at all. I keep really busy. I'm working thirty hours a week. I have one advanced writing class. Doing great. And I'm making new friends."

"I'm glad, King." Their hamburgers arrived. King was relieved, because his dad was buzzing from gin. King was, too. They ate like they drank. Quickly.

"How about you, Dad? How are you?"

"Your mother say anything?"

"No," King lied.

"It's no secret to anybody I'm looking forward to retiring. I hate my job."

"You do?" King felt appalled.

"Some days." Jim smiled. "Not always."

"Do you miss being your own boss?" He knew how hard his father had worked as a newspaper man. How tough it was, but probably deeply satisfying.

"You're asking if I have regrets."

"I guess."

"I wish I'd spent more time with you and your brother when you were young."

"It wouldn't have changed anything," King said.

"Yes," Jim argued gently. "It would have. Now that I've gotten to know you, I see what working six days a week putting the paper to bed cost me." He lit a cigarette. "You and your brother are pleasant company. Your mother kept trying to tell me. 'Enjoy the boys.' Luckily, she benefited. She was around for you. You'll always be close."

"Dad. We're close, too," King chided him. King sat across from his father, wanting to tell him how much he loved him. To relieve him of his guilt. The great benefit from that horrible night the family sat around the table to talk about its gay sons began King's new-found relationship with his father. Where before Jim had been distant, if not a little cold, overnight he became loving and forthcoming.

He called once or twice a week from his office. He and King started having lunch together.

"I'd like another drink, King."

How could King tell his father he'd already had too much?

"I probably shouldn't."

King's relief must have been palpable because Jim chuckled.

"I have to slow down. I know that. Probably quit altogether. It's worrying your mother."

King wondered if he'd made his usual stop this morning at the Tip Top. He put his fingertips to his forehead, and thick-lidded, gazed across the table at King. "I didn't have a father. And I owe you an apology."

"No, you don't, Dad."

"See, my father didn't teach me anything about being a father myself. I tried with your brother, I really did, but Neil was so sensitive. The awful hunting trips. I thought he'd get over it, you know, the trauma. But he never did and I insisted that he keep trying."

King's brother Neil refused to ever go hunting again after he shot a rabbit and it didn't die instantly. Jim tried to show Neil how to wring its neck, to put it out of its misery. Neil became hysterical in front of his dad's hunting buddies. Hysterical to the point of needing to be held down, all the while proclaiming his hatred for his father.

"So when it was your turn I didn't even try. I left you both to your mother to raise."

"You raised us, too," King insisted. "We never felt neglected. Neil and I have talked about it."

Neil had recently moved away from the college professor. He called their parents crying hysterically early one morning, and within two hours Jim pulled up in front of his house, and loaded up his belongings without saying a word other than to express support. Neil reported that while Paul, his ex-boyfriend, stood in the kitchen, dressed in a fancy silk robe, screaming graphic obscenities at him (apparently Neil had been caught cheating), their dad moved box after box of belongings out to the van as though he were deaf.

"Did he *fuck* you? Huh? Did he have a *big dick*? Huh? *Huh*? Bigger than mine? Bigger than *mine*?"

King's poor father. Such a man's man. Both sons.

"If you want another drink, I'll have one with you," King offered.

"That would be nice, King. It's a slow day. I won't be missed."

The cocktail waitress quickly appeared with two fresh drinks. "On Leo, Mr. James."

They glanced over in Leo's direction and nodded their appreciation in unison. Father and son.

The following week King's mother called to inform him that his father had been driven home from his office in the middle of the day by a coworker, Phil Jiminez.

"Jim-in-nez." She pronounced it phonetically.

"It's 'He-*may*-nez,'" King corrected her, wanting to avoid the main reason she was calling. "You're pronouncing it wrong."

"That's how Phil pronounces it," she countered. "Don't change the subject. We're having a family meeting."

"No."

"*What?*"

"I don't want to come to another family meeting." King was surprisingly sharp with her. "I won't embarrass him that way."

She was outraged. King could hear her talking angrily to herself.

"You *know* why I'm calling, don't you?" she accused him.

"Yes."

"He was drunk. At noon!"

King felt bad for her. He would allow her to vent.

"I told him, 'I don't need this!' That's exactly what I said. And then I went to the phone book and found the number to AA. I told him, 'I've found the number but you have to make the call!'"

"And?"

"Some men came over. Took him out for coffee."

"Strangers? Why?"

"To support him, of course. That's how it works. He was so ashamed."

"What did Neil say?"

"I can't reach him." Then she began to cry. "What's happened to us? What's happened to all of us? Why didn't you tell me you suspected something?"

"Because we're beginning to understand each other. I didn't want to betray his trust."

She was silent, mulling this over. King sensed she was struggling with feelings of jealousy.

"He admitted he drinks on the way to work. That he stops for martinis near where he parks. In the morning!"

King didn't admit that he knew. He had a horrible feeling in the pit of his stomach. His father drank because of him and Neil.

"Do you blame us, Mom?"

"What a ridiculous thing to say! I blame him. He's a grown man. He should be able to control himself!"

"Alcoholism is a disease. He can't control himself."

"He'll learn to in AA."

In spite of himself, King laughed. And she began to cry.

"I'll come home," King told her. "I have to get someone to cover my shift at work and I'll come home to wait with you."

"No," she said dully. "You're right. We'll embarrass him."

"I'll come, Mother. You did the right thing," King added.

"Did I?" she asked me. "I didn't know. I just knew that I didn't need it right now. I was being selfish. I told him the truth."

"That's always good," he whispered. "I'll call him later. I love you."

"I just didn't need it right now."

King hadn't seen his brother since he moved into his new house, and decided it might be time to pay Neil a call. He lived on Emerson and 13th, conveniently located in Denver's Capitol Hill, in a large brick Victorian house right on the corner. The house was owned by lovers Don and Greg. Don waited tables with Neil at the Brown Palace Hotel. King's brother rented an attic room overlooking a quaint backyard garden and a distant view of the Rockies.

Greg answered the door. In his mid-thirties, blonde, craggy-faced handsome, Greg liked to play when Don wasn't looking. He expressed his intrigue that two brothers in one small family could be gay. He kissed King hello and grinned as he watched him mount the three flights of golden oak stairs. From the landing on the second floor, King glanced down and caught Greg staring at him.

Neil was glad to see King. He hadn't unpacked his boxes and sat cross-legged on his mattress, smoking. He was still distraught about his breakup with the professor. Neil had shaggy dark hair and vivid brown eyes. His features were more exaggerated than King's. Flaring nostrils and big lips, Neil was sensual looking. He loved crafts, and macraméd and tie-dyed endlessly. That night he wore a torn tie-dyed T-shirt and jeans. Heat pumped through a knocking radiator. It was cozy up in his room, the dormer windows smoky with steam.

King and Neil would remark through their lives that they were grateful that fate made both of them gay and not just one. Even if initially it proved more difficult for his parents, King knew they'd probably agree. Since the potential for a stable, longtime relationship was not even considered an option, it was a shared consensus that Neil and King would always take care of each other.

"Did you hear about Dad?"

"Yes." He dragged on his cigarette. Bonnie Raitt's voice drifted like curling smoke up through the house from a room below. Neil got caught up in the lyrics.

He was still hurting from his move.

King waited for more of a response.

"I wish she'd leave it alone," he said finally, with some resentment. "If a drink now and then gives him some peace, he's *earned* it."

"He's going to AA."

"He's only going to AA for her. When she finds out he has to go for the rest of his life, she'll make him stop. She's very controlling, King."

King didn't say anything. King hated it when Neil started in on their mom.

Neil studied him, put his cigarette out. King contemplated his hands. He had very beautiful hands. They were small, like King's, like their dad's, but very strong. Michaelangelo would have loved Neil's hands.

"You want a Coke or something?"

"No."

"Mom told me you asked her if Dad's drinking was our fault."

"I asked her if she *thought* it was our fault."

"Same difference, King."

"It isn't at all. Besides, she said no."

"You're too easy on them. If we have to get used to it, so do they."

"That's not very compassionate, Neil."

"I'm not feeling very compassionate these days. Look at this dump."

"It's a nice house."

"We had a fucking open relationship. He *agreed* that it was healthy for me to explore my sexuality. He was pissed off that I did it away from home. I was supposed to share. He won't even talk to me."

"Paul was so creepy. How could you sleep with him?" Paul had pasty white skin and very fine red hair. The few evenings King spent with him, he was also a crashing bore.

"I loved him," Neil insisted. He misted up a little.

"Then how could you have sex with some other guy?" King was really annoyed by the tears.

"You're such a prude, King."

"I'm not a prude. If I'm single I'm game for anything, but it gets old. I'd give anything to have—"

"To have what Mom and Dad have."

"That's not what I was going to say."

"They're straight, honey. It won't ever happen. Gay liberation doesn't mean conforming to society's norms for heterosexuals—it means celebrating male sexuality. There's nothing wrong with being sexually liberated. Men can't stay monogamous. We shouldn't have to."

"That's Paul talking."

"I learned a lot from Paul about sexuality. You have all the impossible expectations of a teenage girl, King. No man will be true to you. And deep down, you're still guided by outdated Christian mores. They drove you out, King. 'Whips and chains . . .' " He shook his head disgustedly. "Honestly. You've got to loosen up."

"Fuck you, Neil." King shot to his feet, shaking he was so pissed off. He turned to leave.

"Hey, King, wait up. I'm sorry."

"Fuck you." King reached for the door.

"King—listen, I got worked up. You just got so badly hurt by all of it. I want you to develop better defense mechanisms. Wait up. I'm sorry."

King opened the door and ran down the stairs. On the second floor, Gary's door was slightly ajar. Greg stood naked near his bed. He'd been waiting for King. He grinned as if in invitation. He turned, displaying his ass. King knew his brother didn't like him. Neil was watching from the landing above. King decided to teach him a lesson. He decided to make it with Greg. He started toward his door.

"King, don't."

"I'm a prude, huh?" King looked up at him.

Neil pounded down the stairs. "Stop where you are."

Greg pulled on his robe and stepped into the hall. "What's the problem, Neil?"

"I was saying good-bye to King. He's going back to Boulder."

Greg studied King longingly. "I think he'd like to stay."

"He's going back to Boulder."

"That's for King to decide," Greg said ominously.

"That is not for *King* or *you* to decide," Neil growled back. Neil had always been very protective of King as a kid.

"I don't like being *admonished* in my own house."

"Jesus fucking Christ, Greg. You just had a hustler in here two hours ago. You think I'm gonna let you lay a *hand* on my little brother?"

King's head reeled. This was all too new. They were fighting over him. He didn't want Neil to screw up another living arrangement.

"I'll take off, Neil. It's okay." King looked at Greg. "I'm taking off. Sorry."

"Your brother should learn some manners."

"It's my fault."

"No, it isn't your fault!" Neil erupted. "Jesus, King! You don't get anything I've been trying to explain to you. Do whatever the hell you want." He turned and stomped back up to his room.

Downstairs, a key turned in the front door. Don was coming home early. Greg abruptly closed the door in King's face. King headed down the stairs. He and Don came face-to-face in the hall. Don's face was red from the cold air. He was ten years older than King, plaid shirt, clone handsome with a mustache and thick wavy hair.

"King . . ." he said warmly.

"Hey."

"Visiting Neil?"

"Yeah. Just leaving."

"We're so glad to have Neil living with us. Two beautiful gay brothers. You're welcome in our home anytime." He smiled pleasantly as King passed him. In the mirror, King followed his gaze upstairs to the closed door of the bedroom he shared with Greg. Worry tinged his brow but he saw King watching and checked it.

"Baby?" he called up the stairs. "I came home early," he added, mounting the stairs loudly, almost as if in warning.

When King got to his car, he sat for several minutes till he calmed down.

He decided to go to the Back Door. The Back Door was exactly that, a bar customers entered through the front of a bar call the Door. The Door was a block north of Colfax on Broadway. Upon entering the Door, King always lowered his eyes, hurrying past the dregs of Denver's drinking underground—prostitutes, pimps, smack addicts, and petty thieves—and across a tiny dance floor to a heavy swinging door hidden to match the wall. You had to know it was there to go through it.

And once he did, another scene altogether. The horror of what King escaped gave way to a cramped but inviting cabaret space with café tables and stools lining a tiny stage. This was the Back Door, and although King had the option to park in the alley and enter through the rear and skip the front altogether, the rush of entering through a secret passage appealed to his covert sensibilities. King loved the Back Door.

King took his usual seat at a stool by the stage. A waiter rushed over and he ordered a shot of Tanqueray. When King arrived, the room had been relatively empty. Now it began to quickly fill up. The clientele of the Back Door was always unpredictable. For King and his old friends, the Back Door was always the first stop on their way to dance clubs like Doc Weeds or the Broadway, or leather and denim cruise bars like the Triangle and the 1942.

The shows always started early. The waiter returned with King's drink. The heightened energy in the room could only mean one thing: Scotti was back.

The curtain opened, creaking somewhat, to reveal a scuffed, empty wooden stage.

"Ladies and gentlemen," a deep feminine voice announced over a tinny PA system. "It gives me great pleasure to welcome back the greatest female impersonator west of the Mississippi, the fabulous, the divine, the *diva of the beevahs*, Miss Scotti!" And out she stepped, dressed as a man from head to toe.

Looming 6'2" in dress shoes and a businessman's suit, with slicked-back hair, Scotti towered over King, basking in resounding applause. To his limited knowledge, Scotti had been a hermaphrodite until recently deciding to choose her more feminine side. With hormone shots and recent surgery, Scotti was now officially a woman. A woman impersonating a man.

Several other drag queens had threatened to quit the show, arguing if she was really a woman she couldn't legitimately call herself a female impersonator and what was so tough about her act. But Scotti had originally opened the Back Door, and the new owner, Buzz Conaway, an old cowboy who lived an ordinary rancher's life out near Golden, threatened to close the club if Scotti wasn't permitted to perform.

"I used to say I had my mother's features and my father's fixtures . . ." Scotti grinned, "but now I'm all mixed up! I came in male drag to show the other bitches that Scotti will always be a crossdresser no matter what the plumber has to say about it!"

The room snickered.

Scotti told a few more jokes and then began to emcee the evening. "We have a special treat tonight . . ." She recognized a few friends and waved to a table near the back by the bar. "Stephanie found a ladies big and tall shop in Cheyenne, which means she'll finally be able to change her shoes. Don't you hate it when these tall girls come out in costume after costume but they're still wearing the same big white scuffed high heels?"

"I heard that, you bitch!" a woman cried from backstage. "My shoes are always polished and beyond reproach."

"Whatever you say sweetheart. With no further ado—what's ado, anyway? The opposite of *adon't?*—I give you Princess Stephanie!" Scotti zipped offstage.

The music cranked up and Stephanie overtook the stage. Black and lean, for her opening act she always wore a white sundress like Marilyn Monroe in *The Seven Year Itch.* Dancing and twirling so the dress whirled up high enough for all of them to see her flat panty line, Stephanie knew how to please her audience. An older fat guy several stools down offered up a five-dollar bill. Stephanie swooped down on it like a falcon grabbing a kitten. Tipping was expected from the patrons riding the stools, most of whom were straight middle-aged traveling salesmen. King liked Stephanie the best so he always tipped her more. She knew he'd wait till later in the evening, when she'd come out as Millie Jackson.

He glanced down at his watch. It was just after ten. King felt bad that he and Neil had argued. He thought about calling him at the pay phone but was afraid Greg might answer. Stephanie wound up her act. Millie Jackson was apparently on vacation. It was Nina's turn next. Nina was Mexican-American, and loved Vicki Carr.

King decided to head home as Nina launched into her passionate interpretation of "Let It Please Be Him."

King had to work in the morning, which never stopped him before, but tonight he was tired. There was so much he didn't understand. So what if he wanted a lover to settle down with? Neil had been so vehement that no guy would ever stay.

King paid his tab and left.

King ended up having a cheeseburger at the Old Grist Mill at Speer Boulevard and 8th Avenue. The Old Grist Mill was a twenty-four-hour coffee shop which catered to an after-hours gay crowd. After doing the rounds at the clubs, Lex, Mari, and King used to stop there for something to eat before heading back to Boulder.

Mari was an old friend of Lex's from Berkeley. Persian, Mari always wore the same short, white cotton dress. She was big-breasted, had great legs, and long, thick, black hair. Mari personified *droll*. She loved to dance, but more than that, Mari loved the Back Door, especially when Stephanie sang Millie Jackson. She always cried when she sang "If Loving You Is Wrong, I Don't Want to Be Right." Stephanie had their number and knew if she played to Mari, she could always count on at least ten bucks in tips.

When King and his friends discovered that Nina, Scotti, and Stephanie all frequented the Old Grist Mill, they always stopped before heading back to Boulder. It was a good idea, given how drunk they were. They liked to sit in the booth next to the drag queens and eavesdrop. They never said anything too significant, but Neil, Mari, and Lex hung on every word. Occasionally they tried to engage them in conversation, but were always politely dismissed.

Tonight King was the only gay customer in the joint. King and one hermaphrodite who decided to engage him in conversation.

"You look a little depressed tonight. Need a shoulder to cry on?"

King looked up. His name was Connie. "His," because tonight he was dressed like a man, but clearly had breasts. King had seen him in there, but never at the Back Door. He was older than King, probably by twenty years. Looked like Truman Capote. He wore a cowboy shirt and jeans rolled up at the cuffs. Like Marilyn Monroe in *The Misfits*.

"I'm okay," King said. "I'll live."

"Man trouble, honey? He leave you at the altar?"

"They all leave, don't they?"

"I've been luckier than most. My man and I just celebrated sixteen years."

"Where is he?"

"He's a truck driver. He's probably pulling into Wells, Nevada, as we speak. I'm waiting for his call. I know the night manager. He always lets me know if Wesley's calling."

"Why don't you wait at home?"

"I'm an insomniac. Always have been. So if I'm really lonely, I hang out here till the sun comes up. I can always sleep when the sun comes up. I even help out some. I fold napkins. I like the company. Or the promise of company."

"Well, I'm just heading back to Boulder."

"I wasn't coming on to you."

"I didn't think you were."

"Heavens, Wesley would kill me. And I'd never do that, I just wouldn't."

"Do you think he's faithful to you?" King had heard rest stops were pretty rowdy.

"If he's ever succumbed, he has the class not to tell me about it. I keep my own side of the street clean. That's how I save my sanity. If I succumbed, I'd start wondering what Wesley was up to. I'd get obsessed, and before you know it, I'd be in my car driving west down the interstate till I caught up with him in Salt Lake or Elko. I did it once. I'll never do it again. It wouldn't be worth it. Not even if the boy was as sweet and pretty as you. Who's broken your heart, sweet and pretty? You want me to break his legs?"

King laughed. "No."

"I'm a little psychic. You know what I think?"

"What?"

"I think he'll be back. The question is, will you want him, then?"

King thought of Matthew. He would.

"He's away, huh?"

"Yes. I hardly know him. He doesn't even live here."

"And things are complicated for him."

"Yes."

"He older?"

"Yes."

"Wait for him. But enjoy the wait, that's my advice to you."

The telephone rang. Connie looked eagerly toward the cashier. Someone wanted to place an order to go. Connie slumped in defeat. He and King smiled at each other miserably. When King stood to leave, Connie squeezed his hand.

"I hope he calls tonight," King told him.

"I do, too. Oh, I do, too."

Chapter Nine

King was the first male operator hired at the university switchboard, which was housed in the basement of the architecture school. His supervisor Arlene was a pretty older woman who loved men and wore ornate bifocals hanging from her neck on a glasses chain. She liked tight dresses and twisted her gray hair into a chignon.

Arlene sat at a desk near a pentagon-shaped console where King sat with four women—good-looking, perfumed, grandmotherly types who doted on him, Dorothy, Marge, Joni, and Ruth. The university didn't have direct dial numbers. All calls were routed through a central switchboard.

King liked talking on the telephone so he loved his job. He was quick, efficient, and personable. The switchboard necessitated twenty-four-hour coverage, and Arlene liked him because he always volunteered for tough shifts. Christmas Eve, for instance, and Saturday nights. King liked the overnight shifts. The student operators were allowed to sleep as long as the phone was answered. A well-worn foam pad, a pillow, and an old blue blanket made a cozy bed. King usually slept on a cafeteria-style folding table, which he dragged next to the console and could roll in his sleep to put calls through.

The best perk was free long distance. The university paid for WATTS service, monitoring long-distance calls on time cards which were metered manually. If no record of calls got recorded, no one knew the difference. King loved making prank calls. He used to connect his friend Ann with the White House or the Pentagon.

If two friends weren't speaking, he'd call them simultaneously and eavesdrop while they bickered about who had called who first.

And King was generous about long-distance calls for his friends. On Saturday nights he'd have sleepovers. Mari would bring pizza and they'd drink beer till the switchboard quieted down, falling asleep under the console till morning.

The ladies were sweet. King basked in their dotage. They'd gossip between calls. Tell jokes. Swap recipes. They'd ask about his girlfriends. He'd smile and evade. The job paid one of the highest hourly wages on campus. Because his parents paid for his expenses, King always had money. Always.

In addition to the old ladies, the twenty-four-hour shifts were supplemented by student operators. In addition to King, they had two black students, Fatima and Polly, the first black operators at the switchboard; Lisa, married and from Palo Alto; and Peter, Tim's boyfriend.

The morning King arrived for work, Peter came in late, apologizing like hell and looking like it, too. Arlene was gracious. She liked him but chided him to call next time. He was visibly upset. King and Peter sat next to each other. The best and worst aspect of the job was the monotony. Hour after hour of answering calls, taking requests for WATTS calls, giving out extension numbers.

Today, kindly old Marge shocked King when she commented that Fatima was sweet, but in her words "gorilla ugly." Peter overheard her and began to laugh.

Dorothy, the assistant chief operator, looked up, and to quell further outbursts from Marge, hastened to agree how sweet Fatima was, and that she disagreed. She thought Fatima very pretty in her way.

"Very pretty," the other ladies agreed.

Marge looked around blankly.

Peter was laughing so hard King thought he might start peeing in his chair. After a minute he calmed down.

"King, maybe you and Peter should take your breaks together . . ."

King knew Arlene. She wanted to find out what was bothering Peter. King already guessed. He was drunk and he hadn't slept. They went to the break room and King closed the door.

Peter broke down.

"What's this about? Why haven't you slept?"

"Tim was arrested last night."

"Arrested! For what?"

"Lewd behavior. He got caught fucking some guy behind the Taco Bell on Baseline."

"Who caught him?"

"Cop car."

"Jesus."

"He told me he was at the library. He picked the guy up and they were so hot for each other they couldn't fucking wait. His pants were down around his ankles. They had to pull 'em apart."

King had been fucked by Tim at a party in North Boulder, he reflected privately. Tim enjoyed fucking in public places. He happened to mention that he liked Joni Mitchell, and asshole that King was, he bought him *Blue* and took it over the next day. King didn't know at the time he was seeing Peter.

"Who gave you the details?"

"Sam. He bailed him out. He doesn't have a chance. He may get expelled for being a sex pervert. That's what goes down on your record. 'Sexual deviant.' "

"What about the other guy?"

"He took off. Got away. Tim didn't even know his name. Cops thought he was lying to protect him. You know what else? They beat him up. Said he resisted arrest."

"Jesus."

"Broke a rib. Saved me the trouble." Peter swooned down in a chair.

Arlene knocked on the door of the lounge. "Time's up fellas . . ."

"Sorry, Arlene. Look, can I do anything?"

"Nah. He fucks everybody . . ." Peter stared blankly into his lap. "He told me about you."

"I didn't know he was seeing you. I'm sorry—"

"Don't worry about it."

"I'll tell Arlene you're sick. You can't work. Take a nap and I'll walk you back to your apartment over lunch. They really beat him up?"

"Unbelievable, huh? Sam's freaking out. He wants to protest at the cop station."

Arlene tapped again. "We're starting to gossip about you out here. Maybe you should come up for air."

King opened the door. "He's got some twenty-four-hour flu. I told him I'd drive him home over lunch."

She peered at Peter over her bifocals. "Better take him now. I've been married seven times. I know what kind of flu he has. Take your time, King. We can cover for you."

"Thanks, Arlene," Peter whispered.

"You come back when you're feeling better, dear," she said kindly.

King guided their fallen operator through the main room and out the door. The ladies smiled sympathetically.

Peter and Tim lived on 20th, only two blocks from King's apartment. "Is he home now?" King asked.

"Yeah."

"Would you rather go to my apartment? Get some sleep?"

"Nah. I've done this millions of times. He swears he loves me, King. You think I'm a joke?"

"No!"

"Everybody sticks up for him."

"Who sticks up for him?"

"You know, Rod and Tony. Sam. They all told me that if I couldn't accept that part of him, it was my fault for sticking it out." He looked up at their apartment door. "I guess they're right. I haven't exactly been Mary Poppins, myself."

"You aren't gonna drink anymore, right? You need to sleep. Sure you don't want to hang out at my place?"

"Nah. Thanks for getting me home, King." He reached across the seat and hugged him. His breath was sour from Wild Turkey and cigarettes. "You're a good guy. Why do you hang back so much?"

"Hang back?" King knew fully well what he was talking about.

"Don't be such a loner, King. You act like you're afraid we'll all bite your head off. Some of the guys think you're arrogant. I tell 'em you're just shy. We should hang out together. Listen to me. I gotta get a life here myself." He gazed up at his windows. "I do love him. If that makes me a sap, then I'm a sap. Still can hurt, though."

He opened his door and started across the frozen grass to the stairs. He turned and waved to King.

Slowly, King drove away.

That night King took Jen to Rudi's, a vegetarian restaurant on lower Spruce. Rudi was a swami, a Hindu priest, and the restaurant was owned and operated by his followers. In the last several years the face of Boulder had changed significantly. Boulder was fast becoming a bastion for alternative religions, and these groups had money. Many were buying up old office buildings and apartment houses. Conservative townspeople began to squawk but nothing could be done. As for King, it only made Boulder more intriguing.

He often ate breakfast alone at Rudi's on weekends. It was beautiful to sit near the window on a bright Boulder winter morning, sipping coffee and pretending to read a book. At night they served Indian and Greek dishes. Spanokopeta, doma and vegetarian curry. Great hot squash soup with a hint a ginger.

Now that Jen was starting to show, she seemed excited about the pregnancy, assured that she was healthy and so was the baby.

"I talked to your mother today. She thinks you're mad at her."

"Why doesn't she ask me herself?"

She studied the menu. "Are you mad at her?"

"No. Yes."

Jen glanced up at him. "She doesn't have the language we have. She didn't take psychology courses. She doesn't have a women's group. She's so frustrated. You have to be patient with her. I wish my mother was cool enough to call a family meeting to discuss how they could all be more supportive to me."

"She wasn't necessarily gathering all of us to do that."

"At least she was willing to dialogue."

"*Dialogue?*"

"Psych 403," she smiled. "Don't they serve anything with meat?"

"This is a vegetarian restaurant. I warned you."

"I'd love a pork chop. Do you think they could make me one?"

King shook his head. She was ribbing him.

"Did you know your mother is knitting me a baby blanket? She asked me my favorite colors."

"She knits beautiful afghans." King looked up at her. Jen's brow was furrowed as she studied the menu. She looked angelically innocent. "But she isn't as nonjudgmental as she seems."

Angry then, Jen looked up. King wished he could jump across the table after his words. He was being cruel trying to undermine his mother's friendship with Jen. He knew it was terribly important to both of them.

"I'm sorry," he muttered. "Maybe I'm jealous."

"Of who more?"

"I don't understand."

"Are you jealous that your mother is doting more on me than you, or that I can give her an experience you and your brother are cheating her out of?"

King blinked. He didn't know how to respond. Her comment was, in fact, meaner than his. Suddenly dinner didn't seem like such a great idea.

"We even?" Jen asked King.

"I think you won." His tone was quiet and bitter.

"Your mother told me she kicked you out because of that Lex guy. She told me you tried to kill yourself afterward. She hates herself for it."

"I don't want to talk about that. I never discuss that."

"I know how you feel, King. It really hurts." Her faced pinched up, like she might cry. "At least your mom came around. My mother isn't even calling me."

"I'm sorry. I started this. I'm sorry."

"Your mom calls me every day. She missed one day and I was so freaked out I started bawling when she called the next day. That's how much her friendship means to me! I don't expect that she'd approve of my situation anymore than she can be expected to approve of yours. She can't catch up in an afternoon. It's asking too much. But I give her all the credit in the world for trying to understand. To anybody looking, my parents would seem much more sophisticated than she is. But they aren't. They're just bigoted. They're hateful. And so is the father of this fetus!"

"Don't call your baby a fetus." King looked away from the table.

"I'm frankly hurt about something else, King."

"What?"

"You aren't around very much. This is the first time I've seen you in a week."

"I'm sorry."

King didn't want her to say anything more. He was remembering his mom, a year ago, screaming at him in the garage to *get out, get out of her house* and *never, never come back.* King just stood there and stared up at the rafters. He couldn't believe what he'd just heard. *Never, never, never.* He certainly wasn't going anywhere. His feet were numb. To placate her, he may have inched slightly toward the driveway.

He'd been abandoned by his friends. And then Lex, who couldn't take the heat. Through their entire affair, Lex never lost a minute's sleep. Nicholas never called his parents. He never sought their guidance. His mom never cried. He never missed a class, or dropped out of school. He never contemplated suicide, as King did, often.

He just grinned his way through the whole damn mess. When King was out of the picture, he started seeing King's best friend since grade school, Lucy, who King had introduced him to.

King's childhood hung from those rafters. His first bike. An old pair of ice skates. A saddle from a horse they had in Wyoming. A hangman's noose he and Neil crafted from an old clothesline rope for Halloween. It was still hanging there, tangled up and gathering dust. As a joke, they'd stuffed old clothes and attached a plastic Halloween pumpkin to the body, to scare the neighborhood kids when they came to their house for trick or treats. Neil, wanting it to appear realistic, had meticulously followed a diagram he'd found in a knot-making book.

He even cajoled King into slipping it over his neck while King teetered on Neil's shoulders, to test it to see if it would hold King's weight. The trusting, giggling, young King obliged his older brother, but Neil's knees buckled, and for a horrible instant, King found himself, feet thrashing, dangling at the end of a hangman's noose. Luckily, Neil found his balance in time to bolster his little brother and loosen the slack, while a choking King loosened the knot and yanked it over his head.

They laughed and laughed about that one. Neil tossed the noose up into the rafters, but over the years, it had worked its way down again, unnoticed as the family had gotten on with their lives. They'd learned one thing for future reference, which King remembered now. The nylon rope could easily sustain a teenager's weight. That and much, much more.

As King evaluated the rafters, he also remembered freshly slaughtered deer, gutted and hanging from their antlers as blood drained, dripping into a metal bucket while Neil cursed his father.

As Jen studied him, King recalled standing and looking up at the wooden beams, and wondering how he'd look, hanging there next to the skates. Next to the imaginary deer.

"Don't," he pleaded softly.

"Don't *what*, King?" Jen asked.

"Don't make me leave."

"Nobody's making you leave. King! King! Who are you talking to?"

But King was imagining his mother, without answering him as she slammed her way into the kitchen. It was nearly five, and time to throw the damn supper on the table. He had just told her that his love for Lex had gone beyond the platonic, information she hadn't asked for or especially needed to be spelled out specifically.

"I didn't like it so much," he offered by way of explaining his candor. He thought it would reassure her. Instead, the idea sickened her and she ordered him out of her house.

He would later claim that he didn't remember climbing up on the workbench. What he remembered was the sensation of dropping, the plummet. Had his life flashed before his eyes? No. It felt like exhilarating, like he imagined sky diving would feel, or cannon balling off the high dive at the neighborhood swimming pool. But it also felt justified. Required. Needed to make things right.

A punishment equal to the sorrow he had caused his mother, to pay for her sin that she would be pushed so far as to evict him from her life. In King's mind, that action, a mother throwing her child away, was as contrary to nature as the homosexual sex act. Two heinous crimes against God had been committed, but only hers was justified, King thought. He would free her by taking his own life, and sparing them both further judgment and heartache. He couldn't find any blame, any responsibility to share with her. He was evil, she was good. King was dirty, but the queen mother was white, like a virgin, even after bearing two sons.

"I saw his eyes," King told Jen. "As I was dropping."

"Whose eyes?"

"I thought they were God's."

"What? King, you're scaring me!"

"They were a brilliant white, and coming at me with amazing speed. I got taken up by them! I was hanging there, my breath nearly gone and I saw the eyes and I was lifted up, saved."

"King," Jen muttered. She said it so softly. "King!" she called a little louder, and the turbaned head of the waitress turned, wondering if she'd heard a voice at all.

"I'm okay," King told Jen. He relaxed. He waived the waitress away.

"How can you say you're okay! I half expect your head to spin around."

"I'm okay," he repeated. "The eyes."

"What about the eyes?"

"They're weren't eyes at all. They were the headlights of my dad's van. I tried to hang myself from the rafters of our garage. After our fight. After she went inside. I climbed up, put the noose around my neck. I jumped. He drove up at exactly the same time."

"He saw you dangling there?" Her voice was hushed, but horrified.

"He kept driving," King nodded. "He drove his van up under me. The rope slackened. I found myself on my knees on the hood of his van. I dented it. That's why he got a new one. Too many memories." King shrugged. "If he'd been a minute late, you'd be sitting here alone."

Jen just stared at him. After a long silence, they both started laughing.

"What happened then?"

"My mom came to the door when he was cutting the rope off my neck with his Swiss army knife. We had dinner. We pretended everything was normal. I think they watched TV. I went to my room. I fell asleep. I woke up and they were fighting."

"He tried to hang himself," King remembered his mother screaming. "They need to lock him up."

"It'll be on his record," his father yelled back. "Forever!"

"He needs more help than we can give him!"

"*No*," Jim roared. "We need to give him more help."

And he manhandled her down the hall to King's room. King's bedroom door burst open. He sat up in bed, a young adult in his childhood twin bed.

His father switched on the light. His face was ashen, his mother's arm red where he was gripping her. "We have to get control of this situation! That means you too, King. I don't know what went on between the two of you, but it stops now. Do you both understand what's at stake here? Do you know what it's like to have a family break up? I do. I do! And I'll be damned if it's going to happen to me again! I'll be goddamned!"

"And then my dad broke down and went to bed."

"What did your mother say?"

"She said she was sorry. I told her I was sorry too." King whispered hoarsely. "I decided I should get some help."

King told Jen he went to a therapist at Wardenberg Student Health Center who asked why he allowed men to fuck him if he didn't like it. He wasn't really a psychologist. He was an MD studying to be a psychiatrist. He thought King was pretty intriguing, and asked if he'd like him to practice on him.

In the very first session the doctor explained he was bisexual. "If we find ourselves attracted to each other, we need to set a ground rule that nothing can happen. In the confines of these sessions, at least."

Seemed to King he was leaving a window open. They just couldn't fuck in his office. He liked to tell him about his own sexual escapades. He told him about fucking his girlfriend one warm autumn afternoon on the roof of his house, where they'd just built a sweet little sundeck.

King didn't know that this completely violated all the basic ethics in a therapist–client relationship. He always left the sessions simultaneously aroused and agitated and after a few of them, didn't go back.

"And a couple days later, I talked Lex into going to California for the summer with me. He had family there. Then after quitting five jobs, I decided we should come back to Boulder to finish school. We lived together for a month. Then he left me for a friend of ours, a girl I'd introduced him to. Someone I grew up with in Denver. And then I moved in with Teddy. Then I danced with Sam. Then I moved out."

A surprised King started to cry. Several others noticed, looking at her sympathetically. Jen stood up and moved next to him, reaching down and cradling his head in her arms.

"I'm so sorry, King. I'm sorry everyone got so hurt." She knelt down and began kissing his forehead, the side of his face. She was crying, too.

"Everything okay?" the nervous waitress asked.

"Hard day," Jen smiled up at him, wiping her eyes with her sleeve. "Maybe we'll order."

"Yeah," King agreed. "Let's order."

*   *   *

When King got home that night his phone rang. It was Sam. At Boulder Community Hospital. Calling everybody. Outraged about Tim's beating from the Boulder PD. He'd started hemorrhaging tonight.

"He's in ICU," Sam told King breathlessly. "His parents are coming from Houston."

"Is Peter with him?"

"Yeah. He's wasted."

"You need me to come by?"

"It's pretty late to ask you."

"I'll come," King told him.

"I called a few other guys. They're all still out at the goddamned Denver bars."

King pulled on his jacket and went back out into the freezing night air. Jen's light was still on. He decided to let her know where he was going. She answered in her nightgown. King could see her rounded belly underneath the flannel. He explained what was happening.

"I think from now on I should let you know if I'm away at night."

"Did I ask you yet?"

"Ask me what?"

"I remember you used to go to mass all the time. I'd see you. I want you to be my baby's godfather."

"I'm not really Catholic."

"I know. You never took communion. Doesn't matter."

"I'd like that."

"My sister's going to be the godmother." She smiled at him. "Well, I hope your friend will be okay. If you plan to protest, count me in. Good night, King."

King trudged to his car. It was still warm from their drive to dinner. King headed up Canyon to Broadway and turned north. What a night. Now he struggled again with motive but shook it off.

Sam hugged him tightly when King came wandering into the waiting area. His eyes were red. He'd been crying. He was horribly upset.

"Peter's asleep on the couch. I don't think we should wake him. He's drunk."

"He was drunk this morning at work." King studied Peter's sleeping form, stretched out with Sam's coat draped over him. The waiting room lights were dimmed. Other than Peter, Sam and King were alone.

"We can't see him. He's through those doors. They have him connected to all kinds of tubes and machines. I think he might die." And his voice broke.

"His parents are coming?" King asked in a small voice. He reached for Sam's hand and squeezed it.

"Yeah. Tomorrow morning. It was too late to come tonight. I told them I'd wait with him."

Sam put his arm around King. He gazed down at him appreciatively, a day's growth of beard on his chin. He kissed King, brushing the hair out of his eyes.

"I knew you'd show up, King. You want some coffee? It's gonna be a long night."

"I'll get it. You?"

"Yeah. Please. It's down the hall past the elevators."

King didn't have to ask how he took it.

The corridor was empty, save for a wheelchair sitting abandoned near the men's room door. The temptation to try it out flickered across King's brain. He found the coffee machine and came back.

They sat hunched next to each other just out of earshot of Peter.

"Cops are saying he resisted arrest. That he fell against a rock while he tried to struggle away. There's a huge bruise over his kidney, where the rib is broken. The rib probably punctured the kidney. This is all such bullshit. They'd never arrest heteros. For fucking in a parking lot? Please. They were behind the goddamned Taco Bell in a dark car. Cops pulled him out by his feet after his trick ran off."

"Do his folks know any of this?"

Sam shook his head. "I don't know if they'll pursue it. Peter says they know about Tim, but they're pretty homophobic."

"Is he conscious?"

"Not since about seven. He's pretty sedated. I tricked with the night nurse once. He promised he'd come and get me if he thought I was needed."

"Needed?"

"If he falls into a coma. I'd have to wake Peter." Sam looked around. "If he doesn't make it and his parents don't insist on an investigation, I'm taking matters into my own hands after they leave."

Wheels whirred in his head as he planned to avenge Tim's beating. It gave King pause that he could be overtaken by pragmatism at a time like this. He was already writing the speech.

Sam read King's mind and quieted suddenly. He squeezed King's hand and looked away. Since King's arrival, he hadn't let go once. They could hear Peter snoring softly. The heat whirred on and drowned him out.

"Rest," King told him. "I'll keep an eye open."

Sam looked around. "Maybe I'll stretch out." Without asking, he pulled his knees up on the sofa and curled into King, his head on his lap. King resisted the urge to stroke his hair.

"Kiss me good night, King." Sam gazed up. "I used to like your good night kisses. The last little gentle one before we'd fall asleep."

King knew what he meant. He leaned down and kissed him gently. More of a peck, really.

King began to trace the bridge of Sam's nose with his index finger. For an instant King could remember the smell of Sam's dorm room. The radiator heat and his toiletries. He traced Sam's lips, those pretty lips.

"King?"

"Yeah?"

"Don't be a hero. Wake me when you get tired."

"I will."

He kissed the tip of King's finger with his lips.

King's thoughts drifted to Tim and the night they tricked.

He'd seen Tim around campus, drawn to his Irish confidence. Tim was usually laughing, always surrounded by several pals. He liked hanging around the UMC fountain court. Always after guys. Liked getting laid.

They finally spoke at a Hidden Valley dance, held in a circus tent on a small ranch north of Boulder. King had maneuvered his way into his line of sight. They danced for a while. Tim asked if King had a car, would he like to go to a party. Off they went. His whole crowd was there. Tony, Rod—a few notorious frat boys who ditched their girlfriends and swung from the rafters once they came into an all-gay scene. King hadn't met Sam yet.

Tim disappeared for a while and King gave up hope. King got really wasted. Ended up making out with a catering chef. Decided he didn't want to go home with him. He was headed out the door when Tim intercepted him. Tim was really stoned. Was King just planning to leave him stranded out here?

Tim asked King to help him find his coat. They went upstairs to one of the bedrooms.

"Grass make you horny? It really makes me horny," he said. He sat on the edge of the bed. It was piled with coats. "There's a lock on the door. You into it?"

King could still picture Tim smiling at him as he sat on the bed. He turned to lock the door. By the time King turned around, Tim was pulling off his clothes. King kicked off his boots and went to join him. It was important to Tim that one of them got fucked. King reflected that some guys didn't think sex had happened unless someone got a poke. Tim volunteered King to be that guy. They didn't have any lube.

"I usually don't need it." Tim hiked up King's ass. "I get so hot my cock lubes itself."

Tim struggled and struggled but without success. King was tight as a drum. "Can't you relax? I've got to get in there."

King's resistance was turning him on even more. Tim yanked on his pants. King started to get dressed, feeling like he'd failed as a fuck buddy.

"I'll be right back. Don't go anywhere."

Somebody knocked. "I need my coat."

Tim went to the door. "What kind of coat is it?"

"A red North Face parka, man."

"You can have it on one condition. Go down the hall and find me some Vaseline."

"You're fucking on our coats?"

"Not yours, if you hurry."

Tim scrambled back and dug through the pile of parkas. He found it and they waited for a knock on the door. When it came, Tim opened it and a hand waved a rank-looking jar through the door. Tim grabbed it, and tossed the parka over the guy's head. He slammed the door and locked it.

He came back to bed and straddled King.

They fucked on Gortex and motorcycle leather while the party raged on.

King drove him home later and they talked in the car, the windows steaming. He told King how much he loved Joni Mitchell and

Laura Nyro. King liked him tremendously. He called King "cutie"— *I wondered who the cutie was*—and wanted to get together again. They exchanged numbers. The next day King bought him *Blue*. He found out about Peter at the following Friday Night Coffee House. King felt really guilty and horrible. He had dreams about Tim's Japanese bridge erection. His kisses.

King stirred awake to Peter, standing over them and begging them to wake up. Tim had just died. Sam struggled to his feet and began howling.

WINTER

Chapter Ten

Talons of icicles dripped to the steaming sidewalk as King ventured down the walkway toward his apartment. He checked Jen's windows. Her drapes were open. She stood in full view, obviously watching for him. King noticed how pregnant she suddenly looked. Her belly was swollen, and she clasped her hands beneath her chest as if resting them on a small shelf.

He was relieved to see her. She slid open her door and stepped into the sun. Just as she did, a long icicle crashed to the sidewalk, shattering near her feet. They both jumped.

Then Theo, too, appeared, having observed King pull up in the parking space under his window.

"I want to go to breakfast," King told them. "Then I'll come home and sleep."

"I can make omelets," Theo volunteered. Theo hadn't known Tim very well. In fact, he once remarked that he thought he was a light-weight. Counterproductive to the cause. Still, King could tell he felt bad.

"Let's go out. I want us all to go out. Then I'll sleep," King said again.

"I'll drive," Theo offered. "Where shall we go?"

"King likes the Village."

Jen knew his morning ritual by heart. King went out for breakfast everyday. Usually to the Village Coffee Shop at Folsom and Arapaho. He customarily sat at the counter, closest to the door. His stool was always waiting. Breakfast for King was an event. Something terribly special to do. He'd spend his last dollar on breakfast out. At breakfast, King could figure out what to do.

His regular waitress was Sally. Sally was a Newport Beach surfer girl who fell in love with a ski patrol guy on a trip to Vail one winter. She had long blond hair, blue eyes, and her skin was already sun damaged, even at thirty-three.

She liked him. King was her regular and they always exchanged quick intimate details of their lives over his eggs and toast.

"Mitch fucked me last night. Thought he'd rip me in half."

"Wish he'd rip me in half."

"I'd ask, but I don't think he'd be cool about it."

"I'll take my chances."

"I wish every guy could get fucked just once. Then they might show a little consideration before forcing themselves inside a woman."

Mitch was hot. Sun burnished with a handlebar mustache and crinkly green eyes. Newport was only twelve miles from Laguna Beach. Sally knew the score. She'd had lots of gay friends. She liked to ride her bike down to the Boom Boom Room and play pool in the afternoons. Mitch put a stop to it when he asked her to marry him and move to Boulder.

With Jen and Theo with King, they needed a booth. The place was packed. Sally saw him and winked. She'd seen King with Jen a few times before. She saw the expression on his face and didn't rib him that morning. She just took their order and brought the food. When she brought the check she touched King's shoulder kind of lightly.

Sally told him the only thing she hated about being a waitress was the feel of gravy on the sides of a customer's dirty plate. She hated accidentally touching gravy. Hated it. King thought of Sally every time he ate breakfast.

Tim's death made the evening news. It would have made the morning edition but the Boulder Police Department managed to keep it quiet until Sam notified the *Denver Post*, the *Rocky Mountain News*, the *Boulder Daily Camera*, and Channels 2, 4, and 7.

Gay student kicked to death by Boulder Police, charged homosexual activist Sam Ford.

The Boulder PD public information officer denied Sam's claim. They said Tim, while engaging in lewd contact behind the Taco Bell on Baseline Road, resisted arrest. His fierce struggle to escape was the cause of his injuries. No police officer at any time struck or kicked him. His injuries were consistent with those of a fall. An internal investigation, however, was underway. The arresting officers would not be suspended. All were still on active duty.

An attorney for Tim's parents was interviewed briefly on the five o'clock news. They were deeply saddened by the loss of their son, but did not hold the Boulder Police Department culpable in any way. They did not support the efforts of subversive campus groups to blow this terrible tragedy out of proportion. In fact, they wished that all members of the Boulder community respect their right to privacy and allow them to grieve quietly the loss of their wonderful, albeit misguided, son.

They would be returning to Houston with Timothy's body as soon as the coroner completed his investigation, anticipated to be within twenty-four hours. They planned to cremate him in Colorado, apparently to save the cost of shipping.

King got a call from his parents about two minutes after he and Jen watched the news. When the phone rang they gazed at each other. Both knew it was them.

After Tim died, King dropped Sam off with Peter at Tim and Peter's apartment. They planned to meet Tim's parents at Stapleton International Airport in Denver later that morning. Sam planned to keep an eye on Peter in case he started drinking. He didn't want him drunk when he met Tim's parents for the first time.

Sam didn't want King to wait with them. He was cool and distracted. That much was clear. King thought Sam might be afraid he'd gotten the wrong idea about the kiss. About the holding. Maybe King was being paranoid. Sam sensed that King's feelings were hurt which made him feel selfish on top of everything. King liked Tim. He wanted to stay focused on him. His life. King never knew anybody his age who died before.

He didn't think it possible.

As the phone continued to ring, Jen asked if King wanted to be alone while he talked to his parents.

"Would you answer it?" King asked her.

"If I answer they'll think something's terribly wrong."

King nodded and reached for the receiver.

"King?" His mother spoke his name before he even said hello.

"Yeah?" King sounded tremulous. Matthew's voice suddenly rang through his brain. *Affirm your life, King. Affirm your life.* "Yeah," King said again, this time more forcefully. Jen nodded in silent support. She lay huddled on his bed with her back to the wall King shared with Theo.

"King, did you know this boy who died?" Kay asked.

"Yeah," King said again.

"*You keep just saying 'yeah,*' " Jen stage whispered critically.

"Yes, he was a friend. I was there when he died."

This bit of information stunned them.

"*You mean you were there at the hospital,*" Jen coached him again.

"I was at the hospital. A friend called me to come over . . ."

"You were *that* close to him?" King's mother queried, somewhat alarmed.

"Well, yes, Mom. I was. I work with his roommate, Peter."

"Did he call?"

"No, that was someone else."

"The boy on the news?"

They'd seen Sam on the news. Jen and King had missed him.

"You met him. Sam. When we found Jen her apartment."

"The handsome one?"

Jesus, King thought.

"Let him talk, Kay." King's father was on the extension. King was vastly comforted.

"Jen is here. She says hello. She met him, too."

"Do you want us to come up, King? Do you want to come home?"

"No," King said. "Jen's just across the way. A few of us might get together later anyway."

"The boy on the news. He seemed like an agitator."

"We don't want you to get into any trouble, King," Jim said. "His tone was threatening."

"They killed him, Dad."

"We're coming up!" Kay announced.

Jen could hear her from the bed. King held up the phone, choking back emotion. She moved to take the receiver.

"Hi, Kay. Hi, Mr. James. It's me, Jen."

And King watched her calm them down. She told them he was upset but wouldn't do anything foolish. She'd stay right with him.

She told them she agreed that Sam seemed pretty serious, but he was like that. He was overreacting for the press. Tim's parents weren't pressing charges. They'd be gone in the next day or so and it'd all blow over.

"Tim was a nice guy," she said finally, gazing sadly over at King. "He didn't deserve to die."

When she hung up, Jen and King both knew they were afraid for him. Afraid of what he might do if any protesting started up.

"You have to remember, King, as far as they're concerned, it might have been you."

"It may well have. It may well have."

The phone rang again. This time it was Neil.

"Mom and Dad are fucking scared to death. You planning anything foolish?"

"Not yet." King and Neil still hadn't spoken since they'd fought.

"I'll come to Boulder."

"You don't need to protect me anymore, Neil."

"Yes, I do. I'm always your older brother. I want to be there for you."

King stared into the phone. "I haven't heard anything yet. Tim's parents are against it. Nothing like this has ever happened here."

"I've met someone."

"Yeah?"

"A friend of Don and Gary's. From California. Laguna Beach. His name is Vince. He was here last weekend. He's coming back at the end of the month. Just to see me. Don and Greg are shitting bricks. They had him fixed up with three different guys. Then I came in and he asked about me. He's great. Really different from Paul."

"Anyone would be an improvement over Paul."

"I think he's the one. I may move, King."

"After a weekend?"

"Somehow you know."

"To California?" This seemed impossible. Neil leaving King behind.

"We've talked about it. He has a hair salon in Newport. I'd get my license. We'd work together. You'll like him. He wants to meet you. We'll take you to dinner."

King heard Neil take a drag off his cigarette.

"Who's the hot guy with the mustache screaming on TV?"

"Sam." King shook his head. Even his mother and brother were affected by him. "I was with him at the hospital. I used to see him for a little while."

Neil's silence proved King had his respect.

"Seems pretty hotheaded. Don't let him talk you into anything. All this shit goes on your record. You can get expelled."

"Nothing is going on."

"You call me. If I hear about it, and I will, I'll come up and find you. Call me," he said again, this time more reasonably. "I'm still your big brother."

King didn't say anything.

"You've been through enough, King. Don't put yourself in jeopardy."

"He was a nice guy," King began.

"We're all nice guys," Neil said gently. "That's why we have to take care of each other. If a demonstration is organized, maybe I'll come to Boulder. We'll walk together, King. The James Brothers."

That's what Neil and King called each other when they were kids. The James Brothers. Then Neil bought *Simply Streisand* and life for the James Brothers was never the same. They'd sit in their finished basement and listen to it over and over and over again.

"King, maybe if I move to California you can come after you graduate."

"I've been to California."

"This time I'd be there," Neil told him.

Occasionally it occurred to King to move from Colorado. But Boulder was great. Where would King ever find another Boulder?

"It's a big world, King. I'd watch out for you."

Better two than one.

King didn't call Neil to come to the march, afraid if there was trouble, both his mother's sons would be culpable.

Because he was president of the BGLF, Theo addressed the group of demonstrators politely but forcefully in the parking lot of Boulder's Taco Bell. They were to think of this march as a political funeral, he said, a new phrase he had coined. They weren't to be baited by harassment from onlookers. They would move cohesively—as one body. They were showing the community their faces as a unified group. They were coming out of the closet.

At rush hour, about six o'clock, the group carried candles and marched from the Taco Bell on Baseline up to Broadway and followed it all the way to the Boulder County Courthouse. About a hundred people walked. Sam and Theo led the procession with Peter as the grieving mate close behind them. Peter staggered and lurched so much Rod and Tony stepped up to bolster him on each arm.

"He's truly hurting," Jen murmured sympathetically.

"He's drunk," King whispered back. On cue Peter began to vomit on the lawn in front of the registration building. Sam looked frankly disgusted. "I wish Tim's parents were here. It'd be a whole lot more powerful. More emotional."

"Yeah, on them," Jen whispered to King.

"Sam asked for some of Tim's ashes."

"*No!*"

"He wanted to scatter them on the steps of the Boulder Police Department."

"Fuck!" Jen couldn't restrain herself. They started laughing.

Theo had asked King and Jen to take up the rear of the line to herd any stragglers forward so the group appeared as one body.

"Keep it moving," Jen ordered a pair of sorority girls who'd got caught up at the back of the procession.

"We aren't in line," one of them argued. "We're trying to get through."

"This is a funeral procession!" Jen barked. "Show some respect or get the hell out of here." When she explained whose funeral it was and why they were protesting, the girls squealed and ran off. "Jesus," she hissed. "Was I that much of a dipshit?"

Jen clearly enjoyed her new radical status. She even sported a black beret, which offset a shock of blond hair she'd put up under the hat. She told King she wanted to look like she was a member of the French resistance. It was cold and she wore her long black cashmere overcoat with black leather boots.

"You look more like the French fashion police."

"Look, there are some days I don't want to look pregnant," she said.

"Those days are numbered."

"Thank God! I'm glad I live alone. You wouldn't believe all the farting at night."

Theo requested that all members of the procession wear black. About ten people were asked to carry red lanterns, contrasting with the white lighted candles to signify Tim's spilled blood.

Of course King never took his eyes off of Sam.

Brooding and solemn, Sam towered at the head of the procession, like a handsome Abraham Lincoln. He, too, wore a long black car coat with a white shirt and black tie underneath it. He carried a sign: GAY RIGHTS ARE HUMAN RIGHTS. JUSTICE NOW!

King and Sam hadn't really talked since the night Tim died. There had been too much to do, to plan. Theo called an emergency meeting of the BGLF. They met in his apartment. The gathering was very emotional. Some members called for civil unrest. A few lesbians volunteered to chain themselves to the railing on the front of the Boulder Police Department.

"This is our first public march. I favor restraint."

"They're ignoring Tim's murder."

"Fuck, yes!"

"This is our first public forum in Boulder," Theo reminded them. "It's historic. We can't swarm a police station."

"There might be violence anyway," Sam observed quietly.

This caught the group's attention. They looked at each other.

"He means against us," Theo explained.

"You aren't suggesting we not defend ourselves."

"Tim couldn't defend himself," Sam said.

"You also need to be prepared for possible arrest," Theo added. "None of us has much experience with civil disobedience. We have only forty-eight dollars in our treasury. There isn't any money for bail or legal fees. An arrest will go on your record."

"I'll take that chance."

"And we'll bail you out." Rod and Tony smirked.

But Sam didn't smile. He was dead serious. They debated and argued for hours.

Given the sordid nature of the events preceding Tim's death, getting caught butt-fucking behind a Taco Bell and all, the founding fathers and mothers of the BGLF thought it best the demonstration stay dignified and restrained.

Sam's speech was eloquent, elegiac, and emotional. By the time they arrived, the march had swelled to more than two hundred people including the news crew from Channel 9 in Denver. Sam's picture appeared on the front page of the *Boulder Daily Camera,* page eight of the *Rocky Mountain News* and wasn't covered by the *Denver Post.*

Homosexual Death Ruled Accidental capped a follow-up article in the *Camera*. News references to homosexuality weren't common in 1974. Uncharted territory, Tim's death would have the effect of referring to homosexuals as *gays* in the Colorado media.

King still hated the word *gay*.

But there it was, and so was he.

The next day before King went to work, he decided to go to mass at the Shrine of St. Thomas, a small beautiful Catholic church overlooking Boulder. In his sophomore and junior years, it wasn't uncommon for King to attend Mass once a day, sometimes twice, depending on his schedule.

This was before Lex. Before Nicholas and his other old friends. Before King lost them to being gay. He enjoyed daily Mass at St. Tom's. The priests were usually young and cute. Because Boulder was a university town, they were loose. The homilies dealt with current events. Social issues. Politics.

Weekdays, attendance was modest. No more than ten or twelve people at best. King usually lit a candle and took his seat in a pew behind the others. He'd kneel and pray for God's will to be done. He'd offer the peace of Christ to his pew mates.

He'd listen and think. Sometimes he'd come to the sanctuary in the afternoon, and satisfied he was alone, King would sing from the choir loft. St. Tom's had beautiful stained glass windows and rich, dark wooden pews.

King loved lighting candles for his family and friends. Because of the anxiety he felt over his burgeoning sexuality, it always felt so safe and quiet. King felt like God loved him. It was magnificent that such a sanctuary existed twenty-four hours a day for someone like King to come and pray, meditate, or sit quietly and enjoy the flickering candles while it snowed outside.

Now he was back.

It felt safe and familiar, the way the floorboards creaked as King made his way over to the candles where he lit one for Tim. Poor Tim. King's emotions were mixed. He couldn't give himself completely up to old beliefs. He didn't resent St. Tom's or the crucifix of Jesus hanging over the altar. He didn't resent the priests or the parishioners of St. Tom's who freely attended mass on a daily or weekly basis.

As he knelt near the candle he lit for Tim, King felt overcome, convicted, they used to say, by a keen sense of self-hatred and recrimination. The church and his old friends were certainly homophobic. He'd been treated horrifically. But worse than their ignorance, their prejudices, worse than all the hatred the world had for minorities, homosexuals in particular, was King's own ambivalence. His own nagging abhorrence for being gay.

King sat quietly in the rear pew of St. Tom's and watched the snow fall against a small clear pane in a stained glass window, which had apparently been temporarily repaired. It had been a stormy winter. Snowfall most every afternoon. The sun shining only briefly in the morning. Never enough to melt the hard, yellowing base which was always freshly blanketed by evening.

King reflected on these truths. He watched Tim's votive candle flickering under the statue of St. Thomas Aquinas, the scholar and scientist. A good saint for the confused. King's patron saint.

The door creaked open and a woman entered, followed by an elderly man King often saw at noon Mass. The noon regulars began to come in. King hadn't been to Mass in over six months, but most of the faces were the same. Candles were lit by an altar boy. An older priest appeared, someone he didn't recognize. The mass began.

King knelt on the hassock, comfortable in his anonymity. He prayed his usual prayer. He thanked God for his family and asked for them to be blessed. He prayed for general forgiveness. For God's will in all his decisions. He prayed to be filled with God's spirit. The priest instructed each parishioner to offer his neighbors the sign of peace.

After doing so, inexplicably, King stood up and walked out.

He stepped onto 11th Street and headed toward campus. A quick burst of cold wind came up. King was reminded of his dad the morning he saw him leave the bar and head toward his office. This moment felt as cold and lonely as that.

The ladies at the switchboard stared at King when he came in. Peter hadn't been to work since Tim's murder. They might have seen him on television, standing behind Sam on the steps of the police station. King didn't know how they figured the whole thing involved him, if at all, but they knew Peter and King were friends. King pulled off his coat and hung it up in the back room.

Arlene followed King into the lounge and closed the door.

Her face was etched with sympathy. She took off her bifocals. "Can we talk a minute?"

"I'll be late for my shift."

"I'm your supervisor, dear. There's no way you can be late."

King waited for her to collect her thoughts. On any given day King would have loved to entertain a discussion on everything that had happened in the last several days. King loved to discourse. King didn't particularly care about the mundane details of someone's day. What interested him was what they thought about those details.

Now he just wanted to answer the phone and give out information.

King felt deeply fatigued and sad.

"We're all very concerned about Peter. Is he doing okay?"

They knew.

"A friend of ours is staying with him. I haven't checked in with them today."

"He hasn't called, but I've covered his shift. Frankly, I don't know what to say to him. I want to respect his privacy."

She crossed her arms, almost wistfully. She could read King's body language, by how guarded he stood.

"I'm concerned about you, too, King. You know we care about Peter. But we love you. You're our favorite." She hesitated. "I've never been so fond of a student operator. You're a wonderful young man. Sometimes though, I worry that you feel you can't be yourself with all of us."

Emotion choked his throat.

"Oh dear," Arlene whispered. She reached for a tissue from a box of Kleenex near the coffee urn. She took one for herself and offered the box to King. Instead King wiped his cheek with his hand.

"King," she continued. "What I'm trying to say is that even though you have a perfectly wonderful mother, we'd like you to think of us like grandmothers or—in my case," she joked, "your older sister. We're family, all of us. You're part of that, no matter what. When I got my last divorce, Dorothy spent a week with me and covered for me at work. We all know June's an alcoholic. She's finally gone to AA. Marge drives her there every morning before work. We've lived long lives. Them longer than me. We're not simple-minded, shortsighted old ladies. Do you get my drift already?"

King nodded.

"Do you think I can call Peter and tell him we miss him and to take his time? He still has a job when he feels up to coming back."

"I think he'd appreciate it," King whispered. "I know I do."

"It takes getting used to, doesn't it?"

To King, Arlene was the smartest woman on earth.

"Yes," he nodded. "But I'm working on it."

When King followed Arlene into the main room and took his seat, the ladies smiled as he adjusted his headset. His first line lit up.

"Hello, this is the University of Colorado . . ."

Through the basement windows of the office, snow began to drift, and for the first time since he'd slept with Matthew, King felt safe, cozy, and warm.

Chapter Eleven

When King got home that night, Theo was loading his skis onto the ski rack of his BMW. "You ski? I'm heading up to Lake Eldora."

"My skis are in Denver in my folks' garage. They aren't that great anyway."

"You can rent. You ever night skied before?"

King hadn't. Lake Eldora was a small ski area only thirty minutes up Boulder Canyon. It was the only night skiing available in Colorado.

"I'm not much more than a beginner."

"So ride along anyway. I'll give you a few pointers and I'll go off on my own. I want to get out of Boulder, and somehow the mountains feel a little more pure than the dungeon at the Triangle." The Triangle was a leather bar in the Five Points section of downtown Denver.

"Should we ask Jen?"

"She's studying for a test. Besides, she's pregnant." Theo stopped what he was doing. He seemed exasperated.

"What's wrong?"

"You seem to have this aversion to spending any time alone with me."

"That's not true."

"I'm not after your ass."

"I never assumed you were."

"Look, it's none of my business, but you're wasting your time, waiting for Sam. He's not gonna come around. He's got a boyfriend in Denver. I hear he's moving."

Hell of a day. *Hell.*

At least it explained why he'd cooled after the night in the hospital. Sam probably thought he was using him. King felt sick and ashamed. In the aftermath of Tim's death, he'd been pining for Sam without even admitting it to himself.

"So let me get my gloves and a sweater."

"You'll go?"

"And if it's okay by you, I'd like to at least tell Jen where I'm going. We have a deal."

King headed down the sidewalk toward his apartment.

They decided to stop at McDonald's before heading up Boulder Canyon. Theo's BMW, a silver-blue 2002, purred as it edged up the mountain. Occasionally the car would skid on a patch of black ice and careen toward the banks of the Boulder Creek. King would clutch the armrest, but Theo kept the little sedan under control. King glanced over at him. Theo seemed intent on the road ahead. He had a nice profile. He was a good-looking guy in a scholarly way. He played it down with his wire frames and black clothes. He'd spent a winter semester studying in Paris. He smoked Gitane cigarettes and read a lot of philosophy books.

"I wouldn't have pegged you for a skier."

"How about a football player?"

"Nope."

"I was homecoming king in my senior class. I was the captain of the baseball team."

King laughed. He thought Theo was pulling his leg.

"Not because of me, mind you. But my dad."

"Who's your dad?"

"He manages a major league baseball team." Theo told King his name. King never heard of him, or them.

"Is that why you don't tell him you're gay?"

"Kinda makes sense. He's retiring next year. My mom asked me to wait. At least till he's out of the spotlight."

"Would he be so embarrassed?"

"No. He'd overreact in the other direction. He'd bend over backwards to make sure nobody thought he was embarrassed. And then I'd be embarrassed. And so would my mom."

This seemed incongruous to King. Theo, the president of the

Boulder Gay Liberation Front, saving his prominent father the embarrassment of a gay son.

"Is that why you let Sam step out in front when cameras are nearby?"

"Sam wants that kind of attention and he's articulate. He's good for us. I could get all jealous and power hungry, but I don't. I want what's best for the movement. I've seen quite a bit of him lately. We're writing the first gay rights legislation ever to be put on a state ballot. It'll protect us in jobs, housing."

"You'll coauthor it, though."

"Of course. But no way in hell will it pass."

They drove in silence for ten more minutes. The heat blasted under the dashboard of the Beamer. Occasionally King could feel Theo glance over at him, almost as if searching his face for something.

"I don't know if I ever thanked you for extending yourself before I moved."

"You thanked me," he said.

"Still, it's been good for me."

"I like having you around. Jen, too. I didn't have much in common with my other tenants."

"Your tenants?" It sounded proprietary.

"I don't tell anybody this, but I own the building. I don't usually tell 'em who my dad is either, but I wanted you to know. All my life I've been treated differently because of my family. Coming out has been great. I don't like stereotypes, but fact is, not many gays give a shit about baseball so nobody knows who we are."

"I like baseball players' butts."

"I could tell you stories about going into the locker room with my dad."

"I hear plenty through your wall."

"I don't hear anything through yours. You've got to change that, King. Enjoy your body. Your young gay life."

Theo didn't take off on his own like they'd discussed. After renting his skis, he stayed by King's side the whole night. Someone on the lift said the wind chill was below zero. Only the beginner and intermediate slopes were open, softly lit by amber lamps. It was incredibly beautiful, skiing through the night, the ski lodge muting in and out, miles below the top of the lift.

Theo was a gifted skier, a natural athlete. He gave King pointers on paralleling. He'd wait patiently if he fell. If Theo skied ahead he'd always turn around, watching King's form, calling out polite suggestions, ideas for improvement. They skied ten runs before they bothered to take a break.

King was struck by Theo's comment that purity was the order of the day. In the ski lodge they ordered hot mulled cider. They clomped over to the bench near the fireplace in their ski boots. The room seemed occupied by couples. The atmosphere felt rugged, almost romantic. A ski instructor they noticed earlier massaged the foot of his client, a pretty woman with a Texas drawl.

"You want your foot massaged?" King asked Theo.

"No, but I wouldn't mind the option if I did."

Theo became agitated. "You think we'll ever see a day when two men or two women can be affectionate in public without getting killed for it?"

"I don't know."

"Fucking asshole cops."

"Let's go back up," King said, standing to his feet. "We came to get away, remember?"

Theo gazed up at him and nodded. The firelight illuminated the side of his face, glinting in his hair. On impulse, King leaned down and kissed him. As he stood back up, he made it a point not to look around to see if they'd been noticed.

On the ski lift, nothing was said. The cloud cover had disintegrated. Black, black evergreens framed the starry night sky. Although the temperature must have dropped another ten degrees, they each removed a glove, holding hands silently on the gently swaying ride to the top of the mountain.

Theo made a ground rule about sleeping together. They weren't falling in love. They were only men enjoying the mysteries of another man's body. They had to be adult about it if they weren't successful lovers.

They pulled their wet sweaters off. They untied their boots and kicked them away. They unzipped their ski pants and stepped out of them, hard-ons poking through their jockeys.

Theo laid King out on his bed and studied him intently. Theo's body was pale, but surprisingly toned. He had the first washboard stomach King ever encountered. King eased out of his shorts. Theo kissed him, kneeling next to the bed. After Theo made certain every inch of King's skin was satisfied, he lay quietly on top of him, King's semen sealing them together.

"I want you to come, now."

"I will," Theo whispered back. And then he began to tighten his grip. Theo was strong, pressing himself onto King with as much force as he could, and then, motionless for several moments, began to ejaculate onto his abdomen.

"A Zen orgasm," King whispered wonderingly.

"Yes." Theo smiled down at him. "I can levitate, too, if you give me a chance."

The next morning Jen observed King leave Theo's apartment. She was up early for a chemistry midterm.

"Unbelievable," she called from her door. She took a swig of coffee from a mug King's mother had given her. King knew it was his mother's because he'd given it to her two years ago for Mother's Day.

"I thought long and hard about my privacy when you moved in. I could have stopped it but I didn't!"

"Theo," she called. "*The-o . . .*"

Theo poked his head through the door. He was naked and he held his drape over his torso. He looked at Jen, then at King.

"What?"

"Nothing," she shrugged.

"That's right," King said. "Nothing."

"Thanks a lot."

"You set the ground rules," King answered back, half joking, half not.

"What are the ground rules?" Jen felt playful and wanted to start a deal.

"Theo told me we can't fall in love!" King's voice ricocheted between the two buildings.

"Why can't you fall in love?"

Theo's smile dimmed. "Am I the only one who knows the answer?"

Taken aback, Jen took another gulp of her coffee. King didn't say anything, probably because he knew the answer.

"What's the answer, King?" Jen asked.

"Because King is love with Sam," Theo barked. "And no matter how much caring and affection anyone pours on him, he won't be dissuaded. I know it, you know it, and Sam knows it."

"I have to study for my test." Jen retreated into her apartment.

"You've talked about me?" King felt humiliated.

"Come back inside."

It was all too confusing. King ambled back to Theo's apartment. Theo held the drape open for King. He was naked, just getting ready to take a shower when he'd heard Jen calling him.

"Lemme pull on a pair of shorts."

"I know it isn't going to happen with me and Sam." King watched him rummage through a pile of clothes in a hamper. He had a beautifully shaped ass. He found a pair of CU gym shorts and stepped into them. His cock was engorging and he tried to hide it. He wanted to keep this conversation serious.

"Your head knows it."

"Why are you making such a big deal? You made all the ground rules last night. 'We can't fall in love. We're only two men exploring the mysteries of another man's body.' You didn't ask me. You *told* me."

"Are you saying you want us to be more?"

"We had a good time."

"King! You need to look at something." Theo sat down. "You have an ability to create intimacy, real fast. You don't make small talk. And you listen carefully when others speak. I watch you."

"And this is a detriment? A character flaw?"

"You're a serious, romantic man. You've only just come out."

"Hey. I didn't only just come out. I was never really in. I've always been honest about who I was."

"I think you shouldn't be so forthcoming."

"Why?"

"Because you'll be hurt by it. Sam told me he thought you were needy. He liked you, but he didn't trust your motives. He didn't want to move so fast."

King was stunned. Nobody ever told him they didn't trust him. It made him sound so cloying. So manipulative.

"He called me to come to the hospital. He laid his head in my lap and asked me to kiss him."

"He needed comfort. Reassurance. That's all."

"You talked about that, too?"

"Yes. He feels really guilty. But he's also a little pissed at you. He thinks you used the thing with Tim to try to get close to him. He thought afterwards you were a little inappropriate."

Tears sprang to King's eyes. His body rippled with humiliation. Theo wasn't telling King anything he hadn't already accused himself of. But he never totally believed it. King always questioned his own motives.

"I *liked* Tim. I had a thing with Tim."

"Yeah, and afterward you went out and bought him a Joni Mitchell album. You fucked each other at a party, for Christ's sake. He was after sex. Not a marriage. Couldn't you tell the difference?"

"Is there anything you don't know about me? Do you all sit around and compare notes? Why the fuck am I so goddamned interesting?"

"Because you are interesting," Theo said. "Why do you think I stopped you that day? Moved you in here? You think it was all altruistic? A brother helping a brother? I wanted to get in your pants."

"Well, mission accomplished." Stung, King sat on the edge of a kitchen chair. This made no sense at all. He was outraged about Sam. *Outraged.* Now he hated him.

"And if I'm going to be a hundred percent honest here, I must admit I want more . . ."

King glanced up.

"But I think you need to be single for awhile. See what's out there. That's what I meant last night. I don't want to get clobbered. When I find a lover, I want it to be for keeps. You equate sex with love."

"That's because I was in love with the first person I had sex with."

"How can you really believe that?"

Lex. Again.

"He was my very best friend in the world. We knew each other for *years* before we touched each other. We waited. We faced terrible obstacles. Have you ever waited to have sex with someone? Has Sam? You fuckers don't know what you're talking about. You don't know the difference."

King stood up and walked out. Fucking Lex. Fucking Lex. He'd fucked King's sex life up forever. All these guys whose first sexual encounters were anonymous and furtive. Public rest rooms, porno movies, steam rooms, parks—they knew something King would never know for certain. Until now, King never had sex with anyone without some sense of promise, or hope. Neil was right. He had all the expectations of a teenage girl. King's case was unusual. He didn't know of anybody who'd say they were in love the first time they made love. Maybe after, but not *before*. He was hopeless. Hopeless. It would fuck up his fucking around for the rest of his life.

King was grateful to Theo for one thing. Now he was over Sam, astonished such huge feelings could evaporate so quickly. King had used Tim. But Sam used Tim to get his face on TV and his picture in the newspaper. He was about as spontaneous as a pyramid.

If Sam and Theo and Neil all thought he should fuck around before settling down, King decided to take them up on it. Before King slammed his sliding glass door, he heard Theo's voice. Something he didn't quite hear. Jen told King later what it was.

"Something like, 'Now I *do* know the difference.' What'd he mean by that?"

King knew, but Theo had ruined his chances with him. That night King decided to go to the baths.

At the mouth of Boulder Canyon and 9th Street stood an unassuming industrial warehouse with tin siding. It had no sign, or even a street number visible from the intersection. Because of its proximity to the mountain roads, it looked like it sheltered snow plows.

The parking lot was behind the building and would curiously fill up later in the evening. Mostly past ten. Before Lex explained what it was, King thought they plowed through the night. There are a few concepts in life which seem inconceivable till they take some time to settle in. Sexual intercourse between a man and a woman is probably the first one. How a television works. Sexual intercourse between two men.

Lex taught King about that without warning him. Boy, was King surprised. Lex liked getting fucked more than he liked anything else. It was laughable that he went back to women. King bet he was still a virgin.

So when Lex explained what a bathhouse was, King was stupefied. And now, thanks to his chat with Theo, King knew why he was stupefied.

Fourteen-year-old girls don't engage in same-sex orgies after they hit the locker room after gym. Instead they tape pictures of teen idols inside their lockers. They wrap themselves tightly up in towels and take private showers and have bathroom stalls with doors. The boys weren't afforded such privacy. For such a homophobic culture, much sexual tension was created for the teenaged boy.

For King, junior high meant sprinting to his locker, spinning his padlock, hoping his towel would conceal his adolescent erection. The trick was getting his underwear pulled up before the towel fell off. Then King had to decide which he could do faster. Jump in his jeans or pull on his sweater, all to cover his swelling shorts.

One guy he knew wasn't so lucky. His nickname was Billy Boner. He didn't even have the wits about him to try to hide it. When he'd hit the showers, wagging his flag pole, the whole class would run laughing and screaming back to their lockers. The coach excused him from gym for the rest of the semester.

How could King describe the secret pleasures a locker room provided for a gay man? Imagine a hot-blooded heterosexual male wandering at will through a shower filled with wet, naked, lathered, and shining women, bending, stretching, reaching, and squatting. In high school, gym teachers often showered with the last physical education class of the day.

Oh, joy! When the beefy coach would amble naked, his dick wobbling, from the showers to his office, they all stared, not just the gays, but everybody. They all checked out the coach's cock. Sometimes he'd move so slowly, in King's mind, it had to be purposely seductive. King's first semester in college, he signed up for weight training, and the instructor cornered him one morning and told him he wasn't working hard enough. King explained that he worked the night shift, and got very little sleep. He told King to meet him in his office later that day so they could talk about it.

When King arrived, he'd left a note. He'd just finished a game of racquetball, wanted King to meet him in the showers. You guessed it. He knew King was coming, figured he'd be on time, and asked him to wait while he finished his shower. They were the only ones in the locker room, him naked and King watching. It was now clear to King he was trying to seduce him, but at the time, no such thing occurred.

Later, for a short time, King worked as a janitor at the university recreation center. The men's showers fell under his purview. He probably disappeared into the janitor's closet four or five times a shift to jack off. There was also an observation window in the bottom of the swimming pool. During certain hours men swam naked, and King used to watch them flutter by, their tight bodies shimmering like marlins in the blue, blue water.

People asked why King seemed to like being a janitor so much. They even admired his humility. He always looked forward to his work.

A red light over a metal door beckoned to King from across the parking lot. It was another freezing cold night. What the hell was he doing? King wondered. King stopped, deciding to turn back. Because he was focused on the red light, he was surprised when another door, obscured as if part of the structure's wall, opened and a tall man stepped outside. He paused when he saw King standing in the shadows near the back of the parking lot. It was too cold for someone to be cruising. Did he think King was dangerous?

King weighed his options. He could go home and write, which he should have been doing the last two months. He had several stories he could use from last summer but wanted to write something new, something post-Sam.

Whatever King thought about Sam, he represented a turning point. It all changed when King met Sam. But now he was cold and had to make a decision.

King headed for the red-lit door.

The stranger hesitated as King approached. If he thought he could pick King up in the parking lot when it'd taken this much courage for King to get out of the car, he had another thing coming. King was going inside.

When he passed, King muttered, "Hullo."

"Boring," the stranger said.

Me or the goings-on inside? King wondered.

King ignored him and opened the door. A naked lightbulb illuminated a small vestibule, no bigger than a coat closet, with something akin to a takeout window and some young guy in a leather vest sitting behind it.

He looked up expectantly. Behind him small tubes of lubricants and assorted brands of poppers lined a shelf. King had only done poppers once with Lex.

"Card?" the teller asked.

King was sure he looked as simple as a kindergarten drawing. To top it off, his teeth started chattering. He felt a sudden urge to use a toilet.

"I don't have a card."

"It's ten bucks to join. Three with a card. You have ID?"

King struggled with his wallet. A wad of cash fell to the rubber-matted floor. Instead of picking it up, he managed to fish out his driver's license.

"Get your money or someone else will. This your first time, baby?"

King nodded.

"You're in for a treat. First, I have to ask you to lift your shirt."

"What?"

"You gotta lift your shirt."

"Why?"

"No femmes or fatties are allowed."

"*What?*"

He shrugged. "You want to come in or not? I've gotta do a load of towels."

King shook his head, lifting his shirt. King still hadn't taken off his parka.

"Nice enough," he nodded. "Fill this out."

King scanned the card. "What do you need to know all this for?"

"In case of fire." He popped his gum. "And I keep your ID and personals in a lockbox. Only you have a key. You're lucky. We still have rooms. Number nineteen. Same key fits your room door. Keep it locked."

At this rate, King didn't think he could ever maintain a hard-on again. He pushed back the card with a ten-dollar bill. He stuffed his keys and wallet in the lockbox. He closed the lid and removed the key.

The clerk grabbed the lockbox and tossed King a towel. "Enjoy yourself. Frankly, you look a little tense." He winked and turned away. King pulled off his parka and opened the door.

What he saw amazed him.

Chapter Twelve

King's eyes adjusted. He wandered down a narrow, dimly lit corridor with numbered doors, no further apart than large storage lockers. He concentrated on finding his room number. A few men passed him, towels wrapped loosely at the waist. They slowed as they passed. One of them massaged his groin. The air was warm and steamy. King was sweating in his heavy parka, his jeans, and hiking boots.

The smell of poppers and weed wafted to his nostrils. Muted, generic disco music pulsed overhead like a fast heartbeat. He heard moaning as he passed one room. The door was partially open and two guys were fucking. King paused. Someone rear-ended him, he was following so close. King found this funny and started to laugh.

The tailgater dropped his towel and stepped around him. He entered the cubicle without being asked. Soon a small circle of men stood outside the open door and started beating off. These were the rules. Anything goes.

King passed another open door. A naked man basked on a narrow mattress, an open jar of lotion ready and waiting. He didn't look up and King didn't stand around. King kept moving. A man came toward him. Ignoring King, he glanced inside the open room. He disappeared into it and closed the door. The room numbers were getting lower instead of higher. King was going the wrong way. He had to turn back. He rounded another corner.

This suddenly seemed like an idiotic idea. King was gonna strip, walk around barefoot on rubber matting gunked up with God knew what? King could hear doors opening and closing. It was fantastic. Fantastic that such a place existed. Especially at the throat of Boulder Canyon. King wondered why it wasn't being stormed by the police.

He decided he should cut his losses and leave. Maybe Jen was still up. King was only here because he was pissed off at Theo. And Sam. If King could find his way out of this maze of corridors, he'd leave. King turned another corridor. Five or six guys were pissing on some black guy while he beat off. He lay prone in a metal trough. King gagged and kept moving.

Another group ahead.

King's anxiety mounted. Last night Theo and King were on a ski lift, swaying above a pure white mountaintop. How could he sink so low? This was Sodom and Gomorrah. He saw an exit sign out of the corner of his eye.

King turned and found himself face-to-face with a University of Colorado football player he knew from classes and a few Bible studies. They'd been friendly, if not friends. His name was Barry Adams. Fully dressed, he had to duck his head to accommodate the low ceiling of the halls. Barry seemed genuinely happy to see King. Behind him a few guys gathered in hopes he'd be taking off his clothes. Barry ignored them.

"King. I thought that was you in the parking lot."

"Was that *you*?"

"Sure." Barry grinned. "You seemed embarrassed, so I didn't say anything. I'm not out, you know," he added conspiratorially. "I've never seen you here before."

"I won't say I saw you, if that's why you came in to find me. This is my first time."

King had to admit to himself he was pretty shocked. Barry had watched the entire debacle of him and Lex unfold right before his very eyes. He'd been particularly considerate with King. He never judged. Always offered to come over and pray with him. Take him to church. He even hooked King up with a minister who preached to the University of Colorado Buffs. This was right when King came out to his parents. After he told Nicholas, it was all over Boulder. Friends from high school confided they were hearing rumors about him. "Is this *true*, King?"

Barry came to visit King at his dorm a week later. He'd sat quietly in the chair at King's desk and suggested he meet Brother Casey, the team pastor. He thought Brother Casey might have some insight for him. Would King like him to call?

Brother Casey had a nondenominational parish in Louisville. Barry himself drove King out to meet him. He was fat and wore a horrible toupee. King couldn't imagine the coach of the Colorado Buffs letting him near his locker room. The three of them prayed together and Barry excused himself. Brother Casey and King needed to convene in private.

King wept when he found himself alone with him. He told him everything that had happened. How it came up in a prayer session, that he'd never consciously admitted it to himself. How Lex's hands started shaking. How chaotic it all became. How hurt King's parents were. About his brother. How much King didn't want to be gay, and did Brother Casey think he really was? Would God take it away if they all prayed hard enough? Lastly, King proclaimed how much his faith meant to him and would he lose that, too, on top of everything else?

King reflected he was sure he was an interesting case.

Brother Casey then explained something fascinating to him. He, too, had experienced similar anguish, which for reasons he didn't understand till now, Barry was privy to. When God didn't change him, he prayed for an explanation. The answer came to him through a series of meditations. Casey would be allowed to keep his feelings of love for men, if he used them in an appropriate, loving, unsinful way.

The way was shown to Brother Casey, when his church assigned him the position as special minister to the members of the University of Colorado football team. Brother Casey would have full access to the locker room, anytime he liked.

"Imagine, King," Brother Casey exclaimed. "I have the best of both worlds. I love men and I'm around the most beautiful men in the world. I use my emotions to understand them. I have a special gift as long as I don't cross the line. As long as I understand that the gift comes from God. And to this day, I've never abused it. As gay men we aren't inherently separated from God. Being gay is not a sin. Acting on it is."

King found some temporary relief. In a second session, Brother Casey made a startling suggestion.

"I want you to go home to your mother and ask her what she's keeping secret which frightened her so."

"How do you know she's afraid of something?"

"Just ask. You'll see."

And King went home to ask her.

"Are you keeping a big secret from Neil and me?"

"What kind of secret?" she asked.

"My minister told me to ask. He thinks something happened in your past that's made you afraid."

"What business is it of his?"

King shrugged and didn't push it. Kay went to the kitchen to start dinner. Jim was on a business trip. King had come home to keep her company. Watching her from the dining room, he could tell she was rattled.

"You can tell me," he said. "I certainly have no secrets left from you."

She laughed ruefully. "Why would he think to ask you that?"

"What is it?" King asked her again. "I won't tell Neil."

"You can't tell anyone. Even your minister. If your dad found out, he'd be hurt. Can you keep a secret, King?"

King had such a big mouth, he wondered why she planned to trust him. He nodded, just to make her feel better.

"Your father tried to kill himself when you were a baby. Neil was three. We were living in Montana. It was winter. Ten below. He got fired. His boss was jealous of him. He didn't come home. When he did, he told me he'd been out all night, trying to drive himself off the road. He finally ran out of gas. He couldn't even do that right."

"Oh."

"We agreed to never mention it again. He got his job back, and then a better one, so we moved. Your father comes home every night like clockwork. He never gave me another reason to worry."

"But still you do."

She shot him a scathing, sarcastic look. "Yes, King. I still do. I've got to say, your father and I are a little dismayed about this religious obsession of yours. I suppose there are worse things you could get into, but frankly, I'd like you to take it a little easy around here. And tell your minister to mind his own business."

Barry didn't call again after that, and King didn't call him.

The group behind them started to dispel. King and Barry were talking too openly, like they'd just met at the Auto Club and not in a bathhouse.

"You want me to show you around?" Barry smiled. "What's your room number?"

"Nineteen. But I'm not staying."

"Nineteen." He ignored King. "It's back here. Hidden." He grinned. He had college good looks. Perfect white teeth. He held out his arm and ushered King down the corridor. They arrived at his room. King fumbled with the lock. Barry took the key and swiftly opened it up.

King's own narrow mattress awaited him. He wondered if the sheet was really unused. Barry waited for King to step inside, leaning against the doorsill. King could see him reflected in a small mirror, smiling good-naturedly. King had no idea what Barry intended for him to do. He turned around and shrugged.

"Throw your parka on the bed, King. Mind if I come in?"

"Well. Sure."

Barry sat on the edge of the mattress. Several guys gathered at King's open door. Barry reached over, closing it in their faces.

"Look, King," he said seriously. "Here's the thing. I'm not out. I'm bisexual, see. I only have sex in the baths. I have a girlfriend. Holly at the Tri-Delt house. We're planning to get engaged over Easter."

"I know Holly," King said dryly. "Congratulations."

Barry patted the edge of the mattress. King sat down obediently. "I have to be practical because Holly and I have a lot of sex. I can't be bringing home VD. It'd mess up pretty much everything. So when I come to the baths, I only jerk off. Guys can watch but they can't touch. Not if I don't know 'em. That's the only way I can do this. You'd be surprised, by the way, how many guys on the team do the same thing. It's like a natural progression, really. We get all worked up on the field, come back, and shower together. But see, we're all Christians and we can't get involved with certain activity. We can't lay with a man, see what I mean, King?"

King understood completely. Taking scripture so literally had gotten him in big trouble before.

"So what *can* you do?"

"I've prayed about it, as I'm sure you have. I've searched my heart and found there are one or two things I'm comfortable with doing." He looked at King a little nervously.

"Yeah?" King asked.

"King, we were friends. You went through a lot. We have no secrets now, right?"

"I suppose not, Barry." King folded his arms. He resisted the urge to start laughing.

"Would you like to take off your clothes with me and suck me off? I'm afraid I can't help you that way, but I'll hold you while you satisfy yourself. How would that be? In friendship."

"That'd be pretty good."

"Remember Accounting last spring? You wore shorts one day with no underwear. I was sitting across the room from you. I never forgot it. I always liked you."

He pulled off his shirt. He helped King with his. He kicked off his shoes, scuffed, snow-stained saddle shoes. He stood up and dropped his jeans. He wasn't wearing underwear. He faced King. His cock was huge. He pushed himself inside King's mouth, rotating his hips and squeezing King's head like a muskmelon. He finished in seconds, spurting what seemed like gallons of semen into King's throat.

Barry handed King his towel. "Spit it out if you need to."

"I want to swallow you." King gagged.

Barry squeezed King's shoulders and waited politely till he got his load all down.

"Now for my part of the bargain." Barry sat down on the mattress and opened his legs. He pivoted King away from him. He sat him on his knee like Charlie McCarthy. "Lean back into ol' Barry. Lean your whole weight against me, King."

King complied. King began to massage himself. All the while Barry whispered to him, "Let me rest my chin in the crook of your neck. Let me smell your hair and your skin while you jerk off. Let me stroke your calves, your inner thighs. Lean your ass against my cock. I'm still hard for you, King. Feel my hands on your belly, King? Shall I squeeze your nipples? They still hard from the cold? I was so happy to see you outside, King. I came back in here just because of you. Keep working it, King. Keep working it. Lean back into me, King, against ol' Barry's chest. You're safe with me. That's right. That's right. That's right."

King and Barry went for coffee at the International House of Pancakes on Baseline. Barry seemed rested and happy. He told King his plans after graduation. In all likelihood he'd be drafted by a professional football team. The pro scouts had been flirting with him for years. It had been in all the papers. Had King read anything about it?

"After all King, I threw twenty-two touchdown passes with only six interceptions last season. Plus, I look like a franchise quarter-back."

King knew what he meant but asked Barry to explain it anyway.

"Not to brag, but I'm six feet four and weigh two hundred fifteen pounds. I know I'm a walking around good-looking guy, King." He grinned winningly, flashing his white teeth.

"Like a regular Wheaties box." King smiled back. He had to admit, Barry was very engaging.

If it didn't work out, which was very unlikely, Holly's dad had an accounting firm in Chicago. Best independent firm in the state of Illinois. He'd study for his CPA examination on the job. He'd work his way up, that much he insisted on. If he didn't earn his own way, he didn't deserve to make partner. After a couple of years he figured they'd move to New York. He was interested in investment banking. That's where the money was.

"I've done all the talking. I can tell you like sex. I'd make an ex-ception with you, King. I'd see you away from the baths. I never of-fered that to anyone. Don't answer me now. It's just sex, remember? But I would like to see you. Normally I don't like sweetness in a man, but with you it's been different. I don't have a gay friend. I have all kinds of straight friends. Why shouldn't I have at least one gay friend? No crime in that. I've accepted my bisexuality. Lord must have a purpose for it. Besides"—he winked—"I know you can keep a secret."

The next morning, King and Jen drove up Sunshine Canyon. It was a bright cold day. The sun was shining and they liked to have coffee in Gold Hill, a ghost town which had been reclaimed by hip-pies and dropouts. There was a sweet little café with a nice wooden deck and a spectacular view of the Continental Divide. Jen and King loved the view. The road was always rough. It was only paved part of the way. There was still a lot of snow, but mostly it was just slushy mud. King worried about the Capri, but that's what a car was for, to take them where they wanted to go.

"I just serviced Holly's boyfriend."

"Barry? You mean his car?"

King winked at her, suggestively.

"King! Since when do you act that way?"

"Since *now*. Since I apparently read like a judgmental prude. Since Theo told me Sam dumped me because I seemed too desperate. And then, top this, I used him the night Tim died. Not to mention he's moving to Denver with a boyfriend he met he never bothered to mention."

"I've had sex with Barry. He came pretty fast."

King's mouth still tasted like Barry. He grew somber. "What's wrong?"

"I was supposed to keep it a secret."

"He asks everybody he fucks to keep it a secret."

"It was pretty exciting, I've got to admit. A linebacker."

"Quarterback."

"He wants to see me again."

"On a date?"

This hadn't occurred to King. "I think just friends."

"No offense, but Barry doesn't have friends like you. You must provide pretty excellent felatio."

"He did all the moving around. I was just a hole."

"Welcome to the world of most women everywhere."

"He told me he couldn't lay with me."

"It'd be an affront to his coach. So what *did* you do?"

"I sat and he stood."

"That's what we did. He's huge, isn't he?"

"The biggest I ever had. And I'll tell you what. I want it again. He's come up with a few ground rules to ensure I won't fall in love with him. See, that's what I'm known for. Thinking having sex means making love. So from here on out, I'll only fuck with people."

"Theo's serious about you."

"I'll only fuck *with* people, and I'll dump 'em the second they act halfway interested. I'm changing my major."

"Changing your *major?*" Jen laughed her head off. They neared the top of the hill. The clouds rolling over the mountains meant snow tonight. King would call his folks when he got home. They always knew how much it would snow.

"So you're having a pretty good time," Jen commented. "It sounds so fun." She smiled at King wistfully. "I miss having sex."

"You'll have sex again."

"I worry about my body after the baby's born. It never comes back all the way."

"Yours will."

"There's more to think about than a flat stomach anyway. Look at the hawk, King." She pointed way out over the canyon. A hawk circled and dove, descending like a stone and catching a current of wind, soared higher than before. Lex wanted to be an ornithologist. He could tell King what kind of hawk it was, even from this distance. He loved the outdoors. Sierra Club posters of the crashing surf at Point Reyes Peninsula and the emerald green marshes of Yosemite's upper meadows adorned Lex's walls. When Lex hiked, he clattered with binoculars, cameras, and a clipboard to record sightings of trap-door spiders and coyote scat.

King and Lex loved to camp. Grabbing North Face sleeping bags and their cooking gear, they'd drive up Boulder Canyon at sundown and pitch camp in the dark. At night they'd bake potatoes in the embers of their campfire and later make smoky love in the firelight.

The next morning King and Lex would be back in Boulder, sitting in class, the wilderness just a minute away. King thought Lex would always be there, like the wilderness.

"What did you say back there?"

"Where?"

"When we were driving. About Theo."

"He's in love with you."

"How did you know?" King pretended to be disinterested.

"He was pretty frantic when you didn't come home last night."

"I came home."

"But not till four-thirty."

"Barry trains every morning at five."

"I *know*."

"How's he do that?"

"Probably white crosses."

"What are white crosses?"

"Speed. God, King." Jen shook her head. Her hair was long now, and she didn't curl it. She just brushed it every night. She'd even taken to wearing granny glasses when an eye doctor told her she needed a slight correction. Jen was turning into a flower child before King's very eyes. About ten years too late. "You never took speed to cram for a test?"

"No. I always just studied."

"God, King." She lifted her face into a blast of cold wind. "Theo's really in love with you. You can't hurt him. He's very real. He's had a bitch of a childhood. Sorry, that was a sexist statement. Did I tell you I joined a women's group? I'm a feminist now."

"Let's get going. I want to be home before it starts snowing."

Gold Hill was really only two streets. It had a restaurant, the Gold Hill Inn, the café, and maybe twenty log cabins. Most not winterized. Luckily the café was open. They kept a potbellied stove burning on the patio. King and Jen pulled their chairs toward it and huddled together. A girl in hiking boots, a down vest, and batik skirt took their order. Jen asked her where the restroom was.

"When are you expecting?" the girl asked King when Jen was gone.

"She's having the baby. It isn't mine."

"Oh." She smiled, somewhat embarrassed. "You looked happy together, that's all."

"We are. We're best friends."

After she left, King smiled when Jen came back. He told her about the mistake. "I was tempted to not correct her. Sometimes I like people thinking I'm the father. That we're together."

"I kinda wished you hadn't said anything. She changed when you told her. I caught her staring at me inside. It made her sad." Jen put the lip of her mug to her mouth and blew to cool it.

King studied her swollen belly. "Does the baby keep you company?"

She smiled radiantly. "Yes."

"Guess I'll never have a kid."

"Who knows, King."

"I know."

"Do you want to be my partner through this?"

"You mean your beard?"

"No. My Lamaze partner. You'd coach me during birth. We'd start classes at the end of my seventh month. It's a lot to ask."

King contemplated the fire. "Did you mention this to my mom?"

"Your mother didn't put me up to this."

"I'd want to do it even if she did."

"Your mom doesn't want to change you. She wants your happiness. So do I, for that matter."

"I know." King studied the fire. "You know your own mother will be back in the picture when the baby's born."

"Probably. After your mom's done all the hand-holding."

"It'll be hard on my mom."

"Not if the baby's named after her." Jen smiled. "I have to tell you. I wanted it to be a surprise, but I found out today. She's a little girl! I'll have my girl. I'm relieved. I don't know why, but I think it'll be easier to be a woman alone with a daughter. That's what my feminist sisters say. God, some of 'em hate men."

"The dykes."

"Can you please not use the word dyke when I've just told you I'm having a daughter?"

"I'm sorry." King smiled. He reached over and kissed her cheek. "I'm relieved too. I hate men. I guess I'm a closet lesbian."

"It's not just the lesbians. Not at all. They know who they are. What most of us hate is needing and *wanting* men. We despise that."

"Don't despise me for asking about my mother."

"I don't, King. And if it makes you feel any better, she isn't entertaining any fantasy that this is her granddaughter. She told me all her friends hate their grandchildren. She hears they're highly overrated."

That night King wrote a short-short story about Jen. In King's story, Jen was a white trash girl named Darla. Darla had gotten herself pregnant by some jerk who ditched her and moved up near Leadville. King called the story "The Sleeping Porch." He wrote it present tense, longhand, in pencil, on narrow-lined school paper.

THE SLEEPING PORCH

A lilac bush blooms just outside the sleeping porch. It grows right up the side of the screen so that the blossoms are pressed against the wire mesh. Darla is awake and thinking: DAMN YOU, BABY, DAMN YOU, DAMN YOU, DAMN YOU. Since the baby waits inside, it knows her thoughts and kicks her hard enough to make Darla gasp. A breeze, bearing the smell of lilacs to her nostrils, comforts her. She relaxes, thinking: I'M SORRY, BABY, and the baby rests.

The baby lies curled within her. Darla lies on her side, snug beneath the blankets of her narrow bed. The bed nearly fills the sleeping porch. At one end sits a chair. At the other, a china lamp. The room is very crowded, very secure. The sleeping porch emerges from the house. There are screens on three sides, a peninsula; it holds fast to the main island. The house feeds the sleeping porch warmth and brakes the winds from the west end, the street side. White clapboard, paint peeling, the house is surrounded by dense foliage. Clinging ivy, thick shrubbery, the lilac bush and climbing roses all envelop it. Breezes sweep through the brush, air currents caress it. At night, blackness shrouds everything.

The baby stretches in Darla's womb and she rolls over on her other side. The bed quivers and the timber creaks below the sleeping porch. The foundation of the house settles and the ivy grips tighter to its walls. Darla sleeps. The baby listens to her dreams.

King felt pretty satisfied. For a first draft King was pleased. He already had two other stories in mind to write. One about Matthew. The other about a mother—his mom—coming to the heart knowledge, before being told, that her son is gay.

King got a call about eleven-thirty. "Hello?"

"King? It's Barry. Barry Adams."

"Yeah?" What could he possibly want?

"I was thinking about you today."

"I thought about you, too."

"It's late," Barry said, his voice brisk, customarily direct. "I'm wiped out. But I wanted to call. I was thinking about last night. It was pretty great." He hesitated. King could hear him tapping his fingers on his desk. "It was more than great. You were perfect."

"My lips are still humming."

"I enjoyed having coffee with you at the pancake house. I enjoyed it very much."

"I liked that part, too." King kept scanning his story about Jen, looking for misspelled words. King had a friend named Missy who typed all his papers. She typed everything word for word, even if a word or a sentence didn't make sense. She charged extra for editing.

"King?"

"Yeah, Barry?"

"Do you ever get confused?"

"All the time."

"I wouldn't have thought so. You seem like your ol' noggin is screwed on pretty tight."

"My teeth were chattering, I was so nervous last night."

"My teeth chatter like that in the locker room before every game. Sometimes I get so scared I'm afraid I'll mess my pants."

"But you never do."

"No."

"What's that like, playing football in front of all those people?"

"You try to forget about 'em. You try to stay focused on each play."

King told him about walking outside Folsom Field that afternoon. How much King felt like an outsider, how big the roar of the crowd seemed. So big King could see it rise up out of the stadium. "Maybe they were cheering you."

"Or booing me." Barry cleared his throat. "I must seem pretty corny to you. My life all mapped out. Engaged to Holly. Drafted by an NFL team. Good job waiting for me at an accounting firm if that fails. No more surprises for ol' Barry. What will you do when you graduate?"

"I might move to California. But I'd stay this time."

"California! You're a wild man, King."

"There's a chance my brother might move there. I'd like to be close to him."

"I'd miss you if you moved."

There it was.

"You hardly know me."

"I used to watch the clock till you came into the Bible studies. I used to hold my breath. When you stopped coming it killed me. I thought I was worried about your soul. Now I know it was more than that."

King's defenses shot up. He'd heard this kind of talk before. "I never knew."

"King, would you like to come with me to the Boulder Open? I have box seats. This Saturday. Do you like tennis?"

If King had been standing in a bar, he'd be turning around, looking for the guy he was really talking to. King couldn't believe Barry was talking to him.

"Why aren't you taking Holly?"

"I want to take you. I'll meet you outside the stadium. Five-thirty sharp, ol' buddy. We'll grab a bite after. Maybe you'll show me where you live. 'Night, sport." And he hung up.

Chapter Thirteen

King's father called to ask if he would watch him take his thirty-day chip in AA. King couldn't believe he hadn't taken a drink in a month.

"Are Mom and Neil coming?"

"I'm afraid your mother isn't taking it so well."

King hesitated. Neil had been right. She was jealous.

"She didn't know she'd be trading a stay-at-home drunk for a stay-away husband who left her every night to sit in AA meetings."

King felt bad for him. "But you're happier, right?"

"Not so much happier. Just more comfortable in my skin."

"Did you ask Neil?"

"I actually wanted just you this time. I don't want to hurt him. I'd feel more comfortable if it was just you, King." He paused, emotion catching in his throat. "There's a spiritual aspect to this process that I was unprepared for but I find I like—you understand these things. You're more open about your feelings. Your brother is quite cynical. I'm ashamed to say he learned it from me. I have much to make up to him. And to your mother. I believe you've forgiven me."

"I'll come, Dad. I'll keep it between us."

"How's school?"

"You know. Coming down to the wire. I'm only taking one class. I'm working full-time."

"How's the writing?"

"I haven't been too inspired lately."

"Don't worry. It'll come when the time is right. I've been thinking of a few things I'd like to write myself."

*   *   *

The AA meeting was very moving. King drove to Denver and met his father in the lobby of a small bank building near Wadsworth and Jewell. The meeting was held in a small conference room in the basement. King didn't know how he expected a room filled with recovering alcoholics to look, but he was surprised how ordinary they seemed. In the hallway outside the meeting room, a table was set up with a coffee urn and paper cups. King scrambled for some change. Behind him, a pretty, middle-aged woman told him it was free.

King poured two cups and went to look for his father, who was surrounded by several men. King was struck by his father's laughter. He was telling jokes and his friends were laughing.

"You had me on that one." One of the men laughed raucously. He studied King when he came up to greet his father.

"This is my son, King."

"King?"

King smiled. "Family name."

"I'm Gill. Your dad's doing real, real good."

King gazed over at his father. King tried not to appear unnerved, but didn't think he was too successful. His dad was always his own man. Always independent. Even on a snowy Denver dawn, leaving a bar before he walked to work.

"He always done real good by me."

"Well, I'm sure your support and high opinion mean a lot to him. He knows I'm not so lucky with my people." Gill grinned meaningfully at King's father and strode into a throng of friends. The room filled up quickly then. Everybody began to pull padded blue office chairs away from the table and take their seats.

At exactly six-fifteen, Gill picked up several pieces of paper and called the meeting to order. "My name is Gill, and I'm an alcoholic."

He asked the woman who told King the coffee was free to read from the Big Book.

"What's a big book? A Bible?"

"No. It's like a reference book for AA."

She introduced herself as Irene, an alcoholic. She began to read an excerpt from Chapter Five.

King glanced over at his dad. This was suddenly terribly personal. King wondered if his father regretted having him come to the meeting. He'd credited King with understanding vulnerability and being free with his emotions.

"Are there any newcomers or returnees with less than thirty days of sobriety?"

No one raised a hand.

"Any visitors who wish to identify themselves?"

King sat mute and his dad didn't nudge him.

Gill reached for a baggie filled with colored poker chips. "Anybody care to take a chip for thirty days of continuous sobriety?" He grinned at Jim. King's dad stood up. He was trembling. The room burst into applause. King tugged lightly on his coat sleeve. He rounded the table and waited while Gill fished out a blue chip.

"My name is Jim, and I'm an alcoholic. I'd like to quickly thank everyone for all their support this past month. I particularly want to acknowledge my son King for coming out tonight to support me. I don't deserve it, but he's here." His voice broke.

Everyone clapped again.

When King's father sat down they didn't acknowledge each other. Jim clenched the chip in his fist till his knuckles turned white. For the remainder of the meeting, members "shared." It was over in forty-five minutes.

King and his dad went to a Luby's Cafeteria on Sheridan after the meeting. They stood in line to pay, King's Pepsi lurching back and forth on a wet red tray. King ordered the fresh roast turkey. Jim had beef stroganoff and peas. King's father loved canned peas. He didn't seem like himself tonight.

"These are together," Jim told the cashier.

"I'm paying," King told her.

"No, King."

"Yes, Dad." King's money was already out. He paid with a ten and she gave him back three ones and some change. His dad looked embarrassed, like King had bought him a Cadillac or something. "You shouldn't have done that," he told him. They scanned the dining room for an empty table. It was busy, filled with overweight working-class families dressed in heavy sweaters and blue jeans from Sears. King noticed before that the husbands in these families could often be very cute. Trim in plaid wool shirts, slightly balding, a day's growth of rough beard framing bright white smiles. The wives, as a rule, were horrible, with short, frizzy, hair, or frosted and teased up in front and flat in back like they'd slept on it. Forget their children.

Monsters, all.

King wondered if Jen's baby would be a monster. Not hardly. She was beautiful and so was Teddy, if he was the true father. Jen would never let herself go like these women. At twenty-eight, life was over. King scanned their faces. They ate looking into their mashed potatoes. Nobody talking. They should be scared about keeping their husbands.

"This isn't Leo's, I know," King's father observed. He'd been reading King's mind and felt guilty. They found two seats at the end of a big community table.

"It's like a prison movie," King laughed.

"Just don't make a play for my bread."

At Luby's, some folks ate right off their trays; more fastidious customers made a big deal of organizing their plates and silverware like they were at home, or eating in a better restaurant, and putting the empty trays on a clean table nearby.

There were five or six empty trays on the stools where they intended to sit. Instead of removing them and putting them in someone else's way, Jim put his plate down and walked them the entire length of the room to the dishwasher conveyer belt. This was the dignity of his father, King reflected. The humility. King was reminded of him scraping his windshield.

It was a trait King inherited and would probably always bedevil him. Already King was giving out mixed signals. The arrogant ones were luckier, King thought. Even if eventually they were going to hell.

"I've put you in a position. I owe you an apology. Of course I'll take responsibility for it with your mother."

"I won't tell her, Dad."

"But I should tell her. And Neil. She's terribly angry at me now." Jim pushed his peas around on his plate. "Which is why I didn't want her to come tonight."

"I'm sorry, Dad."

"It isn't her fault."

"Or yours."

"I'm sure she regards it as a character flaw. No matter what she reads. She misses our Friday night sundowners." King's parents always had a bourbon and water together every Friday after he came home from work.

"No more than you probably miss your morning day brighteners."

King got him to laugh.

"They miss me at the Tip Top. Ray, the bartender, called me at the office to ask why I didn't come in anymore."

"Have you been tempted?"

"Only for the company. See, I didn't really have any friends of my own," he commented. "Neither does your mother. That's why the meetings are troubling to her. I've promised I'll cut back. I shouldn't leave her alone at night."

"You shouldn't cut back on the meetings if they're making you well, Dad."

"Well, we'll see." He pulled out his chip.

"Can I see it?"

He handed it over to King. He recited the inscription. " 'The best of everything is getting well.' "

He started to cry softly. Embarrassed, King stared at his food, and like the other patrons at Luby's he had judged that night, he and his father finished their meal in silence.

Theo stopped King on the stairs. King heard him slide open his door. He pulled back his drapes. "You planning to stay mad at me forever?"

King waved his hand in irritation. It was cold and King was having trouble with his key.

"Would you please come inside before you go to bed?"

King shook his head. He didn't want to cheapen the evening he'd just spent with his dad talking about who was fucking who, and who said this or that. He wanted to work on his short story about Jen. He needed to finish it so Missy could type it by Friday.

"I have to finish my short story."

"Is it about us? A short story?'

"A short-short. Less than five hundred words." King finally managed to turn his key. He slipped into the warm dark cave of his apartment. Inside he was surprised at himself. King was normally pretty forgiving. Justifying. Theo had ultimately been so kind to him. Why was King acting like such a dick?

He decided to talk with him.

King knocked. "It's me."

Theo was on the telephone. King heard him beg off. He came to his door. All he wore was a pair of gray sweatpants with the university emblem on them. King sat on the edge of his bed and stared up at Theo. He started to get a hard-on and sat down abruptly, perched on the edge of a folding chair.

King smirked.

"Sorry about the way I said what I said."

"But not for the content."

"No."

King stood up.

"Can we be adult here?"

"Fuck you."

Theo grabbed his arm when King pushed past him. "Stay. Please."

"You know what I think? I think you made it up. Or at least exaggerated it. I thought about it. It doesn't sound like Sam at all. 'King used Tim. King was inappropriate.' "

"Maybe he didn't exactly use those words."

Relief flooded King but he checked it. "What words did he use?"

"He took part of the responsibility. Said he might have confused you. He really only wanted comfort." Theo scratched his stomach. "He thought you both were inappropriate. Peter yelled at him later. When he found you both curled up together."

"He was probably drunk."

"You haven't been to see him."

This was true. King had to ask himself why. He figured Peter would be surrounded by all the guys who intimidated King so. Rod and Tony. Sam.

"I've had some things come up with my dad. I've been a little preoccupied."

"I'm glad we talked. You coming on Friday night?" The Friday Night Coffee House at the church.

"I have a date."

"Ah." And Theo looked so mournful.

"It's not really a date," King corrected himself. "I don't know what it is. Maybe I'll come later."

"We're planning to go to the Boulderado after. Maybe you can meet us there."

"Do you really believe in a different set of rules for all of us?"

"Ultimately."

"I don't. I think I have a right to expect all the stability and consistency anybody else does."

"I hope you find it," Theo nodded.

As King left, he reached out to pat Theo's side. Theo had been good to him. King was happy for the night skiing. He was happy that they'd had a night together, that even though they slept less than two feet away every night, they'd had one night without the wall between them.

Later that afternoon King turned in his short story about Jen. He got an A. Professor Sloan even suggested that it might be publishable. King was ecstatic. Coincidentally, that night as King sat alone at the New York Deli on the Pearl Street Mall, Maddie came in with a tall, slightly older man, very handsome with graying temples and blazing brown eyes. King approved because he'd lay money on the fact that he probably had a great hairy ass.

"King! Can we join you? We've just been to see *Women in Love* at the UMC film series. Glenda Jackson and Alan Bates! Promise me you'll see it. This is Robert." Robert shook King's hand. He had powerful sensual hands. Maddie scooted into the booth. Robert reluctantly sat next to her, looking somewhat annoyed. Animated and smiling vivaciously, she squeezed his forearm, as if asking him to lighten up.

"King, Robert is a very renowned poet. He was my professor at the University of Iowa. I've convinced him to transfer to Boulder. We've just got engaged!"

They both watched King's face fall. He tried to disguise his distress, but his reaction came over him so fast he didn't have time.

"King, what is it?"

King watched Robert's annoyance convert to intrigue. He sat back and almost smirked. "I think I heard a bubble burst," he murmured to her.

Maddie searched his face. Smiling vivaciously, she reached for his hand. "King! You're happy for me, aren't you?"

"Sure." King tried to smile. He wanted to be happy for her. He loved her. "Best of luck to you both."

Still holding his hand, Maddie said, "King is my favorite student, Bobby. He won a full-tuition writing scholarship."

"What's your favorite medium?"

"Short-shorts," King told him.

"I sent you one of his stories. Remember?"

"The one about the mother of the gay son . . ." Robert's voice trailed off. "Say, I hope she asked permission to show it to me."

"I didn't, Bobby. I owe King an apology."

King felt mixed up about this vampire reading his work. He was so dark and intense. An image of them making love flashed through King's mind. He was so much larger than Maddie.

"King, should we go? "

"We intruded on you, after all," Robert added. "Maddie has spoken of you in such high regard. You *are* her favorite student."

King smiled at her. "She's my favorite teacher."

"We were actually on our way to the Boulderado. I just saw you in the window. Allen Ginsberg is doing an unadvertised reading of excerpts from his latest book of poetry in the small bar on the main floor."

"Le Bar?"

"You know it?"

"I hang out there."

"Of course you would. Of course."

"Why don't you join us, King?" Robert straightened up. "I've acted badly. I guess I'm a little jealous."

"Bobby!" Maddie shook her head. She seemed used to it, tired of it now.

King had been hearing about Ginsberg for years. He never saw him around. This was a great chance.

"I'd like to go," he told them.

Maddie in the middle, the three of them walked arm-in-arm down the mall toward the hotel. Robert lightened up. They told King they'd just made an offer on a great old house on Mapleton, a beautiful old street in North Boulder which fed into Sunshine Canyon.

"We'll have five bedrooms!" said Maddie. "And a study for each of us. You can visit whenever you like. We both have so many friends back east who've never been to Colorado."

"You could even spend weekends," Robert offered.

"Yes!" Maddie agreed. She seemed so genuinely happy to have King along. "This coat is so beautiful, King. Did you get it from Lawrence Covell?" Lawrence Covell was a leather store so intimidating King had never been in. As King thought about it, this coat did look like it came from Lawrence Covell.

"No," was all King said. "It was a gift."

"Secret admirer?" Robert smiled over.

"I bet King has all kinds of secret admirers," Maddie said.

"I bet," said Robert.

The tiny bar was jammed with chairs. A small platform with an easy chair rested in front of the stained glass window on the east wall of the room. When they entered, or when someone spotted Robert, King noticed a table magically opened up at the foot of Allen's chair. There were three seats waiting.

"I need to use the restroom," Maddie excused herself.

Robert quickly acknowledged a few friends close to their table, and then turned his full attention on King. "We mean how welcome you'll be at the new house, King. Is King your real name?"

"Yeah."

"You can call your memoirs, *King James Version.*"

"I've already thought of that."

Robert continued to study King intently, and King would swear he was clearly flirting with him.

"Maddie doesn't have as many close friends here as she did in Iowa. And I only know Allen and a few other poets. Here's Allen now." And with that, Ginsberg entered the room. He was short and round, wearing drawstring pants and a Mexican wedding shirt with layers and layers of beads. Bearded, sporting tiny, round wire-frame glasses, he stopped at their table and surprised King by kissing Robert full on the mouth, the only person in the room he kissed. As he was situating himself in his chair and someone brought him water, Maddie entered, edging through the chairs and tables to take her seat. When Ginsberg saw her, he touched his fingers to his lips and blew her a kiss.

"Allen and Robert are terribly close, King. He was in San Francisco the night Allen first read "Howl." I'm so happy we ran into you. We're all incredibly lucky to be here tonight."

Robert placed his arm over her shoulder and she nestled close to him. His reach extended to King's upper arm. Gently he pulled King closer into Maddie. His hand rested past her shoulder and behind King's neck the entire reading. King couldn't remember a word Ginsberg read. He only knew that occasionally Robert would tug at the little tendrils of the hair at the nape of King's neck, and to his great consternation, yet again King found himself aroused.

*   *   *

King reported this to Jen, who was furious that he hadn't called to ask her to join them.

"I'm arty now."

"What was going on?"

"They're into you."

"No." It seemed so sordid. King was bleak with disappointment in his wonderful Professor Sloan.

"You look so sad. What's wrong?"

"I was so embarrassed for her. She had to know."

"Of course she knew. She probably procures him boys." Jen adjusted herself on her sofa bed. King felt horribly hurt.

"No. No, no, no, no."

"King, this is the seventies. Swapping and menages are very common. I *told* you about me and Teddy. It's very common." Then she grimaced. "Yeow!"

"What's wrong?"

"The baby's kicking like crazy these days."

"I forgot to tell you. I got an A on my story."

"She probably wants to stay on your good side." Jen laughed. King got so mad he left.

King lay low for the next couple of days. He took long drives in the mountains. He'd bring his notebook and a couple of sharp pencils, thinking he'd do some writing, but his confusion and sadness weren't of the creative variety. King felt blocked. Instead of writing, he'd find himself sitting over a beer or a mug of coffee in some mountain bar, staring out the window into a pine forest and just thinking. It was dawning on him that in a few months he'd be graduating from college. He'd have a liberal arts degree with no job prospects. He knew companies came to interview graduating seniors, but King didn't have a blue suit. He also didn't have the slightest idea what he wanted to do other than write.

Arlene pointed out that a full-time operator at the university switchboard could earn seven thousand dollars a year, more than enough to live comfortably in Boulder. He figured she was hinting that a space was available if he wanted to stay after graduating.

Graduate school was another option. Maddie had once offered him a good recommendation if King wanted to apply to Iowa, where she had pull. Boulder didn't have a good graduate writing program. As much as he poured over every beat, every nuance of the other evening, King couldn't believe she had any alternative motive in her head. They were Bohemian, she and Robert. Intellectuals. So what if Robert was kissed by Allen Ginsberg and liked the wrestling scene in *Women in Love?* King had run over to the UMC the next night to watch it. He spent the night beating off to fantasies of wrestling with a naked Robert in front of a roaring fire.

King knew he could never acquiesce to a threesome with Maddie and Robert. It was ridiculous to be so preoccupied with it, as if it presented itself as the weightiest proposition on the table.

Why, King wondered, had he met so many men lately who were married or engaged to women? He wished he could talk to Theo about it. On a rock overlooking a waterfall in Boulder Canyon, images of Matthew sitting perched on the end of his bed while they said good-bye suddenly overwhelmed him. Matthew had been the personification of sorrow and regret.

King wondered if Matthew thought about him. Since that morning, King wore his coat like a second skin. It was never far away from him. Matthew had been so insightful. He'd wanted to be remembered by King. The coat was aging nicely, spotted by occasional snowfall. It had darkened even further, felt less fancy and more comfortable to King.

Matthew hadn't called, and King felt amazed he'd had the presence of mind not to call him, not once, but he carried his card in his wallet. Occasionally King fantasized that if he was ever unconscious in an emergency room, Matthew would be notified in Pittsburgh. His was the only card King carried. On the back of it, sitting at the bar, King wrote sentimentally: *In case of emergency.*

"Ralph Goodhue?"

"Yes?"

"This is the emergency room at Denver General Hospital. Do you know a Kingston James?"

Would he remember? Would he come?

Chapter Fourteen

King, Jen, and Neil were invited to dinner by his mother. Jen hadn't met Neil and King knew she was pretty curious. She'd seen pictures of his brother and remarked how different he and King looked.

"Are you sure one of you isn't adopted?"

"No. I look like my dad's side of the family and he looks like my mom's."

They took the back road, Highway 93 from Boulder to Golden, rather than the Boulder Turnpike. Jen wanted to drive. She hadn't driven a car since her father had her Mustang repossessed. King was pretty possessive about the Capri, and didn't hide his nervousness very well.

"Jesus, King, I've driven back and forth to California a hundred times. I've never had a ticket. Have you ever had a ticket?"

King admitted that the year he got his license he rolled a stop sign.

"Then I'm obviously more qualified to drive."

"It's a dark and winding road."

"You sound like Edgar Allen Poe. I've driven it a thousand times, coming home from ski trips. Sometimes we were so drunk, it's a wonder I didn't kill us all."

"Just don't kill me and your baby. My mother couldn't stand it."

Jen floored the pedal as they crested the rise overlooking Eldorado Springs. Lights twinkled in the dark vista. Beyond it, the silhouette of the front range of the Rocky Mountains. The Capri shot forward and careened around a curve Jen hadn't anticipated.

"Jesus, Jen."

"It's not the Mustang, but this baby has a little punch and pull."

Soon they were flying past Rocky Flats, Colorado's own nuclear power plant. Last year, Joan Baez held an impromptu concert outside the gates. A crowd of over a thousand protesters managed to close the plant for twenty-four hours. King didn't attend. He was too busy having a nervous breakdown over Lex.

They continued on. The drive to Golden was probably only fifteen minutes. Neil once commented it was the most beautiful highway in Colorado, roping its way along the foothills, with mountains to the west. Plains to the east. He liked the geological juxtaposition of the drive.

Because Jen came from money, King was a little embarrassed by the small tract house he'd grown up in. Every third house on the block was the same. His was overgrown with shrubs and tall trees, tall for a relatively young housing development; the crazy house on the street. Bird feeders were hanging from the naked apple tree in the front yard. One year for Mother's Day King gave his mother a Jonathan apple tree, which his father told him later was pretty neurotic.

"The tree, not you," Jim explained. He'd been annoyed when King brought it home, which in turn annoyed King's mother because she worried about his feelings, but every winter his dad fought like hell to keep it alive.

For Father's Day, King gave him a Sunburst Locust, which he knew pleased him tremendously because of how hearty it was. They planted it in the lower backyard and every year it got taller and taller, sprouting yellow, fern-like leaves. The James family garden was like a horticulturist's family album. Climbing trumpet vines from King's grandparents' farm in Minnesota. Lilac bushes imported from the old house in Wyoming.

They were all dormant, now. Nothing softened the house in winter but snow.

Tonight Neil planned to tell their parents he'd be moving to California. King could tell by his mother's expression that he already had. When they drove up, Neil appeared at the front door, peering out at King and Jen through the screen, pretending to be a ship captain in a storm.

"He's cute, King. Much cuter than you."

"I'm usually told the opposite."

Jen opened her door.

"Let me come around. The street might be slick. Black ice."

"Black ice?"

"My father always warns us about black ice. Thin ice you can't see on the blacktop."

Obediently, Jen waited. A neighbor came to her door and peered out as King was helping Jen out of his car. This lady was a horrible gossip, one of the few women on the street King's mother would have nothing to do with. She made no attempt to disguise her curiosity. Here was King with a pregnant woman, obviously made pregnant by him.

They mounted the steps, Jen protesting she was fine and King fussing behind her.

"Nice public relations stunt," Neil observed. "You get to look virile and doting when obviously this girl is far too pretty for you."

"I am pretty, aren't I, King?" Jen smiled back at King.

"I always said you were the most beautiful girl at Boulder."

"Really?" Jen giggled. "Did you?"

"This is making me sick." Neil held open the door. "Get inside before you ruin all our reputations."

"King is really the father of my baby," Jen said as she came through the door. His mom stood in the living room.

"I wish," Kay said dryly.

"How are you, Kay?" Jen smiled.

"I'm fine. How are you?"

"Pregnant." Jen sighed. "King let me drive."

"Take her coat, Neil."

Neil smirked at them and helped Jen off with her coat.

"Before he comes in," Kay whispered, "please don't mention drinking."

"Anybody care for a drink?" King's dad appeared at the kitchen door.

"No. Nobody needs anything." Kay spoke for them all.

"She thinks nobody should drink if I don't."

"I don't think it's fair, that's all."

"We always have a drink on Friday nights," Jim explained to Jen. "Ever since we were married. Would my sons please have a drink with their mother?"

"Jim. I told you it isn't necessary."

"And I'm telling *you* that it's a tradition I'd like to see honored tonight. We have our sons and an honored guest. Have a drink with your sons, Kay."

She glared at him, exasperated.

"I'd like gin," King said. "On the rocks."

"I'm afraid I don't have any fancy gins at home, King. It's just Gilbey's."

"Fine, Dad. Jen? What would you like?"

"Oh." She moaned. "I'd like a Bud with a shot of Wild Turkey, but I'll have milk instead." She smiled at Kay. "I'll keep him company."

"One milk it is. Neil?"

"Bourbon and water. Like Mom."

"I'm not having anything."

"Yes," his father insisted. "You are. Come and help me, King."

"I don't like to see him tempted," she muttered as King followed him into the kitchen.

"Have a drink with King and Neil," Jen whispered to her. "Don't make such a big deal of it."

King was struck that Jen could so calmly offer advice to his mom without fear of reprisal. They were truly confidants. They could hear them talking plainly in the kitchen.

"If you think so," Kay said. "I just haven't known what to do."

"He seems fine, Kay. Don't worry so much."

"This house isn't that well built," Neil called out. "We can hear you."

Jim shot a glance at King. King was embarrassed for him. He punched him lightly in the arm.

Before dinner, Neil and King each had two full cocktails. Their mother refused to take one sip from her glass. She gripped it tightly in her fist, her eyes anxiously darting from Neil to Jen to King and back. Jim was barbecuing the turkey, something he liked to do, even if it was freezing in the backyard.

Neil and King showed Jen the basement, which their dad had converted into a family room with a fireplace and a spare bedroom, which Neil and King shared as kids.

"Can you believe how tiny it was?" Neil remarked. "No wonder I wanted to kill you."

"Did you guys fight much?"

"He hated me so bad he moved into the utility room," King told her.

"Why didn't one of you take the other bedroom upstairs?"

"The doors are veneer in this house."

"Puberty, huh?" Jen smiled.

"So what's it like to be pregnant?" Neil asked. They filed out into the family room. Jim had built a fire. Jen inspected the bookshelves flanking the fireplace. All of Jim's prizes and trophies were displayed on one side.

"I wish the circumstances were a bit more traditional, but untraditional is what I have and I'm dealing with it."

"We could say the same thing, huh, Neil?"

"I'll take the road less traveled any day of the week, thank you."

"Your dad was a newspaper editor?" Jen asked. "Why'd he give it up?"

"No money in it. He gave it up so we could go to college."

"How'd they take it?" Jen asked him. "You moving to California."

"Mom thinks King will follow me as soon as he graduates."

Jen smiled at King. Her eyes were questioning. Jen and King never discussed what they'd do when he graduated. They never talked about what kind of jobs they'd get, if they'd still live in Boulder or even stay in Colorado.

"Would you, King?"

"I've thought about it."

"Don't you have family in Los Angeles?" Neil asked.

"No," Jen answered lightly. "Not anymore."

"But King said you did."

"He was wrong." She smiled. King could tell she was upset. "I think I'll go help your mom." She disappeared into the hallway. Neil and King could hear her slowly mounting the stairs.

"Sorry, King." Neil reflected. "I guess she's counting on you more than you thought."

"I guess so," King said, downing his drink.

Kay was subdued over dinner, but their dad seemed more talkative and animated than ever. Without any alcohol his spirits had lifted. Kay's seemed to sink. Neil talked in graphic detail about the life Vince had described for him in California. "It overlooks the ocean. You're all welcome anytime you like. Wouldn't it be great to come in the dead of winter? Get out of all this snow?"

"I've been to Laguna," Jen commented. "It's very pretty."

King wondered if Sally at the Village knew Vince from the Boom Boom Room.

"I'm sure it's very nice." Kay stared at the wall. "Maybe I'd like my drink after all. With my meal."

They all jumped to retrieve it. King was up first so he escaped, Neil and his dad sinking slowly into their chairs.

"My turkey is perfect, Mr. James."

"Jim cooks a good turkey," his mother announced as King handed her the drink. The ice had mostly melted but she accepted it anyway. She took a big gulp.

"Well, I really appreciate a home-cooked meal." Jen patted her hand. Kay smiled, but King thought she was going to cry.

"Yeah, thanks," King murmured.

They didn't stay for pie.

Jen and King didn't say much on the drive home. Finally, as they crossed the bridge over the Coal Creek River, King asked if she was upset.

"I'm sober," she answered evenly.

"I know. You only had milk."

"That's not what I meant and you know it. This curve is so beautiful during the day. I like to take it fast. The canyon walls and the little creek. Whenever I drive through here I always think the same thing. How beautiful and a little dangerous it is. You know the train tracks at the top of the hill? Once when I heading back to Boulder, I nearly hit a train."

She stopped talking. The Capri raced up the hill.

"And?"

"Well, it's easier than you think to hit a train. You think you'd see it, plain as day, but when it's moving, and you aren't expecting it, the only way I can explain it is that even as big as it was, it was out of context and my mind wouldn't accept it. Plain as day and I didn't see it. I nearly overturned my car, slamming on the brakes."

"Wasn't there a signal crossing? Didn't the horn sound?"

"No," she mused. "See, it wasn't really moving. It was just parked there, before the intersection, and I didn't see it because I never saw one there before. I guess I was daydreaming. I nearly rolled my car."

When they got home, she headed for her apartment without any fanfare.

"Jen. What's wrong?"

"I just realized how alone I really am. After the baby's born, we'll be totally alone and I'm scared."

"I'm sorry about the thing with California. I guess I did figure you'd probably go back. Because of your family."

"My family has disowned me, King. Don't you get that? My father isn't just testing me. I'm dead to him. And since he controls all the money, I'm dead to the rest of them, too." She turned to continue down the steps to her door.

King wanted to call after her that she wasn't alone, but it would have sounded condescending. He wasn't the father of the baby or her boyfriend. She was alone, and needed to face it. For that matter, so did King.

King felt claustrophobic in his room. He decided to go out. He didn't want to drive all the way back to Denver to the bars, so he decided to walk over to the Boulderado. He called Jen.

"I'm going out."

"Fine," she said. She hesitated. "Maybe it isn't necessary for you to report your comings and goings. You must feel pretty trapped by me."

King opened his drape to see if hers was open. It was drawn shut.

"I don't feel trapped."

"Maybe I feel a little trapped," she said, her voice tinged with annoyance.

"What's that supposed to mean?"

"I don't know what I'm doing here. Pregnant, in this dump. Your world so big across the way."

"So big?"

"Yeah. We didn't even *know* each other last summer. Now I'm all caught up in your bizarre lifestyle."

"You came to me for help and you *got* it. That's more than I got from anybody last year."

"You've had your parents and your brother the whole time."

"Not right away, I didn't. I lost everything until my dad intervened. I'd be dead now if it weren't for my dad."

"Well, you seem to be doing okay now. Look at you. You're going out again to pick somebody up. You can't stand to be alone for a second."

"Why should I be alone if I don't have to? In the first days since I came out, my mother and my friends all warned me I was looking forward to a long, lonely, empty life. How do they know? What makes everybody such an expert on me?"

"Because you ask everybody what they think."

"No. I tell people what I'm feeling and they mistake it for weakness."

"I don't want to fight anymore. Go out, King. Maybe tonight you'll meet Mr. Right. I was so naïve. I get so lonely." She started to cry. "I thought having the baby inside would be some company, but it isn't. I never dreamed I'd feel so lonely."

"I'm coming over."

"No. I won't let you in."

"I'll stand outside till you do." King hung up, grabbed his coat, and stomped over to her door. He knocked lightly. She didn't answer so he knocked a little louder. Finally she let him in.

Jen's face was blotched and red from crying. "It's just hormones. They warned me I'd get emotional."

"You got upset because of my family. We aren't the Waltons, after all." By her reaction, King was apparently dead right.

"You all still hurt so bad." Jen sank to her bed. King moved to sit down next to her. He placed his arm around her shoulder and they rocked together slightly.

"That's why Neil's moving. He wants to get away."

"But you all love each other so much."

"Yes." King nodded. "We do."

"Shouldn't that fix it? I guess I thought you'd all accepted everything. It gave me hope for my family. At least your parents are liberal. It just hit me tonight. All the kindness you've shown me. Loaning me your mother, for Christ's sake. It's still not like I have any guarantees. You might move away. I've laid such expectations on you. That's all I'm saying. I have to rely more on myself."

"I don't think that's ever a bad idea. But I promise you this. I'm not going anywhere till the baby's born. My mom's not going anywhere ever."

"I've tried to understand my dad's position. And my mother's. But I just can't. If I could just understand the thinking. I'm their only daughter. I'm on welfare. I pay for food with food stamps. *Food stamps.* I was with Holly once at the King Sooper's on 28th. We were buying margarita mix. A girl was paying for her food with food stamps and I remember thinking what white trash she was. She had to give something back, like a roll of toilet paper, because it wasn't allowed. Holly made some crack and the girl looked back at us. She was so *hurt*, King. All she wanted was to wipe her ass. When we left the market, we passed her waiting at the bus stop with her groceries. The top was down on my car. I had to stop for the light. I couldn't look at her. I wondered what she thought of us sitting in my new red convertible. A chill went through me. When the light changed, I stepped on it. I remember thinking I was hell-bound, then. *Hellbound* if I didn't shape up. If I didn't stop being such a fucking spoiled bitch."

"When was this?"

"Right before I found out I was pregnant." She grimaced, like something was hurting her. "This kid is doing somersaults."

"Can I feel?"

"Yes."

She exposed her belly. She took King's hands and placed them over her belly button. The baby kicked. He yanked his hand back. A foot appeared, disappearing just as quickly. King started to laugh. For the next half hour they lay next to each other and watched the baby undulate. It was as mysterious as watching an aquarium churning with exotic fish.

"It's late, King. And you wanted to go."

"It's too cold to go out. I'll stay."

"I'm sorry about what I said."

"I just wanted to shake off tonight. It was hard. She was being so hard on my dad."

"Go out, King. My good humor is coming back to me. I think I'll call your mom. She was low. She says I cheer her up."

"Let's call her together, and then I'll go."

"That's a good idea."

King reached for Jen's telephone and dialed home. Kay answered on the first ring.

"Mom?"

"Neil?"

"No, it's King. I'm here with Jen. The baby's kicking like crazy. I felt her foot."

"Did you, King? Did you really?" His mom started laughing. Jen grabbed the receiver.

"We had a great time tonight, Kay! Yeah, she's really kicking. Can you come up next week? Or I can borrow King's car and come to you." Jen shot King a look of defiance. She pointed to her door, waving him away. Before King crept out, he kissed the top of her head.

"Have a good time," she whispered. "Maybe you'll run into Maddie and Robert." She resumed her conversation with King's mother. He could hear her laughing as King climbed the stairs to the walkway. Theo's light was on. King could see two figures moving in silhouette behind his drapes. Theo was over him.

What else was new?

It was too late to drive back to Denver. King decided to walk over to the Boulderado. The lobby was empty. Upstairs on the mezzanine, several couples lounged in rattan chairs overlooking the railing. King figured Le Bar would probably be dead. If it was, he'd cruise once through the Catacombs and head home, just to prove to himself that he'd made an effort.

King hesitated at the entry to Le Bar. The air was thick with cigarette smoke. He could hear energetic conversation. He peered in. Nearly every table was occupied. A large group had claimed the corner, and in the center with his back to the wall was Allen Ginsberg. When he saw King, he nodded. King didn't know if he placed him from the other night with Maddie and Robert or if he just placed him as a single gay man.

Next to Ginsberg sat poet William Burroughs, who King knew lived in the hotel. A few women listened raptly. Lastly, the only man with the back of his head to King turned around. Of course it was Maddie's fiancé, Robert. King searched the table for Maddie. She wasn't with him, and there was no sign of an empty chair waiting for her to return.

King stared at them and they stared back. Finally Robert whispered something to Ginsberg. Ginsberg responded, and although King couldn't make out exactly what he said, the sonority of his voice reverberated across the room. Robert waved King toward them. He sprang for another chair, and stood while King fidgeted with his coat.

King was younger by half of anyone seated at the table. Robert introduced him around. King was grateful that he opted not to use last names. "King, this is Allen, Bill, Anne, Peter, and Rachel." King recognized Rachel, a folk singer King often heard at Tulagi on the hill. For some reason, she impressed him more than anyone else.

"King is a student of Maddie's. He's a very good writer," Robert explained. "I've read his work. He won a creative writing scholarship at the university."

They murmured their approval.

"Does the university nurture young writers?" asked Burroughs.

"Financial aid informed me. I'm lucky because of Professor Sloan."

"You should consider Naropa." Robert laughed with a hint of irony in his voice. "They'd take good care of you there."

Ginsberg studied King as if he were a curiosity somehow. He felt completely intimidated. He only knew them by their book jacket covers. Frankly, King had read Kerouac because he was so handsome. And Kerouac wasn't coming tonight or ever.

They resumed their conversation. Robert poured King a glass of wine from what seemed to be a never-empty carafe. The bartender, the same fellow who'd been working the night gay liberation overtook Le Bar, kept filling and refilling it. King wondered if he recognized him.

"Where's Dr. Sloan?" King whispered to Robert.

"She flew to Phoenix to be with her family," Robert told him. His hand moved to the back of King's chair as he leaned forward to make some terribly vital point. King was embarrassed. Instead of listening to him, they all followed Robert's overly animated gesture of claiming King as taken—by him. King was certain Ginsberg even grinned sympathetically, but he checked it when Robert noticed.

Burroughs was tired and wanted to beg off. Allen and Peter had walked over together from Ginsberg's house at Pine and 22nd. Rachel and her friend reached for their coats. The bartender appeared with the bill. He made a big deal about collecting before anyone left. They all dug apologetically in their pockets. Robert ended up paying.

Ginsberg smiled obsequiously at Robert. He patted King's shoulder and no one else said good-bye. Soon Robert and King were sitting alone.

"I was hoping you might drop in tonight." Robert searched King's face. He still reminded King of some hairy Satan. He felt malevolent. King wanted to excuse himself. "Why do I make you so uncomfortable, King? Is it because of Maddie?"

King didn't know what to say.

"Maddie and I have a very clear understanding. She knows and accepts my bisexuality. Truly," he added. "Ask her."

Ask her, King would never do.

"You clearly have a crush on her. If you can have a crush on Maddie, then why can't I be attracted to you?"

"You can think or feel whatever you like," King stammered.

"Maddie has feelings for you, too."

Oh my god, King thought. *Please shut up. Please shut up.* "She's been a good teacher. My favorite. She feels that and responds. I'm sure it's nothing more."

"You're combative." He nodded approvingly. "I was worried you might be too passive."

"People mistake me for being passive all the time," King spoke sharply. "I'm usually just trying to control a very bad temper."

"Are you angry now?"

"Yes."

"Why?"

"I'm sick and tired of cowardice. I don't buy your bisexuality for a minute. I think you're using Maddie. I don't want to see her hurt."

He reeled back in utter shock. "How dare you?"

"How dare *you*?" King stood up. "You fucking bastard!"

The bartender watched them with interest. He was wiping down his counter and stopped. Robert glanced past King into the hotel lobby.

"Burroughs is coming back. Control yourself."

King turned wildly toward the door. Now he could leave without more of a scene.

"Bill." Robert smiled charmingly. "Did Allen forget his glove?"

"I'm not Allen's runner, Robert," Burroughs said flatly. There was no love lost between him and Robert. "If Allen lost his glove he'd come back himself to find it."

"Oh." Robert sniffed.

"I came back myself to say we'd been rude to your friend. I'm sorry." He reached to shake King's hand. "Robert has a bit of a reputation. Not that Allen isn't still smitten by him. We were unfairly judging you by the company you keep. Please come and visit us anytime. Allen meant it about Naropa. We'd like to read your writing." He simmered at Robert, who sat, completely aghast, alone at the table they'd all just shared.

"Thanks," King said. "Thanks."

"You need a chaperone?"

"No. We're fine," King said. "Robert's being a perfect gentleman."

"That's not like Robert. I think you're the gentleman. Good night, then."

King watched him go. He turned and found himself embarrassed for Robert. He stood up and pulled on his coat. "I'm sorry," King muttered. "I do care for Professor Sloan."

"So do I," Robert hissed, pushing past him. "What's so difficult to understand?"

Chapter Fifteen

Two days later King had his tennis date with Barry Adams to contend with. King was only going for the sex. After his run-in with Robert, King felt like a hypocrite about seducing Barry, but Robert was Robert and Barry was a goddamned football player. He'd come to his senses pretty soon, so King figured he may as well drink while the bar was open. They met in front of Balch Fieldhouse, promptly at five-thirty. Barry wore his bathhouse saddle shoes, the tightest Levi's King ever saw, accentuating every crack, bulge, and crevice of his lower body, front and back. So tight King could make out the head of his penis, mushrooming below the stitching of the crotch of Barry's jeans. He wore a University of Colorado Buffalo letter jacket with a hooded white sweatshirt underneath.

King was glad Barry's hair wasn't all combed and sprayed. He'd just come from the gym and it was still damp from the showers. Barry's teeth were the color of his sweatshirt. He smiled brilliantly as he saw King head up the walk past Folsom Field.

Barry's anticipation, King's anticipation—King couldn't explain what charged between them, but he knew he felt absolutely electrified when he saw Barry again. King didn't understand why he hadn't looked more forward to seeing him.

King reflected quickly. There was the Holly business, of course. His own history with Holly, not to mention Jen's. Now here King was, plotting to suck him so dry there'd never be a drop left for poor Holly's vaginal passage. She'd never be satisfied with another man's cock after Barry had stretched her all out. How she could walk? King wondered.

Then there was also the born-again thing. And all the golly-gee-whizzery of Barry's IHOP banter. Recently, King sat at the knee of Allen Ginsberg while he recited poetry, surrounded by Boulder's best scholars. What would Ginsberg do? Would he compromise his core belief system just to have sex with a dumb football player?

Someday King hoped to ask him. Not to mention Barry's closely held belief that two men couldn't lay with each other. That nagging repugnant-to-God thing. An abomination, in fact. Barry wasn't out and he was a religious fanatic, as well. Politically, King was heading way in the wrong direction, but he kept walking. Barry was clearly happy to see him. And because of that, King was now in love with him.

These were the feelings King believed everyone was trying to warn him about misinterpreting: King's pounding heart. His hurried breath. His cock writhing inside his Jockeys, wanting to express itself. But more than that, more than the sexual reinforcement, King realized that Barry's acceptance might be his downfall. King knew, unless he blew it totally, that later tonight Barry would ask to see where he lived, which would lead to something sexual. More plans would be mulled over. They'd see each other again.

And King had a history of telling people during sex that he loved them and having to laughingly apologize for it six minutes later. Sexual acceptance was the ultimate for him. To be accepted physically was the highest he could go. He knew intellectually that this was inherently wrong, but not emotionally. What, then, was the source of self-esteem so deprecating his heart could be sold for a genuine smile?

King didn't know. He managed to calm down when Barry reached him. Barry, too, had probably been marveling over similar facts. They both sobered slightly. They stood facing each other without speaking. Barry, the taller man, talking to the air above his head, the whiff of sexuality in the air. Like a junkie arranging a drug deal.

"We've got to use these tickets," Barry apologized, finally gazing down at King. "The president of the bank gave them to me. It's a front row box."

"We should go in." King nodded. Hoards of tennis fans crushed past them into the field house. Some greeted Barry. Some recognized him, respect flickering in their eyes.

"I don't want to go in, King ol' man." He nudged his thigh with his knee. "But we should."

"We should," King echoed. The match was sponsored by the United Bank of Boulder. These were the president's tickets after all.

They sat in a box set up for six, just the two of them, a chair in between, Barry's arm draped over it so he could lightly tap King's shoulder. King slumped down, crossed his arms, his legs wide, his boots propped up on the railing; pretending to be riveted by the game of tennis.

King didn't look at Barry once. He doubted Barry looked over at him. Thank God Bobby won easily. They found themselves walking toward Barry's GTO by quarter to seven.

"I'd like to go someplace dark," Barry said. "Walrus okay for you?"

"Great."

A basement restaurant, the Walrus sat at the corner of Walnut and 7th down the street from Scornovacco's and a block over from the Pearl Street Mall.

The GTO was parked in a special parking lot reserved for CU football players, a half block away from the stadium. He popped the gleaming gear shift into drive and roared down Folsom, past the chapel where the Friday Night Coffee House would be held later tonight. Barry placed his big, pigskin-pitching hand on King's thigh, and didn't pull it away till they got to the restaurant. It didn't grope, massage or wander—it just lay there.

Since they met outside the field house, King didn't think more than a few words had been exchanged. They were shown to a booth in the back. The hostess knew Barry, asked about Holly. Several other tables recognized him and hooted greetings. He waved good-naturedly but they kept walking.

"Let me know if you need anything, Barry." The hostess smiled at King and disappeared. A waitress came up. Barry ordered a Budweiser with a shot of Wild Turkey.

"The same," King said.

Instead of downing the whiskey, Barry nursed it, tempering it with his beer.

"So, King," he finally said. "Good to see you."

"Same here."

"I almost canceled, but I didn't."

"I think I understand."

"I'm used to getting everything pretty easy, and I like it." He stretched. "By coming out with you tonight, I'm heading down a road that could change all that."

"Count on it."

"You suffered pretty publicly. I'm sorry I didn't call you again."

"I wouldn't have expected you to do more than you did."

"Still," he said. "I'm sorry. You ever see Lex?"

"No. Lex lives somewhere on the other side of 28th. I think he may be living with a girlfriend."

"You don't talk at all."

"No."

"And Nicholas? I see him around."

"He is engaged to Leslie." Leslie was once a good friend of King's. They once drove to San Francisco on a whim. King had never laughed so much in his life.

"I heard what Nicholas did to your mom and dad."

"None of us had any experience with what we were up against. He thought he was saving my life."

Barry's eyes softened with admiration.

"I saw you on that march to the courthouse. You and Jen passed right by my car."

"I told Jen about the other night," King confessed, suddenly. Barry rubbed his jaw and mulled this bit of news over. "She's my best friend. She lives across the way from me."

"I like Jen. She got a raw deal, too. Jen is one of the most terrific girls on campus. I guess you two take care of each other."

"I'm sorry I told her."

Barry finished off his shot and smiled. "I don't mind. Jen and I have our own history, but I guess she probably mentioned that."

The waitress came back to take their order. They hadn't even looked at their menus. "A well-done burger's fine with me. How 'bout for you, King?"

"Same."

"How is it, then? The road you've gone down."

"It's good," King said, and meant it. "Now."

"Your folks know. I understand they've stood by you."

"Yes."

"And you've made new friends."

"That, too."

"I don't know if I could do it."

"If I had it to do over again, I wouldn't make it such a big deal."

"I don't know. There's Holly, after all. I care for her."

"But you don't love her."

"No."

"That's a tough one."

They sat quietly for a while, nursing their beers. King figured the mood had been blown. Fuck. King could never be light and airy. Theo was right. Five minutes with King and Pollyanna would turn into Sylvia Plath. Nobody sought King out to have fun. They needed King to confide in. Nobody had taken it closer to the edge than old King and lived to tell about it. Tell *him* what's on your mind. King's definitely no one to judge.

Fuck me, fuck me, fuck me, King lamented. He looked up at Barry. His life was made for him if he just stayed the course. He could just fake it for the next fifty years. Maybe it was for the best. Nicholas was right. King was the devil. He deserved to be driven out of Boulder with whips and chains.

"I'm wondering if I can spend the night with you, King."

Ah.

King fidgeted in his chair. The waitress came back with their hamburgers. They were thick and juicy, with big steak fries on the side. King liked to order hamburgers in nice restaurants. The meat was so good.

"Jen lives across the way," King reminded him. "She won't say anything, but she'll probably see you."

This sobered him.

"You know what we could do?"

"What?" Barry asked.

"Maybe we could rent a cabin. It's Friday night. I'm not working tomorrow. We'd have some privacy."

"Yes." Barry grinned. "Yes. I have some spare gear in the car. We can swing by your place and get your toothbrush."

King hesitated. Much as he wanted to get Barry's dick in his mouth, he wasn't up for a long drive, a quick blow job, and a guilty ride home later that night.

"I should clarify something first. I want to sleep with you. In the bed. Laying down. If we can't do that, maybe we should call it off." King thought he'd feel evil, but didn't. He felt honest. And courageous.

"I don't know how to do much more than what we did the other night."

"Have you ever kissed another man?"

"No."

"Have you wanted to?"

"I want to kiss you."

"Everything else will be okay after that."

King knew what Barry was going through. In Barry's mind, he thought he was risking the wrath of God. And for King, what was worse, the loss of God's friendship. All those prayer breakfasts, the youth groups, the invocations at the football games, the bargaining with God if we can only win this game, the Sunday school classes he liked teaching, Easter sunrise services, the Bible studies, praying on his knees every night, rejoicing in his Lord.

The smug security of being saved.

The proprietor of the cabins was an old hippie who didn't blink an eye when he saw two men standing on his porch.

"Didn't expect any business tonight," he commented. "Might snow. You have chains to get out of here tomorrow if it does?" The smell of grass wafted into the night. Inside his front room King saw a cat curled up next to an old dog lying by a happy fire. "I have a nice cabin next to the river, but it's mostly frozen over. It'll heat up pretty fast. Got a wall unit and a big fireplace. Wood's on the back porch."

King and Barry rushed down the path.

The firewood was dry, and with plenty of kindling, soon the room heated up. They never switched on a light. Barry lit a candle next to the bed. The cabin was only one medium-size room, with a big stone fireplace, a brass bed, a rocker, and an easy chair. An old Kelvinator refrigerator, like the one King had grown up with, hummed in the corner. A two-burner stove and a small sink was all it offered by way of a kitchen. Barry stepped into the small bathroom to pee. He didn't close the door, which King liked. When he came out, they undressed unceremoniously. Barry kept his socks on and climbed under the quilt. The bed was tiny for the two of them. King jumped under the covers. Barry sat up and looked around with slightly wild eyes.

"Barry. Aren't you going to lie down?"

"I didn't say my prayers."

"Then let's say them. Get out of bed."

"When's the last time you prayed, King?"

"Last night. I still pray every night. So can you."

Barry slid out of bed. King slipped down next to him. They were bare-ass naked except for Barry's white socks. While the image looked ridiculous, to King it wasn't. It was poignant.

"What should we pray for, King?"

"That the sex will be blessed."

"Amen." he laughed. They crawled into bed. Later King would write:

I am facedown in a canoe on a lake. I am facedown in a canoe, hollowed out, silken with exquisite woods. I am facedown in a canoe, the hollowed-out shell silken with exquisite woods, and the sun is warm on my back, and the canoe rocks gently on the clear mountain lake, and envelops me like the body of brutal man at rest.

I am facedown in a canoe on a lake and the canoe overturns, but the water is warm and I have gills and the canoe holds me close and I don't drift away because it rights itself and suddenly the sun is warming my back once again.

In the morning King restricted their lovemaking to the neck up.

Barry sat cross-legged and King straddled him, lotus-style, face-to-face. They wore cotton gym shorts, T-shirts, and white tennis socks. True to his word, Barry had lay down with King. Now, snow-bound in a cabin warmed by a morning fire, Barry and King faced off.

King recalled being told by a girlfriend that the most sensual area on her body was her face. If her face was on fire, she could peak almost instantly. Because it was so forbidden, Barry was having the same experience. King was reassured by his size, his physical mass. Unshaven, Barry scraped his jaw in the hollows of King's cheekbones. He traced King's forehead, the bridge of his nose, his lips and his chin with his jaw. Barry offered up his neck, a neck the size of most men's thighs, and allowed King to lavish it, like a thirsty horse, lapping at a salt lick.

Barry reached for King's groin. King stopped him.

"Only faces."

Barry didn't protest but the intimacy challenged him. Chin to chin, King brushed Barry's lips with his. Barry hadn't permitted kissing last night, avoiding it apologetically.

"Barry," King whispered. "Would you open your eyes?"

Obediently, they flickered open.

"What does a big man do when he wants to be held?"

"What are you getting at?"

"I think I'm luckier, being smaller than you. You'd have to find a giant to hold you the way you held me last night."

"You aren't a small man, King."

"No, but I fit inside the circle of your frame."

"I'm the house. You're the room."

"That's okay with you?"

"Yes." He pulled King closer. Lip to lip. Eyelash to eyelash. King and Barry began to kiss. They made out for an hour and not once did they fumble with their clothes.

They checked out of their cabin and drove back down the Foothill Highway toward Boulder. The eastern plains were dusted with snow. The sky churned. Thick gray-green clouds threatened more weather. Barry drove with his arm over King's shoulder, which made King feel like his girlfriend. King felt guilty that he liked it, but he did.

King remembered from before that Barry was by nature a very affectionate man. If he sat next to King in church or a Bible study, he always draped his arm over King's shoulders. Athletes had a largesse that they didn't get enough credit for. They touched freely, and not just the joked-about ass-patting. They shook hands. They kissed each other on the cheek when they were handed some trophy. They bear-hugged each other and everyone else.

So anyone driving by and noticing that Barry Adams had his arm around King wouldn't have thought a thing about it. That was just Barry. Athlete, Christian, good citizen—a credit to his mother and father.

They stopped at the Village for breakfast. Sally and Mitch were huge CU football fans. She recognized Barry, who held the door for King, but in her mind didn't put them together. When she noticed King, she nodded toward his usual stool at the counter.

"We're together."

"Take the booth in the corner," she said, cool about it. "More leg room."

Barry saw a few buddies across the room. He excused himself politely. Went to glad-hand.

"You're kidding, right?" Sally came up behind King.

"Kidding about what?"

"King. *Barry Adams?*"

"We're friends."

She snorted. "You must have an asshole as big as Texas this morning."

Unfortunately, King blushed and she was on to them. There it was. Barry was a famous athlete and King was a famous homosexual. Being seen publicly with King compromised him.

"Look," King stammered.

"Mitch is gonna shit bricks." She glanced over to the grill. "My order's ready."

Barry and his friends were still laughing. Apologetically, he winked at King. Sally followed it.

"Please don't say anything."

"Like I would. I know how all this shit works. But tomorrow I'll need details. I tell you about me and Mitch. Maybe we can double-date. Mitch's a *huge* fan of Barry's and so am I." Grinning, she walked away.

When Barry drove King home, King prepared himself for "the talk." Barry had been quiet over breakfast. Mostly he'd chatted to other tables, or friends who came in. He even autographed a few napkins. King didn't think Barry looked at him once. In the car he kept both hands on the wheel.

"The talk" would consist of a few polite assessments of the facts. Barry was a public figure and therefore a role model. He was engaged. He'd be moving to Florida after they graduated at the end of the semester. While last night had been "different," he was still a Christian and the homosexual lifestyle was directly in conflict with his core beliefs. He would repent and pray that King would also.

What King would pray for, he decided, was compassion and understanding. Hadn't he stood in exactly the same shoes? Hadn't King weighed the severity of the path he was "choosing"? The worry of his parents? The reaction of friends? The conflict with his faith? What would King's financial future be if he couldn't, or wouldn't, stay in the closet?

On the basis of one blissful winter's night, King couldn't ask Barry to come to terms with all that.

He could hear Neil's voice. "So you think you're in love again, huh, King? Who's the lucky guy? How long have you known him? He out? Comfortable with it? Ah. Sounds positive. Sounds like you *have* changed."

And hadn't King made fun of him with Jen? And in King's own mind? Didn't King think of Barry as a "dumb athlete," even if he once heard his scholastic average was a 3.9. How would Barry fit in with King and Jen? With Theo and Sam? With Maddie and Robert at Le Bar?

What did King and Barry have in common but mutual confusion about sex and spirituality? King felt suddenly overwhelmed with sadness.

Barry wheeled the GTO onto Goss, the side street by King's building.

"So I guess we should talk," King told him.

"There's something I need to do first." Barry leaned over and kissed him. "So King, I don't know how to sift through all these new feelings. Fact is, you're the only one I can talk to about 'em. We have a lot in common. I've always gone with my gut. Last night the sky didn't fall. The earth didn't open up and swallow us whole."

"I swallowed you whole."

"You sure did. There's something I have to do. Can I come by later?"

"Sure," King said, a little surprised. "I'm working till eight. I should be back after that." King opened his door and hopped out. Barry looked pretty grave. He probably wanted to call King to break up. Or he wouldn't call at all. King smiled his best brave little smile. "Thanks, you know. For everything."

"See you later, King." And the GTO roared away.

Barry didn't show at eight-thirty or nine. By ten, King had curled in a fetal position behind his bed, next to the heater. He heard a knock at his door.

"King?"

"Barry?" King popped his head up.

King pulled back his drape. Through the falling snow he could see Jen peering across. He would have waved but Barry looked so awful.

Jen saw King hesitate and understood. King opened the sliding glass door and let him inside.

Barry pulled off his parka. He looked for a space to sit down. King's chairs were piled with books and clothes. Barry sank down on the edge of King's bed. He noted King's family photos with interest. He asked him their names. Asked about Neil. He was surprised when King told him Neil was gay.

Barry seemed somewhat shy. He was big in the room. Huge. Kept reaching for King. Hugging him from behind as he inspected something over King's shoulder. King's piles of handwritten short stories. His books.

"Remember when you told me how different you felt, standing outside the stadium that afternoon?"

"Yes."

"That's me, now. I can see the noise of the crowd, it's so loud. But I'm not part of it anymore. I broke it off with Holly."

His life plan. Down the drain.

"She told me there were rumors everywhere about me."

King laughed. It felt inappropriate, but Barry laughed, too.

"It's a whole new ball game." They quieted. Barry edged back slightly. "You asked me what a big man did when he wanted to be held. I told you that big men never expected to be held. It wasn't an option."

"You were the house, I was the room."

"I was wrong. A big man needs to be held now and then."

"It's late, Barry. Let's say our prayers and go to bed."

In the morning they were interrupted by the sound of Theo's sliding glass door opening. A guy with big work boots stepped past the window. Theo's sexual appetite had been insatiable the last month. He had a different trick over every night.

Barry nuzzled the back of King's neck with his chin. Even his day-old beard was strong. King struggled to pull away from him, but he held fast. Finally King relented. He was joking, but King could feel his fear.

"King."

"What?"

"I want to talk with you about a few things, but I'm afraid."

"Don't be afraid."

He hesitated. King glanced over his shoulder. He could see one blue eye, staring over his burnished cheekbone to the light forming gently in the sky over Jen's side of the apartment building.

"I don't know what our understanding is."

"Understanding?"

"I want us to be faithful to each other." He whispered it so gently King didn't hear him at first.

"We met in a bathhouse, after all. While you were engaged."

"I knew you'd throw that up to me."

"You like sex. It never meant anything personal to you."

"Not till you."

King was flattered as hell. Barry was falling in love with him. He guessed he hoped if he needed to get off, he'd go to the baths like he did before. Keep it quick and anonymous. King wondered then if he was being honest. Did the idea threaten him? Then, was Barry the only one they needed to worry about?

Talk about monogamy could only lead to trouble. Then again, the door was open and they had to go through it.

"You aren't answering me fast enough." Barry rolled away and faced the wall.

King rolled behind him and whispered to the back of his head. "Yes. I wanted to be faithful. I want us to be committed lovers. I don't want to be modern. I want to be one person. I want you to get football out of your system and stay in Boulder and live together with me. I want you to close your eyes in the locker room."

He hiked himself up on one elbow and smiled. "Will you make love with me in the woods?"

"All day long."

"I love you, King. I love you."

The following week, Barry and King appeared at the Friday Night Coffee House as a couple. It was the first time that Barry had openly convened with other gay men and women in a nonsexually compromised situation. They decided to walk over. He was very nervous as they cut through the married student housing to Folsom and up the hill toward the chapel.

Although Barry kept his room in the football dorm, he wanted to spend most of his nights with King. King had to pull one overnighter at the switchboard, and gamely Barry came and slept over, fascinated that he could call anywhere in the United States for free.

Barry, too, had an abbreviated schedule. When King's writing class with Maddie adjourned, Barry was outside in the hall, waiting for him. He walked King from class to class. Invariably someone would recognize him, want to reminisce about the key plays in the Colorado-Missouri play-off game, and he'd oblige them until King appeared, begging off affably and escorting King to his next stop.

King hadn't slept with anyone on a regular basis since Lex. How the two of them managed to get any sleep at all in a twin bed was a miracle, but they managed.

"I want to be as close to you as possible," Barry told King. King's small room seemed like a second skin to them. They were one living organism inside its walls. They read touching, ate touching, and slept touching. Barry liked to shower together.

Barry loved King and told him so, often. After it became obvious that Barry and King were together, Theo grew distant and even cold. He grunted hello, if that. He'd been amazed when Barry and King appeared in front of him at the ticket table at the chapel coffee house. Barry, he guessed, was probably infamous for the size of his dick at the baths. They were notorious as a couple. Absolutely notorious.

They had their reputations. King for being a religious, suicidal, fanatic spook and Barry as the closeted star football player. That night they sat mostly on the sidelines, holding hands on a sofa while watching people dance. King didn't ask Barry if he wanted to dance. He knew how scared he was. He had Florida to consider. They hadn't even discussed what would happen in the summer.

Rod, Tony, and Peter came in. Peter had never come back to work at the switchboard. King heard he'd dropped out of school, but occasionally he'd see him hanging around campus. He wouldn't have anything to do with King after Tim died, and King never really understood why. Then Sam came in with his new boyfriend, Skip.

This was bigger news than King and Barry.

Barry noted his interest and squeezed King's hand. Sam took a mental inventory of who was in the room.

"This is Skip," he said as he introduced him around. Peter, Tony, and Rod already knew him.

He was a few years older than Sam, and pretty slick-looking. King heard he was an investment banker in downtown Denver. Where in Boulder the dress code was jeans and boots, Skip dressed more like Matthew. He reminded King of Matthew, but was much younger. He also had political aspirations. He wanted to establish a gay national agenda, which had attracted Sam to him. Even Theo seemed impressed to have him come to Boulder.

Sam saw Barry and King sitting on the sofa. He nudged Skip. They started over. King didn't know if Sam had heard about him and Barry. King could tell old Skip thought Barry was pretty hot.

"I'm a huge fan. *Huge.*"

"This is King," Sam said. "King, this is Skip."

"Yes, King. How are you?" His gaze swung to Barry.

"So most likely you'll be playing for the Dolphins in the fall."

"Draft is in one month."

"That's *huge*," Skip effused. "Good luck."

King noticed Skip didn't pronounce the 'h'. He kept saying "*yeeooge.*" Sam seemed very smitten by him. King knew Sam's background was working-class. Skipper reeked of money. Tonight Sam wore a cashmere turtleneck with gray flannel slacks. He kept moistening his lips with Chap Stick. Whenever he did, he unconsciously handed it to Skip, who'd make the same application.

Barry glanced over at King. King could tell he didn't like Skip, thought he was a little effeminate.

Sam pulled up two chairs for him and Skip.

"I think you're very courageous, Barry."

"Why?" Barry said flatly.

"You're so visible! A sports figure? It's huge."

King shifted uncomfortably.

"Look," Barry said. "I respect what these other guys have done, but I'm a long way from making any public announcement about me and King here."

King was surprised at the mention of his name.

"What's King have to do with it?" Skip grinned.

"King is the reason I'm here tonight. If you want to acknowledge anyone for being courageous, acknowledge King."

Sam squeezed the back of Skip's shoulders. To shut him up, King thought. If they intended to rush Barry to help the cause, Skip was royally blowing it.

"Not to diminish King's contributions," Skip explained, "not at *all*, King, but what the national gay agenda is looking for are role models as spokespersons."

"I still don't know why you aren't as interested in King. Do you think I've made a bigger contribution because I play football? Trust me, the only people who know I'm out are sitting in this room. It's people like King you should acknowledge. I'm a coward next to King."

"No," King corrected him, his face flushing. "You aren't."

"When King became a Christian, he told everyone about it. Didn't worry what others would think. When King accepted he was gay, he went to his family for support. To his friends. To the church. He's honest that way. No television reporter was interested. No newspaper. I don't have that kind of courage. Don't know if I ever will."

"Your love for King is like gold," Skip mused emotionally. "It's huge." He shrugged. He brushed a tear from his cheek. He leaned over and smooched Sam on his cheek.

"It is huge," King volunteered from the shadows. He knew Skip was wondering about Barry's cock. "It's huge."

Barry grinned at Skip.

Sam, seeing what an ass Skip could be, was obviously embarrassed. He smiled apologetically.

"Fact is, I had something I wanted to ask King to do."

Barry put his arm around King.

"King can do anything he sets his mind to."

Skip looked at Sam wonderingly.

"King is a wonderful writer. I want him to help me draft our human rights correspondence. For Colorado's new initiative."

"We have people who do that." Skip sniffed. "Legal minds. Scholars."

"King wouldn't be the sole author. Neither would you or me. But I want him to put his pen to it."

Skip stood up, completely unnerved. "Boulder is quite the radical nerve center, isn't it? Well, if Sam thinks you're up to it, I'm in complete agreement."

"That's huge of you, Skipper." Barry grinned.

"We're heading for supper. Thought we'd drive up to the Red Lion. Would you care to join us?" Sam asked. "We can get off the subject of politics and talk about sports."

Barry stretched. He flexed his arms. King thought Skip would have a heart attack when he saw his muscles bulge. He drew King close.

"Fellas, I would, but tonight, if it's okay with King, I thought we'd have dinner alone and hit the hay early. Fact is, I can't keep my hands off him. And I don't want to share him for a minute. But I'll leave it up to King."

They waited for King's answer.

"Jen's home alone, tonight. We should get back."

Sam and Skip drifted away. Sam took him over to introduce him formally to Theo. When they left, Theo didn't even say good-bye.

Barry and King walked back to the apartment, huddled into each other as they treaded the path along Boulder Creek. Barry fell silent. Skip's assumption that because he'd come to a gay coffee house he was ready to come out to the press had unnerved him.

"We haven't talked about the summer," Barry said. "Or the fall."

"I was hoping to avoid it as long as I could."

"You always wanted to go to California."

"I already did. Remember?"

"That was with Lex."

"Florida isn't so different from California. We have orange trees, too."

"I don't want to talk about this now."

Tiny buds were forming in the dead branches of the cottonwoods lining Boulder Creek. Spring was just around the corner. King kept walking. Barry fell back several paces. King turned back to face him. Barry was so tall he could hang from the lower branches of his favorite cottonwood tree.

"We should have gone to dinner with them."

"Why?"

"It shouldn't be just me and you against the world. We should make friends. As a couple." King choked on the word couple. Deep down, he was afraid Barry would come to his senses. Wake up. All he had to do was fake it for ten more years, if he made first-string. Maybe fifteen, if his knees held up.

"That guy was a dick."

"Sam's okay."

"You and Sam were involved." He pulled himself up into the tree and hung there.

"Yeah."

"I could tell." He dropped to the ground with a thud.

"Did it make you jealous?"

"Do you want me to be jealous?"

"I want you to be comfortable in your skin."

"I want the same for you."

King was relieved. No fighting tonight. King knew what was on Barry's mind. "I don't expect you to give up Florida," King told him. "Without Holly, you lost your Plan B. Or maybe I'm it."

King hurt him with this remark and felt bad.

"I can't come out to the world and play NFL football, King. As it is, breaking up with Holly was very risky right now. The scouts had already interviewed her—they interview the girlfriend, the family, the minister. All as a test of stability. She could call the scout. Start rumors. Everything gets weighed before they make a final decision. Millions of dollars are riding on it."

"I know."

"There'll be appearances to keep up. That would put stress on us."

King knew what he was talking about. He'd need to find a girl-friend. A beard. He casually wondered aloud if Jen would cooperate. He laughed.

"I don't want to talk about this anymore. But, King?"

"Yeah."

"It may not seem like it, but it doesn't mean more to me than you, if that's what you're thinking. This is all so new."

"How can something you've worked toward on this scale not be the most important thing in the world for you?"

"I explained that to you at the IHOP. It all came easy. I just did what I was told."

"I haven't done anything I was told."

"I'll tell you what to do, then."

"What?"

"For starters, come and give old Barry a kiss. Tell me that you love me."

"I love you." King moved through the cottonwoods.

"I love you, too, King."

Chapter Sixteen

Barry hesitated at King's door. The stress of the entire evening was visible in his eyes. King reflected that he had never seen Barry look depressed or truly anxious before they started seeing each other. He often saw the same look in Lex's eyes. Barry had been light-spirited all of his life. Was King ruining his future? Should he back away, give Barry his privacy back? He'd been so happy roaming the bathhouse that night. Now, after these weeks with King, he'd broken his engagement, ruined his reputation, and put all his plans in jeopardy. King doubted if he was worth all that, but he knew better than to ask.

"Maybe you should go home. Get some rest." King studied his boots. "We've had some night, huh?"

Barry smiled down at him. "I like just us," he admitted. "Any more is a crowd." He kissed the top of King's head.

"I agree, but it won't always be practical."

"I suppose not. You sure I can't come in?"

King paused. "Tomorrow's Saturday. I have to be at work by seven. I'd wake you. You could sleep in at your place."

"Sleeping in sounds good, I admit."

King didn't respond.

"I'll stay if you want me to." He chucked King's chin.

"No." King brightened, wanting to make it easier for Barry to go home. "How are we going to stand six months apart if we can't handle one night?"

"Seems unfair that we have to plan for that. I guess that's what your friends at the coffee house are trying to change."

King smiled up at him. It was honest of him to admit.

"Don't think I believe my career is more worth protecting than anybody else's."

"Just kiss me good night. Meet me at the switchboard at three?"

"I'll call you when I wake up to say good morning." Barry held his face tenderly and kissed him deeply. "What if I get lonely and want to come back?"

King shook his head. Barry grinned and turned up the dark stairwell.

"I'll leave the door unlocked," King called after him. "Let yourself in."

But the wind came up and carried the sentiment off in the wrong direction.

King woke up to flashing white lights, everything white and mirrored. His veins were stinging, and floating above him was a clear plastic pouch, filled with plasma. He lay facedown and hanging over a gurney. He tried to raise his head, but he felt nauseous and laid it down again. He began to revive and he could hear voices. A man's voice urging him to wake up.

"Where am I?" he murmured.

"You're in Boulder Community Hospital. You're in a recovery room. You've just had an operation."

"I feel sick. I'm gonna throw up."

"You can't throw up. You'll pop your stitches."

"Who are you?"

"I'm a nurse. I'm also a friend of Sam's."

Sam's friend from the hospital. The night Tim died.

"Why did I have an operation?"

He knelt down close to King's ear. "Your rectal wall got torn. You've lost a lot of blood." He fiddled with a bag of plasma. "You're damn lucky they found you."

"I don't understand." King tried to wake up.

"Baby, I don't know how else to tell you this, but somebody was fucking you so hard they tore your rectum, you started hemorrhaging, and they left you to bleed to death. Your girlfriend found you, the pregnant one. She's out in the waiting room with Theo and Sam."

King passed out.

*   *   *

In the following hours King was transferred to a private room. After the orderlies left, Sam, Theo, and Jen assembled.

Jen couldn't look at him. She'd been crying. Theo's face was grave, Sam's very sad and filled with concern.

"Jen found you," Theo said. "You were unconscious. With all the blood, she thought you'd been murdered. I heard her screaming."

"Do my mom and dad know?"

"We called your brother," Jen volunteered. "We had to. You'd lost so much blood."

"We left it up to him to tell them," Theo added. "We laid it on him, which wasn't really fair. We thought that's what you'd want."

"You nearly died, King." Sam said ominously. He sat in a chair near King's bed and patted his hand. Then he kissed the top of King's head. "The important thing is you're still alive. And you'll be okay. It was the loss of blood."

"Do my parents *know* how this happened?"

"That's a discussion for later."

King had his answer. He tried to rise up. Sam and Theo leapt to restrain him. Gently they pushed him back down. Jen started crying harder.

"What is it? What's wrong? Something else is wrong."

They looked at each other.

"It's a big mess, King," Sam said. He took a deep breath. "Your brother is with your mom. We told him we'd stay with you. Be here when you woke up. Your dad was killed this morning in an automobile accident. It was snowing and he lost control of the car near Rocky Flats."

A sound came from King's throat he didn't think he'd ever heard before. He had to be dreaming. This couldn't be true. He wanted to shake Barry awake to comfort him. To rock all of this away. Where was Barry? Why were they all in his room?

"King. Do you understand what we're telling you?"

"He was coming here?"

"Your brother called him this morning. He didn't know he'd been drinking," Jen whispered. "We never should have called him, but they warned us you might not make it."

"Did my dad *know* what happened to me?"

They didn't answer.

"Does my mom know?" King found Jen's eyes. "The baby okay?"

"She's fine, King," Jen whispered. "She's fine."

"Can I talk to Jen alone?"

Theo and Sam filed out.

"It was all my fault. Everything has been my fault up to now."

"King, I got a call from the switchboard. You hadn't shown up. I went over to see if you'd overslept. The curtain was closed. When I knocked, Barry started yelling from inside. I opened your door and came in. Barry was trying to stop the bleeding. You weren't conscious. He was covered in your blood. He called the ambulance. He was so distraught. He was sobbing. We both were sobbing. We thought you were dying. We didn't know how to stop it. We were lucky the ambulance came as fast as it did. When we heard sirens, I asked him if he wanted to leave. There was nothing more he could do."

Jen hesitated. Her face was wretched with grief. "Was that wrong of me, King? Do you forgive me? I know he wouldn't have left unless I gave him the opening. He wanted to stay. I was thinking so fast. I thought it would be better if they found me with you. You know, a girl. Pregnant. Pretending I didn't know how it happened. With Barry being famous—I was thinking of you, too. And your family."

"Did you know how it happened?"

"I've been around, King." She waited, wringing her hands. "The police want to talk to you."

"Do they know about me and Barry?"

"I told them he was spending the night with me. From their point of view, you were left for dead. There was blood all over your apartment. There were bloody footprints in the snow."

"Where is he?"

"The police are talking to him. Because he made the call."

King fell silent. The painkillers were scrambling his brain. This couldn't truly be happening.

"I have to fix this. It wasn't Barry."

"I don't think you can, sweetie. The cops think you were raped. You have a bloody lip. Bruises all over your body." Jen began to cry, but collected herself. She was clearly outraged by the act. "Consistent of a forcible rape. That's what it looked like. I wouldn't have let him off the hook if I'd known the extent of your injuries. I heard you tell him you'd leave the door unlocked. Why did it get so out of hand? So violent? If it wasn't Barry, then who was it?"

"He went a little crazy."

"Who?"

"Don't you see?"

"No. I don't. Explain what you're talking about!"

"Maybe for a minute, in his mind, he thought he was fucking the devil."

"That's crazy. You aren't evil, King!"

"Oh no? Then how do you explain everything that just happened? My poor dad," he ruminated. "How can I ever face my mother?"

"She doesn't know the specifics. We have to call her, now that you're out of danger. She's frantic."

"She'll hate me till the day I die."

"I know your mom. You're wrong."

SPRING

Chapter Seventeen

When King was browsing in the religious studies section of the Boulder Bookstore, he was surprised to encounter Allen Ginsberg sitting on a stool, musing over an anthology of Zen poets. Lost in his thoughts, Ginsberg didn't notice King at first, but eventually glanced up just as King was about to leave the section.

"You."

King turned.

"Me," he said simply.

"The young writer. I forget. Prose or poetry."

"Prose."

"Oh. A shame."

King smiled.

"I've forgotten your name. It's unusual, I do remember that. It's a boastful name, a self-aggrandizing name. Not your fault at all, I'm sure. A parental blunder. They must have known that much would be expected of someone with a name like yours. But I still can't remember it. Is it biblical? Joseph? Job? Harrod? Lot? Not Judas. They wouldn't have done that to you. What is it again?"

"King," he replied. "King James."

"King," Ginsberg repeated. "You're Robert and Maddie's friend."

"I'm a student of Dr. Sloan," King replied.

"And no fan of Robert's."

King didn't respond, so Ginsberg pushed forward. "What are you looking for?"

King knew, but he didn't want to tell him. He was here, looking for options. A new path. A new way to think. Something to fill the void he felt within. To assuage grief.

"I've read every book in this section. I could probably help you if you'd tell me more what you had in mind." King studied Ginsberg with fascination. An energy field seemed to emanate from him. A true aura. King felt at once peaceful and electrified. At the same time, he was too tired to be messed with today. Even by a great mind.

"I don't think what I need is available anywhere in this store."

"What is that you're missing?" Ginsberg asked, blinking behind his round wire-framed glasses.

"Bad things have happened," King told him.

"And you blame yourself."

"Yes."

"Would you like to come home with me for tea? It's a few blocks away. I think you'd find it a welcoming atmosphere."

"I don't know anything about your poetry. Or your religion."

"Oh, a virgin," said Ginsberg. "But Buddhism isn't a religion. Its a philosophy."

"I'm not a virgin," said King flatly.

"But you find yourself curious."

"I need a God I can trust."

"I see, I see. We often cry out for God when we find ourselves hurting." Ginsberg stood up. He carefully replaced the book he was reading. "Do you like the store? I'm very proud of it. Very happy Boulder had made space for so many innovative and beautiful books."

King hesitated.

"I don't intend to proselytize or seduce you." Ginsberg smiled at King. "Come with me. Come now."

And King followed after him, Ginsberg smiling and patting hands when customers recognized him as they climbed the stairs to the street level of the bookstore. Outside, tiny buds were forming on the cottonwood trees of the Pearl Street Mall. Ginsberg walked quickly, and King noticed the tender buds of the crocuses poking through the hard winter soil.

They moved swiftly down Pine Street, Ginsberg's sonorous voice commenting on the advent of spring, the beauty of Boulder, and the coming visits of friends from San Francisco and New York. At last,

Ginsberg mounted steps to a pretty Victorian brick house. As they entered, a small statue of Buddha, a modest vase of flowers, and an incense holder with burning incense coiling up through the air comprised a humble entry-hall shrine.

The hallway ran past the ascending oak staircase into the kitchen at the back of the house. Large, beveled glass windows opened out onto the winter-barren backyard. The room was cheerful, with a large round oak table in the center and four padded chairs pushed haphazardly around it. Ginsberg filled a teakettle with water and placed it on the back burner of a gas stove. King hung back, unsure what was expected of him.

Today was his second day out of the hospital. He'd lingered in his dark studio behind closed curtains all day yesterday. Jen mentioned that she planned to study all day. Theo, too, was hanging around planning the BGLF summer calendar. They were both gently letting King know they were nearby.

This morning King decided it was ridiculous to waste a nice day by hiding in his dark room. He wasn't scheduled to work until this Sunday. The ladies at the switchboard had sent flowers. They knew something bad had happened, but Arlene, in her usual tactful way, sent King a note with the flowers telling King to call her whenever he wanted to come back to work. They were very sorry to hear about the death of his dad.

Unbelievably, King had managed to write yesterday. In longhand, on narrow-lined legal pads, King worked on his journal. It was stream of consciousness, a list, really, of happy memories, as far back as he could recall. Whatever came into his mind he wrote down. Camping with his dad and Neil at Kelsey Creek. Singing the lead in a ninth-grade rendition of Gilbert and Sullivan's *Trial by Jury*. The fireplace in his grandmother's Minnesota farmhouse kitchen. His junior prom, when he was class president.

He wrote solidly for hours, not correcting, not even punctuating properly. He'd need the list for later, he knew. It would be dog-eared by the time King stopped needing to refer to it. He'd keep it bedside, for late at night when he couldn't sleep. When King's hand started cramping, seven hours later, he had over fifty pages of good memories.

That stood for something, didn't it? Fifty pages.

Ginsberg offered King a selection of Celestial Seasoning teas. King picked Sleepy Time, thinking of that first night with Sam. Ginsberg poked through a disorganized pantry and found a package of cookies, placing them on a chipped plate.

"You're so sad," he noted. "I'm guessing something very serious has happened, something of the unfixable variety, but I've observed that every time I've seen you, the same sadness has been evident. This dysthymia is organic to your spirit, regardless of the events of your life. I've known people like you. Have you ever tried to meditate?"

"TM," King told him. "I didn't keep it up."

When King was a freshman in college, Neil had paid for lessons in Transcendental Meditation. Neil himself had recently completed the course. He meditated twice a day, Neil reported to King. Fifteen minutes in the morning. The same, early evening. His instructor had given Neil a mantra, a word to meditate on. The mantra must be kept secret at all costs, at risk to one's own central nervous system. Transcendental Meditation was not a religion. It was a scientific fact that it slowed the heart rate. The alpha state, normally to be found only in deep sleep, could be obtained while in a conscious state of meditation.

King attended his first orientation meeting with a high amount of skepticism. The UMC meeting room was packed. After the first hour, King was hooked. He'd never sat with a hundred silent human beings before. Concerted silence. King came back to the next session and quickly paid Neil's hundred dollars.

After filling out an extensive questionnaire, King was assigned a teacher, a slightly balding and pale man named Del. Many teachers had left diverse careers to follow the teaching of Maharishi Mahesh Yogi. The Maharishi had been visited by famous personalities such as Mia Farrow and the Beetles. Transcendental Meditation was a tool. It discouraged the use of drugs and alcohol. It encouraged exercise and a healthy diet. It could cure all kinds of ills if one were disciplined in its practices. Advanced students could experience untold ecstasy, including the ability to float. A film about the Maharishi and TM was shown to King and his fellow students. The floating looked more to King like hopping, but he kept his opinions to himself.

For his third session, King was asked to bring flowers, a piece of fruit, and a white handkerchief. He arrived punctually, and Del ushered him into a small room with a table adorned with a white tablecloth, candles, and a photograph of the Maharishi. King was asked to sit with his feet flat on the floor, his back straight and his hands on each knee.

Did he feel comfortable, relaxed?

"Yes."

"I want you to sit quietly with your eyes closed. After a few moments I'm going to assign you your mantra. It was selected especially for you after careful evaluation of your questionnaire. It isn't unique, but it's unlikely that anyone you know could have the same one. It is imperative that you repeat it only as loud as necessary for me to hear. I need to be certain that you've heard it correctly. After I'm convinced, you'll say it quietly several more times. After that, you'll only repeat it in your mind. You should never speak it aloud again or write it down. Do you understand?"

"Yes."

"Close your eyes, King." And King did. After several peaceful moments, Del gave King his mantra. It was one syllable.

"Repeat it softly."

King whispered the word, a commonly used participle which King needn't worry about forgetting.

"One more time, and then I want you to repeat it over and over again in your head. It may disappear. Don't control your thoughts. Allow it to permeate your inner consciousness. I think eighteen minutes would be an optimal amount of time for you to meditate. When I say 'time,' I'd like you to stop meditating, but sit quietly for a moment or so. Repeat it again, and this time, I won't interrupt you."

And King did as he was told. The word quickly retracted inside his brain, and the phenomenon felt like a spinning top, whirling and whirling deeper inside his consciousness. There was no cessation of his senses. He could smell the incense. The flowers. The burning candle wax. He could hear his own heart beating. Outside in the corridor, he could hear the deeply muffled sound of voices. He was completely awake, but stilled in a way he'd never experienced before.

Thoughts catapulted through his mind. His head began to bob slightly. King remembered not to be dismayed or distracted by it. It only meant his body was shunting off pent-up anxiety. Whatever recognizable thoughts came up were probably indicative of what might be truly troubling to him. He was not to edit or try to control his thoughts. Some practitioners never experienced the head bobbing. Some reported more pronounced motion than others.

When Del told him it was time to stop, King sat quietly for a minute or more.

He opened his eyes. Del smiled.

"The fruit is for you to eat. Wrap the peels in the handkerchief. Take a moment. You can let yourself out when you're finished." Del stood and left King alone with the shrine to the Maharishi.

Several months later, King volunteered for an EKG in a biopsychology demonstration to measure his brain waves. His professor gladly agreed when learning that King practiced TM. No one in the class had previously experienced alpha waves in a conscious state. When King got hooked up, he closed his eyes, silently repeated his mantra, and within a minute, the monitor reported the alpha state.

After King finished his tea, Ginsberg said, "I want you to sit opposite me on the mat in the sunroom."

King complied. The walls were covered with photographs taken by Ginsberg of his old friends. Timothy Leary, Jack Kerouac, Diane DiPrima. Even a young Robert, wearing beads, with flowers in his hair.

"He was very beautiful." Ginsberg read his thoughts. "You don't approve of him."

"No," King admitted.

"Buddha left his wife and family to find enlightenment. Sometimes the search for peace can seem very selfish."

"I think Robert's a long way away from peace," King said.

"So are you." Ginsberg sat cross-legged on the mat. He patted the mat opposite him for King to sit on.

King gamely tried to emulate Ginsberg's lotus position. The tendons in his legs were tight. He toppled forward against Ginsberg's upper torso. Ginsberg caught him, holding him gently.

King didn't pull away. Ginsberg cradled King's head in the crook of his shoulder. He put his arms around him, and for an hour, allowed King to rest in the uncompromised safety of his lotus embrace.

The following day, King was asked if he could be questioned by the investigating officer of the Boulder Police Department about the events preceding his visit to the emergency room. They needed to satisfy themselves, for his sake as much as anything, that he wasn't protecting anyone out of fear for his own safety. King appeared at the Boulder Police Department thirty minutes later.

The investigating officer was a woman, Detective Little, and after showing him to a small interrogating room, she offered him a coffee, which he accepted.

"This is obviously delicate, and embarrassing for me, too," she began. "What I need to determine is if you were purposely injured, as someone has charged."

"Who?"

"I can't tell you. I'm sorry. The party thinks you're protecting someone."

Theo, King surmised. "I think I know who you're talking about. He's jealous."

"A spurned lover?"

"A friend."

"What happened that night?"

"I don't remember anything more than waking up to my friend Jen screaming. Then I passed out, and next thing I recall, I was being revived in the recovery room of the hospital. The nurse told me what he guessed had happened. I think you know what that was."

"Yes. Who were you with?"

"I don't remember."

"Why don't you remember?"

"Maybe I'm too distressed over my dad."

"Could this injury have been self-inflicted?" The detective studied King. He could tell he was gay.

"It could have been. I have a history of depression and suicide ideation."

"Big word, ideation." She blinked. "Trouble is, we couldn't find a tool or an instrument you may have used. You lost a lot of blood. You could have died."

"But I didn't."

She leaned closer to him. "I'm going to break all the rules here, son. I'm going to confide in you, and then you can go home. I think you were with someone and things got carried away. Your doctor says you'll be fine, good as new. Your own physiology contributed to the phenomenon. Fact is, we think we know who you were with. We know why you don't want to tell us yourself. And here's the part that's confidential, if you can agree, as a gentleman, not to repeat what I'm about to tell you."

"Sure," King shrugged. He liked her.

"My fellow officers don't want you to name the guy because of who he is. This is a university town, after all. They were opposed to me calling you in, but I insisted, only for your safety. See to them, you're a throwaway."

"Throwaway?"

"Inconvenient. What I want to say is, you aren't a throwaway to me. Are you hearing me?"

"Yes," King nodded.

"Are you getting help?"

He knew what she meant.

"I have my friends. My brother."

"Then I don't have to worry about you. This guy won't come after you."

"I highly doubt that, ma'am." King looked her dead in the eye. "Given the results."

"I'm sorry about your dad."

"Thank you. Can I go now?"

The Holy Trinity appeared to King in the form of Sam, Theo, and Jen assembling on his front porch later that evening. It appeared that they seemed to think an intervention was in order. For one thing, although fully recovered, the general consensus seemed to be that King had lost too much weight, his coloring was pale, and his mood, sad and remote.

"There's more to life than a steady boyfriend," Theo offered. Theo's reaction to King's incident at first annoyed, then touched King. Jen told King privately that the idea that King had nearly died on the opposite side of an eight-inch wall from Theo had especially unnerved him. Theo was a bit of a mother hen. He liked keeping tabs on his chicks.

"He thinks he caused you to rebound from him to Barry."

"He thinks too highly about his effect on me."

"Let him help," Jen chided him. "We think we need to remind you that Boulder, being Boulder, is loaded with spiritual options other than mainstream religion."

"What makes you think I *need* spiritual options?"

"King." She sighed. "I'm a psychology major with six hours of religious studies under my belt. It doesn't take C.S. Lewis or Sigmund Freud for me to diagnose that you suffer from a God hole."

"God hole?" he repeated.

"Yes, it's a term I've coined. Some people have a special place in their brain, probably in the hypothalamus, which is highly oriented toward spiritual ecstasy. You need God much in the same way you need food, sleep, and sex. You send out the signal. What I'd like to suggest is that we try other ways for you to communicate with God, paths which don't exclude you for being wantonly homosexual."

"And what have you come up with?"

"Well, I didn't exactly call and ask if they accepted gays, but I thought we should try Sufi dancing. Theo found a group meeting tonight. Sam wants to come, too."

"Sam?"

"I thought you'd like that. Then afterwards we thought we'd all go to Rudi's for dinner."

King blinked and nodded. That night he found himself surrounded by whirling dervishes, a few he recognized from nights at Le Bar. It seemed that no matter what one's eastern religious sect of preference, they all liked tossing down carafes of red wine at the Hotel Boulderado.

Jen, in a mother-earth flowing caftan, danced heartily with the other flower children. Because she was pregnant, she was treated with special deference by her fellow Sufi dancers. One esthete asked her to spend the night. He found it particularly erotic to put his seed in pregnant women.

"That's enough Sufi dancing for tonight," Jen announced, holding up her hand. "I'm hungry. Let's walk over to Tom's Tavern."

The four friends strolled several blocks through Boulder's back streets until they came to Tom's. Jen knew King felt comfortable here. They sat by the window. "Maybe you should become a swami," Jen suggested. "They're very peace-loving."

"I don't want to become a swami. I want to be a writer."

"You need life experience for that," Theo offered.

"I think King's had enough life experience for ten writers," Sam volunteered.

"King's writing a short story about me," Jen crowed.

"I'd like to read it after you're finished." Sam smiled.

"I can't finish till after the baby's born."

"Having a baby isn't the end of my story," Jen interjected.

The waitress came. Another New York expatriate in batik with a jewel in her nose. They ordered an assortment of appetizers. The conversation was genial and focused mostly on King.

"Why not try Naropa if you want to write?"

"Why not just write?"

King thought of Robert and shuddered.

"You told me Allen Ginsberg offered to read your writing."

"I don't really understand his writing," King admitted. "So I doubt he'd be any fan of mine."

Chapter Eighteen

An excerpt of a short-short story King wrote about his mother:

KARL

She's upstairs, sitting in the dark, her silhouette blocking the moonlight from the dining room window. Her hair is silver in the light. Her cigarette glows in the dark, an orange ember, and occasionally she takes a puff, throwing her head back and blowing the smoke in the air. Then she flicks the ashes into the ceramic ashtray Karl made her as a scout.

The house is silent, dark, and she sits alone, thinking. Occasionally she sighs, or rocks silently, drawing the quilted bathrobe around her shoulders. The heater begins to hum, the warm air blasting from the furnace. She hears it click on, somewhere in the bowels of the house, and waits for heat to fill the room.

She can't sleep. She knows why, but has not consciously recognized the reason. It hides beneath her heart, this knowledge, and she struggles to disbelieve, to maintain the illusion, reject the truth. All she wants is for everybody to be happy, she thinks. She smokes her cigarette and contemplates this in the dark.

It was Neil who saw them through. For as much as they had in common, Neil and King had not been historically very close. Now everything was different. He spent most of the month of March driving back and forth between downtown Denver to King's apartment, then traversing the foothill highway to Golden and Green Mountain, frantic to reassure them that as a family they still loved each other. In her own way, Jen was doing the same thing, distracting his mother with details about her pregnancy, deluging her with questions she already knew the answers to.

They didn't have a funeral service. King's parents were virtually friendless at that time. Their sons were their lives. But still, King and his mom couldn't bring themselves together to meet face-to-face. It had been nearly a month since his father died.

Jen told King his mother busied herself with paperwork: death certificates, notifying the Social Security Administration, transferring the title of the house into her name, deleting Jim's name from joint bank accounts, adding King's and Neil's.

Neil brought King the bank signature cards. "Here. Sign these."

"Is this in case she dies?"

"Or becomes incapacitated."

"Why's she doing that?"

"Because she *trusts* us, King."

"Well, I don't think I'm needed. As long as you've signed."

"You're needed."

"I just don't see why—"

"Sign the *goddamned* card, King!" Neil towered imperiously over King. His face was etched with grief. King could see the strain that acting as go-between was having on him. His eyes were often red from crying. His cheeks were drawn. His hand shook as King scrawled his name. King overran the small box allotted and looked up at Neil miserably. Then he started to cry.

With that, Neil fell apart and dropped on top of him while they both rocked in synchronized guilty agony. "You have to see each other," he whispered. "It's killing all of us. You have to see her."

"Does she want to see me?" Neil asked.

"She and I just had this same scene an hour ago. She feels guilty she couldn't bring herself to get to the hospital to see you."

"She feels guilty about *that*? Tell her she doesn't need to worry about it."

"No, you tell her."

And King knew they had to see each other.

* * *

King's mother drove up unannounced to Boulder on one of those crystal clear March days. It had snowed heavily several days before, but the wet streets were clear and steaming from the bright sun. King had worked the morning shift and came home about one. She was sitting on a bench in the park across from his apartment complex and watching for King. She didn't even tell Jen she was coming. King knew she'd seen Jen at least twice since his dad died.

Without seeing her at first, King felt her presence. Although the sun was in his eyes, he noticed a round-shouldered woman in a gray parka and a homemade blue knit cap, her silver hair poking out, sitting on a park bench, smoking a cigarette. She stretched her legs and studied her new snow boots, like a girl in grade school waiting for her bus. King wasn't even certain if she recognized him. She didn't wave or call to him. King guessed she wanted to take him in before he saw her; get a full dose of her youngest son.

King reflected back to the family meeting when he and Neil disclosed their homosexuality. Their mom had been so frustrated, so disgusted with their father, who'd sat stricken and dumb at the head of the table. She was mad because he wouldn't say anything. Neil had been barking statistics at her about homosexuality. King felt so humiliated. So compromised.

And now as King contemplated his little mother as she poignantly studied her new snow boots, he felt resentment toward her. If she hadn't really meant it when she told him Neil and King could tell them anything, why did she have to blow it on something so big?

Now here it was. Another family meeting, only this time without his dad and without Neil. Just them. What if she wanted details? How could King explain what he was doing? Why King needed it to be done?

She'd kicked King out of her house, if only in a moment of desperation. He'd been ostracized by all his friends. He'd dropped out of school. His parents, who'd never fought in his presence all his life, were at each other's throats.

King reasoned that he'd been unable to properly explain to her what Lex meant to him, especially under those circumstances. He'd put everything on the line for him. The deed to the ranch. All the eggs. His firstborn. His seat at the right hand of God. How could he allow Lex to escape him? He tried, but King wouldn't let him. He tried to kill himself over him. Lex had to pay, too. That's why King talked him into getting back together.

King trudged across the street and sat next to his mom.

"How are you feeling, King?"

"Fine. Good as new."

"I'm sorry I didn't come to the hospital."

"Under the circumstances, I'm relieved you didn't. People would have stared at you. I'd have hated that."

Kay hesitated. "If they were staring at you, I should have been there."

"I wasn't alone."

"I know." She drew from her cigarette, huddling into her parka. "I got new snow boots."

"I saw you admiring them from across the street."

They both stared at her feet.

"I wonder if the goddamned winter will ever end," Kay said, searching the darkening sky. "It's nearly April and look at the snow. I hope my bulbs don't freeze. Your father planted them so painstakingly last summer. I hope we'll get his tulips for him."

"Neil says you've gotten your financial affairs in order. Are you worried about money?"

"No. I put all of his life insurance money in our checking account. I never have to worry about money again. If you need anything, let me know."

"Thank you."

"I can't say I'll ever understand what homosexual men need from each other," she said, abruptly changing the subject. "We never talked much about sex in our house. Maybe we should have. When we found out about you and Neil, your father and I just buried our heads in the sand. We could have gone to a therapist. Or a support group."

Jen talking, King thought.

"Your father called me before he left for Boulder that day. He told me what had happened. He asked me if I wanted to go. I said no."

"Mom."

"I'm positive he hadn't had anything to drink yet. I'm sure if I'd agreed to come, he wouldn't have. He didn't have his accident till after noon. He called me at nine-thirty. I'm sure he started drinking after we hung up. He would have beaten the snow if he left right away."

King thought about his dad trudging up Broadway past the capitol building toward his parked van. He'd obviously stopped in at the Tip Top. Here was a man, King figured, who was owed a drink.

"I hope they let him drink for free."

"So do I." She laughed. They paused to gather their thoughts.

"I thought about something the other day that I want to apologize for," King told her. "Remember when I first moved to Boulder? My freshman year?"

"You didn't want your father and me to bring you. You asked Neil instead." Her voice became slightly accusatory, but she checked it.

"Why did you think I didn't want you there?"

"I thought you were ashamed of us. So did your dad."

"You're wrong," King whispered. He was shocked. Why would they think he was ashamed of them?

"Then why?"

"There's a very good chance I might have dropped out. Gone home with you. I couldn't stand the idea of leaving home."

"All kids get homesick."

"I was terrified."

She studied King with interest. "Why?"

"I liked being home. I liked you and Dad. And I remember how you reacted when Neil went to school."

When King was a high school sophomore, his brother left and moved to Greeley to attend the University of Northern Colorado. Secretive and somber, Neil was equal parts his mother and father's son. In an early August week prior to his departure, the entire family drove the sixty miles to Greeley to attend Neil's freshman orientation. The day began in a festive manner. Kay was unusually exuberant, having gone to the trouble of making herself a new blue pantsuit for the occasion. King's father wore work clothes; his dress cowboy boots, dark brown dress pants, a plaid shirt, and a bolo tie.

Neil had gotten very drunk the night before with a few friends, and overslept. When he finally appeared, he was waxy and perspiring, and twice their father had to pull over so he could throw up. This blanketed their mother's buoyancy, but once they got to campus and began touring the various buildings—the library, the dorms, the auditorium and the campus student union—her enthusiasm came back.

Kay had saved for years to send Neil to school, and even if Greeley wasn't Neil's first choice, it was a highly regarded teacher's college, and Neil, who wanted to be an art teacher, was lucky enough to be going there. After all, it beat Vietnam. Neil's draft number had been 83. He surely would have had to go. Enough of the poor kids from high school were already serving or on their way. No special exemption status if parents couldn't afford to send their sons to college.

King remembered being particularly smirky that day, not knowing why, but his father finally told him to knock it off. He'd been doing his best to exacerbate Neil's uneasiness by grinning at him behind his Coke-bottle eyeglasses, teasing him whenever he had the chance and effeminately flapping his way ahead of the family as they moved like cattle from one designated stop to the next.

Their mother's good humor couldn't be contained. She asked questions, laughed heartily at the tour guide's jokes, grabbed Neil excitedly to point out the art supplies in the student bookstore. When they were in junior high Kay had taken a job as a school cook. (To Neil's and King's own great humiliation.) Although she didn't make much money, what she earned was to go toward their college education. They would earn spending money at their respective summer jobs, but she and King's father would bankroll their education, including housing and tuition.

Neil never could have risen to her level of enthusiasm, and on the drive home, her mood changed. Mostly she smoked and stared out the window.

"All the smog from Denver blows to Greeley," King commented. In the rearview mirror, his father shot him a look.

"Shut up, King," Neil murmured. He was reading his mother's body language, her rounding shoulders. King saw it, too.

"Sorry," he grunted.

"I'm sorry it can't be an Ivy League school," King's mother commented.

"It's fine, Mom," Neil reassured her.

She shook her head and took another drag off her cigarette. "I guess it's better than Vietnam." And she didn't speak for the rest of the drive home.

In the days that followed, Kay began to retreat. She took long naps in the afternoon, taking to bed with a cat, a woman's magazine, and a bag of candy from Safeway. She always made dinner, but little more than boxed macaroni and cheese, or hamburgers, or pancakes. If Jim came in at five o'clock, she threw supper on the table minutes later. The family would eat in silence.

Neil began packing, but surreptitiously, hiding his boxes under the stairs in the utility room. He told King he'd leave the stereo because his assigned roommate already had one. They had spoken over the telephone. His name was Sherman Levine, an overweight Jew, by his own admission, from Brooklyn, New York. Kay brightened somewhat at this news, commenting that Neil would be exposed to a fascinating new culture. They didn't know any Jews. Wasn't this going to be fun? When Neil didn't rejoin enthusiastically, she retreated as quickly as she'd effused.

King didn't go with them the day Neil moved. He was confused and emotional and about to become an only child. Neil was to be the first man to leave him. King worked that day instead. When he came home, it was over. Neil was gone and their mother in bed. That night, King heard her crying. She cried for days after that. His father told King not to worry and stay out of her way. This was not unusual behavior for a mother when her firstborn left the nest. She stayed depressed for close to a year.

"You thought it was over Neil moving away?" She shook her head, her eyes bright with mirth. "When you have kids, which I'm not ruling out, you too, will be astounded at their conceit. My mother told me that once, and I didn't understand her, but now I do. Neil was my firstborn. Maybe I overreacted, but I got over it."

"You went to bed for a year."

"So what if I did?" Kay shrugged. "It was overwhelming. I'll tell you a little secret. I love your brother, and I missed him, but that wasn't why I had such a hard time."

"Why, then?"

"I was *jealous*," she spat out. "Jealous out of my mind. I wanted it to be me. I wanted to go to college and never got the chance. Your grandparents had money to send one kid to school, so they sent your uncle because he was a boy and would need to support a family some day. Because I was a girl, my education was expendable, even though I got better grades. I was an 'A' student. He barely passed. I was jealous," she said wonderingly.

And she, King reflected, was unable to explain to him how badly she felt that he was squandering her gift of an education. A four-year free ride to a wonderful university. The dignity a degree would bring. The opportunities. A pass to a new world—something she never had. Something his grandparents never gave her, but gave to her brother. Why the *hell* wasn't King having a good time? So much chaos over *Lex? Lex?*

"He's not worth it," she'd observed.

King reflected that Rod, the fellow who's lap he'd sat on and recited poetry to, had made a similar observation. He'd been jealous of Lex about King. He hadn't thought much of Lex, either. Nor had Barry. After him, Lex had bolted back to the closet with one of his best friends.

"I thought you were gonna die over Neil leaving."

"Is that why you were afraid to move away?"

"Yes."

"I'm sorry, King. I wasn't depressed. I was jealous. All we wanted was for the two of you to go to college and enjoy yourselves. Look how it turned out."

"It hasn't all been bad. I have good friends now. I've gotten good grades. I like myself better, now that I know what I am."

"You're a person, not an object."

"*Who* I am," King corrected himself. "Neil thinks if we have to get used to it, so should you."

"He's right. He told me the same thing." Cars rushed past them down Canyon Avenue. "Do you think it had anything to do with Bobby Farrell?"

King laughed. "What did you think?"

Bobby Farrell was King's best friend in first grade. They were living in a small Wyoming town near Yellowstone. King's father was the editor of the newspaper. Bobby was a few months younger than King, and when he moved into the neighborhood, taught the local kids a few tricks.

"Your father and I never discussed it."

Bobby taught King how to play nasty. He liked to take off his clothes. The second he and King were alone, they'd strip. They'd touch each other. They'd press bottoms together. They lay on top of each other. Soon all the neighborhood boys were caught up in it. It was never King's idea, but he always participated. All the parents were scandalized. If they got caught, Bobby'd get spanked by his father. King's parents would never lay a hand on him.

"Jen thinks he was probably being molested," Kay said after a minute. "He was acting out what he was being taught. Joe Farrell was a very strange man."

"No! You've talked to *Jen* about this?"

"I've talked to Jen about everything. I love that girl, King. She's the best gift you ever gave me. I couldn't have survived the last two months without her. Not that Neil hasn't been wonderful." She took a drag off her cigarette. "And don't start feeling guilty. You've had more than your fair share to worry about."

As a prepubescent kid, King used to fantasize about Joe Farrell. He was a big man, handsome, with a Southern drawl. King used to envy Bobby the spankings. At night, to go to sleep, King would fantasize getting spanked by Joe.

"Did he molest you, King?"

King shook his head, certain he hadn't.

"Did *anyone* molest you?"

"No. No one."

They sat quietly. They gave up trying to find reasons why King was gay.

Later they hugged each other. King's mom never mentioned his condition or his operation after hearing he was okay. If she blamed King because his dad came rushing to Boulder on that snowy day, she never said anything, because King could counter that he possibly stopped going to meetings because she was jealous.

They were both to blame. And not. They needed each other more than ever. Before she left, Kay asked one thing.

"Do you think you could lie low for awhile, King? Let the others carry the torch for awhile? I think you've done your fair share for the cause. I think you've given enough."

As he watched her steer her little Dodge into the snowy street, King had to admit she had a point.

Everyone assumed King felt guilty about the death of his father. Or embarrassed about his own circumstances. In fact, King felt quite free from those feelings. He had Jen to thank for that. They both needed someone to cling to as her pregnancy neared its term. Kay drove up at least once a week and took her to lunch.

She always came on days she knew King was working, or had a class. She'd hang around till he came home, but King knew she needed time with Jen alone. She was grateful he was intuitive enough to let it happen.

Kay finished the baby's afghan. It was beautiful, the lightest green and white acrylic yarn.

"I hate pink or blue baby blankets," Jen exclaimed when she saw it. "This reminds me of spring."

Kay never came without a baby gift. A little dress. Tiny shoes. A cup and spoon. A macramé mobile. She and Jen would wait for King to arrive and the three of them might walk across the street to the park, and sit on a sunny bench betting when the crocuses might bloom.

Kay always left before sunset. She called when she got home.

King had a question waiting for her.

"No one else was involved in Dad's accident. Do you think he did it on purpose?" The tone in his voice was so sobering she knew she couldn't evade him with her usual tactics.

"I've wondered the same thing. He didn't spin out. There weren't skid marks. The car just leapt off the road."

"So you think he did?"

"Yes, but not at that moment. I think he died wanting to save you. He made the choice to kill himself earlier that morning. When he chose to drink. If he hadn't succeeded that day, it would have been another. Illness, character flaw, I could care less anymore. You know what I did when he called and told me?"

"What?"

"I shoveled the walk. Remember, you come from me, too, King. There are other ways to handle life's blows."

King fell silent as he contemplated her words. It was true. He did have options.

"You know what worries me?" she asked. "It's the strangest thing. I worry that nobody knows where I am, sometimes. That I'm not expected anywhere. I could come home, way past dark and nobody would bat an eye."

"That's how I felt when I moved to college."

"Guess I never grew up. I moved from my mother's house into your father's house."

"It was your house, too."

"I know that." She puffed on her cigarette. "I'm saying I never lived alone. I feel guilty as hell for saying this, but sometimes I like it."

"Don't feel guilty."

"Don't think I'm asking to be forgiven for it if I do. That's the good thing about living alone, which you already know. You think you can do whatever you want."

Chapter Nineteen

Neil invited King down to meet his new boyfriend, the one from California. Don and Greg were clearly furious that Neil had snatched him from their clutches. After all, Neil was only a renter, an attic rat. Since the little altercation about King, Greg and Neil barely spoke. If Don wondered why, he let it go.

They hadn't seen King since his dad's accident. Or King's. When Don opened the door, King knew he knew the details. He was formal with King, but kind.

"They're upstairs in the library."

Library. It was a converted bedroom on the second floor. It maybe had five novels and an ancient set of encyclopedias in the bookcases flanking the fireplace. The other shelves were reserved for Waterford crystal and Baccarat animals. They were such pretentious bastards.

Greg, who had always lit with sexual desire whenever he saw King, averted his eyes, now saw him as damaged goods. King laughed when he saw his reaction. King had developed a pretty aggressive edge since his dad's death. He wasn't taking shit from anybody. Neil once told King that Greg loved to fuck virgins. King guessed he was pretty happy things hadn't worked out with him. King, bloody and half dead upstairs, with Don coming home expecting his dinner.

King had completely recovered. The proctologist explained that he probably had a thrombosed rectal vein and his partner had simply "traumatized" it. A hard stool might have done the same damage. He explained quite clinically that King's kind of operation was routine in prison hospitals, though such a great loss of blood was quite rare. Had his friends not acted quickly, King probably would have bled to death. He examined King thoroughly and King was free to engage in anal intercourse should he again be so inclined.

Neil was sitting on the sofa, leaning into Vince, the tannest man King ever saw. He was big, taller than Neil, with white teeth and black hair, slightly graying at the temples. He wore tight jeans, a Polo shirt, and boat shoes. He looked like he'd just stepped off a yacht.

He never stopped smiling. He was very masculine, powerful-looking, easily fifteen years older than Neil. He had a casually disarming manner. He was charming.

"Neil's told me all about you. I'm sorry about your dad."

"Yeah," grumbled Don and Greg simultaneously.

"Thanks," King said. Neil and King didn't really acknowledge each other. They didn't need to. They were both inside each other's heads. Neil wanted to get out of Colorado as fast as he could. King intended to follow him as soon as he graduated and Jen had her baby. Their mother would be all right, they decided. Neil predicted she'd stand at the door, cry while they loaded up their cars, and the second they were gone she'd turn up her stereo and have Bloody Marys on the deck with her block mates.

She, too, deserved to be free to heal.

Vince invited them all out to dinner. He doted on Neil. He asked King if he'd ever been to Laguna Beach.

"I've only been to Northern California."

"It's the California Riviera. I have a gorgeous house in the hills overlooking the Pacific Ocean."

"Really gorgeous," Don and Greg chimed in, bitter as hell.

"It has a guest cabana by the pool. I don't have to tell you it's yours to use as long as you like, if you'll move to California and keep your brother company. When you get set up your mother can come, and we'll all be one big happy family."

King noticed how much he liked to drink. Neil was drinking heavily, too, something he swore he'd never do. Since their dad died, Neil called King every day. He'd ask how the writing was coming along, how Jen was feeling. He'd talk about Vince. He'd come to the conclusion King might be right. Maybe a monogamous marriage would be okay after all. Vince had made his wishes clear from the very first day. He was looking for a committed mate.

*   *   *

The next day, King was sitting at his kitchen table, writing the monthly Boulder Gay Liberation Newsletter. Theo thought it would be good therapy.

"You're out and you aren't going back in."

King had laughed. He liked writing the newsletter. He only focused on positive local and national events. When Jen came in, he was scanning the national gay newspapers for inspiration. King gazed up at her.

"I have something to tell you," Jen advised him. "Might be difficult."

"How bad can it really be?" he asked her mildly. "Given everything. Given all that's happened so far."

"Holly and Barry eloped last weekend."

"Oh." King kept reading.

"Someone heard it on the radio."

King kept reading.

"I wanted to be the one to tell you."

He glanced up. "What reaction are you looking for from me?"

"I thought you'd be upset."

"I'm not. He's better off with her."

"I know Holly, King. That's simply not true. She's mean and she's not very bright."

"You don't believe me about Barry. You're testing me. Trying to make me blow his cover."

"King!" She stood up, pretending she was offended. "If you told me it wasn't Barry's fault, that's good enough for me."

"Apparently not, so I'll tell you one more time. He went home. We'd had a heavy night."

"Then who was it?

"I'll never tell you."

"Was it consensual?"

King didn't answer.

"Why should the guy get off unscathed!" Jen railed, betraying herself.

"He isn't," King replied softly. "Besides, how do you know it was a guy?" He smirked at her.

"Then why did you and Barry break up?"

"I insisted. Barry cared for me. Now he's in prison. He has it worse than me."

"How can you say that?"

"He's married Holly. They're moving to Florida. He can never come out. He can never make one false move. He's famous. He can never be himself."

"At least you gave him that. Do you wish he'd call?"

"Yes. I want him to know I don't blame him for the choice he had to make."

"By *denying* you?"

"He risked losing everything he worked for. Life can't always be the way things ought to be. In a better world, he wouldn't have to make that choice."

"Do you miss him?"

"I miss all of them."

All King knew was that when men left him, he died a little.

When King grieved his father, it was difficult not to confuse him with Sam, Matthew, Theo, and Barry. Even Lex. He wasn't ready to talk about that one yet. He just missed them all, and couldn't separate grieving the loss of his dad and grieving the loss of them.

The nurse at the hospital had a big mouth, unless Theo or Sam said anything, but everybody knew what really happened. Even Sally knew, which of course meant she placed King with Barry. Luckily, the story was so intense nobody really liked repeating it.

When it came right down to it, King thought, as far as being gay went, wasn't it the ass-fucking that freaked everybody out? Straight men liked blow jobs. They could even justify giving a blow job to some guy if they were drunk at the time. It was the ass-fucking that blew everything out of context. Out of context, King had to admit, it sounded pretty disgusting.

King's father died from gay sex by proxy. Unheard of. Whoever died of gay sex? King had been surprised to hear he was drinking.

The sound of the typewriter overtook the timbre of sorrow in the room. The tapping of the keys invigorated King as he watched letters and words and sentences fill the page. A feeling of renewal overtook him. He would learn from this event the power that writing had to allow him to escape. Writing, from that moment forward, would be like a fast car escaping the grim realities of a small town. It was the only true solace he had, and he was both unlucky and lucky to benefit from that wisdom at such a tender age. It might guarantee him a lonely life.

Sam, too, had been particularly attentive to King during these days. King knew that Sam and Skip suffered tension in their relationship because of King. When King worked the overnight shift at the switchboard, Sam occasionally arrived unannounced, on the pretext of wanting to make a free long-distance call, but sitting with King until the incoming calls stopped, and King felt it was quiet enough to fall asleep. Sometimes they wouldn't talk at all, sitting quietly while King worked on his stories and Sam wrote his master's thesis. Other nights, Sam talked politics. He was fascinated by the ongoing political strides minorities seemed to be making across the country. Visibility was high for all human rights organizations. Jimmy Carter, a little known Georgia governor, was rapidly moving up in the polls as a potential Democratic candidate for president.

One night, Sam asked King how he'd feel about being on a small panel to speak to a Sociology 101 class the following week. The class, Sam warned, was large. It met in the university theater. There were over a hundred students in the class.

"You think you're ready?" Sam wondered.

"My mom asked me to lie low for awhile," King said.

"If you think you should, I understand."

"Who else is on the panel?"

"Me. Rod. Deborah. You know her, Jen's friend."

"Deborah's so shy. What about Theo?"

"Theo can't, because he has a midterm."

"What would we have to do?"

"Represent the Boulder Gay Liberation Front. The focus is on maintaining visibility. Not so much coming out, but the challenges of staying out."

"Who came up with that?"

"I did. Inspired by you."

"Me?"

"I keep going over what Barry said to Skip the night of the coffee house debacle. About how quietly and bravely you keep showing up as a gay man."

"I've overestimated Colorado."

"Maybe not, King."

"I'm the homophobe."

"No. But your story is pretty classic. Maybe if you get a chance to talk about it, you'll change some thinking."

"How have you felt, now that your family knows? How have they been acting toward you since your trip last semester?"

"They've accepted me. It's been easy. But I know that's not the norm."

King closed his eyes. When he opened them, a call came in, blinking on the console. He answered it. Someone needed to be connected to the Wardenberg Health Center. He dialed the number and put them through.

"I'll do it."

"There's one other thing you should know. We feel we should post our names ahead of time. The professor will announce that we're coming a week before. We'll have fliers printed up. Your name would be on the flier."

King laughed.

There were four chairs set up on the stage; a round, beat-up coffee table with a water pitcher and glasses gleaming in front of them. Students ambled disconsolately into the theater. King watched them with interest. It amused him to see a class from the teacher's perspective. Most seemed sullen; preoccupied. Lacking any animation whatsoever. Some chewed gum. A few chewed their hair. A few squinted in the panel's direction. God, King thought. Was this America's future, assembling before his eyes? His mother was right. Education was wasted on the young.

Sam wore the same suit he wore for Tim's protest march. He'd slicked his hair back out of his eyes. He looked earnest, strikingly handsome tonight. He scanned the students, locking eyes with everyone who would meet his gaze. Rod wore a white T-shirt to show off his chest. He had a great build. He'd bleached his short hair for this occasion. With his strong chin and burnished cheekbones, he glowed under the theater's jelled lights. Masculine but clearly gay.

Meek and studious-looking as ever, Deborah seemed intimidated as the theater began to fill with students. King squeezed her hand and was surprised by the warm way she reciprocated. Deborah, Jen had told King, had admitted to having feelings for her. She'd let her down gently, but worried because Deborah had been a good friend to her. Jen didn't want to hurt her.

"I used to break a hundred hearts a week," Jen confided to King.

"I didn't give a rat's ass who I hurt. Now I'm burdened with *conscience*," she reported. "It's all your fault."

"My fault," King replied. He was astonished.

"Yes, you and your family, thinking so hard how your actions will affect everybody else. All the thinking has to stop!"

"But would you go back to the spoiled, narcissistic way you were before?"

"No, King. Impossible. I'm too evolved to ever go back."

"So what did you tell Deborah?"

"I told her she could touch my breast but it couldn't go any further."

"And did she?"

Jen just laughed.

King had come to the symposium wearing his daily uniform. Sam suggested that whatever he wore, he should feel comfortable, so he picked a blue Lacoste shirt, a pair of jeans, and his Topsiders. Matthew's leather jacket hung over the back of his folding chair.

Professor Carlson-Greene entered the auditorium. Formally Dr. Greene, he was young, in his early thirties, and the first man anybody heard of who'd hyphenated his last name with his wife's. King recognized him from around campus. Slender and buoyant, the class responded to his appearance by shifting in their seats, shuffling paperwork, including the flier King had seen posted earlier on the theater doors: *Gay Liberation in Boulder.* King saw his name listed last.

Dr. Carlson-Greene quickly took the stage and began by shaking the hands of each member of his panel. He turned quickly, taking the podium.

"I'd like to ask you to join me in welcoming this week's panel, representing the University of Colorado Boulder Gay Liberation Front." Tepid applause followed, slightly alarming King. Would they be heckled? Had he read everything wrong again?

Dr. Carlson-Greene continued. He gave a brief history of the youthful gay liberation movement. He marked the Stonewall Riots in '69 as the day the struggle for gay rights came out of the closet and into everyday society. Because of religious mores, "out" gays faced an ambitious, rigorous journey.

He planned to ask each panel member in turn to answer a few of his questions, and then he wanted to open it up to the class. His only prerequisite for the panel had been that each speaker be out to immediate family and friends.

"How soon, after coming to the conclusion you were gay, did you come out to family and friends?"

Sam answered first. "For me, coming out was not an instantaneous decision. Until recently, I was engaged to my high school sweetheart. I thought I loved her. We had an enjoyable physical relationship, but something was missing. I'd had occasional dalliances with college buddies, usually associated with alcohol. The sex was always quick. I regarded it as nothing more than letting off steam. But then I read about Boulder and how progressive Colorado was about gay rights. I decided to come here for graduate school. I recently went home to tell my parents."

"So media exposure about gay issues helped you? Gave you more courage?"

"I would say most definitely."

"And do you find Colorado to be as open as you hoped?"

"In most ways, yes. If you told me a year ago I'd be talking about gay sex in front of a hundred strangers, I'd have thought you were crazy."

The audience chuckled. King could see why Sam was such a good candidate to be a spokesperson for gay liberation. Rod, on the other hand, wouldn't prove to be so gentle on the ears.

"I knew I was gay when I was fourteen. My best friend's dad used to fondle me when we'd go camping. When my friend would fall asleep, his hands would start wandering."

"You were being molested?"

The audience fell silent. Emboldened, Rod spoke very frankly. And graphically.

"I didn't think so. I don't think so now. It was hot. We went camping every weekend that summer. My mom was single, and she was glad I had a male figure in my life. Sometimes we'd even go without my friend. I have great memories. He'd let me explore his body. He basically taught me how to fuck a man. By that, I mean how to give and get pleasure from a man's body. I consider myself lucky. I'm a great lover because of him."

"You seem pretty cocky," the professor laughed, easing the tension. "And what does your mother think?"

"I've never had sex with her. How would she know?"

"But she knows you're gay."

"Most definitely."

"Does she know about the man she entrusted you to as a minor?"

"Yes. She and I don't talk anymore."

"Let's ask a woman her take on coming out."

"I'm a lesbian." Deborah spoke softly. "I grew up on a ranch in southern Wyoming. My mother died when I was four. I had three older brothers, and could handle farming equipment as good as any of them. I was often mistaken for being a boy. I still am. Not all gay women look like me. If you think they do, you're probably in for a big surprise. I was pretty lucky with my family. A frilly little girl wouldn't have been practical where I grew up. My dad needed all the help he could get. He knows who I am and values me because of it. He told me he always knew. I called him before I came today. He told me to be honest, like I'd always been. He told me he was proud of me."

"Let's hear from our last panel member." Dr. Carlson-Greene turned, nodding to King.

From down the row, Sam smiled encouragingly. Just as King was about to speak, he noticed a face he recognized in the second row. It was Nicholas. King's old nemesis. The born-again Christian who'd threatened King's parents.

What possible reason did he have for being here? Nicholas's jaw was set, but his eyes reflected concern, and not outright hatred for King.

Down the row, Sam noticed that King was thrown.

"Go on, King," he urged him.

"Things haven't gone so smoothly for me," King acknowledged.

"Enlighten us," Dr. Carlson-Greene said.

"Whatever difficulties have arisen, I place them squarely at my own door. Being of my own doing."

"What difficulties, King?"

"I didn't know what was happening to me. I never knew any gay people before. If I had urges, I didn't consciously entertain them. I kept them hidden."

"But you felt something was different about you."

"Yes. I also have a gay brother."

"Really."

"I had no idea about him either. We never discussed it till I told my parents about me."

"And how did they react? Two gay sons. You have any other siblings?"

"No." King took a deep breath. Every eye in the room was trained on him. He was having trouble choosing his words. Nicholas just looked at his hands.

"They were afraid for us."

"Are they still afraid?"

"My dad recently died. I know that he was very afraid the world would hurt his sons. I think my mom is handling it better. She thinks we should stand on our own two feet."

"In retrospect, do you wish you hadn't told them?"

"If I hadn't, I think my dad would be alive today."

"What do you mean? How did he die?"

"I had been injured. I was in the hospital. He was coming to help me and died in an alcohol-related car accident. He drank heavily after I told him about me and my brother." King gazed out over the sea of somber faces. "He was a good guy. He blamed himself."

"It seems to me that he responded like any good parent would. A kid in the hospital. You come."

"My injuries were unique."

"Unique?"

"Of a sexual nature. And I don't want to go into any further detail than that. Yes. I feel very responsible."

"How are you coping?"

"With the love of my mom and my brother. And I have good friends."

"Thank you, King. Any questions from the floor?"

"I'd like to ask King a question."

King looked up. It was Nicholas.

"Go on."

"If you could change your nature, would you?"

"That's impossible to answer," King replied.

"And why is that?"

"My nature is God-given," King said firmly. "And I accept it. Your question is moot."

King happened to be getting coffee at the Alferd Packer Grill when a roar came from the UMC television room across the hall. A gangly freshman rushed into the grill, yelling that University of Colorado quarterback Barry Adams had just been named the first draft pick of the Miami Dolphins. The grill emptied as students and professors crammed into the smaller lunchroom. Cheers continued to erupt. King found himself standing alone in the empty cafeteria.

Over the din, he could hear Barry's reaction in a televised interview by a local Denver news station. Barry said it was a dream come true. He and his new wife Holly were looking forward to the Florida climate. Words couldn't express his gratitude. Without the love of his family, the support of his teammates, the guidance of his coach, and the inspiration of his minister, Barry wouldn't be standing here today.

King smiled. Nothing Barry said was untrue. King reflected that once again he was standing alone, on the periphery of a joyful melee. As Barry's voice faded to the dinning cheers of his fans, a young woman entered the grill.

Other than the cashier, she and King were the only people in the entire place. King was startled to see that it was Holly, Barry's new wife. The look on her face was one of utter distress. She wasn't crying, but she was close to it. She didn't seem to recognize King.

If there ever should be enemies, King and Holly qualified. King stared her down. He'd seen her at the dance, and once or twice at Teddy's. Certainly the day of the tailgate party. They hadn't been introduced. Teddy didn't introduce him to anyone. He passed her heading out the door as she was she going in. He'd heard Jen call her name, *Holly*, and for some reason his memory stored her image. She had dark hair and gray eyes. She was big-breasted, and King recalled that intermingled with her perfume was the unmistakable smell of cruelty. She was rank, this one.

She was startled by his hostility, had no idea who she was to him, what trouble she'd caused for him and his family. Why was this stranger staring at her with such hostility? King couldn't imagine how she'd know who he was anyway, unless she'd seen him with Barry, before their marriage quelled the rumors about his sexual orientation. King was surprised by his own rushing emotion as he clapped eyes on her.

She decided to ignore him and walked quickly past the cashier to the coffee urn. Shaking, she poured coffee into a small Styrofoam cup. She paid for it, tossing a dollar on the counter, ignoring the cashier's offer of change. She'd already forgotten King, returning to the morass of her own confusion. King noticed her wedding ring. It was a simple gold band, hastily purchased, no doubt. This girl hadn't earned her diamond.

She sat at a table in the far back of the grill. She was encased in shadows, and King could barely make out her face. She must have heard the announcement about Barry, even his remarks referencing her. Why hadn't she been there, on the podium with him? Wouldn't a girl like Holly have eaten up the opportunity for so much attention? Her face on the news. Her picture in the paper.

King watched her sip her coffee. She stared at her hands, studying the ring finger, twisting the gold band as thoughts churned in her head. Finally she twisted it off, placing it firmly on the table in front of her. In astonishment, King read her thoughts. She was trying to make up her mind to stay in the marriage. King's malevolence for her vanished.

Suddenly her thoughts became his. *What am I throwing away by marrying this man? I know who he really is. I know he doesn't really love me and never will. Is the fame worth it? The glamour? The stature? The money?* She knew Barry could make a kid with her. Maybe two. After that, the sex would stop. He'd travel without her. Stay busy. She was set dressing. And not pretty enough for that. Even Holly knew who she was. Barry could do much, much better than her, so why didn't he? A drunk sorority sister had asked that very thing last fall. They all knew what Barry was. And by marrying him, they knew what she was, too.

She looked up. King was still staring. He was reminded how he felt with Nicholas's eyes on him, sitting in the shadows of the sociology class while King poured out his innermost feelings. To be kind, King looked away.

She dabbed her eyes with a napkin and stood up. Without looking over at him, she walked swiftly toward a side exit, leading into the main corridor of the UMC.

"Holly," King called.

She stopped. How did he know her name? She turned, peering across the gleaming linoleum tables where King was backlit against the sun-drenched entrance to the grill.

"What? Why are you staring at me? What did I ever do to you?"

"Your ring," King mentioned.

"What about my ring?" her voice echoed.

"You forgot it," King told her. And he stood up and walked out.

Chapter Twenty

When King came home, Theo knocked on his door.

"I'm calling an emergency meeting. My place in an hour. This is big. Has national importance. And its happening right here in Boulder."

Later, King heard conversation outside his door, he peered out. Sam had arrived with Rod and Tony. Deborah and a few lesbians were already there. King came outside and joined them.

Theo appeared at his door. "Come in. Let's get started."

He moved anxiously, impatiently ordering the group to get seated and listen up.

"I've just been notified that the Boulder county clerk will issue marriage licenses to same-sex couples. She thinks she's found a loophole in the law. The Boulder assistant district attorney concurs. There's no way they'll let her keep doing it, but as a political gesture, she's laying her career on the line."

The group was dumbstruck. No one uttered a word. The several pairs of lovers eyed each other circumspectly. Who was ready to make that kind of commitment? Should it be sincere, or political? They all started talking at once.

"There are apparently a few out-of-state couples on their way," Theo told them. "An Australian man, about to be deported, seeks permanent residency by marrying an American male. We see this as a seventy-two-hour window. Maybe a week. Prospective couples will need blood tests."

"To protect us from having two-headed babies?" Tony teased him.

"Can first cousins marry?" someone else asked.

"The state assembly will surely kill it before it gets any bigger," Theo smiled. "Even so, I've never been prouder to be a Coloradan."

"Well, we're going for it for sure." Rod gripped Tony's hand.

"I'm not marrying you. I'm an Italian Catholic. It'll kill my mom. My dad's a New York cop. Besides, I don't want to get married now. I'm too young!"

And they started arguing.

King gazed around the room. A few of the women conferred in the corner, sitting on Theo's bed. Peter began crying about Tim. If only he were alive. They could get married and finally be happy.

King, too, felt emotional. What an amazing opportunity for those who wanted it. How many times this year had he been accused of adhering to the heterosexual model of coupling? Other than Theo, Sam and his brother Neil were now in committed relationships. And King was alone. Wanting it but without a partner.

King found Sam's eyes. He seemed shocked. He was sitting on the floor, leaning against Theo's sliding glass door. He saw King staring at him, and looked away, brushing his hand through his hair.

"What about you and Skip?" Theo queried. "This seems right up Skip's alley."

"He's out of the country," Sam said. "Gee, I'd hate to miss this chance. I have to call him. See if he can come back."

Sam's eyes found King, who hadn't looked away. Out of the group, three sets of couples agreed to apply. They all quickly dispersed. Only King, Theo, and Sam remained. Reading the energy between Sam and King, a hurt Theo made excuses about calling the head of Denver's gay coalition.

Sam and King ambled out to Sam's car.

"Big news, huh?"

"Never thought I'd see it in my time," King concurred.

"I've got to try to reach Skip. It's late. He'll probably be asleep." Sam leaned down, kissing King."

Sam climbed in his car and pulled away. When he drove away, he and King exchanged a final complicit glance.

"I'll marry you."

"What point is there to that?" King asked Jen. "You're a woman."

"I'm glad you noticed."

King smiled at her.

"But see, we aren't really together. Wouldn't it be political enough that one of us was gay?"

"Not the same."

"I think you're being very mean. You'd be lucky to marry someone like me, King."

"I know that," he told her wearily.

"What's eating you?" Jen was sitting at his kitchen table.

"I feel so sad."

"Tell me something new. You wish you had someone to marry, don't you, King?" She softened. "You're so traditional. Trapped in the body of a male whore."

"I'm not a whore, Miss Not-sure-who-the-father-of-her-due-anytime-baby is."

"King! I never told you that so you could throw it up in my face anytime you liked."

"Face it. We're both whores."

"I know," she said glumly.

"I wish I could, though," King said softly.

"Maybe someday." She patted his hand.

That night, King got a call from Sam. "I have a pretty bizarre request to make of you. Don't hesitate to say no."

"What?"

"Skip's on a business trip in France. Otherwise he'd do it."

"What?"

"You know what's going on at the Boulder county clerk's office."

"Yeah," King said.

"Well, it got leaked to the *New York Times*. She can't keep issuing licenses. We have to go right away."

"What are you talking about?"

"I want us to get married. I've talked it over with Skip. He's not happy about it, but this is historic and I want to be part of it. It's strictly political."

But not very romantic, King thought.

"Did you ask anybody else first?"

"Other than Skip?"

"No."

"Do I get a wedding night?"

Sam fell silent.

"Just kidding. I'd be honored."

Sam and King were issued a marriage license by Clela Rorex, the
Boulder county clerk, the seventh couple to be granted such a request. They waited in line behind an irate cowboy looking to marry
his favorite horse. The request was denied on the grounds that the
eight-year-old mare was underage.

As witnesses were Jen, sworn on her baby's life to never tell King's
mother; a bickering Rod and Tony, fighting because Tony had refused Rod's proposal of marriage; Deborah and her new girlfriend
Suzy, who happened to be a photographer for the *Boulder Daily
Camera* and took lots of pictures, and lastly Theo, tending to a very
drunk Peter, lamenting that it should have been him and Tim.

By now these marriage licenses had been played out in the press,
but Suzy's photograph of the cowboy and his horse would get
printed by AP all over the world. King was just as glad. Later that afternoon they were married by a lesbian pastor against the backdrop
of Boulder Falls. Jen was King's best man. Theo attended as "a political statement," nodded his approval and left during their kiss.

Sam and King were both particularly moved by the experience.

"Are you sorry it couldn't be Skip?"

"No. That's not it. I'm sorry that they'll probably annul this in
less than a month. I'm sorry that I can't stay married to you because
we're both men. Wouldn't it be wonderful, King? To be allowed to
marry anyone you loved?"

"Yes." King smiled.

"Do you think I used you?"

"No. You could have asked ten other guys. I'm political, too."

"I was glad Skip was out of town. I'd never marry Skip. I already
know I've made a mistake. He threw out my mung beans."

Sam grew bean sprouts in a big jar on top of his dresser. He was
very proud of his green thumb. King couldn't imagine Skip liking
that for an instant. Even King thought they smelled too much.

"I'm probably going to head back to New York next month. I'll
move out before he comes back. I guess I looked pretty silly. I was
impressed with his pretensions. He wanted to change me. I'll always
be the son of a blue-collar family."

"And I'm heading for California."

"Really? You haven't said anything and I'm your husband."

"My wife."

"That remains to be seen."

"I miss your old room."

"I miss it, too."

They fell silent. There was strong sexual tension between them.

"Maybe we should just keep it political," King said.

"You'll come to say goodbye?"

"Yeah."

"I've enjoyed being married to you." And Sam leaned down and kissed him.

The next day King drove up past Lake Eldora to a great hiking area called 4th of July Campground. There was a short, beautiful trail leading up to a small, pristine mountain lake. King started climbing. It only took him twenty minutes. He crested a hill, and saw the lake below, shrouded in pines. A hiker was climbing up from a sandy beach near the water. King couldn't make him out, but something about his gait seemed so familiar. He was concentrating on the path in front of him, deep in thought. As he got closer, King cleared his throat, not wanting to startle him. He looked up, surprised.

It was Lex. King hadn't seen Lex or Lucy since last summer, nearly a year ago. He was wearing a backpack, probably loaded with books on birds and botany. A pair of binoculars dangled from his neck. A canteen latched to his belt. In his hand was a tube of Chap Stick. Lex was always applying Chap Stick.

"Oh," he said, but it sounded more like *Uh-oh*.

"Hello," King responded. Lex and King had not parted on good terms. If he remembered correctly, the first time King was screaming after him to come back, to not leave, to stay like he promised, while old friends rushed Lex away and he kept going. He was tired of King. And later King tried to hang himself. And they got back together. Went to California. Came back. Then Lex left again. And then King got better. And then he killed his dad.

All of which Lex had to be thinking about now.

Lex and King met through Nicholas, his roommate at Kittredge Commons. Lex had curly brown hair, blue eyes, and a self-deprecating sense of humor. He was fat as a kid, had since outgrown it, but still carried the extra weight as an emotional burden. He didn't think he was handsome, which he was.

He played the guitar and sang, not as well as King sang, but okay.

People who sing and play the guitar always want to perform. They dragged out the guitar at the slightest prompting. They brought it to parties and camp outs. They never offered to play while someone else with a nice voice sang, hogging the spotlight to themselves. They sang one song too many, losing all sense of propriety. King hated people who played the guitar. King didn't hate Lex. Not for the guitar. Not for anything.

Lex always smiled. King reflected on this, because he would eventually wipe that smile off his face. Not forever, King wasn't that powerful, but for a time. Had Lex never met King, he wouldn't have lost an hour of smiles. Thanks to King, it cost him close to a year. Knowing a king was always a rough ride. Kings, Lex had found, just wouldn't be ignored for a minute.

"Are you graduating this month?"

"Yep. Finally."

Lex folded his arms. "How are you doing, King? We heard about your dad. I'm sorry."

"Thank you." They continued to stare at each other. "How's Lucy?"

"She's fine. We aren't together anymore."

"Ah."

"She moved to Denver. I'm going up to Eureka for graduate school."

"Neil's moving to southern California. I'll probably follow him."

"Did I hear you were seeing Barry Adams?" He said this incredulously. King could tell he wanted to be conspiratorial, like girlfriends gossiping at ten thousand feet.

"No," I shook my head, wanting to protect Barry's privacy. "I don't know who started that rumor. I'd sure like to," King said. "I hear he's got a huge cock. You still see the group?"

"Not since Lucy and I broke up."

"No?"

He kicked at a rock. "I gotta tell somebody. It may as well be you. I owe you that.

I broke up with her." He moved to sit down on a log. "Lucy and I never had sex."

King resisted the urge to laugh.

"She wanted to."

"But you wanted to save it until marriage."

"It was as good an excuse as anything to avoid it," Lex shrugged.

"I've gotta be going." But King hesitated. "Hey, Lex. One question. Why did you leave me?

And Lex got angry.

Humiliated, King started up the path. As he neared the fork to go back to the campground, Lex yelled something. King pretended not to hear him, but did, and if possible, the truth of it hurt him more than the worst event of the many which occurred over the past several years.

"*I couldn't take it,*" he called after King. His voice was shrill with resentment. "*Not after the year I had with you.*"

And damn the Rocky Mountains, if it didn't echo ten times, a hundred times as King stormed down the path.

King rewrote the short story about his mother. If a short story could be a painting, that's what this was. A portrait of her. He decided it was so good he might try to get it published. When he went over to Sam's to say goodbye, he asked him to read it. It must have been pretty good because Sam cried.

"You should show this to Rod. Maybe he'd publish it in his paper."

"You think it's that good?"

"Yeah, King," Sam smiled. "I do."

His studio was loaded with boxes. He was packing for his move to New York. "I hope you'll come visit," Sam said.

"I'll come," King said airily, and his eyes fell to his single bed.

"You miss Barry?"

"Yeah." King hesitated. "Do you think it's odd, after all that happened. After my dad?"

"For you, King? No. It makes sense."

"How do you mean?"

"It makes sense that you'd let him slide. I think in a way if you hadn't, it might have ruined his life. If you don't forgive him, he may never have been able to forgive himself."

"It wasn't Barry."

Sam studied King circumspectly. He calculated whether to press harder. He decided to drop it, but wanted to ask one more question.

"Why did he drop you? If you care about someone, and you

know everything that happened, wouldn't you at least come to the hospital? Or call to ask what happened?"

"I didn't call him to explain."

"What did you need to explain? The nurse says you had to have been attacked. I've slept with you King. I think I'd know if S&M was your thing. Do you honestly think any of us believe it was consensual?"

"I told you, I don't remember what happened. Maybe it was the devil," King grinned. "I'm fine now. I want to get past it."

"One more thing and I'll stop. We all think Barry getting married showed a lack of character."

"You still think he should come out?"

"Yes." He reached for a hanging macramé plant holder. "Guess I'll have to store this. Plant's been dead for a month. I haven't been here except to pee."

King loved sitting with Sam while he continued packing. He wore a tank top and cutoff jeans and King remembered what it felt like to have Sam's long legs wrapped around him. He hadn't packed his teapot and he made some tea. The door to his room was open, drawing the breeze in from the window. Outside, instead of snow, the trees were leafy green and rustled from the mountain winds.

Sam continued working while King nursed his Celestial Seasonings. They didn't feel the need to talk. It was nice, watching Sam move among his belongings, laboring over items to keep or give away. Sam was a pack rat. He saved newspaper clippings, and magazines. Rolls and rolls of drafting projects were stacked in the corner, waiting to be tubed.

Occasionally Sam glanced over, smiling warmly. King started to feel aroused, wondering if he should go before he ruined everything. King had nearly finished with his tea. He got up and went into Sam's bathroom. He closed the door. He actually needed to take a break. King often hid out in someone's bathroom, just for a minute of privacy. To ponder his feelings. King was always pondering feelings. He flushed the toilet without using it and decided he'd go. Sam had to finish packing.

When King came out, he noticed the door to the hallway was closed. He looked around. Sam was in bed, sprawled facedown, his nude body sheathed in a thin white sheet, pulled up to the cleft of his butt. The curtain fluttered gently overhead, the afternoon sun flooding the end of the narrow bed.

"We're married." he spoke into the pillow. "I have my wifely duties."
He opened his eyes and smiled lazily.

"Are you sleepy, King? You looked so cute, sitting there with your mug of tea. You want to fool around and take a nap? We could have an early dinner and then I'll head to Denver. If you don't have plans. And if you don't feel used."

King didn't know if there was a name for sleeping with an old lover, but there should have been one, some elaborate French or Latin sounding word as beautiful, say, as *pentimento,* the concept which of course King learned from the Lillian Hellman story by the same name, which Maddie had suggested he read.

There should have been another word for the phenomenon of knowing, inside the moment, how lucky you were to be doing whatever it was that's so special, precisely because fate was affording you an opportunity which probably wouldn't come around again.

King knew a girl, Cindy, who swore she could climax in a concert of classical music. This same girl smiled when she kissed, because King kissed her several times, but that was off the subject.

King really adored Sam, and he was moving to New York and Sam and King wouldn't really be in each other's lives.

So this act of him offering King the afternoon and early evening was a gift, a wink from God.

See King, it isn't all suffering and discipline and hard work with me, God was saying. *Here's Sam again. Enjoy.*

The pages of King's short story fluttered to the floor.

They went to dinner at the Red Lion Inn up Boulder Canyon, a cozy rambling restaurant with porches and wooden shutters set in the woods above the river. They sat at the lowest level of the restaurant, in a private corner not visible to the rest of the room. King could smell the spray of the river as the sun began to set.

Sam reached across the table and held King's hand, even as the cocktail waitress took their order. He seemed inordinately sentimental about his move.

"I have everything that I hoped I'd have," he told him. "I'm out to the world. I didn't think it'd be this easy."

"Has it been easy?" King queried.

"I know it hasn't been easy on you, King."

"I didn't mean for it to come out that way."

"I know you didn't. I'm being glib." Sam hesitated, looking for words. "Thank you for today. For coming to dinner."

The waitress returned with the drinks.

"Thank you for inviting me."

"I was pretty tacky. You should have walked out." He studied him. "I know it was hard for you to forgive me."

"What did you do?"

"I ended our brief affair."

"I wasn't even sure you thought we *had* a brief affair." Then King laughed.

"Yes, King. We had a brief affair."

"So I never really asked. Why *did* you end it?"

"I knew I wasn't finished with screwing around. I wanted to fuck every guy I met last fall. You weren't someone I'd do that to." Sam smiled warmly. "Today it was nice being with you again. It felt familiar. Maybe I'm a little vulnerable. You're an amazingly sensual guy."

"This has been the craziest time. I thought the last four years were confusing. Can I admit something?"

"Sure."

"I love men. I love you. I loved Barry. I loved Matthew."

"Matthew?"

"He's from back East. I met him after you. Tim saw me with him one night at the Broadway. He was more along the lines of Skip, only nicer and better-looking."

King smirked at Sam and he laughed.

"If he'd just leave his wife and come straight to Boulder. He's great. He's probably better equipped to handle me than anybody."

"Who else do you love?"

"I would have to say Lex, my first boyfriend. And Theo."

"Theo was crazy about you."

"Theo has been great to me. And Jen."

They fell silent. The water rushed below them. The tables around them began to fill up. They studied the menu. Drank their drinks. They held hands. Finally they ordered.

"So what's your take on everything? Am I in love with everybody or nobody?"

"How can you fall in love so fast?"

"I just do. I just know."

"If you had to choose, who would it be?"

"Heart of hearts?"

"Yes."

King allowed himself to imagine him and Barry walking in the woods along the river after the coffeehouse. All the making out. The cabin that first winter night. Then he thought of Matthew, sitting opposite King when he told him about his dad. The texture of his hair. The way they fucked while the snow fell against the window of the hotel.

King recalled holding hands with Theo on the ski lift. The surprise in his eyes when King kissed him in front of the fire in the ski lodge. The way he pressed into King when they made love. Coming to King's touch.

And then King's first night with Sam. The dance. The walk home. The invitation up. The sweet smell of his room. Watching him move. Kissing him. The thrill of being with him.

And Lex. His first true love. The hard heart lessons learned from him.

"King?"

Sam shook him out of his daydream.

"Yeah?"

"Where'd you go?"

"I was thinking about my first lover."

"I never met him."

"His name was Lex."

Sam nodded. "I shouldn't have asked you that question."

"It's okay. But since we've been so honest, I want you to know that I love you. How I'd compare that I don't know, but the price of the day is that. I get to tell you I love you. I hope you'll be happy. I hope you'll have a good life."

"Same here." Sam smiled.

"Can I kiss you goodbye?" King asked. King reflected that he always waited to be kissed. Waited to be asked. Waited till it was safe. This was new. Asking Sam.

"Please." Sam nodded.

And King did.

Chapter Twenty-One

The lilac bushes lining the Broadway perimeter of the campus began to bloom in late April, early May. They'd first appear as hard, tiny, dark green buds, and eventually, optimistically, turn to dark pink, then purple grapelike strands of fragrant flowers. Lilacs in bloom portended new beginnings. They lined the sidewalk running the perimeter of the Broadway side of campus, past Ketchum Hall, past the Mary Rippon Shakespeare Theater, and onward toward the Hill.

King's backyard at home was lined with lilac bushes. A late snow could kill them, but this year, unlucky in so much else, fate saved his mother the lilacs. Jen was now in her eighth month and counting the days. She, more than King, was glad for spring.

They often climbed from the caves of their subterranean studios and drove up to Chautauqua Park, the threshold to the Flatirons. The pastures rising up to the mountains were already green and sprinkled with wildflowers like Indian paintbrush and Colorado columbines. Today they took a small picnic.

"God, King! Isn't it glorious?"

They gazed out over the city of Boulder, the flagstone university enshrouded with pine trees and newly budding elms. The sky was brilliant blue with great white billowing clouds rolling east toward Longmont. Lakes and reservoirs sparkled in the afternoon light. A breeze cascaded down the slope behind them.

"It makes me never want to leave," King told her.

"I'm not leaving," Jen said, crunching an apple.

"No?"

"I got accepted to grad school. I've been waiting to tell you. After that, I'm going to medical school. After meeting you, I want to be a psychiatrist."

"How can you do all that with a tiny baby?"

"Grammy Kay is going to baby-sit."

King had to hand it to her. "Did you start making plans with my mom in the car leaving Teddy's that day? Is this the culmination of your master plan?"

"No." She held out her apple. King took a bite and handed it back. "But it's really working out neat, isn't it?"

"You don't feel guilty at all, do you?"

She reflected. "No. Not anymore. Not after I saw people for what they were."

"I wasn't implying that you should feel guilty," King asserted.

"No more than I'd imply that you should feel guilty. Do you feel guilty?"

"No," King told her.

"There you are, then. Fact is, except for a few rough nights, which thankfully you, your mother, and Theo got me through, I've enjoyed being pregnant with my little girl. Frankie the fetus . . ."

Frankie was King's mother's nickname in high school.

"You're naming her Frankie?"

"It's cute, isn't it?" She bit into her apple. "I love it and I love her. King! Look at me! I'm radiant."

She was right. She was. Sometime shortly after Jen and King drove home from dinner at his parents, her spirits lifted. She'd made the conscious decision to enjoy her pregnancy, forsaking the mantle of the "fallen woman." The women's group she attended continued to make a huge impact on her. She saw them once a week.

Jen had read Betty Friedan and Gloria Steinem. It had been difficult at first to count herself as a feminist. When she carefully read the Equal Rights Amendment, she finally concluded that feminism only meant a women's right to equal pay for equal work.

"King," she'd announced dramatically through the sliding glass door to his apartment. "I am now a self-pronounced feminist."

"You already told me that last winter. Up on Gold Hill."

"Well, now I know what I'm talking about."

Jen and King began their Lamaze lessons together as planned. The other couples were mostly in their mid to late thirties. A few were hippies who lived up Boulder Canyon. Some planned home deliveries. The Lamaze instructor's name was Babs. Within five minutes, Babs had every expectant mother convinced that she'd die from the pain of childbirth unless she followed her Lamaze training to the letter. Not only that, if the mother caved and demanded an epidural, the baby was certain to be born lethargic and slow-witted.

Jen and King decided they'd explain their relationship if asked directly. King was the baby's godfather. Jen's sister Anne would be the godmother. Anne was coming back from Paris at the end of the summer.

"I thought your father gave orders to stay away."

"Anne is my half-sister. We have different fathers. My mother had her before she married my dad."

"Your mom was divorced? I thought your father was Catholic."

"She had Anne on her own. Before they were married. The father was on a PT boat in the Pacific. He died shortly before the war ended."

"Then your mom knows what you're going through?"

"I would think so, King." Jen folded her new baby afghan from King's mother. "What's your point?"

The baby was due June 2. Babs, the Lamaze instructor, was continuing her campaign of terror.

"Theo says I can stay in the apartment with the baby. I'm worried that it might be too small."

"I liked our studios in the winter. Now I think they're too dark. I feel like we're bears. We've been hibernating and it's time to come out and play."

Jen held her face up to the sun. Her hair cascaded back behind her. She'd kept it long and free. She hadn't gained any weight in her face. King studied her body. She reminded him of a horn of plenty. A rush of emotion overcame King. He was grateful she'd come to his door the night of her personal storm. King reflected he'd probably never be allowed this point of view of a pregnancy again. This proximity. He was privileged to be her birthing partner, according to Babs.

Babs had sized King up right away. "You're lucky fate is affording this experience to you, King."

"What's to say I won't have a chance with my own child someday?"

"King." Babs stroked his cheek. "Let's face facts. You're out and you aren't going back in."

"That doesn't mean I can't father a child."

"No, probably not. Would you like to have your own children? I know single women who want to bear children who'd like a caring partner to sire them."

"I'm not a prize bull."

"No," Babs observed critically. "You aren't, exactly. But you're healthy enough, and generically appealing. How's your ejaculate?"

"I never had one I didn't enjoy."

"King, can you be adult here? Is it sizable?"

She was asking him about his load. If he was potent.

"I thought it only took one sperm."

"Small, then." Babs studied him critically.

Actually it wasn't. King didn't come as much as Barry, but generally he came quite a bit.

"I saw Barry the other day, sitting at the fountain outside the UMC," Jen read King's thoughts. "He was signing autographs. Just as I was about to go talk to him, Holly showed up. She's gotten so fat."

"Did you talk to her?"

"I said hello. She didn't seem the same at all. I felt bad for her. I don't think she knows who she is. She apologized for not calling me. Holly and I were friends." Jen reflected on this.

"Did they ever kick her out of your sorority house?"

"Not when I moved. They needed the dues."

"Did you sit down with her?"

"She didn't want Barry to see me with her. She asked if I ever heard from Teddy. I told her no. Then she apologized again. I told her not to worry. I told her I had lots of support. Lots of new friends."

"What'd she say?"

"She made some excuse about being late and left. She didn't look very happy. Neither did he." Jen hesitated. "If Barry wasn't the one, who was it?"

"This isn't a joke to me."

"It isn't to me either, sweetie. You still aren't telling me who it was."

"I have my reasons."

"But you knew him?"

"Yeah." King smiled wistfully at Jen. "My mind is unkind to me. Barry is a simple man. He would have stayed if I asked him too, no questions asked. There will always be a modicum of trouble around me. I pushed him away. Made him leave. I know he loved me because I was his first. I know that I truly cared about him, but I couldn't go where he was going, and I don't blame him or me for that."

"But who," Jen started to interrupt, but King stopped her.

"Things got out of hand. I don't know how to explain this, but even I, with all that I've pulled, all the drama I've perpetuated, even *I* didn't want to admit I was probably raped. I have a shred of dignity left. In a weird way, it gives me hope that someday, I'll be a man."

King closed his eyes, laying his head in the fragrant grass, the sun warming his face. The breeze rushed over them. For a moment he imagined that he and Jen were attached to the mountain, unshakable as geological matter, no different than the most significant rock formations, no less than the forested hillside; rich as the fecund earth.

Jen rolled back on the blanket. "You know, King, if you'd told me last September that in May I'd be single, out of my sorority house, eight months pregnant without any help from my family, I probably would have killed myself. But I've done okay for the most part. Haven't I King?"

"You've done great."

"So have you. Teddy and I used to feel sorry for you. You seemed so lonely. So lost."

"You never talked much to me."

"Who knew what I was missing," she mused.

"You've done great, Jen."

"I think you've done great too. Given everything."

"I miss my dad."

"You'll always miss your dad."

"I'm grateful though. We got to know each other, just in time. I liked him tremendously. I know he accepted me." King hesitated.

Jen smiled over at King. They sat silently and watched the clouds.

King thought again about what Babs said. About what a privilege it was to be Jen's birthing partner. Without asking, he reached over and stroked Jen's belly. Her eyes were closed. King wondered if his touch felt invasive to her but she didn't register any surprise. Instead she clasped her hands over his.

"A man's touch is important to little Frankie," she murmured.

*   *   *

Jen went into labor several nights later. When she called, all she said was, "My water broke. It's time."

They were dignified on the drive over to the hospital. King asked if she wanted him to wake Theo, and she said no. He could call him from the hospital. She just wanted the two of them to drive over together and didn't want any awkwardness between him and Theo. Not on such an important occasion.

Jen had insisted on taking a shower. It was nearly four in the morning.

"I can't have Frankie seeing me with dirty hair. Heat up my curlers."

"You're curling it, too?"

"*King*," she sang in a tone that meant business. King obliged her while she took her shower.

On the drive over, Jen told King several things.

"I know you well enough, so I'm going to answer all the questions which must be going through your mind. Yes, I miss Teddy, but not in any really aching way. I wish we were married, that Frankie had been conceived inside the framework of marriage, but that isn't the way things worked out and I am totally okay with that. I feel sorry for Teddy," she told him, and her voice caught a little. "There's no way this baby isn't his."

"I knew you were only giving him an out to test him." King said.

"Now, as for my parents, I suppose if things were different I'd wish they were meeting us. I wish my dad was all blown-up and proud. I wish my mother would stroke my cheek and call me Jenny, but they aren't here and I've accepted that, too. I know you judge them, but don't. I give them all the credit in the world for creating me, and I want you to give 'em credit for that, too. Because, King, as you know, I'm a terribly wonderful girl and I can be every bit as forgiving as you."

"Yes." King nodded. "I know."

"Are you looking forward to meeting Frankie?"

"Yes," he told her.

"Yeow!" Her face contorted with a contraction.

"Gee, they're coming kind of close." King scanned the empty streets of Boulder. They were nearly at the intersection of Broadway and Canyon. King decided to run the red light.

"King! How exciting!"

Sure enough, a cop wheeled out from a narrow alley and pulled up behind the Capri, lights flashing. King rolled down his window as the cop approached. "I have an unwed mother in labor."

"King!"

"Sorry. It just slipped. We're heading for Boulder Community!" He panned his flashlight over to Jen. "Follow me."

Frankie, born five hours later, had a police escort to her birth. It was a dream delivery, by everyone's standards.

King's mother came to pick him up later that day. As excited as she was, Kay allowed King to catch up on his sleep the afternoon after Frankie was born. She'd cut fresh roses from her garden and commanded him to hold them so the vase wouldn't roll and break.

Kay and Jen had already conferred. They'd called her at six this morning to tell her Jen was in labor. King had promised not to leave Jen's side till Frankie was born.

On the drive over, Kay asked how he felt about it.

"Pretty miraculous," he told her.

"How was Jen about her circumstances?"

"She was pretty matter-of-fact. You know Jen. She wants the baby. She doesn't feel victimized."

"She shouldn't."

They fell silent as they sliced through downtown Boulder in Kay's Dodge.

"Did she call her parents? Do they know?"

"If she did, she didn't mention it."

"They don't know what they're missing. When Neil was born, your grandparents drove through the night to be at the hospital. It was so comforting to have my mother there. I'd only held a baby once before I held Neil," she mused, smiling at the thought. "And all the physical demands. Breast-feeding was so strange." She took a drag off her cigarette. "I guess I'm being a little frank."

"Speaking of a little frank, do you know what she's naming her?"

"No."

"I'll let her tell you."

"I hate my name. Tell me it isn't Kay."

"It's not Kay."

"Good."

*   *   *

"Why Frankie?"

They were walking down the hallway to her room, and King was doing that voyeuristic thing people always do in hospital corridors: scanning open doors to see all manner of humanity in varying states of diminishment or grace. An older woman clutching the hand of a terminally ill husband, with pumps and tubes and machines burping all over the place. A young mother and father holding out a teddy bear or doll to a small child contained in a child's bed. A figure, silhouetted in the frame of the window, peering out at the mountains, back to the person confined in bed. Bored kids staring at the infirmed. And always bits of conversation.

Nice view of the hills. Do you need magazines? When do you get out? Are the nurses nice? Is the food just terrible? You look tired, I think we'll be going now . . .

"Why, Frankie?"

Jen's room was at the end of the hall, an overflow from maternity.

King's mother was as perceptive as he was. It was a woman's voice. Slightly chiding, slightly disappointed.

"Why Frankie?"

They both froze. Who could be visiting Jen? Then another word, murmured, an observation of fact, not really, if King heard it properly, mean-spirited.

"It's sweet really. Too bad it's acrylic."

King wanted to spin his mother off in the other direction. He wanted to stop her in her tracks to save her any more bitter pills.

"It must be her mother," he murmured.

"Now that the messy part is over," Kay replied and to her infinite credit, kept moving.

Jen's mom resembled Michele Phillips from the Mamas and the Papas, only in golf clothes. They entered the room wanting to hate her, but her resemblance to Jen made this impossible. It was also immediately clear that she was an emotionally battered wife. King and his mother discussed this at length later.

"This is why," Jen said calmly when she saw Kay and King. She knew they had to have heard, as did her mother, and where her mother quivered with retched embarrassment, Jen played it calm, thereby keeping King and his mother calm.

"Why what?"

"Why Frankie. This is King and his mom. I couldn't have made it without both of them."

"Then, thank you," her mother whispered. "As you know, her father and I let her down." And she stood up and came over to kiss Kay's cheek.

Chapter Twenty-Two

Graduation was on June 8. King was finishing his sixth short story to turn into Maddie, along with his journal. The journal was over three hundred pages, typed single-spaced. Her only admonition was honesty.

"You will only be graded on the short stories," he remembered her saying on the first day of her advanced creative writing survey last September. "There is one caveat. If I sense any deceit in the journal, I'll knock you down one grade. Deceit is how anyone normally defines the term. The journal is not meant to entertain me. Cute, clever, shocking, I can smell insincerity a smile away. The short stories will only reflect how you're doing now as a writer. The journal, as a practice of honesty, portends your future as a writer. It's very important. I want daily entries. Even if all you report was what you ate for dinner."

Now, as it became time to hand in his pages, King was growing increasingly agitated. Jen, captivated with Frankie and trying to study for her chemistry final, noticed something was wrong.

"I have to turn in my short stories to Dr. Sloan."

"You never showed me the one you wrote about me."

"It's good. That's all you need to know."

She was about to nurse Frankie. "Turn your eyes."

"You're nursing her, for Christ's sake."

"Nobody gets a gander at these babies but Frankie and my future husband."

"Got anybody in mind?"

"No, King. Are you offended that I don't have a crush on you?"

"Why'd you bring that up?" Now King was offended.

"On the other hand, Sam is a dream boat."

"I have to finish retyping my stories."

"Who else inspired you?"

"It's pretty obvious. You. My mom. Sam. Matthew. Neil. Barry."

"Not your dad?"

"Can't do that one, yet."

Frankie finished and Jen placed a towel over her shoulder to burp her. After she was finished, she held Frankie up to King. "Who's that? *Who's that*? Is that your uncle King? *Is that your uncle King?*"

"I'm gonna barf."

"Is he a mean man? *Is he a mean man?*"

King hesitated outside Maddie's office door. He could hear that she was on the phone. The conversation was heated, and personal. He knew who she was talking to without hearing her specific words. He waited until she hung up. Then he tapped softly on the wall by her door.

"King?" Smiling, she came to the door.

"How'd you know it was me?"

"The mirror over my bookshelf." She gestured to a small ornate mirror sitting atop the cluttered credenza. "I keep it there for exactly that reason. As you know, I don't like to work with my door closed. I like my view of the commons. So I keep the door ajar and I can tell who's out here by my little mirror. The mirror was a gift to my mother from Rose Kennedy."

"I wasn't eavesdropping."

"I know that, King." She continued to smile, but King could read pain in her eyes. "Come in. I'm making tea. I'm glad it's you. Relieved, even. I suppose you gathered it was Robert. If not, you must think I'm having a very unhappy affair with somebody else. So, are you turning in your assignment?"

He proffered his pages.

"What's wrong, King?"

"I think my stories are quite good."

She reacted. "How confident."

"I'm not turning in my journal."

She plugged in her electric teapot. Reaching for two cups, she arranged them on a small tray. She had a silver bowl with assorted sugar packets. She didn't use milk and remembered that King didn't, either.

King glanced around the room. How he loved it in here. Maddie had rearranged it so the appointments of her office looked to the windows. They were slightly ajar, and a lilac-perfumed breeze swept through, pulled by the open door into the corridor. Maddie closed it behind them.

"You moved everything around."

"Yes. I decided to be selfish. Why should my students have the pleasure of the garden outside my windows? I had my desk moved so my back would be to the door and I could see the green. I think the chairs are lovely under the window. I don't ask all my visitors to sit with me there. Certainly not my students. I have this hardback chair reserved for them. That way, all they can see is me and the door *out*."

She emphasized the word out. King wondered where he would be invited to sit. She seemed out of sorts. She handed him his cup of tea and motioned for him to take a seat under the window, where her two cracking leather club chairs faced each other, with a small coffee table in between.

"These chairs came from an old hotel in Telluride. It's so beautiful there. They're planning major redevelopment. I hope you go before it all changes. Everything's changing so fast."

"My father lived in Telluride for a short time."

"You never talk about your father."

King was stunned. Surely she knew.

"What's wrong?"

"He recently died."

Her head snapped back in astonishment.

"Since this year?"

"Three months ago."

"Why didn't you say anything?"

"Everybody knew. It was in the paper. Car accident on his way to Boulder."

They stared at each other like strangers.

"I'm sorry," she said. Distressed, she sipped at her tea. After an uncomfortable moment, while she struggled to compose herself, she asked, "So why are you holding back the journal? Having read the first drafts of your short stories, you've undoubtedly earned an 'A.' A lower grade could keep you out of Iowa. Without the journal, I'd have to drop you to a 'B.' "

"I wasn't dishonest in my journal."

"Then what's the problem?"

"I don't want you to read it."

"Why on earth not? Your stories are clearly autobiographical. You couldn't shock me if you tried."

"I could hurt you."

"Why would you want to hurt me?"

"That's the point."

"Why, King? Don't you care for me?"

"I don't want to hurt you. In my way, I love you."

"Schoolboy crush. Robert's so jealous of you." She smiled, blowing on her tea. "I'm flattered. I thought I was safe with you."

"You are," King advised her. "Are you really going to marry him?"

She glanced up. "Of course I am."

King fell silent.

"Don't you approve? I know he's difficult, he's a very complex man, the most brilliant poet I've ever known, let alone read. The university is thrilled to have him. He could teach anywhere in the world. Cambridge. Harvard. He gave up a lot to move here. I certainly can't compete at his league. I'm lucky Boulder wants me."

"Do they want you because of you, or him?"

"King!"

"You're good enough without him."

She relaxed. "I'm prepared to take my share of the responsibility for introducing you to Robert. Maybe I crossed a professional line. I thought you deserved the opportunity. You aren't very worldly, King. I don't say that to be condescending. You have a gift and you need to see the world. Expand your horizons."

"Are you saying I'm unsophisticated?"

"Yes." She nodded. "But that's also part of your charm. You're authentic. And very intuitive."

He blinked. He was hurt. Unsophisticated? He saw himself reflected in the Rose Kennedy mirror.

When King had first visited Maddie in her office, the Clifford Irving plagiarism scandal had recently broken. Irving had edited a

Howard Hughes autobiography which was deemed a hoax. Irving and his blond girlfriend, Nina Van Pallandt, for a time frequented a small island off the coast of Spain called Ibiza. The beautiful island was a sun-soaked enclave for expatriates. It was very inexpensive. All the beautiful Bohemians hung out there for a time.

When King expressed his desire to go there, Maddie begged him to follow his inclination.

"You can live there so cheaply. I had girlfriends who paid for lodging by making baskets of cookies. You never saw a place so beautiful. The locals are wonderful. So many writers and actors. It was the most beautiful summer of my life," Maddie confided. It solidified her intrigue with King, especially after reading his material. When he applied for her advanced writing course, she accepted him immediately.

Shortly thereafter, he became involved with Lex. Those issues became the focus of King's direction. He stopped writing. Stopped studying. He was consumed with his obsession for Lex, consumed and distressed. The family meeting followed. The fights between his parents. The loss of his friends. The call from Nicholas. The banishment by his mother. His suicide attempt. And that was only junior year. There was so much more to come.

"I want the journal, King. Do you have it with you?"

"No."

"I'll fail you without it." She softened, adding, "The loss of your dad notwithstanding."

"Fail me! But you said our stories counted one hundred percent of our grade."

"I haven't read your stories. Maybe they aren't the caliber I hope they'll be. If they're poor, you might end up with a 'D.' Without the journal, you won't pass at all."

"Why do you want to read it?"

"Remember when we discussed pitching ideas for possible publication? You have to grab your editor in the first three sentences. You've done an excellent job. I must read it. This is horribly manipulative of me, but I think you can be accused of doing the same thing. Get me the journal."

He rifled through his backpack. He handed her his short stories, bound in a folder. He hesitated.

He tossed them on the desk. "I never manipulated *you*."

"The grades will be posted outside my office in a week."

He walked out. In the hall, he stood in the doorway, giving him a view of the cozy office as it was reflected in the mirror. He knew that she, too, could see him if she bothered to glance up, but she was too busy rifling through his pages.

SUMMER

Chapter Twenty-Three

Later that night, King lay on his bed, contemplating the end of his years in Boulder. Four years. It seemed more like twenty. King had applied to the University of Colorado only because his high school best friend Rita told him it was cool. She for one, was not going to Greeley or Fort Collins. She was going to Boulder and King was coming with her. He didn't bother applying any other place.

Was destiny truly that? King wondered as he tossed on his mattress. Had he elected to go elsewhere, would he be out? Would so much be up in the air? Would his father still be alive? Was that the turning point? The decision to come here?

King had selected Kittredge Commons as his dormitory. Kittredge was an elite, newer complex comprised of four dorms, two men's and two women's. The following year all the campus dorms went coed with the exception of one, Hallet Hall, for women. Kittredge was separate from the main campus, and built around a man-made pond. It was luxurious by campus standards, slightly more expensive, attracting a fair amount of out-of-state students. Barry lived there his freshman year. He and King met at a Bible study, just the way Barry and Holly met.

King's friend Rita applied late, and ended up in Williams Village, across the freeway from the campus. It was walkable, but a trolley was available on bad weather days. The day Neil checked King into his dorm room had been emotional. He'd prepared his parents, a week before, that he'd rather Neil bring him up. They'd been politely good-natured about it. King had no idea until now how much he'd hurt them, and for reasons he never intended. How could he tell them he was so afraid to leave home that if they came to Boulder, he would climb back in the car with them, never to leave them again? His dad had ribbed him about his new roommate. All King knew was that his name was Dow. Dow Fulbright, and he lived in Missouri.

"He'll probably be a rich football player," his dad joked.

When King opened the door with Neil lugging his stereo, Dow sat perched on his desk, apparently already claimed. He wore a high school football jersey. He had dark curly hair, blue eyes, and a pouting lower lip. He smiled warmly, got up and shook hands with Neil.

"No," Neil said. "I'm not the roommate. My brother is. This is King."

Dow nodded. "Who made you King?"

Neil left a few minutes later. King walked him to his car. Words evaded him.

"It'll be all right," Neil reassured him. "He's clearly a nice enough guy. You could do a lot worse."

"Will they be okay ?" King asked him.

"Who?" Neil asked him. "Mom and Dad? King, what's wrong?"

"You don't know what it was like when you left. She didn't get out of bed for a year. Are you sure they'll be okay?"

Neil hugged his younger brother, patting him on his back. "They'll be fine, King. They'll have to be. And so will you. If it'll make you feel better, maybe I'll go back home and spend the night. I'll go back to Greeley in the morning."

"I'd appreciate it." King choked up. "Maybe I'll walk over to see Rita."

"This is the best time of your life. Just enjoy it."

When King arrived at Rita's room on the ninth floor of Williams Village, he was informed by her Japanese roommate that Rita had gone home.

"Did she forget something?" he asked incredulously.

"No. She checked out."

"Checked out? That can't be possible. I only came here because of her."

"She said she missed her mother." The Japanese girl shrugged. "She's gone, man. And I have this whole room to myself. Guess you'll have to make it on your own."

*   *   *

"King? Am I calling too late?"

King knew the voice.

"Matthew?"

They fell silent.

"This is awkward. I know I haven't called."

"No," King said without animosity.

"Well," Matthew continued. "I'm in town."

"At the Hilton?"

"No," he said. "I'm in Boulder. At the Boulderado. I think that's very close by."

"You're *here*?"

"Yes, King. My wife and I are divorced. Amicably, I'm happy to say. I would very much like to see you. Would that be possible?"

"Where're you going?" Jen called out to King. Her mother had checked into the Harvest House Hotel and had gone back to her room. "It's late. Where are you going so late? Are you hungry? I'm hungry. Can I come with you?"

King hesitated. "You have a baby now."

"I'll bring her."

"Sorry. Something's come up. Can't explain now."

"You've been entirely frank with me for the last six months. After everything that's happened, what could possibly be so tricky you can't tell me now?"

"The leather jacket."

"You lost your leather jacket?"

"No. He's back."

"You can't see him."

"I'm not going over to *see* him, see him. I'm going over to talk to him." King shook his head. "You're making more out of this than there is."

"King, you were crazy about this guy. He never called you. Don't go. It'll just confuse everything."

"Why are you giving me lectures? I shouldn't have told you."

"No, you shouldn't have."

"I want my privacy back!" he said sharply, hurting her.

"You've got it." She turned around and walked back inside her apartment. King cut through the alley to his car.

*　　*　　*

Matthew's room was on the top floor of the hotel. When the desk clerk told King the room number, he mentioned that it was the only suite in the Boulderado. There was one tiny elevator in the hotel, and to use it required an elevator operator, an old black porter King had seen many times dozing in a leather chair near the lift. He decided to take five flights of stairs instead of disturbing him.

The lobby was quiet, but he could hear voices and laughter coming from Le Bar. Maybe Matthew and King could have a drink. He hadn't even thought to have Matthew meet downstairs first. King took the steps two at a time. By the time he reached Matthew's room he was out of breath.

The door opened and Matthew's eyes lit up when he saw King. His expression converted to concern when he saw King breathing so heavily.

"I took the stairs."

"The porter napping?"

"Yeah. Lemme catch my breath."

"Come inside. I'll get you some water."

The suite had a cozy sitting room with Victorian furnishings and a skylight. Through open double doors King saw a king bed and a smallish window with a fire escape outside. Matthew moved to a dry sink and poured him a glass of water from a crystal pitcher. He held it out to him.

Matthew's hair had just been cut and he had gained a couple of pounds, but he still looked the same. He seemed to be searching King's face for some hint of how he was feeling. King thought he wanted to see if King was everything he remembered.

King knew from his walks across campus that he looked tan and healthy. Matthew was still winter pale. When he finished his water he took the glass and set it back on the dry sink.

"Is this too awkward? Should we go downstairs and have a drink? I hear Allen Ginsberg hangs out in the bar off the lobby."

King laughed.

Matthew laughed, too, but he couldn't have known why. "You look wonderful, King. I must look awful."

King's mind raced with memory. He could smell Matthew's hair. He could feel it brush across his cheek. He could taste his semen. He could hear his breathing as they made love, and later while he slept.

"Can I sit down?"

"Please."

King sat on the sofa. Matthew pulled an easy chair from the wall and sat opposite him. They sat quietly for several moments and stared wonderingly at each other. Matthew broke the silence, with what ordinarily should have been a casual question.

"How are you King, since your dad?"

And without asking how he knew, King told him.

It was quite a scene in Le Bar. When they entered, Allen Ginsberg stood up, walked over, and kissed King sweetly. Sneaking a look at Matthew, King could tell he was intrigued.

"King," Matthew whispered, "I'm so impressed."

Matthew enjoyed himself immensely. Allen was talked into reciting a new poem, and just as he was finishing up, Maddie and Robert came in. She kissed King sweetly and smiled beautifully when he introduced her to Matthew. King could tell she thought him very handsome, and this made Robert jealous. They had no idea who he was to King. Robert warmed up when Matthew recognized his name. Hadn't he just read a poem in the *Atlantic Monthly*?

"That was last month," Maddie interjected. "He got June's *New Yorker*. It's a wonderful poem. It's about me."

"How are you and King acquainted?" asked Robert.

"We met in Denver last fall. I missed him so I came to town."

"What line of work are you in?"

"I'm a divorce attorney. I own a firm in Pittsburgh. I did, until my own recent divorce, at least."

"Ouch," said Maddie.

"Guess I shouldn't have represented myself." He shrugged. "Doesn't really matter now."

"You really just got divorced?"

"I did." Matthew nodded, taking King's hand. "And I'm thinking of relocating here in Boulder."

"Really." Maddie smiled. "Seems sudden. Why Boulder?"

"Why not Boulder? It's an affluent, beautiful small city. Growing faster than it should. Should be plenty of divorces in a trendy city like this. If I want to open a practice, I won't have any trouble. I just don't know if I do." He turned and smiled. "Close your mouth, King."

King closed his mouth.

"So why'd you get divorced?" Robert had been drinking.

"Robert," Maddie rebuked him.

Matthew cupped his jaw in his right hand. "It's okay. He can ask. It's a boorish sort of question, but so much energy is bouncing around the table I'd like to bite. When my wife and I got married, we took a calculated risk. We decided that we'd try to work around whatever sexual preference issues might come up during the course of marriage. Of course, I'm talking about me. I'd experimented with same-sex partners in undergraduate school. I liked it okay, but didn't feel compelled to orient my life to that end. I liked women, too, and in fact, when I met my wife, had no doubt that she was the ideal mate for me. She was beautiful, ambitious, artistic, and intellectual. We came from similar backgrounds, had similar goals. Walking in, she knew about my sexual predilections. And I, hers. Physically, as it happened, we were a fine match."

"But no fireworks." Robert smirked.

"I wasn't looking for the fourth of July. I've met hundreds of divorcing couples and boredom is the number one reason most seem to want out. It makes me sad." He paused to take a sip of wine.

"Were you and your wife bored with each other?" Maddie asked. She had edged slightly away from Robert's side. She seemed to be leaning into King.

"No. We were frustrated. In different ways. My work took me away quite frequently. We had an active social life. Because of our family backgrounds—I hope I don't sound pretentious—we were socially prominent. At first we liked it. She still does. I found it increasingly tiresome. Traveling so much, I found myself wanting to stay in more. I encouraged her to find other escorts, which naturally offended her."

"Of course." Maddie nodded.

"And my desire for men seemed to be increasing. I didn't tell her at first. I took care of those needs when I was out of town."

"That's how you met King," Robert observed.

"In fact, yes. But King was special. I knew I had a problem." He put his arm around King. "I didn't ever mistake sexual passion with love. I'm ultimately too analytical for that trap."

King winced, and Robert, fuck him, noticed.

Matthew smiled. He glanced up, caught Maddie's gaze. She seemed pained by the conversation. "I've been too blunt, I'm afraid."

"No, Mr. Goodhue. You've been just what the doctor ordered."

"What do you mean by that?" Robert demanded.

"The poem in the *New Yorker*," she commented, sipping her wine. "Is it really about me?"

"It says so under the damn title."

"I found the poem a little homoerotic," she said, staring at her hands. "It's a funny thing. All of us at the table have had warm feelings for King."

"She's had too much wine."

"Maybe if Mr. Goodhue read it, he might agree."

"I'll pick up a copy. I'll let you know. "

King began to fidget.

"King." Maddie smiled, taking King's hands. "You aren't the source of any distress between me and Robert. Not on my end, anyway." She smiled over at Robert. "But I do think the poem happens to be about King. It was a little derivative of Jack Spicer. Do you know his works, Matthew?"

"Yes." Matthew nodded slowly. "He wrote my favorite poem."

"What poem?" Robert said darkly. "I knew Jack Spicer very well."

"Robert had a brief affair with Jack Spicer when he was living in San Francisco and very young. He's very proud of it," Maddie scolded.

"I have a favorite Jack Spicer poem," King volunteered.

"What is it, King? Maybe it's the same as Matthew's." Maddie laughed. "I have an idea. Robert, give me your pen. They can both write the title on separate pieces of paper so we'll be sure they're telling the truth."

"This seems very childish."

"Please. Indulge me."

Robert handed his pen to Matthew. Grinning, Matthew carefully scrawled the title of the poem on the cocktail napkin, not wanting to shred it. He handed the pen over to King.

"Give me your napkin," Maddie ordered. She was especially girlish tonight. Her cheeks were flushed, her eyes were shining, and she hadn't stopped smiling all evening. She took it, scanning it quickly, and folded it up.

"Now, King."

On King's napkin he wrote, *Poet Be Like God*. He handed it to Maddie.

"You're so lucky! You're both so lucky! You each love the same poem!"

"That's everybody's favorite Spicer poem," Robert growled. He was very annoyed with her.

"Is it yours?' King asked, somewhat insolently. "Or is it too honest?"

And Robert threw his drink in King's face.

Shocked, King sat back. Maddie began screaming at him. "How dare you do such a thing! How dare you act this way?"

Matthew stood up. "Bring a towel," he shouted at the bartender, the same hippie bartender who always tended bar. He moved quickly. The wine had stained King's leather jacket. Looking at it, King became filled with such terrible sadness. A wave of fatigue rolled over him. He thought he could fall asleep in his chair.

"King," Maddie cried. "I'm so sorry."

"Let's go." Robert tried to take her arm. "I'll send him a new coat in the morning."

"Aren't you even gonna apologize to the kid?" The bartender observed. "He never takes it off. It's his favorite coat!" The group stared at him. "You're eighty-sixed from here, man," the bartender waved his hand. "Get out for good."

"I'm so sorry, King." Maddie said again.

"Yeah, me too," Robert said breezily. "If I remember, the coat was a gift."

"It was a gift from me," Matthew said ominously.

"I *figured*," Robert said icily.

"You drunken old bore."

Robert exited, leaving Maddie in his wake. She gazed at them helplessly.

"Please get me your journal, King. I'm begging you." She gathered her coat and ran after him.

King looked up at Matthew and smiled.

"He was the man in your room."

"Yes," King nodded. "He drinks. I think he was in a blackout. There's something more." And King told Matthew the events of that evening. His appearance with Barry at the Friday Night Coffee House. Sam and Skip. The political pressure Skip put on Barry. The sad, lovely walk through the dry riverbed back to King's place. Deciding to sleep apart. To think things over.

"After Barry left my room that night, things were pretty much up in the air. Because of me, he was risking everything he worked for, his destiny. I didn't want that responsibility."

"You think he might have chosen you over that?"

"I didn't want to put him in that position. I cared for him."

"So you made the decision for him."

A waitress came and cleared the table of their empty wineglasses. She didn't offer another round. Matthew handed her his credit card and she quickly hurried away.

"Yes. So I walked over to here to find Robert. I knew it was his night off from Maddie. I knew he'd be here. He was drunk. I brought him back to my room. Things got carried away. He got violent. I didn't exactly stop him."

"Or couldn't, King. He's a big man."

"I do know one thing."

"He knew he left you at great risk."

"Yes. And I couldn't call Jen. I was worried about her pregnancy. I was passing out. I called Barry. He came. He called the ambulance. He waited till Jen made him go. He endured a police interrogation. He was forced to lie about him and me."

"But not for his sake."

"No. For mine. He was heartbroken. I'm good at that," King said bitterly. "But I'm not sorry. At least he'll have a taste. If it doesn't work out, I won't have cost him that. One of his dreams has come true."

"And Maddie?"

"She doesn't know. And I didn't want a scandal about Robert to hurt her position with the university."

"Do you think your silence is really protecting her?"

"I have a way for her to find the truth if she wants to see it in black and white. It's her call when she's ready."

Matthew smiled back and kissed him. "You have an effect on people, King. It's really the strangest thing."

They woke the elevator operator and went upstairs to Matthew's room.

King climbed into Matthew's bed, as proprietorial as the family cat. Matthew reached for him, pulling him into the contours of his own warm body. They had only slept in the same bed twice, but it felt deeply and sweetly comfortable to them both. Matthew kissed King, but restrained his passion. He was so grateful to have him back in his arms.

"I thought of you a hundred times a day," he told King.

"Same here. You were clever with the coat."

"I hope the coat wasn't the only reminder."

"No." King stroked his face. Matthew's beard was starting to darken. Matthew kissed him gently as King continued to talk. "I fell in love with a few people since I last saw you."

"Love is such a strong word. How can you fall in love so easily?"

"Everybody takes off anyway. What's the harm?" King observed.

"Did you think I took off?"

"Yes."

"You didn't, somewhere in your heart, think I'd come back?"

"I hoped. I have witnesses."

"What have you learned from all your lovers, King?"

"To count on my friends. And my family."

"You haven't asked how I knew about your dad."

"How?"

"My card in your wallet. Someone from the hospital called. It was a mix-up, because they were already in contact with your brother."

"It could have been a note I wrote on the back of it."

"What did it say?"

"It said, 'In case of emergency,' " King grinned. "I was drinking and feeling sorry for myself. I really liked you."

"I gave you some time, but I kept tabs on your recovery. You apparently have quite a few friends. The nurses station said you had a constant stream of caring visitors."

"Was it hard to leave your marriage?"

"Yes. Very."

King traced the outline of Matthew's lip with his finger.

"We were very fair with each other. Our divorce was friendly. Quite sad, but a relief to us both. She'd actually been seeing someone. She seems very much in love."

King rolled away from Matthew. Matthew pressed himself against King's back, kissing the nape of his hair. He prodded King with his erection. King glanced over his shoulder in astonishment.

"You must be joking."

"You told me you were completely recovered," Matthew smiled. "But yes, I am joking."

"Maybe for now, I could just fuck you." King laughed as Matthew's eyes widened with alarm.

"I don't really like getting fucked."

"C'mon," King urged, manipulating his body on top of Matthew. "You're so lovely. If you let me, I'll stay another day." He grinned down at him, recalling the night Matthew begged to have intercourse with him. Matthew laughed.

"I'm used to being on top."

"Then you don't know."

"Know what? King."

"How to trust. It takes a lot of trust to allow a man to put his dick inside of you. I've read a little about it. It compromises everything. The domination of body and spirit. You've never been fucked, have you?"

"No," Matthew whispered.

"Let me."

"I'm a grown man."

"Let me," King lapped at the side of Matthew's jaw, greedily penetrating his ear with his tongue. Matthew groaned. King reached down, hooking Matthew's inner knees and hoisting them upward. King worked his way down Matthew's torso to his belly button. Continuing downward, grazing his cock, King lapped at his balls like a loving golden retriever. He dipped lower, causing Matthew to arch away.

"No," he whispered.

"I want to know you this way," King wheedled.

He flicked at the narrow ridge, just beneath Matthew's testicles. King reached for a nearby dollop of lubricant.

King sprang forward, lapping the entire surface of Matthew's stomach, his pectorals, his neck, his chin, and as he plunged his tongue inside Matthew's mouth, he pinned him against the humid sheet, and gently inserted himself into Matthew's warm, humming body.

King let himself out just before dawn and walked back to his apartment on Canyon Avenue. A predawn walk after making love with Matthew seemed to fit. His leather jacket was stained with red wine, but only faintly. Matthew told him eventually it would add to the natural aging of the leather. King liked it because it looked like blood.

As he walked, he was hoping to see his dad strolling toward him from the opposite direction, only vigorous and tall this time. He

stopped off at his apartment to retrieve the tattered pages of his journal. Then he trotted up to campus and slipped them under Maddie's
door.

Creative Writing 403/405
Dr. Maddie Sloan, Professor
Fall/Spring Semester 1974-1975
University of Colorado, Boulder Campus

"King James Version"
A Journal

Kingston James
2000 Canyon Avenue
Boulder, Colorado

Two excerpts of King's daily journal, which he dropped off to
Maddie's office, on a spring day in Boulder in 1975. On the last
page, to be extra dramatic, King pricked his finger and embossed it
with his bloody fingerprint, thought better of it and replaced it with
a clean one.

February 26, 1974 (Written on March 1st)

*Later that night, I brought Robert back to my room. He
smelled like Scotch. I was tired. In a half dream state. I wanted
to get it over with. Then I wanted him to go. It was only supposed to be quick sex. He was big in the room. He knelt next to
my bed. He took my face in his hands and kissed me, hard,
forcing his tongue inside my mouth. I could taste cigarettes, and
the Scotch. I came fully awake.*
"Fuck! You bit my lip."
"I've waited so long for this," he whispered. "To hold you."
He unbuttoned his shirt.
*"Maybe this isn't such a good idea. You've had too much to
drink."*
"It's okay. Feel this. Feel what I have for you."
He grabbed my hand, skating it over his naked chest. He

seemed like a giant to me. I was afraid. His free hand found my neck. He was breathing so loud I thought the whole world would hear him, come in and stop him.

"You're trembling. Don't be afraid. I won't hurt you."

But he reached under the scramble of my blankets, cupping my body in his arms, wrenching me free from the bedclothes. Kneeling next to my bed, he pulled me from the mattress, cradling the weight of my body on his knees, against his bare chest, all the while pressing his thumb against my trachea.

He kissed me again, his hands roughly searching my body. He pinched me, manipulating my muscles between his fingers.

"Why are you doing this?" I asked him. "Stop."

"It'll go much easier if you give in to it," he lamented. "I always wanted to be this close to you. Closer."

"Robert! Stop."

He kept stroking me, massaging my musculature, my shoulders, the deltoids on my back. I was in such physical pain that I acquiesed, wanting him to get it over with and leave. He began to lap me with his tongue, all the way down to the base of my spine, the cleft of my buttocks. I began to quiver. Nothing I'd ever experienced felt like this before. I'd heard about sexual pleasure from pain. This was it. My guilty truth.

"I want to fuck you," he whispered urgently. In his free hand he held up a bottle of poppers. Uncapping it, he held it up to my nose. I figured they might help. I wanted him gone but I knew I could never overpower him. I decided I had to go with it. I breathed in.

My heart started to pound. I could feel my head swelling up. My body felt like it was going to explode.

Robert tugged at the short hairs of my inner cheeks with his teeth. His tongue started to probe deeper into the rounded globes of my buttocks.

I groaned, laying on my stomach. He undid his pants, kicking off his shoes. He climbed on top of me. He yanked my head back by my hair.

"Come here, King." He shoved the bottle under my nose again. He leaned up swiftly, violently sweeping the inside of my mouth and throat with his tongue.

He reached around behind me. Grabbing the seamed fabric of my underwear under each side of my butt, he slowly started to rip it away. He found lotion and spurted some over his cock. He smoothed it out. Then he shoved himself into me with long even strokes. He started to get excited.

I swiveled my hips, allowing him to slowly burrow his way up inside of me. I had the weight of his entire body on me.

He began to thrust slowly, the momentum picking up. Soon he was savagely fucking me and I didn't care. How can I explain the phenomenon of this man inside of me? Was I allowing this or being forced against my will? My mind raced as he moved on top of me. A sense of urgency took hold. Our autonomies subsided. And for me, a cessation of all my deepest longing and loneliness for male love. I resisted the urge to ejaculate but I think I did. I wanted to be linked like this forever. My dirty secret. Being degraded by heterosexual male power.

I became lightheaded. Euphoric. The bed shuddered from the spasm of Robert's body. He came to.

"Jesus Christ," he muttered. I felt him jump up. I heard water running. The hushed, hurried rustle of him dressing. The sliding door. My sheets felt wet, inordinately wet. I reached down, under my thigh. I brought my hand up. It was covered with blood. I may have fainted, but I revived. I called Barry. "Help," I remember whispering.

I felt myself draining away.

February 27, 1975 Dad Died

When he arrived at his apartment, Jen's curtains were open, but the light was out and she and Frankie were nowhere to be seen. Where could they be at this hour?

He studied Theo's sliding glass door. Should he knock? He did.

Theo pulled back his drape. His didn't open the door. "She's moved into the hotel with her mother."

King reeled back. Had she been that angry?

"What about her stuff? She's coming back for it, isn't she?"

"She told me to keep what I wanted and donate the rest to the Salvation Army."

King peered through her undraped windows. There were gifts from his mother in there. She was just abandoning it all?

"Didn't she say anything else?"

"It's early. I don't know anything more about it."

King unlocked his door and slammed into his apartment. She was leaving? Just like that? His telephone rang. Who'd be calling so early this morning?

"Hello?"

It was his mother's voice. She was crying.

"Mom! What's wrong? What's happened?"

"Did you hear?"

"About Jen?"

"Yes," she cried. "About Jen. She's catching the next plane with her mother. She's not even staying for graduation."

"What about her father? Graduate school?"

"What about *me*?" Kay demanded through her emotion. "She told me she's had enough of your self-destructive behavior. She thinks you're dangerous. Bad for Frankie to be around! What are you doing that makes her think such a thing?"

King was speechless.

"I know about your speech to that sociology class. If you don't respect your privacy, what about your father's? What about mine?"

"I was completely respectful in that lecture. Who told you about that? Jen?"

"No. That Nicholas character thought I'd like to know."

"He's been calling you again? You allowed him to speak to you?" Instead of rage, King's voice dropped an octave from the emotion he was feeling. He became chiding and parental. Disappointment in her dripped from each word.

"He apologized for his earlier behavior and I accepted it," she countered defensively. "He cares about you. He felt awful about your father. Whether you believe it or not, he's still your friend."

At least it wasn't Jen, King thought. Jen wouldn't purposely upset her just to punish King. Then, "Jen told me about your gay wedding. To that boy we saw on TV."

Maybe King had given Jen credit she didn't deserve.

"I went to the Jefferson County Library. I looked it up in the *Boulder Daily Camera*. Your name was in the *Denver Post* and the *New York Times*. Thank God my neighbors don't read newspapers."

"You think that's a good thing? Dad was a newspaper editor, or don't you remember. It was just a political gesture. There's nothing between Sam and me." And when he said it, acceptance flooded over

King. Sam was truly out of his system. It had the effect of calming him down. He didn't want to hurt his mother, as angry as he was. He wanted her to understand him.

"Don't patronize me, King. You broke a promise to me and you know it. You told me that day in Boulder that you'd lie low. Stay out of the spotlight. Haven't you learned anything, King? After everything I've done, now this. I blame it all on you! I did all the work, and her mother gets all the joy! All because of you! Because of your sexual addiction. It's unsavory. I wouldn't want any baby of mine around it either! She's right to leave. But why does she have to leave me too?"

"She wouldn't leave you. She loves you." Did she? King now wondered.

"Big deal. She's going to California. That's a thousand miles away. She's not even staying for graduation. She's not even coming to say goodbye. I looked so forward to helping her. To taking care of Frankie. She'll probably change her name, now. There won't be any Frankie at all. I'll never forgive you for this, King! Never in a million years," and then his mother hung up.

So it was King's fault, again, he reflected as he walked back over to the Boulderado to spend the day with Matthew.

Matthew was loving, allowing King to think it through.

"What if she doesn't come to my graduation? Maybe I shouldn't even bother. I never felt like I belonged here anyway."

"It isn't my place to tell you what to do," Matthew whispered, kissing King gently on his forehead. They were curled into each other, fully dressed, on top of the sheets. "But you've worked so hard. This is an important ritual. Whether you believe it in your heart, you do have a right to sit with your peers and be acknowledged for the last four years. Did you really just do it for your mom and dad? I don't think so."

King gazed wistfully into Matthew's eyes.

"What if I decided I didn't want to stay in Boulder. That I wanted to move away."

"Are you asking what I'd do?"

"Yes."

"I'd stand on the sidewalk and wave till you got out of sight. Then I'd give you the same amount of time you gave me and I'd follow you. I love you King. I want my future to include you."

King considered this. "And if I don't really want to go, if I decide to stay in Boulder, maybe work for Rod's newspaper and earn my living as a male switchboard operator till I write my first novel; if I really want to stay around for my mom and Jen and Frankie; if I stay because of you, is that okay? Is it okay to stay?"

"Who ever told you it was mandatory to *go*?" Matthew smiled.

"I don't know. Maybe from the Bible."

"Prodigal son stuff, huh? Forty days in the desert?" Matthew stroked King's hair, drawing him close. "In answer to your question, yes, King. It's okay to stay. Most people only leave to find the things you already have, to learn what you already know."

"I love you, Matthew."

"We have to face facts. My real name is Ralph. Can you accept the Ralph in Matthew?"

"Do I have to call you Ralph?"

"I'm not kidding, King."

"Hey, Ralph," King smiled happily. "Give me a kiss."

The day before graduation, Matthew offered to walk King across the campus to see his final grade from Maddie. King allowed that he wanted to go alone, but he'd meet him back at his hotel later.

The famous Boulder wind careened down from the foothills where Jen and King dreamed their spring dreams, waxing about love and forgiveness. Leaves from the campus cottonwoods whipped from their branches, raining down on King as he shouldered himself from the Colorado Chinook wind. The wind was as the ghosts of his past, lined up, elbowing past him; even the wind would yet disappear.

As King entered Hellums Hall, he was reminded of his first semester, and the pleasure he derived at seeing his name on the Dean's List. A 3.5 GPA was required. King had a 3.8. When he and Rita received their acceptance packets from the University of Colorado, a schedule was included which statistically calculated their probable scholastic performance. King, apparently, would only fare average, according to the correspondence, which was calculated by his high school grade point average and his SAT scores. His dad, upon reading the letter responded happily, "they don't know my son."

The postings were long gone. King, in spite of his emotional burdens, had done well enough to qualify for a certain level of graduate school. A good Masters program like the University of Iowa required writing samples, a high GPA and professor recommendations. Although he'd abandoned the idea of entering grad school in favor of staying in Boulder to be near Jen and his mother, he wanted the option, should he ever change his mind.

That option now hung pinned on a sheet of paper outside of Maddie's office. King hesitated before he searched for his name. Last week Rod had called to say he was publishing King's short story about Kay. He offered King a job with his paper, which was mostly copyediting and photo captions. He could pay him a little. Was he interested? Was this God again, showing him the way, bolstering him up against impending disappointment?

He took a deep breath and stepped up to the page. Kingston James. 'A.'

Next to his grade, a handwritten note from Maddie. *King, I'm here for you.*

When King entered the lobby of the hotel where Jen's mom was staying, the same hotel which evicted Jen only eight months before, Jen happened to be in the lobby, pushing Frankie in her stroller toward the elevator door. Jen didn't see him.

Knowing her as well as he did, King could see that she was agitated. She also seemed to be trying to avoid the attention of a young, pimply desk clerk, as if she was trying to sneak past him, to avoid the subject of her old unpaid bill. He glanced up.

"I remember you."

"I remember you too. You were the one who kicked me out of this hotel. My mom's a guest here. She paid my bill!"

"I know," he muttered. "You were pregnant, huh?"

The clerk studied her, more out of curiosity than suspicion, King noted. Even as angry as he was at Jen, King couldn't check his empathy. He was watching Jen relive the memory of what it felt like to be kicked out of the hotel into that snowy Boulder dawn. The humiliation, desperation and loneliness. She had been driven by her best instinct to King's door. It had been his best instinct, he reflected now, to let Jen inside.

"You've changed," the clerk told her.

"I just had a baby," Jen sneered. She reached the elevator door.

"I don't mean that," he called after her. "I can see you've just had a baby. You look a little more seasoned, that's all."

"Are you trying to insult me?"

"No," he said calmly.

Furiously, Jen punched the button for the elevator.

"My mother is staying in the most expensive suite in this hotel. I'm not still that girl you threw out in the snow," she shouted back at him.

"No," King called out to her. "You aren't a girl anymore."

Both Jen and the desk clerk turned at the sound of his voice. King now stood boldly in the center of the lobby floor.

"Then who am I to you?" Jen demanded.

"You're the woman who survived her winter."

Later, King begged off a night with Matthew. He could imagine his mother, at home in Green Mountain, sitting on her new redwood deck, smoking cigarettes and drinking coffee. Her garden would be in full bloom. He pictured her gazing down the block, judging her neighbors' manicured, uninspired lawns.

King had called theirs the crazy house on the block. He was right.

So King had saved himself long enough to graduate. His mother had savored this day, but by her own actions, now held herself apart from it.

Jen tearfully admitted in the suite of her mother's hotel that she'd told Kay that King was seeing an older man, a lawyer in his mid-thirties. Jen hadn't met him, but he'd probably promise to divorce his wife for King.

"They did get divorced. But not over me. You also told her I got married to Sam."

"She knew the day after. I felt so close to her. She got me laughing at myself. It slipped out. She always told me I could tell her anything."

"That's what she told me, too," King observed. "So she knew and she didn't say anything. Pretty good. My mom's still a great actress. That's what she does. She invites trust and betrays you for it."

Jen gazed at him miserably. "I knew it was a big mistake. That's why I overreacted about you going to see Matthew. I was a coward. I picked something minor, to make you the fall guy. Because I knew you'd eventually find out that I'd told her about the wedding."

"It's cruel to hurt her as a way to hurt me. You can't do it again. I know in the scheme of things, what you'd been through, what you've given up to have Frankie is pretty big. What I've given up to be honest with myself about who I am, and learning how to stand up for myself is just as big to me. If I seemed selfish, living my own life, I was only learning how to survive. I'm not so sure you really were getting that."

"I'm so sorry, King. I do get it, now."

"She's your friend, but she's my mother. You owe her the apology. Not me."

"I have. I invited her to come to California. Can you forgive me?"

"Yeah," he reflected. "But I haven't forgiven her, yet."

"You *have* to," Jen's mother appeared in the doorway to her bedroom. She was holding a cocktail.

"Oh, God," Jen shuddered.

"Furthermore," she addressed Jen. "You and Frankie aren't coming back to California. You're staying here. You're going to graduate school. You have the financial aid. You don't need us. You've learned to count on yourself. If you backslide now, it'll be the biggest mistake of your life. And I don't care if you don't wear your cap and gown tomorrow, but we're going to watch King graduate. You and Frankie can keep me company in the stands."

An obdurate King stood his ground. Behind him, through the windows of the hotel suite, a magnificent view of the Flatirons.

"What's *your* problem?" Jen's mother asked him. "It's all settled."

"Why do I have to forgive my mother?" King demanded.

"Because for people like you," Jen's mother observed, taking a slug from her drink, "I'm afraid it's simply irresistible."

As King lay on his bed that night, he could hear Theo having sex on the other side of the wall. He covered his face with a pillow to drown out the noise. What sordid business, his mother must be thinking. At least King felt absolved that he hadn't cost Kay her friendship with Jen. She hadn't been abandoned. Her efforts on Jen's behalf hadn't gone unappreciated.

King thought again about his mother's yard. It had been the family yard, his, his dad's and Neil's. Now it was hers. At least she had the apple tree he gave her. The anxious tree had proven his poor father wrong, outliving him even. When King gave it to her he told her he wanted something living she would always remember him by.

"Are you going somewhere? What kind of mother would ever forget her son?" she'd teased him.

Tomorrow was graduation. After King got out of the hospital, she'd told him in the park that if she'd known people were staring at him, she should have been there to stare back. She'd been a good mother, as good as any mother could be. As a child King never missed a meal; always left the house in clean clothes and neatly combed hair. The family attended every science fair, every school play, every parent-teacher conference. His teachers reported that he was very intelligent, was attentive and polite but tended toward sadness. He didn't have many friends, but seemed more comfortable with girls than boys.

She broached this last subject with him, one snowy afternoon. Whenever King came home, he was always genuinely happy to see her. He liked to talk to her, ask about her day. This day, she sat him down, and with false enthusiasm, told him all the nice things his teacher had to say about him. He had the highest grades in his class. She expected that King could look forward to an Ivy League school.

A dismayed Kay explained there would never be that kind of money, not with two sons to think about. The teacher, Miss Dunn, explained that his continuing high grades could make a big difference. Scholarships and financial aid could always be found for gifted students.

"She says you're gifted, King."

King was embarrassed. As it was, his grades made him different from his schoolmates.

Kay handed him his handwritten evaluation. He scanned over the expected compliments. Then he came upon a wounding comment. *Competes with girls*, Miss Dunn had written. She didn't go one further on that score. It was probably damning enough, standing on its own.

"What's she mean by that?" King asked his mother.

"I was wondering if you knew. I didn't ask her."

"Lucy and I have the highest grades in the class. She's who I compete with. Is something wrong with that?" And King had been insulted, and hurt. "None of the boys are as smart as me. Besides, what's wrong with competing with girls?"

King was a feminist at twelve years old. She should have known then. Maybe that's what his teacher was trying to tell her.

"Good grades don't necessarily make you smart," Kay explained.

"Then what do they make you?"

"I didn't mean it the way it sounded. Good grades are very important. Your dad got 'C's and even a 'D' in high school. He's smart, isn't he?"

"What about you?"

"I always got straight A's. You get that from me."

"I still don't understand. What's wrong with competing with girls?"

"It's okay," Kay explained carefully. "As long as you remember you're a boy."

"I still don't understand."

"Why don't you go downstairs and play with your brother?"

A few moments later King was listening to Barbra Streisand's recording of *My Funny Valentine*.

Now, King thought about Jen's mom, her comment about his insatiable need to forgive. He did forgive his mother, no question about it. The difference, he reflected, was that now, King knew he didn't have to go through life apologizing for who he loved, how he lived or who he was. This was a gift from his father.

The ceremony was hot and boring. A congressman spoke, decrying the recent trend in social liberalism. The very fabric of American society was at stake. Many in the audience booed. His speech was cut short. The procession to accept diplomas began. King walked through the motions in a dream. He heard his name, and somewhere in the crowd, Matthew and Neil howled.

He looked up in their direction, knowing in advance which section they'd been assigned. Sitting in a row were Jen's mom, Jen, Matthew, and Neil. Not present were his dad, and lastly and most significantly, that same mother, King's mother, boycotting the day she dreamed for him since even she was a child.

He gazed at Jen. Who was taking care of Frankie? Jen watched him scanning their laps for her. She motioned to the fence near where King was standing in line, holding his diploma.

He glanced over. His mother stood, just inside, on the grass of the football field, holding Frankie. Mother and son calculated one another, nodding begrudgingly like two longtime adversaries who deeply respected the skills of their foe. King held up his diploma. He pressed it to his lips.

As best she could, juggling the baby, his mother began to clap wildly for him.

*   *   *

When Kingston James entered the University of Colorado in 1970, the Stonewall riots were only a year old and he had not come to terms with being gay. He was twice a virgin, had yet to experience sensuality with either man or woman. He had yet to fly in an airplane, actually saw one crash before he himself had flown. He hadn't seen the ocean. He was as unsophisticated as Maddie suggested. He was unworldly and innocent. Nothing had happened of note to this boy.

He came from a simple family; intellectual but unschooled and unpretentious. To King he'd had the most normal childhood a boy could want. Not programmed for high achievement, happiness would be the true marker of success. His parents required neither fame, fortune or power for their boys. They just wanted them to be happy. Now, King reflected, his mother would settle for being happy herself. It had been too much of a burden, to love her sons while envying their youth and opportunity. Who could blame her? he thought. He would continue to confer about this with Jen.

As he bowed his head for the closing prayer, King was reminded of one other thing. When King was a sophomore, he became a religious fanatic, hiding his sexual preference for men behind Christian theology. It was important for him to note that although he, and others, fell away from the church, a few remained loyal to their faith.

In King's hand he held the old bible from Celine, the Canadian woman, who gave it to him because he loved it so much. A King James Version, mistakenly bound backwards and frayed, it had a quirkiness they both liked. It had traveled with her all over the world and she'd annotated in her own handwriting. King hoped one day he could get it back to her because her faith was sincere, as was his, and she'd cared unconditionally for him.

Later, when the black caps of the graduating class of 1975 were tossed high against the blue Colorado sky, the majestic Flatirons jagged against the background, it seemed like an eternity for his tasseled cap to fall to the earth. It seemed like a metaphor for his entire past, soaring up and spiraling down, and as King watched it, he prayed for a gust of wind, a serendipitous blast of air, to refresh his spirits, to keep him sailing longer.

As it plummeted to earth in front of him, he snatched it, quick as a cat, before it hit the ground. Holding it up victoriously, he began to cheer, his voice blending with his fellows, his brother-men, his sister-women, rising high above the stadium as one.